MICHAEL PRESLEY'S

BLACKFUNK II
NO REGRETS / NO APOLOGIES

Revised edition with an excerpt from Tears on a Sunday Afternoon.

Blackfunk Publishing
P.O. Box 23782
Brooklyn, NY 11202
www.Blackfunk-book.com

Acknowledgements

I would like to thank all the readers who have made *BLACKFUNK* a success. I enjoy writing and I look forward to bringing you a lot more endearing stories. Special thanks to my brother, David and sister, Patricia. Kwesi for creating Blackfunk-book.com. Thanks to all my friends especially, Paul, James, Eleise, Chris and Diane in Atlanta, Nigel, Kirk and all my friends who continue to support me.

I think the most important thing in writing is to have a good editor. I think I lucked out when I met Chandra Sparks Taylor. Chandra, thanks for being a friend and a wonderful editor, I look forward to working with you on my future projects.

Dedicated to my mom
whose strength continues to inspire and amaze me.

About the Author

Born in Grenada, West Indies, Michael Presley immigrated to the States (Brooklyn, New York) in 1978. Upon graduation from George W. Wingate High School, he proceeded to get a Bachelor of Arts degree in English Literature at Stony Brook University. He has written various short stories, specializing in fiction. He continues to live in Brooklyn where he is working on his next book.

"Damn bitch. She called my wife and told her everything," George McLeod said as he paced up and down in front of his friend Rashaun Jones.

"That's fucked up. You can't even say it wasn't you," Rashaun said, smiling, enjoying his friend's discomfort.

"Rashaun, this shit ain't funny. Joanna kicked my ass out the house and you making a joke out of it," George said as he continued to pace Rashaun's small law office.

"Relax. Give her time, she'll forget about it."

"Rashaun, you have any Heiny?" George asked as he looked around the small office.

"George, did you see me bring a refrigerator in here when you helped me move in?" Rashaun asked.

"I forgot you are a struggling lawyer now. No more six-figure salaries."

"I will survive," Rashaun said, hating himself for sounding so much like a girl-power record.

"I still can't believe it. Our friend Tyrone Wheatley on trial for fucking a woman to death. This got to be a dream. My brother, you are a hell of a man quitting your job to defend our brother pro bono."

"Sometimes you just got to do what you think is right. Don't worry about me. I'll be all right. Your ass, now that's a different story."

"You don't think she'll divorce me, do you? I can't afford to lose my family," George said, sitting down on a soft red chair for the first time since he walked into the office.

"George, I hate to tell you I told you so but when you play with fire, sooner or later you're gonna get burned."

"But Rashaun, I'm a good father and a good husband. Fine, I like some extra pussy on the side sometimes is there anything wrong with that?"

"George, you're a Muslim. No one put a gun to your head. You got married, you know the rules. You got caught, now deal with it," Rashaun said as he looked at his watch.

"You know what, she going to beg to have me back. You think there are any good men out there. I took care of the house, my son. I took care of everything. If she wanted to go out, I had no problem staying home with the baby. I cook, I clean, I do everything she wants. Now she's going to give me up over this stupid bitch."

"What happened between you and Debra anyway? I thought she knew the rules."

"The bitch flipped, that's what she did. She fucking flipped!"

"What you mean she flipped?" Rashaun asked.

George shook his head and placed his chin between the palms of his hands. He rubbed his hands repeatedly over his face. He hadn't slept since he came home the night before and his wife had changed the locks and had come to the front door when he rang the bell. She was in tears and used the door for support as she spoke to him. He didn't argue or apologize. He didn't ask her to come in. When she had finished saying her piece, she closed the door in his face. He stood outside stunned. He waited until the lights went totally out in the house before he got into his Lincoln Navigator and drove off. He spent that night in the truck, parked on a small scenic area off the Belt Parkway where seniors come to look at Manhattan from a distance and young people came to take the itch out of their clothes.

"I've been fucking Debra off and on for more than two years now. I don't know who she's been talking to lately but all of a sudden she wants me to leave my wife. You know me, Rashaun, I don't go for that bullshit."

"No you didn't."

"Fuck yeah, I told her to go fuck herself. I told her that before when she started her bullshit. But I don't know what the fuck happened this time. She called my wife. And the bitch told me she was going to call my wife, too, but I didn't believe her. But once I had to ring my doorbell when I got to my house I knew shit had changed."

"Did you say it wasn't me?"

"Fuck you, Rashaun. This shit ain't funny."

"I'm sorry I just had to say it again," Rashaun said laughing.

"The bitch told her everything. She even told her about the trip to Jamaica. I mean she told her when and where we fucked, where I took her to dinner, what I bought her, I mean every fucking thing she could remember."

"That is fucked up," Rashaun said, shaking his head.

"After that there was nothing for me to say or do. All I did was wait for her to shut the door in my face. I didn't even get the chance to say good night to my son. Damn, I felt like killing that bitch Debra. But I chilled. I got on the Belt Parkway and went to that spot to enjoy Brooklyn at night."

"You not talking about that fucking spot off the belt, are you? People be fucking in the open over there, cars be jumping like they competing on the West Coast. No George, you didn't?"

"I told you I went there by myself," George said and looked down on the recently carpeted floor.

"George you know the hookers be knocking on the car glass over there. If you not interested you keep your windows up or you blow your horn. Don't act all dumb, George. You went there and fucked a whore."

"Man, she was sweet. Nice ass, small waist and perfect tits. Not R. Kelly young but a little more than two or three above legal."

"You are a sick brother," Rashaun said.

"It wasn't Blackfunk but I'm sure she'll remember the Navigator. She could barely walk when she left."

3

"I hope you gave her a tip at least."

"Fuck no. What for? She said a fuck was fifty, and that's what I gave her. I'm sure she wouldn't return money to a man who fucked her for two seconds with a small dick."

"My brother, whether your wife accepts you back or not, you definitely have issues to deal with."

"I know. You want to see the videotape?" George asked and started to head out the door.

"No. Lately all I have been doing is watching videotape," Rashaun said, a look of exhaustion on his face. "I guess you still have that camera hooked up in your truck."

"Yeah, man, these women out here are crazy. They be calling you on things you never even do, especially black women. Their pussy be having price tags way above the mileage on them. Even the EWP. The shit ain't good and you still got to pay for it."

"I think Peter is going to divorce his wife because of that."

"Are you serious?" George said, forgetting his own predicament.

"You mean this little girl have an extra-wide pussy?" George looked as if someone had caught him jerking off.

"That's why no sex before marriage won't work with me."

"And Peter suffers from SDS."

"We all know that, George. Small dick syndrome and extra-wide pussy don't work."

"So what the fuck did you tell him?"

"I'm a lawyer, I'm not a psychiatrist. Personally, I would file for a divorce based on the fact that she purposely deceived me. Can you imagine, wedding night and the honeymoon?"

"Just a pebble in a well, that's all it is, just a pebble in a well."

"Talking about starting out your marriage on a sour note. I hope they work it out. Too many marriages are failing."

"Why you looking at me like that? Let me see when your ass gets married. By the way if Joanna calls to ask you..."

"Don't insult me, George. We go too far back for that. Go get a shower, man, you starting to funk up the place."

After George left, Rashaun sat back in his big black leather chair. It was the only thing he went all out to buy. The chair cost him $895, which was a little less than the rent he paid for his small office. Everything else in the office he and his fiancée, Andria Jackson went bargain-shopping for. Andria had spent a few days decorating the office for him even though she didn't agree with him leaving the firm. He had decided to leave after he asked his boss for him to take on Tyrone's case for a minimum fee. His boss refused so Rashaun decided to leave. It was a simple decision; he would defend his friend with everything he had. By leaving the law firm he also gave up a lot of resources afforded him through the company. He knew the task ahead of him: he would not only be defending Tyrone, he would also be fighting with his own emotions. Kim Rivers, his ex-girlfriend, is one of the top defenders in the district attorney's office.

He knew she was going to be one of the top lawyers back in law school. Her intelligence was one of the things that attracted him. They competed relentlessly in law school, at first, to motivate each other then after he discovered the Blackfunk videotape, it was for real. She beat him every time. She was the first black female valedictorian of their law school. Her looks combined with her intelligence had every man falling at her feet including him.

Rashaun picked up the phone and dialed his home number. Well it wasn't his alone anymore. It was their phone number. Andria had moved in with him after their engagement. She was the first woman he had live with him. It was rough at first but going home to her put an extra bounce in his step. The answering machine came on and Andria announced to the world

5

that they weren't home. He sat back in his chair and closed his eyes.

The kiss was soft and wet, gliding over his lips.

"What the…" He woke up and there was Andria.

"I thought I would surprise you," she said as she sat in his lap.

"I thought it was my secretary. I was just about to get busy."

"Yeah, with your seventy-year-old part-time secretary. Boy, do you need help?"

"You hired her," he said and kissed her on her cheek.

"Exactly," she said and returned one to his cheek.

"It's tough," he said, looking into her beautiful face for answers.

"I know you're strong," she said, "and sometimes totally arrogant but I love you anyway."

"You have been so understanding," he said as he clasped his hands around hers.

"A month of understanding," she said and kissed him on the lips.

"I know."

"It's burning up in here," she said.

"Yeah, I'm trying to bring the Caribbean to NYC," he answered.

"So it's okay if I take this blouse off, isn't it?" She removed her top without waiting for a response.

"I see you don't wait for answers," he said and started to kiss along her right hand.

"What are you doing, Mr. Jones?" she asked and kissed him along the neck.

"Before we get started, isn't it that time of the month?"

"Very good, but I didn't see anything this afternoon. What, are you scared?"

"Not exactly," he said as he licked around her left nipple. His tongue traced the outside, not once touching the nipple itself.

6

She eased herself off him and quickly unfastened his belt. She unzipped his pants and released his penis from the confines of his boxer shorts. He was extremely hard. His tongue went deep inside her mouth as she pulled on it. She pulled her skirt up so his penis was standing straight up in front of her vagina. She started to slide up and down, letting the lips of her womanhood gently nudge him through her see-through panties. He took his right hand and pulled the panties aside as he inserted his finger.

"Oh, oh, don't stop," she said. She was dripping. She took his penis and ran her hand along the shaft.

He felt like cumming then but he resisted. "It's been too long," he said as he increased the paced with his finger.

She ran her fingers over his head " I like you bald."

"I like you bald too," He said as he removed his finger.

"Just for you," she said and guided him inside of her.

"Damn, this feels good," he said as his butt came off the chair and he thrust upward.

"Fuck me, Rashaun. Oh, fuck me."

He lifted her slightly as he thrust in and out of her.

"Yes, just like that. Yes, just like that," she said as he buried himself inside of her.

He took her and turned her over so that her feet were on the chair and her upper body was lying flat on the mahogany table. He grabbed her butt and squeezed as his stomach contracted to show his six-pack abs, his arms maintained support on the chair handles. He slammed into her, his body soaked and their sweat forming a puddle on his desk. He fucked her like she was the last woman on Earth.

"I'm cumming," he screamed as he continued to thrust into her. She fell forward onto his desk with his last thrust and he fell back into the chair.

"Yes…" she muttered as his action sent the beginning of her orgasm racing through her body. She held on to him even as he was letting go as her body convulsed in unnatural positions.

"Oh, fuck," he said as he looked at his penis. Blood was running down it onto his expensive leather chair.

"I'm…" Andria began.

He took his finger and rested it over her soft lips. "Remember, no regrets, no apologies," he said as he lifted her off the table and into his arms. The blood trickled down from her legs onto the carpet.

"What if…" she started.

Again he silenced her with a finger. "There are no more what if's with us," he said as he ran his finger down the middle of her back.

"I love you," she said and kissed his finger.

"I love you too," he said and picked up her bra from off the floor and put it in his drawer and locked it.

"You are sick," she said, laughing.

"Maybe, but in this world of ours sometimes it's good to reach for something that you can hold on to. You came and blessed the office today," he said.

"I could come back tomorrow and do the same," she said with a mischievous smile on her face.

"Well…" he started but the phone rang before he could continue.

He picked up the phone and uttered some short answers into it.

"It's Tyrone's mother. She said he's acting up again," Rashaun said as he pulled up his pants.

"Damn, I want to hate him but I can't," Andria said as she, too, started to get herself together.

"I know," he said, looking at the confusion in her eyes. "If I thought he had meant to hurt her, I wouldn't be defending him."

"But he did. He killed one of my best friends."

"I'm not disagreeing about that. But accidents do happen, and it doesn't matter how unnatural it is," he said, wondering what Tyrone was doing. He knew that his friend was afraid; he was scared of going to jail. After Tyrone got out of jail on bail he would only leave his house to pick up essentials. Rashaun and George had invited him out many times but Tyrone always refused. Tyrone's mother had to force him to eat and even then he ate very little. Even the mention of pussy would have Tyrone shaking. Rashaun never thought he would see the day when Tyrone would be scared of pussy.

"Be there in a minute," he called out to Andria.

She came out with a washrag in her hand.

"Be where?"

"I'm going to help you clean up," he answered.

"No, you're not. You better get out of here. Your friend needs you."

"And you."

"Oh, I'm finished with you. You served your purpose."

"Then I guess I don't have to come home tonight."

"I guess you don't value your life because if I don't see you in a few hours I'm going to kill you," she said and started to walk by him.

He grabbed her by the hand and pulled her to him, this time letting his tongue explore her mouth like a dental hygienist on a practice exam for the state boards.

"Let me see you do that down there," she said, pointing to her vagina.

"You are sick," he said laughing.

"Maybe we all are. Go see what's up with your friend," she said and headed to the desk.

Rashaun walked up to the small semi-detached brick house on Seventy-seventh Street. The house was located on a quiet block, one of the few in the Canarsie section of Brooklyn without ten or twenty kids playing in the street. Tyrone's parents bought the house in the early eighties before the exodus of the white people.

Before Rashaun could knock on the door, Mrs. Wheatley, Tyrone's mother, opened it. Mrs. Wheatley was a beautiful woman in her mid-sixties with a face etched from the turmoil that had been a part of her twenty-five-year tenure as a teacher in the New York City Public Schools. She had retired a year earlier, three years ago she had started to lose some of the edge that made her one of the best teachers at P.S. 598 in Brooklyn. But as soon as that was over with, then the trouble with Tyrone started and once more the aging process was accelerated.

"Good evening, Mrs. Wheatley," Rashaun said, trying to sound upbeat.

"How you doing, Rashaun? I'm sorry I had to call you but Tyrone wouldn't listen to his father or me. I know you have a lot to do but I didn't know who else to call. He started shouting and banging on the walls. He already took everything else out of the room except for a little cot we had downstairs. I think he is giving up or he feels he should be punished. Rashaun, Tyrone is my only child. I can't afford to lose him."

It was then she began to cry, the tears rolling down her cheeks as her body shuddered.

"Mrs. Wheatley, you won't lose him, I promise. I'll make sure of that. We'll get through this. We will." He hugged her and guided her to a chair in the kitchen. After he sat her down, he proceeded through the hallway until he came to the end of the hall where the door leading into Tyrone's room was painted red, which contrasted greatly with the standard off

10

white color inside the house. Rashaun knocked three times and waited.

There was no answer. Rashaun knocked again, his knuckles rapping hard against the wooden door.

"Tyrone, it's me. Open the door."

"Here, Rashaun," Mrs. Wheatley had regained her composure and brought him a glass of carrot juice. He didn't know what she put in it but she should patent the stuff. It was the best he had ever had. Mrs. Wheatley always gave Tyrone a bottle for him whenever she made it.

"Thank you," Rashaun said and immediately downed half the glass.

"He's in there. Give him a minute to open the door," she said and made her way back down the hall.

'Tyrone," Rashaun shouted again.

This time the knob on the door turned and Rashaun saw his friend.

The first few weeks of the trial were spent picking the jury. Rashaun called Tyrone and kept him updated on the proceedings. Tyrone always sounded fine to him, not like the man Rashaun saw walking back into the stuffy bedroom that smelled like it hadn't been aired out in weeks. Rashaun went straight to the window to open it.

"Please don't," Tyrone said as he went and sat down in the corner of the room.

Tyrone used to be short and thick, benching almost twice as much weight as Rashaun. The man Rashaun saw sitting in the corner of the room was small and frail; a hundred pounds might be too much to have him lift. Even though Rashaun had no intention of calling his friend to the witness stand, Tyrone's appearance was important. If he became too haggard and scary looking, the jury would be afraid of him and would be more likely to lean toward putting him away. He had to get his friend back; he had to convince him that giving up now was to give up on life. Rashaun hoped he hadn't spent too much time on the facts of the case while overlooking the most important element, the person he was defending.

Rashaun hated this part of the job; it was a side the public never saw. Lawyers often became psychiatrists and everything else to their clients. Sometimes lawyers were the only people to whom their clients would listen. They were the invisible fences that separated clients from the real steel bars.

"Why are you doing this to yourself?" Rashaun asked.

"I killed someone, Rashaun. I killed someone I cared deeply for. I go to sleep at night and I see her face, pleading with me not to kill her. Tell me, Rashaun, can you live with that?" Tyrone said, looking out the closed window.

"Tyrone, believe me I know what you're going through!" Rashaun said, trying his best not to raise his voice, "Tyrone if I thought you intentionally killed Judy I wouldn't be here right now. I wouldn't be able to live with myself, much less Andria. Accidents happen. We live in a world where everything that happens to us is not necessarily planned. Can you remember what happened before you went to sleep that night?"

"No, I already told you that."

"Then how could you be guilty of something you can't even remember doing? Come on, Ty, snap out of it. I cannot win this without you; I don't want to win this without you. Stop feeling sorry for yourself; look at what you are doing to your mother."

"I can't sleep, I don't feel like eating. You don't know what it's like. I can't even go outside. My face has been plastered on the front page of nearly every newspaper in town. A woman's group was demonstrating here for weeks. Rashaun, I'm falling apart. I have absolutely no interest in sex. Damn! I don't even look at porno anymore."

"Damn, Tyrone, it's more than ninety degrees in here, open a window or something," Rashaun said, pulling at his shirt collar.

12

"Go ahead, open the window." Tyrone motioned to the window.

"Praise God, I thought the funk in here was going to kill me."

"It does stink in here, doesn't it?" Tyrone said and smiled for the first time.

"Yeah it does." Rashaun smiled, too, feeling a little better as tension exited his body.

"Rashaun, I don't want to spend the rest of my life in prison."

Rashaun walked over to his friend and touched him on his head. "I know, Ty, I know. But, please, I need you as much as you need me. Maybe together we can beat this thing."

"Thanks for everything," Tyrone said, standing up for the first time since Rashaun came into the room.

"You'll be okay," Rashaun said as he hugged his friend.

"Isn't that your boyfriend, Paula?" Andria asked as she pointed to a tall, skinny young man walking on the opposite side of the street.

"Yes, that is Isaiah," Paula said as she and Andria continued to walk down the street.

"Isn't he holding that young girl around her waist?" Andria inquired, stopping briefly to stare at the young couple.

"So what. He can do whatever he wants."

"Are you serious, Paula? When did you become so liberated?"

"I'm not liberated, I just have a little bit more intelligence than the average woman out there. Andria, Isaiah is approaching twenty, not forty-five or fifty. Do you honestly think he would deal with me one on one?"

"Yeah, but what makes him any different from the men you used to date? They couldn't keep their thing in their pants either. What future do you have with him?"

Paula stopped and turned Andria around with her right hand. "I'll tell you the difference. You see that meager boy over there? He can fuck all night. Last night he came seven times and I lost count of how many times I did. There are never any excuses or apologies when it comes to sex. He buys me flowers, comes over and cooks for me. When I'm with him he makes me feel like a queen. You honestly think I believe this young man in his prime will be fateful to a woman like me pushing…"

"Damn, you are liberated," Andria, said.

"No I'm just not a fool," Paula said as they continued to walk down the street. "I'm not waiting and fighting to make someone Mr. Right. Andria, you know what I've been through with men. It hasn't been pretty. If I'm going to have to put up with the bullshit, I might as well get something that's young and sweet instead of some bengay wearing old man."

"Okay, Paula. I get the picture."

"No, you don't, because you still think I should be running behind those older men who have nothing but shit to offer. I met one the other day. He must be old enough to be my father. He come talking about setting me up right. He gonna take care of me. What the hell an old man on Viagra gonna do for me? And you know that old smell they be having, like their skin is rotting or something? I don't want that."

"Paula, we all pick our poison," Andria said as they walked into a West Indian bakery. As usual there was a line, and the people who were serving had the wrong attitude.

"The currant rolls are not what they use to be," Paula said as she positioned herself along the long showcase, had a sign that read, Do Not Lean On Showcase but obviously no one paid any attention to it. If the 300-pound lady in front of them could put both her elbows on it then there was nothing to worry about.

"Nothing is what it use to be, nothing," Andria said, as she reached inside her bag and pulled out her cell phone. She thought about calling Rashaun but changed her mind and returned the phone to her bag. She already knew what he wanted, everything sweet. Andria waited patiently for the woman in front of her to slide the ten hard dough bread loaves she just brought down the showcase.

Andria bought four of the currant rolls, which were not what they use to be; cross buns, bread pudding and hard-dough bread. She knew the bread was full of fat, especially when the cook use lard with all its saturated fat. Paula bought a slice of cake that she closely inspected before the young woman behind the counter wrapped it up. Paula also bought some coconut rolls and some tennis rolls.

As they walked back to the car, Andria saw a troubling look on Paula's face.

"Spit it out, Paula, whatever it is."

"I know you wouldn't like it."

"So, since when has that stopped you from saying or doing what you want to do?" Andria asked as she opened the side door for Paula.

"I'm thinking of having a baby."

"What did you say?" Andria stopped in front of her car door with her right hand on the handle.

Paula also stopped before leaning into the car to look at Andria.

"I knew you would say that."

"Say what? I didn't say anything yet. Paula, have you been using birth control with this boy?"

"Of course. Before I take that next step, believe me, he will have to take an HIV test. I said I wanted to have a baby, I didn't say I wanted to die."

"Times are changing so fast. Sometimes I think I'm way behind in this world. I try my whole life to do things the right way and not to judge others. But day-to-day, I deal with these kids who come from broken and fatherless homes, and I blame the parents. I blame the father for leaving but most of all I blame the women for opening up their legs to those no-good men. And here you are, one of my best friends telling me that you want to have a child for this boy." Andria sat in the car without putting the key into the ignition.

Paula sat down in the car, too, looking straight ahead.

"You don't know, Andria. Sometimes it gets really lonely. It gets so lonely it makes me want to scream. The way life is going I'll never have a man to have a family with. I want a child, Andria," Paula said.

"But, at what cost, Paula? Do you think Isaiah will be there for your child? Do you think a boy can raise a child?"

"To be honest, Andria, I think he'll do a much better job than those so-called men out there. He knew what it was like to grow up without a dad. His dad is serving double life in Rikers. Isaiah is in college now working toward his computer programming degree. Andria, he did it all on his own. I don't think he would abandon his child and just in case he does, don't forget I have a lot of brothers and sisters. There will always be a male role model in my child's life. I promise you that."

As Andria pulled out of the parking lot a soccer ball rolled into the road followed by a little boy on a scooter. She quickly jammed on the brakes to avoid hitting him.

"Fucking bitch," the kid shouted at her.

Andria trembled for a second or two after the kid got out of the road. Andria didn't say a word; she looked at Paula.

Paula looked away.

Three

"Your honor, ladies and gentlemen of the jury, in the next few weeks you will be presented with some very disturbing evidence that will show that the defendant sitting over there, Tyrone Wheatley killed Judy Francis. You will see pictures and hear testimony from witnesses to one of the most horrific crimes of our time. The prosecution will prove beyond a reasonable doubt that Tyrone Wheatley viciously and intentionally killed Judy Francis. He killed her by brutal force and with a weapon that we do not even consider every day: the penis. I'm sure most of you do not even think of it as a weapon but the prosecution will prove that it is as deadly as your hands or your feet. We use our hands and feet every day without hurting or harming anyone but we all know that if we wanted to, they can become a deadly weapon. Mr. Wheatley used his penis as a wife abuser uses his hands to inflict terrible damages on his spouse. He pounded mercilessly on human tissues until they burst and caused death."

Rashaun watched as his ex-girlfriend Kim pounded on the table for maximum effect. She already had everyone's eyes riveted on her. She was wearing a two-piece suit that hugged her body like the scales on a snake. He had seen lawyers in short skirts before but Kim had gone beyond proper court etiquette. Her skirt did not leave more than four inches of her legs covered for the imagination. The judge, a black man in his early fifties, had brought his chair right up to the bench to get the maximum view of the courtroom and Kim's legs. Rashaun had been up against this judge before and he was known for salivating over young women. It was not the judge he wanted for the trial but the roll of the die was to be given him by this judge.

"Then what did the defendant do? He took a nap. He went to sleep as if nothing had happened. After inflicting deadly injuries on the victim in a murderous rage, he took a nap. He did not call an ambulance when he saw the blood coming from the victim. He did not call 911. No, Mr. Wheatley slept like a baby while the victim bled to death. Maybe he thought that's what she deserved, maybe in some sick way he was imposing justice. Ladies and gentlemen of the jury, you will hear alot of questionable things about the victim's character but the victim's character nor her personality is not on trial here. Do not get sidetracked by that. The person who's on trial here is Tyrone Wheatley. Mr. Wheatley is on trial for killing a woman, the mother of a very young child. It is your duty to punish Mr. Wheatley for leaving a husband without his wife and a child without her mother.

"Ladies and gentlemen of the jury, for those of you who haven't heard about Blackfunk, you will get to know it as you know the back of your hand. You will eat and sleep Blackfunk. And if it has the same effect on you it had on me, you will have nightmares about Blackfunk. In this trial you will have an opportunity to strike down Blackfunk. You will be able to set a precedent so whoever tries to use Blackfunk to inflict damage on someone will be met by severe punishment from the courts. This is your opportunity to protect your children and your children's children from pain and suffering. Blackfunk is not a fad; it has been around our communities since slavery. Today it is the leading cause of STD's, sterilization, impotence and strokes. Many lives have been totally destroyed by Blackfunk and many more will, unless you show that there will be consequences for such viciousness."

"And today, Blackfunk has resulted in the ultimate. Today, we are here because the defendant used Blackfunk to commit murder. 'Last night, a man shot and killed his lover in their apartment,' 'yesterday three people were killed in what appeared to be a murder-suicide,' 'a man stabbed his wife to death in a jealous rage...' All these are headlines we are all too

18

familiar with. We shake our heads in disgust as we bury one another. Today, because of the defendant, a child is without a mother. A husband is without a wife. A mother is crying for her daughter. Let's put the suffering of the living and misery away, let justice for those who cannot speak for themselves be heard. When someone dies at the hands of another it is called murder. The defendant committed murder. It might not have been by conventional methods but he nonetheless killed someone.

"The defense will try to tell you the defendant is innocent, it was an accident, he didn't mean to do it. I say whenever you use something to willfully inflict pain and suffering on someone else, there is no innocence. The defense will tell you that the defendant has never been convicted of any criminal activity in his life but tell me isn't there always a first time.

"The same way this is the first time to my knowledge that Blackfunk has resulted in murder. I hope at the end of this trial you set the kind of example that would make it the last time that Blackfunk results in death. Make it the last time that a mother has to cry over her daughter's grave. Make it the last time a husband has to come home and find his wife gone forever. But most of all, do it for that child who will never be able to hold her mother's hand to cross the street, the child who will never be able to come home and tell her mother what happened in school. Do it for the child who will never be able to crawl into her mother's bed and feel the warmth and security of a mother's love." With that said, Kim, on the verge of tears, walked back to her seat. The courtroom was silent.

The judge looked around the courtroom and a full thirty seconds elapsed before he spoke. His words were a repetition of too many cases in a city that cried for justice. This was not Idaho or Atlanta; this was big, bad New York City, where dreams were made and lives stolen, the young and the old were hustlers and only the strong survived. On a moonlit night after 2:00 A.M. you could walk down Broadway in Manhattan and you would be in the company of thousands of people enjoying the beauty of a sleepless night; a city where different ethnic restaurants would be opened to serve people in the wee hours of the morning. The after-hours bar and clubs would be opening their doors a little past 2:00 A.M. to welcome the sleepless, the drugged up and the restless to satisfy their cravings. He looked over at Kim then the defendant.

"Thank you, Ms. Rivers. This court is now in recess until 1:30" With that said his gavel came down in front of him and he rose from his chair.

Andria didn't like it one bit. She was scared of tests and frightened of needles but her gynecologist had told her to come back to the office to discuss her findings after the recent tests. Her exact words to her were "We found abnormal cells in your uterus so we need to run some tests to find out what it is. There is no need to panic, most of the time it's nothing."

Andria wasn't worried about most of the time; her concern was this time.

"Aunty Andria, are we going to buy ice cream?" Rob, Robin's son, asked.

"Yes, we are, as soon as the doctor comes back."

"How come you don't have the same doctor I have?"

"Because you're a child and I'm an adult. There are doctors for kids and there are doctors for adults," she said and held on to his hands as he swung back and forth in front of her.

"What you guys up to?" Robin asked as she closed the door to the rest room.

"Aunty Andria said we're going to have ice cream," Rob said, a smile lighting up his round face.

"Andria!" Robin said and looked at her friend.

"You know I can't resist him," she said as Rob continued to swing in front of her.

"You are spoiling this boy. He knows he can get away with anything around you, and that's what he does."

20

"Robin, leave my godchild alone," Andria said as she brought Rob toward her and kissed him. "You are too cute," she said, pulling on his cheeks.

"And you are going to give him Bubba cheeks."

"Mommy, who is Bubba?"

"Andria, you can come back in now," Dr. Lizah said, opening the door to her office and stepping back.

"Well, Robin, you're on your own with that question. Good luck," Andria said and took the cue from Dr. Lizah.

Dr. Lizah was young, maybe a little older than Andria. Andria knew the woman could not be more than thirty-two. Andria had tried three gynecologists before settling in with Dr. Lizah. The thing Andria liked about her was that she didn't treat her like she was an airhead. The doctor would take her time and explain things. Not the kind of explanation that made comprehension totally impossible, but the kind that made her go *uh-huh, I understand what's going on.* She didn't expect Andria to know medical terms but neither did she intend to leave her in total darkness. She suggested to Andria whenever she was dealing with doctors that she should always get a second opinion for whatever she considered major.

The doctor looked at her and inhaled deeply before talking. "Andria, the test came back positive, I'm afraid we'll have to operate," the doctor said, shifting uneasily in her chair.

"What? Operate to remove what? All you said was that you found abnormal cells."

"Andria, calm down. It's only fibroids. The only problem I can foresee is that you might not be able to conceive." The doctor looked directly into Andria's eyes, which were a mask of confusion and pain.

"Doctor, I want to have children," Andria said, her eyes blood red with unshed tears.

"Andria, I'm not saying that you won't be able to. All I'm saying is that sometimes after patients have these operations they have difficulty conceiving. Everyone is different. I think you should wait until after the operation and see what happens.

We will also be doing some more tests in the upcoming weeks so I suggest you refrain from vaginal intercourse."

"For how long?" Andria asked.

"Why?" the doctor retorted.

"Doctor, I recently got engaged to this beautiful man, you could say a dream come true."

"Congratulations," the doctor said smiling.

"Thank you. How long?" Andria asked, irritation starting to seep in her voice. She liked Dr. Lizah but today she was not Andria's favorite person.

"I think everything should be completed in about six weeks."

"Six weeks? That's a long time. I don't know if I could go that long without sex."

"I said vaginal penetration. Sex encompasses a lot of things. Two people could give and get pleasure in many different ways. I have a few books I would be glad to share with you," the doctor said, pulling open her bottom desk drawer.

"Wait a minute! I know how to please a man without penetration. I don't need a book to tell me what to do. My fiancé is very considerate and I think he'll understand, however, he is also a man, and men are prone to do many questionable things."

"Think of this as a test of fidelity and understanding, two of the most important things in any relationship. If he is the man you say he is, then you have nothing to worry about. However, if he disappoints you in any way then you have a decision to make. I personally wouldn't want a man who couldn't refrain in a crucial time like this. What would happen if you were pregnant? You do know there comes a time in the process when sex is a no-no." Dr. Lizah sounded almost childlike when she made her last statement.

"Doctor, do you know fifty percent of affairs are started during pregnancy?"

"That means that fifty percent of men should not have been married in the first place. Andria, it's your call. You can

22

ignore the problem in your uterus to keep your man or you can have faith and confidence in your man. It's your health at stake here." The doctor closed the drawer without removing the contents. "I think you are making a mountain out of a molehill. Go home, discuss it with your fiancé and see what he says. Like I said before, if he is the man you said he is I don't see any problem." With that said she stood.

"Okay, Dr. Lizah, I'll call you on Thursday to set up the appointment," Andria said. She reached over, shook the doctor's hand and left.

When she got out to the waiting room Robin and Rob were waiting.

"What did she say?" Robin's face was etched with concern for her friend.

"She told me that life is not fair and just when you think you got something good going, there is always a pin waiting to burst that bubble."

Andria noticed the paint had started to chip on the ceiling. It was a long, thin pencil-line crack that extended for about a foot over her head. She wondered why she had never seen it before. Rashaun lay fast asleep next to her, snoring lightly and irritating the shit out of her. She gave him a slight nudge hoping he would stop but all that did was make him turn on his side and continue to snore. She reached over and gently started to run her fingers up and down his back. As she caressed him the snoring dissipated. She should have been able to fall asleep but the last few visits to the doctor were making bags appear under her eyes. She got up and turned the light off. She returned to the bed to retrieve her pillow and planted a small kiss on Rashaun's cheek before she headed to the living room.

In the darkness, Andria found her way to the sofa without tripping over the small side table. She reached over to the table and picked up the Sony all-in-one digital remote control. She pressed a few buttons and the thirty-six-inch Sony

TV came on followed by the satellite and then the Kenwood receiver. There was no sound coming from the five speakers strategically placed around the room. She pressed the display button on the control and some writing appeared on the top left-hand corner of the TV screen informing her that she was watching one of the forgettable black movies that BET clogged the airways with in the wee hours of the morning. At least it was better than the infomercials. She left the sound off and made herself comfortable on the sofa. She looked to the right side of the screen into the white curtained window that kept the unspeakable crimes that happened in the city at this time of night away from her. She stared off into the space reserved for the difficulties of the body and her lack of control over sleep.

"Was I snoring again?" Rashaun asked as he ran his fingers through her hair.

"No, I just couldn't sleep," Andria said as she began to rise from the sofa.

"What's wrong, Andria?" Rashaun took a seat next to her and put his right arm around her, pulling her to him.

"Nothing that I can't handle. Only a little bit of woman trouble."

"Andria, you love sleep I don't know of too many things that would take you away from what you consider beauty rest. The bags under your eyes tell the story of more than one restless night."

"Rashaun, don't you have a big day in court tomorrow? You should be sleeping right now," Andria said as she adjusted herself next to him.

"Don't worry about my case. I'm okay. Let's talk about you." He tried to turn her face toward him but she pulled away.

"I told you, it's nothing!" Her voice sounded hoarse, as if she was about to cry.

"Andria?" Rashaun got off the sofa and knelt in front of her so he could look into her eyes. Tears had begun to run down her face.

"I don't want to worry you." She pulled her knees up onto the sofa, making herself into a tight ball.

"Andria, look at me. Do you think I could go to bed now? This relationship is not about you or me; it's about us. I know I've been preoccupied lately but don't think I've forgotten about you. You are who I live for. I wake up and I know I'm going to have a good day because I see your face." He held her face gently between his hands. The tears had stopped falling.

"I went to the doctor a few days ago and she told me I might have a growth in my uterus."

Rashaun's hands fell from her face. They became cold and clammy, his eyes sunk into his head. His mouth was ajar. He had heard about growths in the uterus, it was the first sign of cancer. The same kind of cancer that had killed his favorite aunt two years earlier. He couldn't look at Andria anymore. He wanted to be strong for her but first he had to be strong for himself.

"Rashaun, I'll be okay." She slid down to the floor to join him and this time she wrapped her hands around him. She traced her hand over his recently cut baldhead feeling the stubs that had started to grow back.

He always liked when she ran her fingers over his head. It relaxed him, almost like a massage. He loved this woman. His heart had stopped beating when she told him about the growth.

"The doctor said it's fibroids and I have to have surgery to remove them." Andria felt Rashaun's body relax as she continued. "The only drawback is that I might not be able to have children. I'm sorry I really want to give you a family."

"Andria, forget about giving me a family, your health comes first." Rashaun stood and lifted Andria up with him. "Let's go back to bed. I'll tell you about the bird in the hand."

"I already know that one."

"Exactly."

"She also said that I won't be able to have sex for a while."

"And that will kill me?" he said as he laid her back down on the bed.

"Who's talking about you."

Rashaun could have made it easy on himself and turned Tyrone down when Tyrone asked Rashaun to represent him. After all, his old law firm had given him valid reasons why he should do just that. Then there was the unwritten lawyer code of ethics, which highly denounced representation of family and friends. And all that other stuff with Andria being so close to Judy should have made refusal easy. But life wasn't supposed to be easy and from the time his black ass was brought into this world it hadn't been for Rashaun. So now as he sat next to his friend in a crowded courtroom Rashaun was going to take all the difficulties of life and combine it with all of his strength and hopefully with a little luck his friend would walk out of the courtroom a free man.

Tyrone sat next to him, his eyes weaving through the courtroom as skillfully as a bike messenger on a Manhattan street during lunchtime. Rashaun patted his friend on the back and stood to give his opening statement. Today Rashaun had on a soft tone brown Italian suit that Andria had picked out for him. It seemed that now that he had a woman in his life he had lost his sense of style. If he had listened to some of his friends he would have put the brakes on Andria trying to change him. They all said it starts when your woman began choosing your clothes for you, the next thing you know she wants you to bring your check home to her. But Rashaun wasn't worried about that—Andria wasn't a control freak. He had known many controlling freaks.

There was this one girl named Kathy he had dated in college. She started by telling him his hair was too long, so he cut it. Then she told him what classes to take and she wasn't even in his major, but he took them. And sex, forget about it! Back then he didn't eat pussy because that wasn't his forte. "Do it this way, do it that way, don't go in so much." Fuck, by the time he came it was a relief not a pleasure. No, Andria was definitely no Kathy. Back then pussy was scarce because women couldn't appreciate a dark skin brother but now Kathy would have had to lick his toes before she could smell his dick. Call it arrogance, but a brother making six figures as a lawyer usually has his pick of the litter.

"Your honor, ladies and gentlemen of the jury, we are here because of a tragic accident," Rashaun said as he walked over to the jury of seven women and five men. Two male alternates were seated in the back of the court. As most jurors called upon to perform their duty, they sat looking as if their time could be better served doing something that wasn't forced down their throats. Most people looking for a break from their job had no problem serving on the jury. It was just that they wanted to do it on their time. Maybe when they were stressed out at work and the boss was on their back like the shell on a turtle, then and there they would be glad to say "sorry Mr. Hendricks but I have jury duty for the next two weeks." But New York didn't give them that choice so here they were Monday morning looking at Rashaun and the shriveled-up boy he was defending. Rashaun knew the jurors were probably wondering how could Mr. Shrivels fuck someone to death? Tyrone's depression might be a good thing after all.

"Did my client have sex with Mrs. Francis? Yes, he did. Was it rough sex? It may or may not have been, depending on whom you talk to. Did he kill Mrs. Francis? No, he didn't. The prosecution would like you to believe that my client willfully and intentionally battered Mrs. Francis until she died. The prosecution wants you to believe that my client is an abuser. They want you to believe that my client deliberately had sex in such a manner that would inflict pain and suffering and eventually death. Not once during sexual intercourse did my client physically abuse the deceased with his hands, feet, mouth or any part of his body that would cause unnecessary pain. There isn't a shred of evidence to show that my client in any way tried to hurt Mrs. Francis. There are many types of sex,

28

some of them you might like, some of them I might like. I'm not going to tell you what you should do behind closed doors and I sure don't want you to tell me what I should do behind closed doors. My client is as much a victim here as Mrs. Francis. For the rest of his life he will have nightmares from this incident. Imagine going to bed after you have had consensual sex, and I do mean consensual because no time in this sexual relationship did my client force the deceased. She wanted to have sex the way it was done. And the defense will prove that the deceased enjoyed that kind of sex. The defense will also show that the deceased pushed my client to that point where he lost control of his senses."

Rashaun walked over to the left side of the jury box and stood in front of a woman who looked to be in her twenties. She was dressed in a long blue-and-white polka-dot dress that revealed a split as she sat with her legs crossed. Rashaun had made eye contact with her a few times before walking over to where she sat. He did not look at her directly when he stood in front of her; instead he continued his opening arguments while scanning the rest of the jury. He was playing with her, showing interest yet not pursuing beyond acknowledgement. In a trial the prosecution and the defense would use whatever it took to get the tide to turn in their favor.

"The prosecution wants you to believe that my client willfully inflicted damages to the deceased's uterus, which eventually led to her death. The prosecution wants you to believe that my client knew exactly what he was doing in regards to the damages he caused to Mrs. Francis. Yet my client called the police to report the woman's death. How many murderers call the cops? The evidence will show that my client was terribly upset when he made that phone call. Do not let the prosecution get into your bedroom. Do not let the prosecution dictate how and with whom you should have sex. There are these lyrics to this old calypso song 'Some like it hot, some like it cold.' We are all individuals and no one should be given the right to tell us how we should like it." Rashaun headed back to the front of the courtroom, his walk was slow and deliberate to give the jurors time for his words to sink in.

"To summarize, the defendant did not cause the death of Mrs. Francis. Mrs. Francis's death was an accident. Was the defendant there when the accident happened? Yes, he was. Could he have prevented the accident? No, he couldn't because he did not know that the accident was about to take place. Was the accident a tragedy? Yes, it was. Should my client be sent to jail for an accident? No, he shouldn't. This is your task, ladies and gentlemen, to decide whether a person should be punished for an accident that he was not responsible for causing. Thank you." Rashaun walked back to the defense table.

Rashaun ate a small lunch with Tyrone and returned to the courtroom at 2:15.

"The prosecution calls Officer Louis Artica to the stand" Kim said as she shuffled papers on her table. She remained at the table while the officer was sworn in.

The white officer stood proudly as the bailiff did his job. He had the look of a veteran who had been in this situation many times before. It was an arrogance that many found revolting in police officers from Long Island who welcomed the challenge of the urban streets. They were usually the first to shoot and the last to get blamed. Their arrogance stemmed from the so-called invisibility of the shield and the power of Guilluanics, which was gun plus white cop equal dead black man. Today he was in court for a different reason.

"Officer Artica, you and your partner were the first officers on the scene?" Kim stood a little lower than eye level to the officer who was elevated on the witness stand.

"Yes," the officer replied, clasping both hands together.

"Was the door to the defendant's apartment opened or closed when you got there?"

"The defendant came and opened the door to the apartment."

30

"Was the defendant clothed when he came to the door?" she asked, walking over to the jury.

"At first, I wasn't able to see the defendant, he back into the room."

"So you didn't know whether the defendant was dressed?"

"No."

When you went into the apartment, were you able to see the defendant then, Officer Artica."

"Yes, he was naked and balled up in the far right-hand corner of the room."

"How did the defendant look to you?"

"Objection, your honor, the officer is not a doctor. He is not qualified to make such an assessment," Rashaun noted.

"Objection sustained. Ms. Rivers, please restate your question."

Kim walked away from the jury back to the witness stand. "Did the defendant appear as if he needed help?"

"Well…" Officer Artica started.

"Objection, your honor, the officer is not qualified to make a medical judgment," Rashaun said standing.

"Your honor, I'm trying to establish the state of mind of the defendant when the officer arrived."

"Continue, Ms. Rivers, but stick to the facts and not opinions. Answer the question, Officer Artica," the judge said.

"He was naked with dried up blood at the end of his penis."

"Did he say anything to you?"

"Yes, he said 'I killed her' and he pointed to the woman on the bed."

"How did he say that he killed her?"

"Objection, your honor, it was not established that my client killed anyone."

"Sustained."

"Officer Artica, what did you do after you walked into the apartment?"

31

"I went over to the defendant and checked for weapons and I told my partner to keep an eye on him while I took a look at the woman on the bed. I searched the bed and I didn't find any weapons then I reached over and checked the victim to see if she was breathing, she wasn't so then I checked her pulse and I didn't get one."

"What did you do then?"

"I told my partner to call EMS while I checked the rest of the apartment."

"Did the defendant say anything else to you?"

"The defendant kept repeating that he was sorry and he didn't mean to kill her. I have never seen anyone get killed by a dick before, unless it's a disease."

"Move to strike from the record. My client did not confess to killing." Rashaun stood and waited for the judge's reply.

"Move granted. The jury will strike the witness statement from the record. Continue, Ms. Rivers," the judge said and once more leaned back into his chair.

"So you did not find anything else in the room that the defendant could have used to inflict the damage on the victim?" Kim asked.

"No," Officer Artica replied.

"Officer, have you ever heard of Blackfunk?"

"Not until recently. When I first heard of it, I thought it was a rap song or a new hip-hop dance craze. But then one of my black friends told me what it was. I don't believe it though. Maybe she had a cut in her vagina or something."

"Officer, please stick to answering to the question," Kim shot back, a look of annoyance clearly visible on her face. Rashaun's face was devoid of expression but inside he was smiling.

"Okay, ma'am," the officer sarcastically answered.

"Officer Artica, did the defendant seem incoherent?"

"Objection, your honor, the officer is unqualified to answer that."

"Okay, your honor let me rephrase the question. Officer Artica, did you request any action from the defendant?"

"Yes."

"And did he complete the action?"

"Yes. I asked him his name and also the victim's name."

"What else?"

"I asked him what happened to the victim and he told me."

"What exactly did he tell you?"

"He said that they were having sex and when he woke up she was dead. He said he thought he had killed her."

"Objection, your honor the—"

"No more questions, your honor." Kim walked quickly to her seat.

"Does the defense wish to cross-examine the witness?" the judge asked.

"Yes, your honor," Rashaun said, standing with a gold pen in his right hand.

"Officer Artica, you said that you don't believe that a man can sex a woman to death."

"Yes, I did."

"Do you still believe that?"

"Well I know you guys are supposed to be well-endowed but…"

"Officer Artica, please answer the question. Do you believe that a man can sex a woman to death?"

"No. Not even a black man."

"Thank you, Officer Artica. No more questions, your honor," Rashaun said and walked back to the defense table.

"Officer Artica, you are excused," the judge said as he looked over to Kim.

"Ladies and gentlemen of the jury, this will be all for now. Please remember your instructions as per discussion of the case. Court will resume tomorrow. Court is dismissed." With that the judge's gavel came down twice on the podium and he rose.

The weights rose slowly, barely reaching the top of the metal stud that signaled to the lifter that his goal had been attained. Rashaun held his hands underneath the rising weight, ready for any sudden movement that would signal the downward spiral of the weight.

"Come on, Peter, one more, don't be a baby. My niece lifts heavier weights than that," Rashaun urged.

As soon as Peter saw the weights were an inch above the metal stud he pushed it back onto the tracks.

"Fuck you, Rashaun. I'm not losing my balls for no metal objects," Peter said, sitting up on the bench. "Remember, I have a wife to support now."

"It's all good. When she leaves your ass for the pectorals-pumping brother down the block, don't come crying to me." Rashaun added more weights to the bar.

"Rashaun, you know something I've been thinking lately about an operation."

"Hold up, Peter" Rashaun turned around to look his friend in the eyes. "You are not telling me there is a woman in you fighting to get out. It's cool. I'll never get on a brother for doing what he has to do but I'm not hanging out with you in any dress. We have a cool brother thing, not a cool sister thing."

"Shut the fuck up, Rashaun, and sit back on the bench." Peter motioned to Rashaun to sit down. "I'm not talking about any sex-change operation. I'm talking about penile enlargement."

"You talking about more meat on your salami, more ounces to the pound, which in your case is a quarter pound," Rashaun said, laughing as he stretched out on the bench.

"I'm serious, Rashaun. What do you think?" Peter asked.

"Me, personally, I don't believe in messing with what God gave you. If it's not broke, don't fix it. Have you done any research on those things? I don't trust half of the shit these white people have out there. Is this shit legal? Look what happened with those women and their breast implants,"

Rashaun said as he adjusted himself so that his forehead was in line with the metal bar that held the weight.

"All I've been doing lately is research. I have been to every Web site that has that shit on it. I..."

"Hold on, Peter, let me do this set before I get cold," Rashaun said as he took the 315-pound weight off the bench and brought it down to his chest. He repeated the same movement ten times then pushed the weight back onto the rack. "Damn, this feels good. You know how long I've been trying to get ten reps at 315."

"I try to lift that shit, my balls would be dragging on the floor," Peter said as he and Rashaun started to remove the forty-five pound slabs of weight off the bar. "But on the serious tip, I think I will do the operation."

"Peter, you ever thought about alternatives?"

"Rashaun, dick exercises don't work. They end in masturbation."

"I wasn't talking about jerking off, I was talking about changing the scenario."

"What you mean, leave my wife?" Peter's face had become contorted as if Rashaun had spoken for abortion at a right-to-life convention. The mere suggestion was appalling.

"I have had my share of ETP [extra tight pussy], maybe there is one out there for you. Or you can have her do the operation. In your case stuff has to be added. God only knows what these doctors are adding to your dick, it could be dog meat. In her case all they have to do is make her hole smaller. I think that's a no-brainer. What do you think?" Rashaun asked as he started to walk toward the incline bench press bar.

"Shit, why didn't I think of that?" Peter slapped his face with his right hand as he followed Rashaun. "You're right, Rashaun. All she has to do is close it up a little bit. Not too much, just a little bit."

"I'll take your word on the exact reduction, Peter. I'm sure you and your wife could come to some agreement on that,"

Rashaun said as he took the twenty-five-pound weight and started to put it on the bar.

"Why you putting on twenty-five pounds, Rashaun?" Peter looked at him as if he had just lost his brain.

"For you," Rashaun answered.

"I'm finished with this weight-lifting stuff. I hate this exercising bullshit. Look at me, I'm skinny and I'll always be skinny, the same as my father and his father and hopefully one day my son. We don't need diet and exercise, skinniness runs in the family." Peter stretched his hands above his head and inhaled deeply. "You ready to get out of here?"

"Naw, man, I have a few more things to do but you can bounce," Rashaun said as he started to replace the twenty-five-pound weight with a forty-five-pound one.

"You sure, man?" Peter asked as he started to adjust his clothes to head out onto the street.

"Yeah, man, go home and take care of your business."

Rashaun stayed an extra hour in the gym to complete his exercise routine. He had already missed Tuesday because Andria didn't want him to leave the house, so he had to make up the time. He invited her to come and work out with him but she told him she didn't like weights. She didn't mind going jogging but weight lifting was a no-no. Then she took the nightgown off and she asked him if he saw anything that needed toning. He didn't but he said yes anyway. So she had him, over very little objections, tone her up.

"The dick is sweet. I can't help myself. My husband comes home and he wants some and I give it to him."

"But Mrs. London you have fourteen children and your sweet dick husband has fifteen more. Nine of your kids are in prison—five of them girls and four boys—and you are pregnant again. Your last child was found wondering in the middle of the street on Albany Avenue. Your house is a known drug-dealing spot. What do you think social services is going to do?" Andria

36

sat across from the forty-eight-year-old woman with the fake straight hair.

"I don't want them to take my baby, I didn't think I could have any more. This is my last one. I promise I'm going to start taking the pill," Mrs. London pleaded.

"Mrs. London, does this sound familiar? Because it should. You have been saying the same thing for the last five pregnancies. Every time you're going to go on the pill, you're going to make sure your husband wears condoms, every time is the same old story. But, here you are pregnant again," Andria said, slamming the pen down on the table. "This has to stop."

"Just let me keep this one, this one is special. I'm begging you let me keep my baby." Mrs. London started to cry. Her tears formed two unbroken lines down her cheeks as they disappeared in her green dress.

Andria was always amazed by the way the lady cried. Mrs. London was the first person that Andria ever saw cry with uninterrupted streams of tears that ran for about thirty seconds then stop right under her eyelids. Andria leaned back in her chair and waited for the episode to pass.

"Are you finished, Mrs. London?" Andria asked. While Andria found Mrs. London's theatrics very entertaining she held no pity for the lady's present condition. Andria was concerned about Mrs. London's baby, an uninvited guest at the world's biggest party. Andria knew the child would be thrown into the system that would make him or her a victim before puberty set in. Rikers, foster homes, abusive relationships were some of the many places that house the uninvited partygoers.

"Go on, Ms. Jackson," Mrs. London said as she pulled a small bag from her big purse. She took a mirror and placed it on the table, followed by an assortment of makeup brushes.

Andria knew the conversation was over—for the rest of the meeting Mrs. London would not hear a word she had to say.

"When is the baby due?" Andria asked, hoping to bring Mrs. London back to the table.

"I think the doctor said in a few months," she replied, bringing the small mirror to her left eye while she used her right hand to apply eyeliner.

"A few months could mean three or four. Mrs. London, you have to be more specific. Have you been going to the doctor for your regular checkups?" Andria asked, wanting to take the mirror from the woman's hand and break it into a million pieces.

"I had fourteen children and I never had any complications. They just drop out one after the other. It don't even pain me to have children no more. The first child was painful but all the others just drop out. I don't even need to go to the doctor but I go, otherwise you people will stop my medical benefits. Yeah, that's why I go because I don't want you people to stop my benefits. My mother had fourteen of us and she raised all of us herself." Mrs. London switched from the left eye to the right. "But because you people give us some pocket change, you all want to tell us what to do with our lives. I think it's a conspiracy, you all working for the white man. You black but the white man is pulling your strings. I know you all going to take my baby but believe me I'm not going to give this one up that easily. I'm going to fight for this one. I'm going to get that black lawyer Cochran to fight for me."

"Mrs. London, how many children do you have living with you?"

"None," Mrs. London said as she put down the eyeliner and picked up a powder sponger and started to pat her face down.

"Yes, Mrs. London, in addition to the drugs and neglect, we took your children away from you because you live in a rat-infested one-bedroom apartment that hasn't been clean for years. You won't let the exterminator in and you barely pass inspection. The only reason why the landlord lets you keep the place is because he is getting paid very well by Section Eight. We don't only pay your medical bills, we pay your gas and electric bills, we give you food stamps and as I mentioned we take care of your rent. Mrs. London, you haven't worked for more than twenty years. You have had a baby every year. So please don't give me this racist bullshit." Andria had started to sweat. "If it were up to me I would take you off all the public assistance. And I wouldn't care if you had to walk the street and sell your body to support yourself, maybe then you would realize what you're doing. And I don't mean what you're doing to yourself. I'm talking about all those kids you bring into the world and abandon."

"I never abandon any of my kids. It's you people who take them away from me. My poor babies."

"Mrs. London when you bring a child into the world and you have no way of taking care of the child, that is called abandonment. When you let the child go days without food, that is called abandonment. When you leave three kids ages one to seven home for two days alone in the house, that is called abandonment. When a three-year-old ends up in the middle of the street that is called abandonment."

"Damn you," Mrs. London said, slamming the mirror down on the table, cracking the flap that covered it. "I was only gone for one day and I was only twenty-three then. It wasn't my fault. I went with my girlfriends and I stayed over a little too long. I love each and every one of my children. It wasn't my fault that one of their fingers got caught in the blender. I told them not to touch the blender. I warned them don't mess with the blender."

"I will see you in two weeks, Mrs. London," Andria said, unwilling to see the tears again.

"I'm keeping my child," Mrs. London said as she gathered her artificial face from the table.

"I'll be calling the doctor to make sure you keep your appointments. You're over forty now, the kids don't just drop anymore," Andria said as she stood up and began to gather her paperwork.

"Bitch, I know how old I am. I don't need reminders."

"Good-bye, Mrs. London."

"Go to hell, bitch." Mrs. London walked out the door, slamming it behind her.

Andria sat back down in her chair inhaling deeply to regain her composure. She had had nightmares before going to visit Mrs. London's apartment. When she went into the apartment she took great pains not to touch anything. She had never sat in the lady's apartment, refusing even bottled water because she didn't know what had crawled around the cap. She couldn't figure for the life of her how anyone could live like that. It was the filthiest apartment Andria had ever seen. Andria was angry that she was part of a system that supported such decay. She didn't know what came over Mrs. London who never loved anything except herself and her husband's wayward dick. She had never wanted to fight to keep any of her kids before. Andria had had cases where unfit mothers had fought to keep their kids and won. The story didn't usually end when the judge give them custody of the kid. No, the story usually ended when the kid came into the hospital with broken bones or a burn that left the imprint of hot metal. Andria knew she had a fight on her hands that did not guarantee the child a great life but maybe a chance to survive in this crazy world.

"Give me a Caucasian minute," the blue-haired waitress said and went to the other table.

"So Rashaun, how's the sex case of the century going?" Paula asked as she adjusted herself on a light blue seat.

"Rashaun doesn't want to talk about the case, Paula. Let's just eat and talk about something else." Andria gave Paula the look that accompanied her statement.

"That's okay, Andria. I have no problem talking about the case. The prosecution has already called it's first witness."

"Judy said she wanted some Blackfunk, I guess she got it. Judy was a freak. We all knew that. Andria, you heard when she said that, didn't you?" Paula diverted her attention from the back of the room where she had seen the waitress disappear. She looked to Andria for confirmation.

"How many of you heard Judy say that she wanted Blackfunk?" Rashaun asked as the waitress reappeared with their lunch. Rashaun had ordered a chicken salad while Andria and Paula had ordered chicken sandwiches with french fries.

"How could you only eat a chicken salad, Rashaun? You on a diet?" Paula asked as a crisp brown french fry disappeared in her mouth. She widened her eyes and sighed.

"Paula, would you testify to what you just told me?" Rashaun drank some water and put a little bit of Thousand Island dressing on his salad.

"That's all the dressing you're going to put on your salad?" Paula asked as she switched from the french fries to her sandwich. As her teeth sank into it a trickle of the honey-mustard dressing fell from the right side of her mouth.

"Paula, can you just shut up and eat." Andria knew that Rashaun would continue questioning Paula but she hoped he wouldn't. She had seen him at work before; he was unrelenting when he got going.

"Paula, you didn't answer my question. Will you testify for the defense?" Rashaun held a fork in his hand, hovering over his salad.

"Go in front of a courtroom with all these people looking at me. Not me, not alone, I will not do it. Why don't you ask Andria, as I said she was there too." Paula continued to devour the sandwich.

All of a sudden Andria did not like chicken sandwiches, it was white and it smelled bad. The honey-mustard sauce that she had drenched it in did not make it any more appealing.

"Andria!" Rashaun spoke a little too loudly for the small table.

Paula stopped for a second to look at the two of them before removing the cap from her diet Pepsi.

"I'm not going to testify against my friend. I'm sorry but I will not do it." Andria pushed the untouched meal to the middle of the table. She did not make eye contact with Rashaun's whose full attention was on her.

"We'll discuss this later." Rashaun looked at his watch. "Ladies, thank you for the meal but I have to leave. Court will be starting soon." He stood, went around to Andria's chair and planted a kiss on her cheek and quickly walked out the door.

"Thank you, Paula," Andria said as she looked over at Paula who was drinking the last of her soda.

"Oh please, girl. Don't worry about that. Rashaun could never stay mad at you for long. Anyway it's getting late, don't you have to go by your mom's?" Paula asked reaching into her purse and pulling out her credit card. "Cash or plastic, lately it seems they're all the same." She flipped over the check, put the plastic back in her purse and brought out a twenty and a ten-dollar bill.

"I don't know what to tell my mom, she really wants me to wear her wedding dress," Andria said as she, too, picked up her purse and checked the contents.

"Do what you think is best" Paula said as she stood.

"I really don't want to hurt her feelings. I'm all she has."

"I'm sure everything will work out. Let's go." Paula was halfway out the door before Andria could respond.

In a city where deals were made and broken and lives were lost and saved in the blink of an eye, the sun had taken its majestic downward spiral. As Andria walked up the steps to her mother's apartment she wanted to steal the setting sun. She wanted to run and get Rashaun and sit on the steps hand in hand watching God's work. *This is why we live*, she thought. *We live for the beauty of the setting sun in a picturesque sky.* Andria did not see the two teenage boys leaning against the wall across the street watching her as she ascended the steps. She didn't hear the argument erupt nor did she notice the tall boy take out a seventeen-inch knife he had cleverly concealed in his waistband. When the door to her mother's apartment closed, Andria missed the knife penetrating deep into one of the boy's stomach muscles as the kid drop to the ground reaching into the arch of his back to pull out a .38 revolver. But his hand never got to the handle because the knife had done its job. His eyes glazed over as he helplessly watched his opponent turn and run into the chaos of the unforgiving streets.

"Hi, Mom" Andria said as she walked into the house. She had called her mother an hour earlier to tell her she was on her way. As usual her mother had prepared a meal for her. A plastic bag with food in a white plastic container was put to the side for Rashaun. Andria was glad she didn't have to cook this evening; she knew she would not be in a good mood. "Mom."

"I'm here." Joyce, Andria's mother, shouted from the bedroom. "Sit down and eat."

Andria poured herself a glass of cranberry juice and took her food from the table and headed to her mother's bedroom.

She found her mother sitting on the foot of her bed, remote in hand looking at the *Wheel of Fortune*. She was dressed in a blue frock and her hair was covered in a head wrap. To the right side of the closet was a long white wedding dress.

43

Andria passed by the wedding dress and sat by her mother, kissing her gently on the cheek before cutting into the chicken breast that her mother had cooked.

"Did you go back to the doctor?" her mother asked still concentrating on the TV screen.

"Not yet," Andria answered before shoveling a forkful of rice and peas into her mouth.

"Your aunt, God rest her soul, died from uterine cancer, you know." Her mother continued to watch the TV.

"Mom, the doctor said it's fibroids," Andria said, before eating a piece of broccoli.

"I hope that's what it is because you are all I have." Her mother's face took on a grief-stricken look. She quickly took the remote and turned to CNN.

"Mom, I'm not going anywhere," Andria said as she put down her plate to hug her mother. Andria wondered if she did the right thing in telling her about the doctor's findings. Andria did not like to see her mother stress herself. It was enough that she had to deal with it, seeing the effect it had on her mother made the food hard to swallow.

"How's Rashaun?" her mother asked.

"He's fine. He didn't come because he was busy at the office." She wondered if Rashaun would've come with her. She was sure that she was not the best thing on his mind, not after their lunch.

"Did you decide?" Andria's mother asked as she turned off the television. The room was now eerily quiet.

"No, Mom, I didn't decide if I was going to wear your dress," Andria said, looking up at the wedding dress for the first time since she had come into the room.

"I know you kids today like all these modern things but this wedding dress is the most beautiful thing I own. Your father, rest his soul, said I was the most beautiful bride he had ever seen. Our wedding was the talk of the village. I will never forget that day." A smile came across her face. For that moment

44

with Andria by her side she seemed to be reliving the most beautiful day of her life.

"Mommy, Mommy," Andria called out, making sure her mother did not get lost in the past. Andria didn't want to wear her mother's wedding dress. She had picked out a beautiful dress at a black boutique in downtown Brooklyn, a long time ago when she wasn't seeing anyone.

She was going to meet Robin at a café on Atlantic Avenue when she saw it in the window. It was the most beautiful wedding dress she had ever seen. She had brought Robin ten blocks back to the store to see it. Andria stood in front the display window smiling like a small schoolgirl. After Rashaun proposed she had gone to the store and spoken to the owner about the dress. Of course it wasn't in the window but he kept pictures of all his wedding dresses. Andria had sat in the boutique for more than an hour looking for the dress. She saw many nice ones and many that death would not find her in. When she finally saw her dress and called the owner over he told her that he hadn't made that dress in years. After Andria refused to buy any of his other dresses he agreed to make it for her. He charged her twice as much as she remembered seeing the dress advertised for but she didn't argue. Andria went in for measurements and left a deposit. She had explained all of this to her mother but her mother was undeterred. She wanted Andria to wear her old wedding dress.

"I hear you, Andria," her mother replied, her gaze returning to the blank TV screen. "Mrs. Oliver died in her sleep yesterday. Nobody knows what killed her. She just died. It seems like death is all around me lately," her mother said, getting up and taking the dishes from Andria. At that moment a siren sounded faint at first then louder as if it was right in the room. The flashing lights from the police car sent cascades of light through the room.

"Mommy, I think something happened outside." Andria got off the bed and went to the window.

"Andria, get away from the window," her mother shouted as she reentered the room. "Just last week this lady heard gunshots and poked her head out the window. Do you know what happened? I tell you what happened. She got killed. A stray bullet hit her right in the middle of the forehead."

Andria got a quick glimpse of about ten police cars through the window with a few officers standing around a white sheet across the street before she closed the blind.

"Mommy, I've been telling you to get out of this neighborhood. It's not safe anymore," Andria said as she followed her mother into the living room.

"Where am I going, Andria? I've lived here all my life. My next address is in the Lord's house," her mother answered as she sat down on the white antique sofa in the living room. Andria had had to plead with her to get rid of the blue-and-gold flowered sofa with the stitching on the side that her mother had had for as long as she could remember. Andria had given her half of the money for the furniture. At first her mother had covered it in plastic but after countless arguments with Andria she removed the covering. Andria's mother very rarely had guests and on those occasions when she did she usually entertained them in the kitchen.

"Mommy, I can't make you move but if you change your mind I will be happy to pay half the rent."

"I know you would, Andria, but all I want for you to do for me is walk down that aisle with that lovely wedding dress in the room."

"Mommy, I told you, I already put a deposit on my wedding dress."

"I will be happy to pay it off for you. Maybe one of your girlfriends would buy it from you. What's that one's name again, the one that could never keep a man? Paulette or something."

"Mommy, Paula is not getting married so she doesn't need a wedding dress. I'm going to go and call Rashaun to come and pick me up," Andria said and went to the phone hanging on the side of the refrigerator in the kitchen. She knew this wedding dress argument would not end until the day of her wedding.

The courthouse was packed as usual. The judge had refused airing of the case on television so the reporters made up most of the audience. Judy's husband never came to the courthouse. The rest of Judy's family, including her sisters and her father, were seated in their usual place behind the prosecution table. Tyrone's mother and father sat behind Rashaun's table. Tyrone sat next to Rashaun in a light blue suit, his hair recently trimmed, which made him look five years younger. Rashaun had recently gotten the list of the prosecution witnesses, most of whom he did not know; neither did Tyrone. There was one exception, though, Natalie, one of Tyrone's old girlfriends. The only thing Tyrone remembered about her was that she had dumped him. But not only did she dump him but she went and told all her friends that he was lousy in bed. Most of her friends were also his friends so he had to chill with the dating thing for a while. He slept with her one more time after he broke up with her and that was a night he would rather forget.

"The prosecution calls Anna Hopkins to the stand." Kim stood between Rashaun's table and hers.

As usual, Rashaun saw that the judge could not take his eyes off Kim. The judge's lust was evident. Today Kim had on a dress that made many men wish a sudden gust of wind would enter the courtroom. The judge hadn't seen a fine piece of ass like that since he was whoring in college. Even on the nights when he left his wife and kids in the five-bedroom mansion in Westchester to prowl the west side highway for high heel shoes he hadn't seen one that look like that. Kim was a thoroughbred. If he had her he would not leave Westchester. But she barely looked at him, all her attention seem to be focused on the defense lawyer. One of the darkest men he had ever seen.

Judging by her preoccupation with the lawyer and the lack of interest in him, she either loved the lawyer to death or wanted to see his head on a plate. Either way she wasn't interested in your lordship, maybe she did not understand what it took to be a black judge in New York. He would love to explain it to her right before he rammed his dick up her hot pussy. *Where is that fucking witness, this lady is getting me hot here,* the judge thought. All he had on under the robe was his boxer shots. He couldn't stand up until thoughts of his wife reappeared in his mind.

Rashaun and Tyrone's heads were glued to the back door where the bailiff had disappeared a minute ago. They and the rest of the courtroom were wondering what was going on. Rashaun knew by the look on the judge's face that he wasn't going to tell Kim anything about the court delay. Shit, Rashaun knew the judge wouldn't mind looking at Kim for the rest of his life. And so would most of the men in the court and some women too. Finally the double doors swung open again and the bailiff's back was exposed to the courtroom. As he turned around he expertly wheeled in a wheelchair carrying a white woman, he straightened it up and pushed the chair down the aisle past gaping mouths. Rashaun continued to scan the crowd until he saw who he was looking for. The man was about seventy years old and he was dressed in a gray suit that had past the fads of time. His baldhead was in staunch contrast to his aged, lined face. He bowed his head slightly after making eye contact with Rashaun; Rashaun returned the acknowledgement and returned his attention to the witness stand where the bailiff had finished swearing in the witness.

"Ms. Hopkins, can you tell us why you're here?" Kim asked as she walked to the witness stand.

"Because I don't want anyone to have to go through what I went through," Ms. Hopkins said, adjusting herself on the chair.

"What exactly did you go through, Ms. Hopkins?"

"Well, I had heard about Blackfunk from a friend of mine. She told me that it was the best sex she had ever had. She told me that you almost lose complete control of your senses when the pleasure becomes unbearable. She said it starts out painful but as the body adjusts to the pain the pleasure comes in spurts."

"Did she tell you who you needed to perform Blackfunk?"

"An angry black man."

"Any black man?"

"Yes, any one of them."

"Have you ever been with a black man before?"

"Yes."

"Have you ever experience Blackfunk?"

"No, the sex was good but never to that level my friend was talking about."

"So you wanted Blackfunk?"

"Yes, you only live once." Ms Hopkins rolled her eyes.

"Continue, Ms. Hopkins."

"My ex-boyfriend had a black militant friend named Leroy. You know, those people that everything for them is black this or black that."

"Yes, I know. Was your boyfriend white or black?"

"White of course! My parents would kill me if they found me with a black man."

"Continue."

"I knew that Leroy was attracted to me but he would never approach me. I think it was that black militant shit more than his actual respect for my boyfriend. My opportunity came when my boyfriend went to the army reserve for the weekend. I never understood why he did it; all they got was this stupid stipend every two weeks. My boyfriend was making a lot of money, he didn't need Uncle Sam's pennies. Anyway, I called Leroy over under the pretense that my purse had fallen behind the fridge and I needed help to move the fridge to get it. He asked me if I could call someone else. Of course I told him I

49

didn't know anyone else. So, he came over, and I was dressed in these short, short shorts with half of my ass showing and if you looked closely you could see pussy hairs and one of those netted blouses with no bra. You should have seen his face when I opened the door, tongue out and drooling. I invited him in and walked from the door to the refrigerator. Now I know some of you all are thinking, white woman, flat butt but look around, these days white women are packing. So we went through the pretense of trying to move the fridge to find the purse. But before he started I gave him a Heineken, which he took care of in about two minutes. He was sweating and it was not from the temperature. In fact, it was a comfortable seventy degrees in the apartment. I was having fun watching this militant brother sweat over some white pussy. Where is the willpower? As I told you before I didn't just want a fuck, I wanted Blackfunk, so I needed to get him angry. How do you get a black militant angry?" Anna stopped and looked around the courtroom as if expecting an answer. There was none forthcoming.

"Your honor, is there a point to this?" Rashaun objected.

"Your honor, most of the jury have never heard of Blackfunk and its inherent danger. Please let Ms. Hopkins continue so that the jury can have a better understanding of the defendant's state of mind."

"Continue, Ms. Hopkins," the judge said.

"So, Leroy and I are sitting at the table. He has another Heineken in his hand and I'm drinking cranberry juice. I asked him 'do you want to fuck me?' He started coughing as if he was trying a cigarette for the first time. I told him to come eat me and I opened my legs. He got up and I was thinking I would make him lick my toes first. But when he came over, he grabbed me by the hair, lifted me off the chair and spread me over the table. So, I say to him, 'you motherfucking nigger.' He says, 'What did you call me?' I said 'I called you a motherfucking nigger.' It was then he ripped off my shorts and shoved this massive dick in me. I wasn't even wet but he kept ramming that shit in me, and screaming that he was gonna kill

50

me. I have to admit it was painful as hell but at the end of the pain there was this intense pleasure. The more painful it became the more intense the pleasure until I almost felt like if he was going to rip out my tubes. He wanted to kill. He used his dick as if it was a weapon. His sole intent was to hurt. But at the height of that pain came this intense pleasure that swept through me. I have never experienced something like that before. It was at that point that I lost consciousness and when I awoke, he had passed out too. But there was something wrong with me. I couldn't move my feet. My upper body worked but I couldn't move my fucking feet. And as you can see, I still cannot move my feet. He took my legs away." It was then that she began to cry. "The fucking black bastard took my legs away."

"Ms. Hopkins, are you okay?" the judge asked.

"Do I look like I'm fucking okay!" she retorted.

"Court will adjourn for lunch, see you back at 2 P.M.

Rashaun declined Tyrone and his parents' offer to have lunch. Instead, he took a walk up to the promenade, stopping on the way to grab a taco at a Mexican restaurant. When he got to the promenade, he looked to his right then his left then he saw him sitting on a black iron bench. Rashaun walked over and sat next to the old man he had acknowledged in court earlier.

"You want one?" the man asked, offering Rashaun a green apple.

"I guess this will balance the taco I just ate," Rashaun said accepting the apple the old man had taken from a plastic bag resting beside him.

"She is good but you know what she's doing, don't you?" he asked. "You see Rashaun white people suffer from SDS (small dick syndrome) and that has caused them to change sex as we know it. Have you ever tried to fuck a woman in the ass?" he asked Rashaun whose apple wasn't fresh anymore. Some conversation Rashaun believed should not be held when a man was eating or drinking. Ass fucking was definitely one of those topics.

Rashaun looked at the old man as if he wasn't seriously expecting a response.

"Like most of us, you did. Moreover, I'll tell you what they said: "are you mad, you not putting that big thing in my ass."

Rashaun smiled as memories flowed.

"Have you ever heard about homosexuality in any part of our African history?" he asked.

Rashaun shook his head. There was no such recollection in all the history books he had read.

"Sex, Rashaun, is about power, and the bigger you are, the more power you wield and if you can't get it one way you get it another. So the white man says to his woman, you not feeling me in your vagina, therefore, I have no power over you. I could have all the money in the world but when I'm naked I'm stripped of my money. I cannot wave a hundred-dollar bill in front of you when I'm naked, therefore, I do not have your respect. And, believe me, Rashaun, we all want to be respected in bed. It's what keeps our chins up. You could be walking around with a million dollars in your pocket and a woman you slept with could be laughing at you. You see, sex is one of the most powerful weapons for either of the sexes if used correctly. Get a woman excited and then become unable to perform, you will become the running joke of many a girls night out." The old man took another bite of his apple.

The conversation was making Rashaun's apple lose the natural organic taste.

"You see, Rashaun, homosexuality started as a power trip between the white man and his woman. It had nothing to do with us Africans. As most unnatural acts in the bedroom, it spread when other circumstances became involved. Man is a survivor; if he can't survive one way, he'll survive another. A clear parallel can be drawn here with drugs, man's constant fight to gain the most pleasure out of life. It's not the poor

52

black and Hispanic people who keep the drug business going, it's the rich people looking for that thrill."

"But I'm sure not all white people suffer from SDS," Rashaun said.

"Of course not. I'm sure there are white men with penises bigger than yours and mine. However, that's not the point, the point is that as in human life there has to be alternatives. There was a problem and white man came up with a solution." The old man paused to put the apple core in his plastic bag and pulled out a yellow pear.

"But there are black homosexuals also. Do they have SDS?" Rashaun asked.

"Not necessarily. Have you ever heard about the husband and wife with the itch."

"No."

"Well the story goes like this: There was a husband and wife who both had an itch. The wife went to the doctor and the doctor gave her medication. Now when she came home, the husband decided to use her medication because he assumed that because they both had the same problem then the solution would be the same.

"Of course, the moral of the story is twofold, one being that just because it itches the same doesn't mean it's the same problem and one person's solution could be another person's problem. You see, while the problem with white men and their women might be a penis problem it doesn't necessarily mean that the problem with black men and their women is the same. So, while the white man might opt for the ass and because both men and women have assholes, his possibilities increase. But the black man, is not an asshole person because physically we were not built for that and in many cases we have to almost be forced into that life. The prisons and broken homes are all ways that are used to make the black man what he is not. Now you see why I said the prosecutor is playing for the white men. White people feel much less threatened when a black man is behind bars. They don't have to keep an eye on their wives who have heard so many things about black men that they are dying to try them. Forget about their daughters. With the advent of hip-hop, exposure to the black culture is scary. White people are afraid of losing their lineage.

"Now what you have to do is make this girl useless to white men. You have to make her believe that she is useless to them and their race. Remember, regardless of how liberal a white person is, he still wants to carry on his legacy. Now once you get them to stop thinking of their girls as white princesses then they will once more feel safe in their world. They will always be threatened but the threat will not be as immediate. In other words, make her into white trash."

"It seems like I have my work cut out for me," Rashaun said, handing the old man the core from his apple. Rashaun had made the mistake of throwing a core from a pear the old man gave him into the street; the old man never let him forget it. He talked about cleanliness from the 1920's to the twenty-first century.

"I'm not sure. Kim seems to want to scare the jury."

The old man took a much smaller bite and chewed on it excessively.

"Nope. She's dividing the jury. Right now, she's going after the three white men in the jury. Those are the only people she cares about right now. She heard the white girl's story before. Yet, she let her tell the whole story without interruption. You do know that the judge would lick her ass. I don't know why you didn't object but that's another issue. What you have to do is devise a plan that will counteract her game plan. You have to make the jury believe that it was an act between two consenting adults that resulted in tragedy. Keep to your accident theory." The old man stood as if on command. "I have to go now. It's about time for me to go and walk my dogs. They're just like humans. They need attention, attention, attention."

"Thanks," Rashaun said and stood as well.

"You didn't need me this time, and maybe you won't need me in the future. I'm very proud of you; you have come a long way. You're still learning and that's a good thing. When you stop learning then you stop growing and that should never happen." With that said the old man turned and headed down the promenade, on a mission to feed his dogs.

"Ms. Hopkins, have you ever cheated on your boyfriend before?"

"No."

"What do you consider cheating, Ms. Hopkins?" Rashaun asked, walking up to the witness stand.

"Sexual intercourse, penetration of the man's penis into the woman's vagina. Doesn't everybody know that?" She rolled her eyes and shook her head.

"Have you ever had oral sex with a man or woman without penetration?"

"Well I had oral sex with this friend from work. He did me then I did him."

"You don't consider that cheating?"

"No, because there was no penetration involved."

"So you do not consider two women to be having sex with each other when they satisfy themselves orally."

"To be honest with you I don't know what two women do, and I don't care what they do."

"Your honor, is there a point to this line of questioning?" Kim objected, standing briefly.

"Mr. Jones, I fail to see the reason for your line of questioning. If there is a point to this I would like you to make it soon," the judge said, staring at Kim.

"Bear with me, your honor. The witness has shown that she is willing to explore numerous territories for her pleasure. What happened to her was an action she willfully brought upon herself."

"Go on," the judge said, watching Kim sit down.

"Ms. Hopkins, did your boyfriend ever find out about your escapades?"

"Yes, I told him. He was angry at first but then he calmed down and we had great sex," she said, leaning back in her chair, smiling proudly.

"Was the friend that you orally satisfied at work, black?"

"Yes, he was. Is there a problem with that?"

Rashaun looked over at the white men in the jury and the expression on their faces showed that they had lost respect for one of their own.

"Do you like black men, Ms. Hopkins?"

She looked around the room, not sure she should answer. "Yes, I do," she said and looked down at the shiny microphone that carried her answers throughout the courtroom.

"Thank you," Rashaun said and walked backed to his chair.

Rashaun arrived at Andria's mother's house at ten and left at ten-fifteen. The ride home was uneventful and the car's motor was the only sound. Andria went to bed at 11:30, leaving Rashaun to stare at the same notes from the woman's testimony. He had read the same page about twenty times since he had gotten home. He had heard when Andria had turned on the TV then later when she went into the kitchen and boiled some hot water. He had heard the tinkling of the spoon against the mug as she made herself a cup of tea.

She should have told him something; she knew how much this case meant to his friend who could be sentenced to twenty-five to life. Rashaun shuddered at the thought.

"Is this how it's going to be?" Andria asked as Rashaun slid into bed next to her at around one O'clock.

"What is there to say? You obviously have made your decision. And you really do not care about the effect that it will have on other people," Rashaun said as he turned to look at Andria, her face hidden in the darkness of the room.

"Rashaun, I accepted your decision when you said you wanted to defend the man who was responsible for one of my best friend's death. I did not get angry and I did not try to stop you. In fact, I supported you because your ex-girlfriend is the prosecutor and I know you guys' history. I could understand you wanting to defend your friend and to win against your ex. What I will never do is to testify for someone who might or might not be responsible for my friend's death. I love you and under most any circumstances, except this one I would go to war and die by your side."

"You are not supporting me. Andria, I think you want me to lose this case. You want to see my friend sentenced to the maximum because you believe that he killed Judy. Don't give me this bullshit about you understanding. I don't give a fuck. I would defend my friend whether you agree or disagree. Your say in this matter means nothing to me."

"Rashaun, why are you cursing at me."

"I don't give a fuck. I can curse if I want to. It is my fucking apartment."

"So that's what it comes down to? It's your apartment, therefore, you can do and say whatever you want? Well I don't need your apartment. In fact, I don't need you." Andria got off the bed and flooded the room with lights.

"Then get the fuck out," Rashaun said, sitting up, his body trembling with anger.

"You can take this ring and give it to your mother. Only she will take your bullshit." Andria threw the engagement ring onto the bed but it rolled off and into the corner of the room.

"Anyone is better than your ass," Rashaun said as he lay down, turning his back to Andria.

Andria took a small suitcase from the bedroom closet and rummage through the drawers. She stuffed some clothes into the suitcase then went into the closet and pulled clothes off the hangers. She grabbed her purse and her keys and slammed the door as she exited.

When she left Rashaun got off the bed quickly and ran to the window. He saw her standing in front the building punching the keys on her cellular phone. He stood by the window watching her. He wanted to go downstairs and tell her to come back. However, he also wanted to leave her alone, let her go back to her mother. He was angry because he was in the biggest fight of his life and he didn't have the main support he needed. He needed her to be by his side two hundred percent. He needed to talk to her about the case and get her reaction. Fuck it. If she wasn't behind him on this she didn't need to be with him at all. Women were a dime a dozen and sometimes a dime could get you two dozen on sale. He watched a few minutes later as Andria got into Robin's car. He walked back into the bedroom and slipped under the covers. He definitely didn't need her. He turned to his right side and closed his eyes. He tried to sleep but it wasn't happening. The next day was Sunday, and he had promised to take his mother to church. He, Andria and his niece were all suppose to be in church the next morning praising God. He would have to come up with something to say to his mother and niece, they both acted as if Andria was already part of the family. He got up and poured himself a glass of Clark's Court rum, the most powerful rum in Grenada. When it hit his throat he winced as if the devil was testing his lungs for fire resistance and he quickly drained the glass. He threw the glass against the wall in the room and it broke into uncounted pieces.

"I don't need her. A blind man needs a cane, a baby needs a mother, the government needs taxes, a politician needs a lawyer but Rashaun Jones does not need Andria Jackson. Rashaun doesn't need anyone." With that said the alcohol reached his brain and he slumped down on the edge of the bed and an eventful night ended.

Andria's eyes were laden with the remnants of a sleepless night. Again, Robin had to rescue her from another man. It was starting to become routine. The whole ride back to Robin's house Andria was wondering if she had done the right thing. She picked up the phone on her desk and began to dial Rashaun's work number. She hung up before she got to the digit. This was not going to work. Who did he think he was? She got up and had to steady herself before walking down the corridor to the coffee machine. Lately she had taken to bringing her sandwich or food from home for lunch in an effort to save some money. It wasn't easy. Rashaun had taken Tyrone's case pro bono and with the high cost of rent for Rashaun's apartment they were barely making ends meet. She tried to get Rashaun to do the same but he would return with his lunch in his briefcase every night. Her stomach was growling because she did not have breakfast. Andria had no appetite when she got out of bed that morning.

"What's wrong, Andria? You look kind of pale this morning." Sandy-Ann, Andria's coworker, asked as she blew on a cup of coffee and took a slight sip. "Good coffee," she said pointing to the cup as if Andria would think she was talking about coffee from mars. Sandy-Ann was dressed in a loose-fitting long skirt touching the top of her two-inch full-length boots. Andria wandered if it was a cultural thing for Guyanese women to be dressed for winter in the summer.

"Nothing. How is your sister?" Andria asked, hoping to take the conversation away from her.

"She just got a restraining order for that dumb husband of hers. I told her not to get married to that fool. I don't know what's wrong with those Guyanese men. They think just because you marry them and you have their children they own you. The girl is in her early thirties and he is running her like she's his maid. Wants her to take out his slippers and to cook for him every day of the week. The girl didn't even finish college, he talking about she don't need to. He beat her the other day and that's when she called the cops and they arrested his ass, then she went and bailed him out. She had to move into our mother's house. I never seen a girl so beautiful yet so stupid. I don't want a Guyanese man. They all better go back to Guyana and get a country girl. I have to run. I have a meeting with a foster mother. She wants to know why she didn't receive her check. I know why, because she don't spend a penny on the foster kids. I'll talk to you later." With that said Sandy-Ann went down the hall with the echoes of boots made for Binghamton snowy winters.

Andria took a paper cup from the small white cupboard located under the coffeepot. She put two spoons of sugar in the cup and gingerly poured the coffee keeping her hand as steady as possible. She didn't feel like cleaning up any mess this morning. After she poured the coffee, she lifted the Cling-Wrap plastic off a straw basket, which contained small brown stirrers. The coffee was the worst tasting shit she had ever had. She quickly headed to the water cooler which was located about two feet away from the coffeepot. She ran the cold water as she emptied the cup of coffee that had left a bad taste in her mouth. Now, she had to go outside to Starbucks, which was two blocks away. She hated going there. It was always too much to pay for a cup of coffee. However, this morning she had to swallow her budgetary restraints and help support one of America's multimillionaires.

"Good morning, Ms. Jackson," the young woman said. Her name was China and she was pregnant with her second child. Her first child was seven years old and was presently with foster parents. China should have been called Chinaqua to reflect her heritage. Her mother was from China, the largest continent in the world, and her father was brought up on the mean streets of Brooklyn. They met in college and married at the New Church, one of the many for-profit churches currently run by the Reverend Steve Grand.

"How are you doing today, China? Since we last spoke you started college at...what's the name of your school?" Andria asked.

"Kingsborough Community College."

"Oh yeah, the one with the beautiful campus. How did you do your first semester?"

"Those introductory courses were very easy. I got a 3.5 average."

"Excellent. Keep up the good work."

"I will but you know my situation. I won't be attending school next year. I have this one coming," she said, rubbing her stomach.

"Well you know we have all the support for you here."

"I know but Keenan takes very good care of me. Ms. Jackson, you know why I'm here. I would like to take Kelly home. It's been over a year since we started having unsupervised visits."

Andria knew the request was coming and she understood why. She knew that China was an excellent mother to her daughter, Kelly, but the incident last year was horrible. Kelly was rushed to the emergency room. Her tiny hand was broken in the middle between the wrist and the elbow. They both denied doing it but their description of the accident left too many unanswered questions. Upon further investigation it was found that Keenan did not like Kelly because she was not his child.

"How's Keenan?" Andria asked.

"Ms. Jackson, Keenan has been very supportive. I think he misses Kelly. I think he didn't like her before because of that whole ego thing. Kelly is the daughter of his best friend who he hasn't spoken to since Keenan and I started dating. Granted it is not the best situation for a child but I think we have gone beyond that. We are a family. Kelly's father is doing a triple life sentence—freedom is not an option for him. Keenan will never hurt Kelly. I will bet my life on it."

"Why isn't he here with you?" Andria asked.

"He's working as a computer technician with Avery and Sons. They wouldn't give him the time off. And you know as well as I do that he hates coming to this office. I think he's hoping you people will just go away."

"I don't think we are getting anywhere, China. I think your boyfriend should start coming here for counseling so that we can observe the interaction between him and the child. The court will not just let you have Kelly back if they are leery of one of the parties that is living in the house. I also will not recommend that the child be returned to the home until you and your boyfriend speak to a psychologist and undergo counseling."

"But you know he wouldn't come to counseling," China said, her eyes bloodshot. "I miss my child, I want her back." She stretched her hands onto Andria's desk, her head buried in her left shoulder. She rested like that for a few seconds then sat up straight on the chair and wiped her eyes with a blue rag she took from her bag.

"I'm sorry. I believe that you are a good mother but you have to convince your boyfriend to take more of an active part otherwise as long as you are with him you will not get your child back. I would love to help you more but I can't." Andria felt for China but she had her reservations about Keenan and he hadn't done anything to alleviate the reservations. She was proud of the young woman that sat in front of her. She had live so much at such an early age. She got pregnant with Kelly when she was fifteen and her parents told her to leave the house. She accepted the responsibility and took great care of the child. Kelly was a happy little girl. Andria observed the child with her mother; a loving mother could only achieve that type of bond. China had made so many sacrifices only to have her precious child taken away from her. Andria could understand the hurt yet she had to look out for the best interest of the child, even though that meant taking Kelly from the person who loved her most.

"I'll talk to him some more, I want my child," China said and got up from the chair. She slipped her Nine West handbag over her fat arm and turned to walk away. "It's hard leaving here without her, I miss her so much."

"I know," Andria concurred, "Just try and get him to come in."

"Where is Aunty Andria?" Sheila, Rashaun's niece, inquired, her beautiful brown eyes looking up at Rashaun.

"She's not coming to church with us today," Rashaun answered, not wanting to lie to the child.

"Why don't you tell her, Rashaun? Tell her your big ego and your fear of feeling for someone has totally destroyed your heart," Rashaun's mother spoke with the compassion of a mother but the words were a scolding from a schoolteacher. "Andria is the best thing that has happened to you in how many years? But you got frightened because your feelings for her were overpowering. So what do you do? Instead of accepting this beautiful thing that was happening to you, you broke it off. Now you're safe again. No one can hurt you. My grandmother always used to tell me a person who cannot be hurt will never be able to feel. You know what that means, Rashaun. When you can't feel you are dead. No feelings equal death." She climbed into the front seat of the car. Rashaun finished buckling Sheila in the back and hesitantly joined his mother in the front.

"Mom, I knew that you liked Andria but I'm the one who has to live with her," Rashaun said, hoping to put an end to the conversation.

"Rashaun, you are a fool. You know how many good women are out there—very, very few, I'm sure you could have a lot of women with your tall, handsome self but how many will be good to you? I knew Andria was a blessed child from the time I first laid my eyes on her. You made my heart strong when you brought her home to me. You know how I feel about your younger brother's wife and I am not a fussy woman. But the woman just doesn't treat that boy right. But Andria is a good woman. She is also a strong woman; you need that in this world today. You will be the biggest fool to let her go. I don't want to hear what happened. I know you, Rashaun. You are my son." With that said she squeezed her mouth shut, veins outlined on her majestic face and stared straight ahead.

"There is nothing left for me to say," Rashaun said looking at the buildings rush by as he went down Church Avenue.

"Uncle Rashaun, you could say something to me. Grandma won't mind," Sheila chimed in.

"I know, sweetie. Uncle Rashaun can always talk to his angel." Rashaun dared not look at his mother.

"Maybe one day you will make one of your own, but you have to get some brains first." His mother opened the door of the car after Rashaun pulled up in front of the church.

It was going to be a long service. His mother would not stop talking to him about Andria until she saw her walk into church with him again. Rashaun missed Andria with all of his soul. What would he say to Andria if he did see her? He wasn't a man keen on apologizing, besides it was she who was being inconsiderate.

"Don't worry, Uncle Rashaun, Andria will come back to you. You won't be lonely anymore." Sheila grabbed his hand and pulled him, following her grandmother's fast gait to the church door. Her rush was more to get away from Rashaun than the Lord's calling. Rashaun followed his mother to the third pew from the front of the church. He hated sitting in the front of the church because he had to get up every time the pastor said rise. Sitting at the back of the church he and the rest of the fake churchgoers were excluded from all those incidentals. Sheila sat between him and his mother and was a welcome buffer. He wasn't sure if his mother was going to reach out and ring his ears the way she used to do when he was a young boy.   The thought of it made him shudder and slid farther down the pew.

The pastor was a rehabilitated drug dealer from Washington Heights, who got his calling in cellblock D of Rikers Island. He stood five feet seven inches with a slow receding hairline courtesy of his father, the retired Reverend Hickers, who was a well-respected pastor in the black community. He started his church in the basement of his house on Fifty-sixth Street. He was a good man who migrated to Brooklyn in 1978 just before America invaded a small island in the West Indies called Grenada.

Reverend Hickers now sat one level down from the pulpit and he looked on with great joy as his begotten son who was now married with five kids, preached the word of God. Reverend Hickers was a proud man and it was all due to the grace of God who had brought a stray home to lead the people of his congregation. The young Reverand Hickers took all of his drug money that the government wasn't able to find and invested it in the house of the Lord. It was his way of trying to ask for forgiveness.

Rashaun was not a churchgoing man but he liked the pastor who was a brother who turned his life around. He drove a 1998 Camry instead of a brand new Jaguar like so many of the other pastors. The pastor had put all of his money into the church and opened a small health food store next door to show and teach black people that just because it was fried didn't mean it was good for you. Pastor Hickers was all right with Rashaun. The minister did not make as much money as the white man with the liquor store one block away but he relished in doing the right thing. All the pastor's children went to public schools in the area. The pastor walked to the pulpit with a small shuffle, a remnant of his life on the street. His eyes swept the congregation like a drug dealer lookout on Franklin Avenue in Brooklyn. When he reached the pulpit he bowed his head and the congregation sat down. From among the many slits in his robe a black Bible appeared in his hand.

65

"Today I am going to put down the Bible but not the word of God. I will talk to you as a man with the same problems you as men are going through. Please don't believe because I am a pastor with a robe on that means I'm different from you." Reverend Hickers' voice was coarse and deliberate as expected of a man who had repeated the same thing over and over.

Rashaun looked at the pastor then at his mother, who was giving the reverend all of her attention. Rashaun wondered if she had called and spoken to the reverend before the service. He would not put that past his beloved mother.

"Church, we have a problem between sisters and brothers and it is tearing us apart. Our families are being divided quicker than shouting police in a crack house. We are breaking up the family and we all are going our separate ways. In a world of increased stress where we need one another more and more, we are giving up on one another. Marriage these days is a time bomb that is exploding and going to pieces by the days, the months and very rarely the years. Brothers and sisters, we have to change this trend, if not for you, do it for me and if not for me do it for the children."

"Amen," a woman with too much makeup shouted.

"Let's look into the mirror and examine the reflection, which is not of a stranger but us. Let's make that sacrifice, turn that selfish, egotistical machine around. When a man meets a woman, it's a beautiful thing and it should be treated as such. Let's start with the five things a man should do in a relationship: "Number one: Respect your woman—and when I say respect your woman I mean to treat her like Einstein and not one of the Three Stooges. Remember, you are with her for her intelligence as much as her body. She is your choice to carry on your name and your father's name. Who else would you give that honor?" Reverend Hickers took a handkerchief from the bottomless slit in his robe and wiped the back of his neck.

"Number two: Honesty. Yes, brothers, I know this is a hard one but remember, a life built on lies is a straw house

66

waiting to be blown down by the slightest wind. Stop looking over your shoulder to see who will see you. Stop covering your face when you pass by the restaurant you were in. Lift your head up, smell the roses and stop sniffing on the ground.

"Number three: Communicate. How can your woman know what you want or what you are feeling if you don't communicate with her? We live in a complicated world. Things are being thrown at us from all angles, and we need to talk about them. You need to say 'honey, this is not working' or 'baby, this was the best.' Contrary to popular opinion women do not read minds. I myself have problems with that. Sometimes I make so many assumptions that I am surprised my wife is still at my side. It's okay to laugh, and most of all it's okay to cry. Only weak men don't show their emotions. I hope that you have nothing to prove to your woman, therefore, you don't need to put on an act for her. She has already accepted you with all your insecurities, so talk to her.

"Number four: Love your woman. Love her with no regrets, and forget about the high school sweetheart that you should have married. Show her your love by your actions, not only your words. Show her that she is the queen of your family. If there is no love in your house, my friends, you need to bring some in A man who has no love is a man who's already dead. A soul that is lacking love is like a man that found water in the desert. He will be able to continue to live but there will be no substance to his life. And remember my brothers, there is a big difference between love and lust. Lust is for a minute but love is for a lifetime.

"But that minute is sure good," a man in the middle of the church shouted. There was a chorus of "uh-huh" after his remark.

"Yes, my friend, but it's like drugs. The feeling is great but it doesn't last. Take my word for it, brother, you do not want to chase the sun because the heat might feel good at first but then it's going to burn you. And finally, my brothers, give your woman the comfort she needs. Every time my phone rings and the other person on the line starts off with, I'm sorry, I know that life has ended for someone. Brothers and sisters, life is so short. Please take comfort in the one you love and let the person take comfort in you."

"Uncle Rashaun, Grandma say wake up," Sheila said, pulling on Rashaun's shirtsleeve.

"Tell your grandma that I wasn't sleeping," Rashaun said, trying his best not to wipe his eyes.

"Yes, you were, Uncle Rashaun, I saw you," Sheila said, looking up at him with her big beautiful brown eyes. Rashaun looked over at his mother and inhaled deeply. He had just nodded off.

"Andria, you haven't gone anywhere since you left Rashaun. You sit in this house playing with Rob day in and day out. Now we're going to Jouvei and I want you to come with us. All the girls are going. It will be the first time we have been together since Judy's funeral." Robin sat on the black leather couch across from Andria. She had her feet tucked underneath her as she occasionally glanced at Regis on *Who Wants to be a Millionaire*. The TV itself was a fifty-two-inch Sony projection set, a gift from Tom, her husband to himself. Robin didn't understand his reasons for buying such a large television. There was nothing wrong with the twenty-five inch they had before.

"I don't know, Robin, I don't think I want to be around anyone," Andria said, lightly rubbing her left eye.

"Stop it, Andria. If you want to go and call Rashaun, go ahead. Here's the phone." Robin took the cordless phone that was nestled on her left side and threw it on the couch next to Andria.

"I can't call him. I don't want to call him," Andria said as she picked up the phone and threw it back to Robin.

"Okay, now that we have settled that, let's talk about what you're going to wear for Jouvei." Robin's smile lit up her soft features.

68

"I'm not going to win this one, am I?"

"Not today. Tonight you'll be a Trini and you're going to show them how to wine."

"Robin, I can't wine."

"Sharon's bringing her friend from the job and I heard she could show anyone how to wine. I think her name is Debbie. But first let me show you what I'm wearing." Robin got off the couch and disappeared into the master bedroom. When she reappeared she had on a pants that barely concealed the crack of her ass and a T-Shirt that read Born American but Trini at Heart.

"You are playing?" Andria said as she looked at her friend.

"No, I'm not. What do you think all that dieting and exercising was for—definitely not for me to wear a nun's robe. No, girl, tonight I'm going to flaunt what my mama gave me and I am going to get on bad," Robin said, turning around and shaking her butt. "And if I remember your size correctly—and I do have to say that I hate you, it is a two."

"Robin, no you didn't," Andria said as she followed Robin into the room.

"I use to have a body like yours but a husband and a kid later I have to just try to keep everything together. But as the young people say, I ain't hating," she said as she reached into the bag on her bed.

"Robin, I'm not wearing no batty rider," Andria sat down on the chair in front of the dresser in the room.

"Andria, don't start. I went and looked all over the place for this for you and I don't want to hear anything except thank you, Robin, it looks really good," Robin said and laid a pair of Capri pants and a white T-shirt on the bed.

"I'm a six, Robin, not two." Andria lifted the pants off the bed.

"They're cut big," Robin said, smiling mischievously.

"I'm sure not two sizes big," Andria answered.

"Girl, just try them on." Robin said pushing the shirt toward Andria.

"Maybe one leg will fit." Andria pulled her sweats down.

"Girl, if I had a body like that I would not be at home waiting for no man," Robin said, looking at Andria's long smooth legs. "Either that or make a few hundred dollars on the Avenue."

Andria took her shirt off and threw it at Robin.

"Not with those panties you're not. I'm sure you have thongs, so go change. You never know who you might see on Flatbush Avenue."

"You know I only want to see one person," Andria answered and started to walk toward the guest room.

"Well, girl, if he sees you tonight, his eyes will burn," Robin said, laughing.

Andria walked into the guest room that Robin had prepared for her. There were two oak dressers and an armoire in the room. The first dresser held Robin's son's clothes and the armoire had Robin's dresses, Andria's clothes was in the second dresser. She sifted through the drawer and pulled out a blue thong. She looked at it and smiled. It was one of Rashaun's favorites.

"I guess half of my stomach needs to be out too," Andria said, looking at herself in the mirror.

"Oh, how I wish. One thing that takes forever to go is your stomach. Why do you think I'm wearing this big T-shirt? Look." Robin untied the shirt around her stomach and lifted it. She had a pouch that diet and exercise did not diminish. "I hate this," she said, pulling on the flab around her stomach.

"Robin, give it time, you'll lose it," Andria said, sitting back down on Robin's bed. "I wish I had a pouch like that, God knows I might never, ever have a pouch like that."

"I was trying to cheer you up and I made you depress. I don't know what comes over me sometimes. I have a husband

70

and a wonderful son. I also have my best friend in the house with me." She moved her hands from Andria's shoulder to her hair, patting it down ever so slightly.

"I'm sorry, Robin. With this surgery coming up and my breakup with Rashaun, I guess I'm a little bit emotional," Andria said, sitting up to join Robin on the side of the bed. "Sometimes I feel like my life is going in circles. It just keeps coming back to the starting point, and I go around again and I'm back to the starting point. My life is going nowhere." She wiped a few tears that had started to fall down her face.

Robin started to laugh loudly.

Andria's eyes grew huge as she stared at her friend.

"Andria, do you see the way Rashaun acts when he's around you? Do you honestly think that Rashaun is going to give you up? That boy is wrapped around your finger. Rashaun adores you I'm sure he's thinking about you right now. I don't see Rashaun leaving you. That bullshit you guys are going through right now won't last. I'll bet my life on it. You and Rashaun will be back together. Now girl, stand up and show me what you working with," Robin said, taking her friend's arm and lifting her up off the bed. "Look at you. You are absolutely beautiful."

"And don't forget smart too," Andria said, smiling as she started to move her waist.

"That's right, girl. Show me what you working with," Robin said as she reached over and pressed the power button on the CD player on top of her son's dresser. She and Andria began to dance as she turned up the volume. Robin had her hands on Andria's shoulder and they danced out of the bedroom into the living room.

"I guess no one cares if I'm home," Robin's husband said as he put his briefcase down and stared at his wife and Andria.

His glance was fleeting over his wife but remained forever on Andria who felt exposed and uncomfortable. She wanted to hide but there was no place for her to go. There was an awkward silence that time couldn't accurately measure.

"Your son is in his room," Robin said angrily.

"Good night, guys," Andria said. "I'm going into my room."

"Don't sleep too long, Andria. Remember we're going to Jouvei even if I have to drag you there," Robin said.

Andria went into her room and quietly closed the door. Immediately the shouting started. She took off her clothes and climbed into bed. She wanted to get up and leave because she didn't want to create any problems for Robin and her family. She heard a knock on the door and it was Robin's son wiping the sleep out of his eyes.

"Mommy said to come sleep with you. I think she and Daddy are fighting," Rob said and climbed into bed with Andria.

Andria hugged him as he buried his head into her chest. The shouting had dwindled to angry chatter, but Andria found herself looking up at the ceiling. She wanted to call her mother and tell her that she was moving back in but lately their conversations were forced and polite. Lots of things had changed since Andria came back from Grenada but her mother hadn't. She didn't realize that she had dozed off until she felt a slight tap on her leg. Rob was snoring peacefully close to the edge of the bed.

"Andria, get up. We got to go." Andria adjusted her eyes to the light coming from the living room. Robin hadn't put on the room light.

"Are you serious? You still want to go?" Andria asked, rubbing her eyes.

"Why wouldn't I want to go? Nothing has changed since this afternoon. If you think my husband was drooling when he saw you, imagine the reaction from all the men on the street."

Andria sat up on the side of the bed. "Robin, to be honest with you I really don't want any reaction from these horny-ass West Indian men who would be lined up on Church

72

Avenue. I think I'll wear something different." Andria walked over to the dresser.

"Don't even think about it. You look great in that outfit. Stop being so stiff. Accept your beauty and enjoy it God knows it doesn't last that long." Robin took the outfit that Andria had from off her son's dresser and put it down on the bed. "Besides, Sharon is coming to pick us up in twenty minutes."

"Robin, you are no good. You know I can't find a new outfit in that time. You purposely waited late to wake me up. I'm going to get you back, I promised," Andria said, picking up the outfit.

"I'm going to go into the room and get my face on," Robin said and turned to go.

"Robin, you're sure that everything is alright? I don't want to create any problems in your marriage. I can always go and stay with my mother." In the streaming light coming in from the living room, Andria looked at her friend's face for any signs of discomfort.

"Andria, my trust in you is unquestionably. I know how men are, and my husband isn't any different. Actually, I would have been surprised if his reaction wasn't so predictable, then I would have to worry about Tom and John," she said, giving one of her trademark relaxing smiles. "Girl, go and get ready."

Rashaun looked at his black Movado watch. The gold dots symmetrically placed to tell time informed him that it was quarter to one in the morning. He was wondering where Lance was. Lance had called and said he would be over at quarter after twelve. Rashaun knew Lance. He was sure the brother was into something and he was about to give the last strokes. The last strokes for Lance could last at least fifteen minutes. But then again Rashaun couldn't complain too much because only Lance was brave enough to take his silver Benz S400 onto Church Avenue. Rashaun went back into his room and looked at his answering machine. Andria hadn't called. He checked the answering machine periodically for messages from her. So far his count was zero. He sat down on the couch in the living room and pressed a few buttons on a large remote-control. The TV, followed by the computer, then the satellite and finally the stereo came on. He sat there smiling like a kid as he remembered teaching Andria how to turn on the various units. Of course by the time he was finished she was ready to throw every piece of electronic equipment out of the window. He did not know how long he sat on the chair not really watching the TV but missing Andria. She hated TV that late at night. She always complained about the *Martin* reruns. She never called Martin's girlfriend on the show by her name, it was either the chubby girl or Martin's girlfriend. When he told her he thought the girl was sexy Andria told him he was only looking at her butt, which in fact was true. After all, what else was there to look at? She had no tits and her face was at best average. This was the first time he had turned on the television since Andria had left. As his thoughts lingered on Andria, he started to remember the night they made love in front the television in plain sight of *NYPD Blue*.

As he started to remember that night he unbuckled his Calvin Klein baggy jeans.

He had gotten home before ten-thirty for the first time in weeks. Andria had been home since six. He had walked in, said hi to her and sat down in front of the TV.

He pulled his pants down to his knees and he could feel himself getting excited beneath the white Calvin Klein boxers. Andria walked into the room wearing a small blue T-shirt, which must have been an extra small because it barely covered her lovely tits. She past right by him smelling of a nice flowery fresh scent and went over and turned the light completely up. He didn't know what kind of perfume or body wash she had dipped herself in but he hope she had plenty more.

He ever so lightly stroked his half-erect penis and started to move under his touch.

74

"What are you doing?" he had asked her as he started to unbutton his shirt.

"Nothing," she said and walked back in front of him. She stood there and with both hands on the TV, she bent over.

Rashaun pulled his underwear down exposing his erect penis. He started to stroke it up and down starting from the base and moving up. His butt felt cool against the leather couch.

"Damn" was all he had said as he saw the most beautiful shaved pussy under the glare of two four-hundred-watt halogen bulbs. His dick had become trapped, twisting and turning but going nowhere.

He lay back on the sofa, his hand stroking his penis, going over the tip then with his index finger then grasping it as he went down the shaft again. It was as if Andria was right there playing with it for him.

Andria had turned around and released the pent-up monster from its cage. She had played with him ever so softly then engulfed him in her mouth. His whole body had come off the sofa as he leaned into her. Rashaun increased the strokes on his penis, as his mind became a vision of memories. His penis responded to every stroke as he continued to visualize Andria.

Andria stopped sucking him because the only other place his erect penis could go was down and he had started feeling that urge at the bottom of his feet. She stood and took her middle finger and ran it down the center of her pussy. Rashaun leaned forward, hungry for the taste of her. She took her finger and inserted it into his mouth. He hungrily sucked on it. She had once more took his penis in her hand lifting him up off the chair. She turned around and slowly she had inserted him into her.

Rashaun could feel himself about to explode. He had never felt something so warm, so comforting. He had found heaven in the canal of birth. The feeling had traveled from the bottom of his feet through his whole body; the initial jerk was simple enough, barely lifting him off the chair. But as he continued to stroke himself his body began to convulse as semen spurted in front of him. He barely heard the bell ring but as he laid back it started to clang in his ear.

"I'm coming," he shouted as he headed to the bathroom.

"Rashaun, what the fuck you doing in there? You jerking off or something," Lance shouted through the locked door.

As Rashaun came out of the bathroom he could hear Lance banging on the door.

He went and jerked it open. "What the fuck is wrong with you? I told you I was coming. Brother, you took your time coming here and now you want to rush me."

"Relax, man, I just don't like waiting," Lance said, talking to Rashaun but looking at his Benz.

"Give me a second, I'll be right there," Rashaun said and went back into the apartment. He knew Lance would not follow him because there was no way Lance would leave his car outside at 1:30 in the night.

"I'll be in my car," Lance said and headed down the stairs.

"This is unbelievable," Andria said as she and the girls tried to walk up Church Avenue. "Look at all these people. It's two in the morning."

"Hell, wait till you get to Flatbush Avenue. You won't be able to walk through the crowd," Sharon said as she walked between two teenagers who couldn't wait for her to pass so they could grab her butt. They both succeeded in doing just that but one got caught by the left elbow Sharon swung as she continued to walk with the group. He went down as the other one laughed at him.

"She fucked you up. She got you good."

His friend had started spurting blood from his nose as he knelt down in pain.

"You all right, Sharon?" Hilda asked as she noticed the commotion behind them.

"Yeah, everything is fine," she said, rubbing her elbow.

The ladies walked in two rows, Andria, Robin and Paula in front followed by Sharon, Hilda and Debbie.

"Hey, guys. Hold on for a minute. Anyone want some roasted corn?" Hilda asked as she stopped in front of a guy dressed in an Iceberg shirt and Roca jeans. He stood over a big oil drum that had been cut in half and had a hole in the top to let out the smoke. Like most of the vendors he was barbecuing chicken on one side and roasting corn on the other.

"How much for the corn?" Hilda asked.

"Three dollars," he answered, wiping his forehead with a rag and turning the corn.

"Boy, you must be crazy. I ain't paying no three dollars for no corn. You think me a tourist," Hilda retorted.

"Virgo, is there a problem." A big woman with a white apron sauntered over to stand between Hilda and Virgo.

"No, Mama, no problem. This lady just wants some corn," he said, flipping the ears over on the grill.

The lady turned to look at Hilda. "Two dollars a corn. How much you want?" she asked.

"How many of you want corn," Hilda asked, pulling a twenty-dollar bill from her pocket.

"That stuff makes my teeth black," Paula said. "I'll skip."

"The corn sweet?" Robin asked.

"It's not that sweet but it tastes good," the lady answered.

"Ma, you too honest. How we going to sell anything if you act like you back home? This is America. You have to change things to make money. Honesty is not the best policy."

Virgo put down the spatula for the corn and picked up the tongs for the chicken.

"Boy, you stupid! Lying to people will only get you a bad reputation. Instead of worrying about me, study yourself.

77

All you do is wear these expensive designer clothes. Look at you. You have on Iceberg shirt and Roca jeans. God only knows how much they cost." Sweat had started to drip down the woman's face.

"I'll take five of your roasted corns," Hilda said, interrupting the banter between Virgo and his mom.

"You see!" Virgo's mom said as she took the twenty dollars from Hilda.

"All right. Mom, all right," he said as he folded the ears in aluminum foil. Robin and Andria pushed two people aside to get up to Virgo who was smiling as he gave them the corn.

"If you all want anything more than corn, you know where I am," he said.

"Yeah, he'll be right here working to pay for that expensive shirt he has on," his mother said as she went back to stirring a big pot of corn soup.

"Mommy, why you got to embarrass me like that in front of these beautiful women?"

"Boy, these women are twice your age. They are not studying you. Keep turning the corn, they burning," she shouted over the pot of soup.

"This corn is good," Debbie said as she bit down on the ear.

"Yeah, it's damn good," Hilda, confirmed. "But my mouth is going to look black when I'm finish."

The ladies continued to walk up until they reached a yard barricaded with a six-foot fence.

"Let me see who they got in there," Sharon said and pulled the fencing back and peeped inside. "They ain't got anybody inside, Shit, let's party outside. We can hear the music just as good."

Robin and Andria squeezed until they found a spot against the wall to finish their corn. "This corn is making me thirsty," Andria said as she bit into it.

"Yeah me too," Robin agreed.

"Water, water, a dollar," a man yelled, straining under the weight of a big red- and-white cooler.

"Hey, let me get some water," Robin said as she gave up her spot on the fence to follow the man.

"Get me one too," Hilda shouted over the thumping soca music.

"Me too," Paula and Debbie said in unison.

"I'll buy for everyone," Robin said.

"Hold on, Robin, before you buy, let me check it out." Andria joined Robin.

Andria took the bottle and brought it so that her eyes and the bottle cap were even. She turned the bottle slowly around looking for a break in the cap. "Next." She gave Robin the first bottle and took the next one from the man and did the same inspection.

"What was that all about?" Robin asked when Andria had completed her inspection and paid for the drinks.

"It's from living with a lawyer. Trust no one, everyone is trying to rip you off. Most people don't even know what they're buying when they get bottled water. Do you know how easy it is to fill up dirty bottles with tap water?" Andria asked.

"I guess you're right but I wasn't thinking," Robin conceded.

"And that's what these con artist live for, a time when you're not thinking. That fool taught me a few things after all," Andria said and twisted the top off the water bottle and took a long gulp.

"Damn look at Debbie!" Robin shouted.

Andria looked over and what she saw was American history. Debbie, a white girl, had a waist that moved like a serpent. Andria and Robin moved to the circle that was forming around Debbie who had put her water on the ground and was wineing over the bottle.

"Go, white girl. Go, white girl," the crowd started to chant.

A short brother with his shirt fully opened exposing his years of work in the gym—or the wonders of anabolic steroids—stepped into the circle with her. He tried to put his hands around her waist but she removed them. She leaned against him and started to wine from his waist all the way to the ground. He tried his best to keep up with her but she moved too fast and at too many different angles for him. Slowly he started to wine back into the crowd of onlookers. Next came a tall brother with fake braids running the length of his back. He came up behind Debbie and started to wine, kicking his foot up in the air as if he was a bucking bull.

"Put it on him, Deb!" Sharon shouted.

"Make him know who his mama is!" Robin joined in.

The crowd started to laugh as Debbie went into a slow grind, making the bull look uncoordinated and wild. He tried to tone down his wind to go with Debbie's but the way her waist alone moved was too much for him.

"Look at his eyes!" Andria shouted.

"Oh no, he's gone." Hilda said, speaking for the first time.

"He's about to embarrass himself in front of everyone," Sharon said. "Work it, girl. Put it on him."

"He should stop," Paula chimed in. " He is going to bust."

As if on cue Debbie moved her waist side to side then up and down. She pushed the man back with her butt and the crowd went wild. The jerking bull started to shake.

"Look, the brother is cumming on himself," someone shouted.

After the brother realized what he had done he pushed through the crowd. The people who saw him coming in their direction stepped aside quickly to let him pass.

"Damn I hope this guy is not from here. He will never be able to live this down," Paula said as she put the water bottle to her mouth.

"Sharon, where did you get this white girl? She'll make sisters handcuff their men," Hilda said.

"Debbie's from Trinidad. Dancing soca and reggae is all that she knows. There's nothing for the sisters to worry about. Debbie already has a Trini man." As she spoke she saw three young boys with do-rags in their pockets start to circle Debbie. Sharon and Hilda stepped in and pulled Debbie away. The boys looked them up and down and the ladies looked back at them the same way.

"I hate to say I told you so," Rashaun said as a cop came up to Lance and told him that his sergeant wanted him at a different post.

"Fuck. What am I going to do?" Lance said as he stood next to his car.

"I would not suggest you try to drive off right now because you won't get too far," Rashaun said, looking at the throngs of people on Flatbush and New York avenues.

"Shit. Someone might see the Benz and fall right in front of the car and try to sue me for hitting them," Lance said.

"What made you bring your Benz on Church Avenue?" George asked, shaking his head.

"Should I tell him or do you want to explain?" Rashaun patted Lance on the back.

"Pussy all right. My car attracts pussy like a magnet. So laugh if you want to," Lance said as he eyed a young boy moving very close to his car. Lance went over to the side of the car and opened the door slightly.

"Doesn't that pretty motherfucker get pussy anyway?" George asked. "He doesn't even have to rap. All these women see is over six feet, light skin, curly hair and straight nose. He don't need no car to get pussy. Me, on the other hand, I need my pussy finder."

"Lance doesn't want to talk to women to get pussy. He wants them to throw that shit at him. He claims he is too old to

81

rap. He wants to be like Puffy and those other rappers but he doesn't have the Benjamins so he leases a Benz," Rashaun said.

"That brother is fucking crazy," George said as he looked over at Lance who stood next to the slightly opened front door of his car.

"I guess the brother is right," Rashaun said as a gorgeous girl came up to Lance and started talking. Lance talked to her while looking all around his car. He went into the car and came out with a small piece of paper that he started to write on.

"That motherfucker doesn't have to say a word. They just slap him in the face with it." George shook his head.

"Yo, guys, sorry I'm late but me and the wifey was getting into something," Peter said, almost out of breath.

"Naw, I won't say anything. This is too easy," Rashaun said as he greeted Peter.

"Where is Pedro? Pete?" George asked.

"I was walking with the brother when he bounced up on something on Utica Avenue and he told me he was gonna catch up with me," Peter said as he pulled out three Heinekens from a knapsack he carried over his shoulder.

"My man Pete. Good looking out," Rashaun said.

"Good looking out. The brother is just cheap. He doesn't want to buy it for three dollars on the street," George said and took a beer from Peter.

"You guys want a bag for that? You know the cops be acting stupid sometimes," Peter said and slid his beer in a brown paper bag.

"Are you crazy? This is carnival time. These West Indians don't give a fuck about the cops. What cop's going to try to bust someone for drinking beer in the street at 2:30 in the morning?" George asked.

"Where's Lance?" Peter asked, turning around and looking at the unknown faces walking by.

"Over there," George said, looking at Lance who was talking to another girl who could have been Vivica Fox's twin.

"I don't know how he does it, but it's ridiculous that a brother gets all that pussy."

"Guys, I'll be right back. Lance is calling me," Peter said and walked over to where Lance and the girl were talking.

He handed Lance a beer and Rashaun and George watched as the girl who was talking to Lance motioned over a friend. This one was a little shorter but also gorgeous.

"Damn, don't tell me he's going to hook Peter up," George said, pointing at Lance and opening his arms. Lance held up his right hand and nodded.

"Peter is getting the digits. What the fuck did Lance tell the girl to get Peter to write a number down?" Rashaun asked as he saw Peter smiling from ear to ear.

After the girls left Peter came back to join Rashaun and George who both looked at him expectantly.

"All right, he told her that I was a surgeon from Boston who came down to visit some friends," Peter said.

"Who did he tell her you were living with while you were down here?" George pressed.

"With him, of course!" Peter said as if shocked that George would even asked a question like that.

"You better put that number in a safe before your wife sees it and jacks your ass up. You know she ain't going for that," Rashaun said as he watched Peter tightly gripping the number.

"I don't even think I'm going to call the girl. Guys, I haven't even been married five years yet. I'm not going to cheat on my wife." Peter said.

"Give me the fucking number," George said and grabbed Peter's hand and tried to peel the number out. "You're a fucking wimp. You scared of that damn woman you have. Give me that number."

"George, relax. Leave him alone, you don't need to be getting pussy from Peter," Rashaun said as he separated George and Peter.

"Yeah, I guess you're right," George said and stepped back from Peter. "Besides, look at all these beautiful women out here tonight."

"There's Pedro," Peter said.

Pedro walked up with a big smile on his face with a woman about twice his size trailing him. She had long hair and two big dimples. Her eyes were a bright white with pinpoint black marbles. She was wearing a skirt that showed her massive legs and her red blouse could not contain her triple D breasts.

"Guys, this is Rita-Ann. We went to high school together back in Jamaica," Pedro said proudly.

The guys introduced themselves to Rita-Ann and Peter handed a Heineken to Pedro.

"You don't have any Red Stripe?" Pedro asked, looking a little perturbed.

"Pedro, you forgot that you were suppose to bring the Stripe," Rashaun said.

"Please, Rashaun, Pedro is the cheapest Jamaican I have ever met," George said softly enough for only the guys to hear.

"Pedro, you love big women, don't you?" Rashaun asked.

"You see, you guys who go with slim women don't understand the benefits of having a big woman. Let me break it down to you. Now, a big woman always provides excellent support."

"Yeah, if you want back problems," George interjected.

"This is where you're wrong. In making love to a big woman you have to take into consideration her weight." Pedro looked over at Rita-Ann and smiled. "Certain positions you would not try with a big woman no matter how nimble she is. You never lift a big woman and put her around your waist. But the thing about a big woman that you can't always get from a slim woman is that she is always wet. The pussy on a big woman is always dripping."

84

"Pedro, shouldn't you go to your woman before she gets irritated standing there waiting for you," Rashaun said, looking at Rita-Ann shift from one leg to the other.

"That's the other thing about big women. You don't have to worry about them, and they have a lot of patience. The other thing is food. A big woman will always have food in her house. And I am talking about real food, not that broccoli and lettuce those skinny women live on. No, when a big woman cooks she's cooking steak and whole chicken and all that good stuff so you're always satisfied. And guys, you all don't want me to talk about the winter months in New York. Just look at the Eskimos. Have you ever seen them with a skinny woman?"

"Now we should take our lessons from the Eskimos who see sunlight once a month," George said, paying more attention to a woman in a multicolored miniskirt walking across the street. "Pedro, just go back over to your Eskimo woman."

"You guys don't understand comfort. You all are too caught up in the superficial, therefore, you do not see the practical." Pedro took another beer from Peter and turned to go.

"Pedro, you know the next round is on you," George said.

Pedro quickly walked over to join his girl.

"I got you, guys. I got you," he shouted over the soca music coming from Lance's car.

"Lance doesn't even like soca music and look at him blasting it." George said.

"If Tyrone was here, Pedro would have never gotten away with this. You know he's going to disappear in a few minutes," Rashaun said as he watched Pedro give Rita-Ann a beer.

"Yeah, he is good as gone," George said as he waved to the girl in the miniskirt. She waved, her skirt rising a little higher with her action. "Guys, I'll be over there," he said, pointing in the girl's direction.

"You couldn't get Tyrone to come huh, Rashaun?" Peter asked with deep concern.

"No, he doesn't want to be social right now. He has too much on his mind," Rashaun said, remembering how much he tried to convince Tyrone to hang out with them.

"I called him the other day but he barely talked to me." Peter said.

"You were lucky. At least he took your call. He has cut almost everyone out," Rashaun said. "I worry about Ty. His mental stability is becoming an issue. I hope he can make it through the trial. I tried to get him some counseling but he refused. I hope I can help him after the trial, regardless of the outcome."

Rashaun knew Peter had asked him a question but he didn't hear him because his mouth had dropped open in surprise. There she was walking with her friends. His whole body felt clammy as he held on tightly to the Heineken. He didn't realize how much he missed Andria until he saw her face. He had always admired the way she walked and that night she seemed to have added a little more sexiness to her strut. And what was she wearing? He had never seen her dress so provocatively before. Her stomach was out and her shirt was unbuttoned right up to her bra.

"Damn, Rashaun, isn't that your girl?" George asked as he hurried over after getting the digits from the woman in the mini.

"Rashaun, you've been holding out on us. I never knew your girl looked like that." Lance had also left his spot by his car to come over on the sidewalk. "You gave that up? What were you smoking, my brother?"

"She commands attention, doesn't she?" Peter said, also caught up in Andria's rapture.

The guys looked at the quickly approaching Andria like she was the only one who existed. Maybe it was because they knew that Andria and Rashaun had broken up or maybe it was because Andria was queen of the group. She had the most complete package of all of them. Her breasts and ass were well proportioned to her frame. Her hair was cut short and permed so that it hung over her ears and brought out the smoothness in her face. She wore a silver necklace with an opal in the middle that matched the silver round earrings that hung from her pierced ears. Her thighs seemed to have gotten bigger than Rashaun remembered.

Rashaun saw Robin whisper something to Andria and for the first time she noticed him. Her eyes burned into him, making him want to look away from her. There were no words for him to say.

"Hello, Rashaun. How have you been?" she asked, not certain that what she was saying was right. She hadn't seen him until Robin had told her. It was then that her body started to tremble and her knees got weak. She mustered the strength and kept walking toward him. He hadn't changed a bit. He did not lose a foot or an eye nor did he bleach himself to get lighter. He was still the tall, beautiful black man that her heart belonged to. He was the only man out of thousands she saw walking on Church Avenue whose arms she wanted around her. She didn't kiss him on the cheek nor did she touch any part of his body. She said hello and stood back. Did he know what she was going through at this moment? Did he even care?

"I've been good, and you?" Rashaun had been prepared for a phone call but not this. Not standing inches away from her, looking in those soft brown eyes, smelling the fragrance of her skin. As a lawyer if he was unprepared he could either win or lose a case but as a man being unprepared could change his whole life. Rashaun had gone through tremendous regret when Andria had left but nothing felt like this now. Her gaze was penetrating deep within him, traveling through his blood.

"Hi, Rashaun," Robin said, breaking his concentration.

"What's up, Robin? How are the husband and the kids?" Rashaun asked, glad to get away from Andria. He was a strong man but Andria was bleeding the strength from him.

"Well my son keeps asking for you. He wants to know how come Uncle Rashaun doesn't come by anymore," Robin said, looking at Andria hoping that her friend doesn't fall apart.

"I've been very busy lately so I haven't had the time to stop by," he lied. Andria's mother and his secretary were good friends and his secretary told him that Andria was living with Robin.

"If you say so. But I think you should give him a call. I'm sure he would love to hear from you," Robin said.

"I promise I will," Rashaun replied, eager to get away from lying.

"Your mom called me the other day but Sheila wasn't there. How is Sheila?" Andria asked, bringing Rashaun's attention back to her.

"Sheila is being as rude as ever. I think she is the smartest kid I have ever known." He said.

"Still spoiling her I see," Andria said, smiling.

"Andria…" Rashaun started.

"Andria, let's go. We have to get to Flatbush Avenue," Paula said and grabbed Andria by the arm.

Andria pulled away "What were you saying?" she asked Rashaun.

"Nothing. Your friends are waiting," he said.

"Take care," she said and started walking toward the group. She waved good-bye to the rest of the men as she got in step with the women.

"Your woman is fine!" Lance said as he watched Andria walk away.

"And she has a head on her shoulders too," George added.

"Only a fool would give something like that up," Peter concluded.

"You guys just don't understand," Rashaun said and for the first time he didn't understand himself.

"The prosecution calls Mrs. Agnes Sinclair to the stand," Kim said.

A tiny lady no more than five feet took a seat on the witness stand. She did not weigh more than 100 pounds judging by the looseness in her clothes. The bailiff went through the swearing in as Mrs. Sinclair took the oath that supposedly made truth the only thing coming from her mouth.

"Mrs. Sinclair, do you know why you are here?" Kim asked.

"Yes, ma'am, to put that bad man away in prison." Mrs. Sinclair looked straight at Tyrone when she spoke.

"That's right, Mrs. Sinclair, but..." Kim said.

"Objection, your honor. My client has not been found guilty of any crime, therefore, he should not be labeled as a bad man."

"Objection sustained. Mrs. Sinclair, please refrain from name-calling. Continue," the judge said.

"Mrs. Sinclair, you were taken to the hospital a year ago. Can you explain why?" Kim asked.

"I had to have my uterus removed."

"Why?" Kim inquired.

"Because it was damaged."

"How was it damaged?"

"I was taken to the emergency room and my doctor told me that it had moved to the point that it just hanged there. He said it could cause further complications to my many health, including an increased risk of cancer," Mrs. Sinclair replied, adjusting herself in the chair.

"Do you want to have children?" Kim asked.

"My husband and I had been planning to have kids for more than a year, but it's not possible anymore. I suggested adoption but he doesn't want to." Mrs. Sinclair lifted her glasses and rubbed her right eye.

"Are you okay, Mrs. Sinclair," the judge asked.

"I'm okay, your honor. It's just this is a painful memory," she said.

"Continue," the judge said.

"Is your husband responsible for the predicament you are in, Mrs. Sinclair?"

"No he's not. My husband is a good man. He's a God-fearing man I love him with all my heart. He would never hurt me."

"Well, Mrs. Sinclair, who caused you to lose your ability to have children?" Kim prodded.

"Some hard old West Indian man. He ugly too." She curled her lip. "He used to work for my husband. His name is Herbert."

"Herbert was responsible for you losing your uterus?" Kim repeated.

"That man is evil." Mrs. Sinclair spoke with contempt.

"What happened between you and Herbert?"

"I think I was set up by my husband's secretary. She is a bitch. Can I say bitch in court? If I can't maybe I could call her a slut."

"It's okay to say bitch, Mrs. Sinclair," Kim said.

"Well the bitch—who I think was fucking my husband but I can't prove it—told me about Herbert. She said he is the best lover she ever had. He was so gentle and sweet. He did all those things that most men don't like doing to women. You know like sucking toes and licking under the armpits. She told me he even washed between her toes and he loved to perform curliness. For those of you who don't know, that's known on the streets as eating pussy."

"Thank you. Mrs. Sinclair, but we know what curliness means. Continue," the judge said, shaking his head.

"My husband is a wonderful man but he is a minute man. And when I say minutes I mean starting at five and working down to seconds. Five minutes is usually reserved for the holidays when he drank wine, so most of the time it's

90

seconds to two minutes. Like I said, I love my husband but I am a young woman with needs. I have been married since I graduated from high school. He was the first man I ever had intercourse with and he doesn't believe in trying different things. I never seen another man's penis before except for the X-rated movies that my sister lets me borrow from time to time. If my husband knew I had those movies he would divorce me but I hide them in the kitchen behind the pots. My husband doesn't believe a man belongs anywhere in the kitchen so he would never find them. I like the Black Taboo series the best. It is perverted but you know."

"Ms. Sinclair please get to the point," Kim urged.

"I am. I don't want you people to think that I'm some sick person. I'm a good God-fearing woman who made a mistake. Well I told Marge, that's my husband secretary, to set something up with Herbert. I wasn't sure if I was going to do anything but at least I would have him do curliness on me. I thought maybe I could give him a few bucks for his family. You know these West Indian men do have a whole bunch of children. Marge told me I didn't have to give him any money because he loves doing those things. I knew that Herbert wouldn't try anything stupid because he didn't have his papers and I could get him fired. It's not easy getting a job in New York without your papers, especially with all those laws passed lately." Mrs. Sinclair started to make a sucking noise with her throat.

"Mrs. Sinclair, would you like some water," the judge asked

"Yes, your honor, I wouldn't mind," she answered.

"Bailiff, get the witness some water," the judge ordered.

"Thank you, your honor. My throat was getting a little parched," Mrs. Sinclair said before proceeding to drink the glass of water.

"Continue, Ms. Sinclair," Kim said as she watched the jury shifting in their chairs.

"Well I invited Herbert over when my husband left for work that morning. He works long hours so I understand when he can't perform his husbandly duties. When Herbert showed up, he had a workbag with him. I was nervous but Herbert calmed me down. He said he was going to give me a body massage so I shouldn't worry about sex. I asked him if he had oils because even though I had never had a massage I know they use oils. He said he had some in his bag but they didn't leave any scent. He told me to go to the bathroom and change, so I did. When I came out Herbert complimented me on my body. My husband never compliments me on my body, maybe my cooking but never my body. So I led Herbert into the bedroom. I know you all are thinking that I am no good but that's not it, I feel safe at home; I would be a nervous wreck anyplace else. Herbert told me to lie down on my stomach and relax. At first that was very difficult to do but once Herbert put his big hands on me my whole body relaxed, I felt like I was floating."

"Your honor, do we have to listen to this story?" Rashaun objected.

"Mr. Jones, please let the witness tell her story. I'm sure she will get to the point soon," the judge said. "Continue Mrs. Sinclair."

"Thank you, your honor," Mrs. Sinclair said as she rolled her eyes at Rashaun. "Herbert used his hands to touch in places I didn't know existed. He turned me over on my back and continued. I did not know when he had started to kiss my breasts my eyes were completely closed. I didn't know when he took off his clothes either; I'm telling you I think he had drugged me with the oils. I had totally given my whole body to him. It was his to do what he wanted with. When he guided my hand to his penis I was totally shocked. He let me start at the base and inched my hand up, I think that man has the biggest penis in the world. I should have taken my cue then and ended this affair but I had come this far I had to see it to the end. I told him to be gentle since I am not use to such big things. He said I

92

wasn't ready. Yet it was then that he took his huge mouth and endless tongue and went to work between my legs. I think I nearly passed out two or three times. After he had done that he started to enter me very slowly. It felt really great at first.

"But then it seemed like he wasn't stopping, he kept pushing it in farther and farther, then he brought it out and it felt good going in again. But then he kept increasing the pace, as I tried to adjust to his thrust. But remember, he was over six feet tall and muscular and there was little I could do. Before you know it I was in tremendous pain but he wouldn't stop.

"I think I told him to stop numerous times but he had this look in his eyes as if he had totally gone insane. It was at the height of that pain that I experienced this immense pleasure. I can't remember what happened after that but when I woke up I was in the hospital with my husband at my side. He told me that he had found me in bed bleeding from my vagina. The doctor was very cordial and he had my husband step out of the room before he spoke to me. He told me that during sex my uterus had been ripped apart. He told me that I would need surgery to remove it completely. I later found out that my husband had fired Herbert two weeks earlier. My husband's secretary is now pregnant with my husband's child."

"Mrs. Sinclair, did you consent to get your womb ripped apart?" Kim asked.

"No "

"Did you consent to be rape?"

"No. All I wanted was to have a little bit of fun. Do something different."

"Was that what you got?"

"Definitely not. I'm scarred for the rest of my life."

"Scarred? By that you mean that you can't have children?"

"No. It means that I can't have sex anymore because my vagina was ripped apart. The doctor said that surgery might be able to bring it back but it would never be the same."

"Do you wish this on anyone, Mrs. Sinclair?"

"No. I wouldn't wish this on my worst enemy, no matter what that person had done."

"No more questions, your honor."

"Does the defense wish to cross-examine the witness?"

"Yes, your honor," Rashaun said, rising and walking to the witness stand. He stood three feet from where Mrs. Sinclair was sipping on her water.

"Mrs. Sinclair, did you consider yourself happily married before your affair?"

"Yes, but I won't call what happened to me an affair. An affair takes time, this was an incident."

"Have you told your husband what happened to you?"

"No."

"Did you press rape charges against Herbert?"

"No. That would destroy my marriage. Right now, my marriage is not the best but I still love my husband."

"Do you consider what happened to you an act of rape or rough sex?"

"I think its rape."

"Why?"

"Objection, your honor. He is badgering the witness." Kim stood from her seat.

"Objection overruled. Answer the question, Mrs. Sinclair."

"Yes, I told him to stop!" If the courtroom wasn't soundproofed Mrs. Sinclair could have been heard three doors down.

"Exactly when did you say no, Mrs. Sinclair? Was it when he was kissing your nipples? Was it when he was licking your vagina? Was it when he pushed it in slowly? Was it when you felt that immense pleasure coming over you?"

Mrs. Sinclair made tight fists and looked as if she was ready to pound on the table.

"Did you say no or stop? Which word did you use?"

"I don't know. They both mean the same thing."

"Why are you here, Mrs. Sinclair?"

"Because I heard what happened to that poor girl."

"Did you know Mrs. Francis, Mrs. Sinclair?"

"No, but I know what she went through and we all are women and women have to stick together."

"So you are here for women's rights?"

"All men should die."

"Excuse me?"

"That's right. All men should die. They are evil."

"Your honor, move to strike that from the witness' last response," Kim said, standing and walking to the judge. "The witness is obviously very upset and is incoherent at this point."

"Defense?" The judge motioned to Rashaun.

"That's okay with me, your honor." Rashaun said "No more questions for the witness."

"Jury, please strike the last remarks from the witness' testimony."

"What is he doing here?" Andria asked as Paul walked into the waiting room.

"I'm sorry, Andria, but I bumped into Paul yesterday and I told him that you were going to have surgery. He asked me where so I told him. Andria, I didn't think he would come to the hospital. I'm sorry."

"Forget about it, Robin. I know how persuasive Paul can be." Andria leaned back in the chair next to Robin as Paul closed the door to the waiting room.

"I'm so sorry to hear that you are sick, Andria I hope you don't mind me being here," Paul said, looking around.

"Paul, you didn't have to come. Flowers would have done fine," Andria said, hoping that he got the hint that he wasn't welcome.

"No, Andria. We have been through too much for me to send flowers. I want you to know that I'm here for you. I brought some Tropicana orange juice for you. Can you drink?" he asked.

"Paul, Andria cannot have anything before the operation," Robin responded

Andria looked at Paul then at Robin. Somehow she was missing something. The pair seemed too cordial. Robin hated Paul's guts but was acting as if he was a good friend. "Paul, I'll be fine. You don't have to stay."

"Andria, I already took the day off. I think in times like this you need your friends. I can remember numerous times when you were there for me when I was sick. Please let me at least show my gratitude," he said, sitting next to Andria and putting her hand in his.

"Andria, let him stay. After all, I have to go and pick up Rob. I want someone to be there for you." Robin tapped Andria lightly on the shoulder.

"I could call my mother and she could come and stay with me." Andria pulled her hand away from Paul's. "I didn't tell her I was going into the hospital because I knew it would stress her, and with her blood pressure..."

"Andria, would you stop it!" Paul said. He looked at her the way he used to do when it meant so much more than comfort. "I'm not going anywhere. I'm staying with you regardless of what you say." He attempted to hold her hand again but Andria quickly withdrew it from within his grasp.

Andria looked at Paul's deceitful eyes and decided there was no room for argument. Besides she was about to have an operation so she needed to relax. "Okay, Paul, you win," she said and looked at the lady in the white uniform behind the big glass window.

A nurse in blue hospital scrubs came out of the door next to the glass partition and called Andria's name.

Andria, Robin and Paul stood.

"I'm sorry. Only the patient is allowed in the surgery room," nurse said with practiced ease.

Robin hugged her. "Everything will be all right," Robin said.

"I love you" Andria said as she freed herself from Robin's embrace.

"Love you too," Robin said as she turned around quickly.

Paul angled himself between the two so that he could put his arms around Andria. "Go get them, tiger," he said.

"I'm sorry if I was rude before, but thanks for coming," she said.

"Don't mention it. Always remember, no matter what, I will always be here for you," he said and kissed her softly on the cheek.

"Got to go, Andria," the nurse said. "There is a cafeteria down the hall if you guys need something to eat. The price is kind of steep but if you really want to it's there for you."

"Hey, you," Rashaun said and planted a soft kiss on her lips.

"Hi," she said, smiling. Andria didn't know if she was still sedated or dreaming, whatever it was she wanted it to continue. She closed her eyes and opened them again. "You're here," she said, smiling. "I thought I was dreaming."

"No you're not dreaming. I'm sorry that I didn't make it here sooner. I wanted to see you before you went in but I was a few seconds too late. It won't happen again. I spoke to the doctor. He said that the operation was very successful and he doesn't see you having any more problems. He said all you need is to rest. I told him that I would make sure of that," he said, smiling.

"You will, huh?" she said, looking up at him with eyes that pierced his soul.

"I don't have to be in court for the next few days, so here I am your servant." He watched her smile create a glow all over her face.

"Where are Robin and Paul?" Andria asked, looking at the door.

"I told them that I would call them after the operation. Robin had to leave so Paul left with her."

"You think you could handle anything that comes up?" Andria asked.

"I'll have to. If not, I'll be a lousy husband."

Andria started to cry at the same time the nurse walked in.

"Excuse me, sir. You cannot stress the patient. You'll have to leave," she said, looking angrily at Rashaun.

"No, it's fine. This is my fiancé. I'm just very happy that he's here," Andria said as Rashaun wiped her eyes with a tissue.

"Are you sure?" the nurse asked still looking at Rashaun.

"I'm very sure," Andria said. " He'll be taking me home later."

"To our apartment," he added.

"I'm very glad for both of you but I don't really need to know anymore. I can see that you guys are in love and all that but this is a hospital for sick people so don't go around with those stupid love smile on your faces," she said.

After she left, Andria turned to Rashaun and asked, "What did you tell Paul? I know he can be very stubborn."

"I told him to step aside. Your man is taking over because he don't know what he got until he lost it," He said. She looked at him and they both started to laugh.

"Isn't there a song by ..."

"Okay you got me."

"Yes, I do."

"I see we have this confidant look on our face now," Rashaun said as he squeezed into the bed with Andria.

"I don't think you can do this in a hospital."

"Do what?" Rashaun asked as he took Andria's hand and put it on his head.

"I don't believe you. You're going to sleep," Andria said as she started to rub his baldhead.

Rashaun pulled Andria toward him. "Yeah. Wake me up when that evil nurse comes back."

Andria dropped a thinly sliced ripe plantain in the hot oil. The phone rang when she had about five pieces in.

"Damn, who the hell is calling now," she said as she put the spatula down and ran to the phone.

"Hello," she shouted.

"Did I interrupt an orgasm? If I did I'll hang up and call back again," Robin said.

"I didn't know it was you. I thought it was one of the salespeople calling to ask for Mr. or Mrs. Jones," Andria said walking back to the frying pan. She quickly flipped the plantains over. "No" she said as she saw that yellow had turn to black.

"Are you okay, Andria?" Robin inquired.

"No, I just burned the plantain that I was frying."

"I told you the secret to frying plantain is to make the slice bigger otherwise they will burn every time."

Andria went into the refrigerator and took out the remaining half of the plantain. She put it on the cutting board once more started to slice, this time making the pieces twice as big as the earlier ones that were now resting in the garbage pail by the refrigerator.

"So what's up, girlfriend? I hardly hear from you since your fiancé took you away from the hospital," Robin said.

"Robin, don't even try that. I spoke to you yesterday morning," Andria said as she once more moved to the frying pan with her plantains. "This better work."

"I promise you it will. What are you cooking?"

"Besides fried plantain, stew chicken, rice and peas, baked fish, mixed provisions and steamed vegetables."

"Okay you've got to tell me. I know you don't need to get the man anymore, you already have him. You do have to keep him but I don't think you need to do it through his belly, so what's the occasion?"

"Hold on," Andria said and clicked the flash button to take an incoming call.

"Hello."

"Hi, babes. What's up?"

"A whole lot but you are too far to get into it."

"You are nothing but a teaser."

"There you go with those soca songs again."

"What can I say? I'm a born West Indian."

"I would love to talk to you but Robin is on the line."

"I don't want you to keep your friend waiting. I'll be home at seven."

"Love you."

"Love you, too, babes. Bye."

Once more Andria pressed the flash button.

"Robin?"

"I'm still here. You gave me time to get my husband and kid in bed."

"Robin, don't even go there. You usually keep me on hold for more than fifteen minutes while you make love on the phone with your husband."

"Well none of that is happening anymore," Robin said in a reserved tone.

"Robin, are you and your husband okay."

"Andria, don't even try to get away from our original topic. My husband and I are fine. Now, what's the occasion."

"Well I went to the doctor and she said everything was okay and we could continue relations."

"You mean you can have sex. You are the only person I know who uses the word *relations* when she is talking about sex. Well I can understand, you got to take care of your man."

As Andria took the plantains out of the frying pan she realized her friend was right. They were a beautiful yellow. She put them on a plate that was covered with a paper towel. After she finished, she took the plate over to the table and placed it next to the tossed salad.

"Finally," she said as she threw the table towel back onto the rack and headed for the bedroom.

"I see you're finished," Robin said.

"Yep. I have some time before I go and reheat some of the food. Do you think these men appreciate the stuff we do for them?"

"No."

"I mean, I don't do this every day but we do so much around the house."

"Speaking of men. I spoke to your ex today. He was very pissed off when Rashaun came to the hospital. I had to go and calm him down. He wants to know who the fuck Rashaun thinks he is to ask him to leave."

"Please. Paul shouldn't be getting upset. I'm not with him. He had his chance and he blew it. By the way, Robin, since when is Paul calling you?"

"It's nothing. He just wanted to talk and I was there to listen."

"Robin, let me warn you. Paul is no good. He's a user and a player. Be very careful."

"Andria, are you jealous or something?"

"No, Robin, I'm not jealous or something. I just know Paul. He will try to find out what you need then try to give it to you and in return he will play you. If Paul needs an ear, let him go to a pastor, that's why they are there and he needs church anyway."

"Andria, I can handle myself, I know what you went through with Paul. I ain't nobody's fool. Besides I don't think Paul is over you. I think he's just trying to get back with you."

Andria walked to the bathroom, taking off her panties and bra as she walked. She reached in the medicine cabinet and took out a shower cap. "Robin, don't let Paul fool you with that

BS. Paul loves one person in life and that person is himself. Please, Robin, just stay away from him."

"Andria, I'll be fine. He also told me to give you his number. Do you have a pen?" Robin asked.

"I don't want his number. I already thanked him for being at the hospital. I don't need to talk to him again." Andria adjusted the shower cap. She picked up the shea butter body wash on the side of the tub and shook it. Rashaun liked it so much on her that they had both started using it.

"Andria, I'm just telling you what he said. Please don't jump down my throat."

"Okay, Robin, if you want me to talk to him, I will. Give me a second," Andria said as she walked back into the bedroom. "Okay give it to me."

"Why are you so worried about Robin?" Rashaun asked as he lay down next to Andria.

"Because I know the type of person Paul is. Robin has no idea what she is getting into. Paul will find her weakness and exploit it. Why do you think I stayed so long with him? He looks, he listens and then he says just the right thing."

"I think you underestimate your friend and her marriage."

"I don't think so." Andria didn't think that Robin had forgiven her husband for his reaction to Andria on the night they went out. She didn't tell Rashaun about the incident but she didn't forget it.

"Why are you so sure?"

"Women know these things. But you know what, I won't let him hurt my friend. It won't happen!"

"Andria, don't get involved in people's business. Believe me, you might be the one getting hurt the most. I'm warning you."

He looked at her lying there next to him where she belonged. He knew she wouldn't listen and he wasn't sure if the shoe were on the other foot if he would listen either.

"Would you stop looking at me that way? You know you make me nervous. Didn't you promise me a full-body massage?" she said as she reached for a bottle of scented oil. "And remember, don't even try to make love to me. I know how you use those hands of yours to seduce me but it's not happening today. You already had me after dinner. Once is enough." She turned over on her back.

"I'm at you service, ma'am," Rashaun said as he took the sheet and covered Andria up to the neck.

"Why are you covering me?" she asked as she turned over, letting the sheet fall below her perfect breasts.

"Because if I don't, my hands will never leave your butt," he said, getting up and turning on the humidifier. "Now lay back, let the ancient massage specialist do his work."

Andria lay back down on her stomach and once more Rashaun put the sheet over her, barely exposing her neck. He took the remote and turned on the CD player next to the bed. The soft, slow, sensual songs of Grover Washington filled the room.

"You got plans for me, don't you?" Andria muttered into the sheets.

"Only time will tell," he said as he straddled her, his knees absorbing all the weight of his body as he took the massage bottle into his hands.

"No hanky panky," she muttered.

He took the massage oil and squeezed some into the middle of his right palm. He rubbed his hands together, warming up the oil. Using his fingertips Rashaun applied pressure down the back of Andria's neck in a smooth, gliding motion. He stopped at the base of her neck and massaged until his fingers touched her hair. He repeated the movements two more times before bringing his right and left palm out in a circular motion, kneading her shoulders. He alternated between his palms and fingers to reach deep within Andria's shoulder blades with a steady pressure to release her tension. He added some more Shea butter moisturizing oil to his hands and continued the massage.

"Yes, right there," Andria, moaned as he continued to knead her shoulder blades with his fingertips. Andria was now lying with the left side of her face on the sheet. Her eyes were closed as she let Rashaun's touch relax her mind and body.

"You are beautiful," he said. He couldn't resist leaning forward and kissing her on her partially exposed lips.

"Let's hope you think the same when the wrinkles appear and the joints become much stiffer," she said, turning her head to the other side.

"Why did you do that?" Rashaun asked.

"You can't kiss half of my lips and expect me to be content, unless you're trying to tell me that my right side looks better than my left."

He laughed as he leaned forward one more time to kiss Andria.

"You start this and you will never finish this massage," she said. She straightened her head so that her face was completely buried on the bed.

"Okay, I get it," he said as he reached over her head for the moisturizing oil. He again went back to massaging, only this time he brought his hands to the middle of her back. He used his thumbs to go straight down her spine with just enough tension to relax her. When he reached to the bottom of her back just above the soft flesh of her butt, he glided his hands up her back, barely touching her. Again, he repeated his thumb action down her back then up with feathery touches. At the top of her back he brought his hands together and started to massage her left side with circular motions.

After he finished with her left side, he brought his fingers over to her right side and did the same. He got off the bed and pulled the sheet off her and removed his Jockey underwear and kneeled to the right of her. He placed his thumbs in the middle of her back while his fingertips were at her sides. It always amazed him how small her waist was. He moved his hands up and down, massaging her lower back and a small portion of her butt.

Slowly he started to extend the coverage of her butt until he was using both his hands to glide up and down using constant pressure. As he moved from her butt to the top of her legs, he used his thumb to slightly touch her vagina. As he did so he could feel himself becoming excited. He moved from the side of the bed to kneeling on the edge, placing her legs between his. As he massaged her butt and down her legs his semi-erect penis touched her calves. He brought his fingers back to her butt and this time as he massaged her legs he glided his thumbs between the lips of her vagina. He continued to go from her legs to the sweetness of her womanhood.

"Rashaun," she called out.

"I'm innocent," he said as he quickly moved his hands away from her vagina to her legs.

"And I'm the Virgin Mary," she said as she parted her legs.

"Beautiful" he said as he rubbed his right hand over her vagina.

"I know you're not talking about my face," she said, trying to muffle her laughter with the sheets.

"Nope, it's your calves. They're the best I have ever seen," he said as he continued to alternate between rubbing her legs and her vagina. He got off the bed and lifted her right leg onto his chest and began to massage her right foot, starting at her knees and going all the way to her toes. He did the same to her left foot and when he finished he brought her toes to his mouth then slowly started to suck on each one.

"Why did you have to go and do that," she said as her feet started to tremble.

He brought her right leg back to his chest then to his mouth.

"You are wicked," she said as the feeling of him sucking her toes went through her body. "Please stop, please."

"Stop what," he said as he began to kiss down her leg.

"You are a…" She didn't finish because he had inserted a finger into her vagina and he was reaching for that spot that he knew so well. She lifted her legs off and knelt with her head on the bed. He took his finger from inside of her and used more to part her vagina, exposing her clit, which he rubbed gently. His erect penis brushed her leg.

"I want you in me," she said, moaning. She grabbed hold of his penis, brought it to the entrance of her vagina and guided the tip inside. Just as she was about to push back he pulled his penis out.

"Rashaun!" She shouted.

"You said we are not going to make love," Rashaun said and got off the bed. "I'm going to the bathroom, I'll come back and finish the massage."

"You are a bastard," she shouted as she quickly got off the bed and followed him into the bathroom.

He grabbed her as soon as she walked inside and lifted her up onto the sink. He spread her legs apart, plunging deeply into her. He grabbed her legs and pulled her toward him as he continued to plunge in and out. His strokes were long and steady reaching deep inside of her. Each time he pulled out and slowed down, she grabbed his butt and pulled him faster and deeper in to her. His chest heaved, his muscles tensed as he brought her into him. He felt like he was about to explode inside of her.

"No you're not," she said and shoved him away from her, almost sending him crashing through the bathroom door. She grabbed him by the penis and brought him down to the cold bathroom floor. "We will do it my way."

"How is that?"

"I want to be treated like a lady," she said, brushing his chin with the back of her hand.

"I thought I always did that."

"No Rashaun, you treat me like a lady but you screw me like a woman."

He started to rise from the floor. "But…"

She pushed him gently back down. "I do enjoy being screwed sometimes, and the feeling of you exploding inside of me over and over is great, but sometimes, I want you to make love to me, slowly and passionately. Like this…"

"Thanks for picking me up after work," Monique, Rashaun's friend from college, said as she got into the car. "I know that I'm very beautiful but I don't think that's a good enough reason for you to want to go to New Jersey. You hate New Jersey."

Rashaun slipped the car into gear and merged into the traffic on Broadway going downtown. "Jersey has always been the forgotten city behind New York. I don't hate it, I just wouldn't live there." He maneuvered the car behind a green Mercedes ML320.

"What's up? And don't tell me you broke up with Andria," Monique said as she put her bag on the backseat.

"Well I did do that but we got back together."

"Did you set a wedding date or are you going to be engaged for a century?" She turned the radio from 107.5 to 101.9. "You don't mind, do you?"

"Monique, you are too much. No, we didn't set a date yet but we have been talking about next year. You know me. I'm not into big weddings."

Monique shook her head in agreement. "Yeah, if it was up to you, the wedding would take place in your apartment with your mother and a few close friends. Praise God the two women in your life will never go for that."

Rashaun laughed. "You make me sound so bad."

"So, everything is good with your mother and family, and you haven't kicked Andria to the curb. I see we're making progress here. Well I don't think there is much left that will make you drive to Jersey in rush hour. So I'm stumped."

Rashaun looked at the slow-moving traffic heading to the Holland Tunnel. "How do these people do this day after day?" he asked as he joined the procession.

"It has gotten worst after the terrorist attack. Me! I like the Path trains. I can relax and catch up on my reading. Yes, Rashaun, I know you have problems with trains and crowded areas."

"Let's say I prefer to drive. If I have to take the train then I will." Rashaun swerved to the left to avoid a driver who suddenly cut in front of him.

"You see, that's the stuff I cannot deal with. That a-hole cutting in front of you. Do you think he just realized that there are two lanes going to Jersey? These idiots, I swear if I had a bull dozer I would ram all of them," Monique said, as she gave the driver the finger.

"Monique, calm down. It's not that bad. I understand that Jersey drivers are the worse so I was ready to make the adjustments," he said.

"Okay, you got me there. I agree Jersey drivers definitely are the worse. Enough of the small talk, Rashaun. What's on your mind?"

"It's this case…"

"Don't tell me you are having feelings for your ex."

"No, it's not that. I think she will always have a little of my heart and a bit of my hate but I love Andria and she is the one who occupies my thoughts. I cannot let any other feelings clog my mind for this trial. I have to admit that sometimes when I look at Kim, I want to…"

"You want to hurt her in the worse way for what she put you through? That's understandable. What you don't want to do is overreact. That won't be good for anyone. I can only imagine what you go through day after day."

"It was very difficult when Andria wasn't there but she's back now and that makes it easier. A woman has never taken so much from me, I will never forget. But that's not what I want to talk to you about."

"I know but I just wanted you to talk about that to kind of bring it out of you because I know it's difficult to discuss it with Andria. Now talk?"

Rashaun inched his car up behind the one that had cut him off earlier. "I'm afraid," he said as he stared straight ahead. "For the first time, I'm afraid of failing."

Monique reached out and patted Rashaun on the shoulder. "That's fine, Rashaun. You're human. This case is not an ordinary one. It's your friend on trial for murder. It's okay to be afraid but turn that fear into the best defense possible. That's all anyone is asking of you. I know you have the ability and so does Tyrone. If he didn't believe in you he wouldn't put his life in your hands."

"I go to court and I see his parents in the courtroom every day. Their only son's life is riding on me. It's a burden that seems enormous at times. What happens if I missed something? There is no 'I'm sorry, your son will be doing twenty-five to life.'"

"Rashaun, you remember when you were in college and you needed that last class to graduate and the only professor who taught it was the one you had that big fight with?"

"Yeah, I remember, Professor Leem. He was an asshole to put it mildly. I don't think any of the students liked him and he failed most of them too. It was the fact that he had tenure, it allowed him get away with murder."

"Yeah, Leem. You came to me and you told me that you would do the work so that the professor wouldn't have any choice but to pass you. I admired that confidence. I didn't tell you then because you would've had a bigger head than you already had."

"That was just confidence that came with lessons from living."

"Whatever you want to call it, but you just were not going to be denied, and you ended up with an A in his class."

"I still didn't like him."

"But my point is that you succeeded, regardless of the obstacle that was in front of you. Rashaun, you have that gift of finding the way that will make sure that you are not denied. I believe that you will win this case because you will refuse to lose. I know this is not college and this is not a three-credit class. Your friend's life stands in the balance but, again, you will succeed."

Rashaun looked over at Monique and smiled. "You're right. The stakes are too high for failure. If I could conquer the so-called curse of the black man, I will definitely make Tyrone a free man."

"Well first you have to get us out of the Holland Tunnel."

"I really don't understand how these people can commute from Jersey. For five days of the week they have to deal with this bumper-to-bumper nonsense."

"Well it's either that or live in Brooklyn and deal with Flatbush and Utica avenues."

"At least if we have traffic jams there is usually something happening on the street that's entertaining. Look. All I see is the brickwork that hopefully won't crumble and make us swim with the fishes. Alas! Light at the end of the tunnel. Now we're about to enter the excitement of New Jersey. By the way, do the cops still do racial profiling? I might have to put on my bulletproof vest because the police aim to kill in Jersey."

"Well you should have had your vest on anyway. In Brooklyn the police want to kill you and the stray bullet intended for the drug dealer on the corner is headed in your direction."

"Only in the bad parts."

"You mean Brooklyn has good parts?" Monique looked at Rashaun as if he had just told her that the Knicks had won the NBA championship. "Let me use your phone. I have to call my husband, Gerry, and tell him to stop at the supermarket."

"What, you ran out of whipped cream?"

"Boy, whipped cream is played out. It's all about the grape jelly."

"What you guys do? Have grape jelly and peanut butter sandwiches?"

"So much to learn," Monique said, shaking her head. "I definitely need to talk to Andria."

Andria looked at her watch for the second time in the ten minutes.

"Do you have another appointment, Andria?" Mrs. Brown, Andria's supervisor, asked.

"No, I guess I just have a few things on my mind," Andria replied.

"Well, I was looking at Mrs. London's file and I think you should try to get the husband in for a group meeting. I think he might be able to convince his wife not to keep the baby."

"The last time I tried to get in touch with Mr. London he was in Georgia. His wife wasn't sure when he was going to be back. I think he has another woman down there who might also have children for him."

"But he has fourteen children with his wife."

"I know but that doesn't seem to mean anything to him. I doubt he cares whether she's pregnant. He doesn't take care of any of his children so I assume that to him they don't really exist. Mrs. London hinted that her husband might have four or five other women who have children for him but it doesn't bother her."

"Does anything bother her? She is about to have another child and the city and the corrections department are already taking care of her litter. I don't understand women like that. Are they stupid? We are in the twenty-first century. You don't have to have a child every time you have sex. There is no rule that says penis plus vagina equals baby. Andria, continue to keep me up to date with this case and if you need any advice, feel free to stop by my office."

"Thank you, Mrs. Brown," Andria said and stood.

"Andria, I meant to ask you how was the operation?"

"It went fine. I have to go to the doctor for periodic checkups but everything is okay," Andria said, taking a quick glance at her watch as she opened the door to her supervisor's office door. She had told Paul that she was going to meet him downtown at Island Hut at 1:45. She went back to her desk, grabbed her bag and headed to the train station.

When she walked into the restaurant, it was fifteen minutes after two. Paul was sitting in the right corner of the room next to a big banana plant. A waitress dressed in a short skirt hovered over him. Andria walked up to the table and stood behind the waitress.

Paul spoke to the woman who turned around and looked Andria up and down before heading in the direction of the kitchen. "I took the liberty of ordering for both of us. I ordered a small stew chicken for you and you know I like my oxtails," Paul said.

"I see you found a friend in the waitress. Maybe now you'll leave my friend alone."

Paul sipped on a bottle of champagne cola? "Straight to the point, no how are you doing and the usual chitchat."

"Paul, our days of chitchatting are over. You were very rude on the phone and you know the reason I'm here."

"That I do. You want to save Robin from the big, bad Paul. You think that I'm out to destroy her marriage and, of course, you don't want that to happen. What if I tell you I really like Robin and I want to start a serious relationship with her?"

"Paul, Robin is already in a serious relationship. She's married with a child. You have nothing to offer her or any other woman."

"Obviously she thinks differently."

The waitress had returned with a glass of cranberry juice, which she placed in front of Andria, almost spilling it on Andria's clothes. "Did you tell her I didn't want your sorry ass?" Andria asked, looking at Paul as the waitress did her disappearing act.

Paul smiled and sipped some more of his drink. "Andria, obviously you're upset. I didn't mean to upset you over the phone but I think you know how to end this whole mix-up. You know I still love you and I want you back. I told you that I was

113

sorry for what I did. Why don't you just leave that loser and come back to me? You know I don't care for Robin, neither did I care for your other friend, the dead one. What's her name again?"

"Paul, I would not go back with you if you were the last man alive. I'd rather sleep with a skunk than you because with a skunk I know what I'm smelling."

"All this is not necessary. Let me tell you what. Let's have one night together, if after that you're not feeling me. I'll leave you and your friend alone. One night, just for old time's sake."

The waitress brought the food and set it on the table.

"Paul, you are not serious. You honestly think that I'm going to sleep with you? Tell me why, Paul. Why would I sleep with you?" Andria asked, pushing away her plate.

Paul took his fork and dug into the rice and peas. "Let me tell you what I know about women. They don't fall out of love. What they do is suppress their feelings. Andria, we were together too long for you to tell me that you don't have any feelings for me. If I thought that was the case then I wouldn't be here. I wouldn't be messing with your friends and sitting here having lunch with you. You know what I can do in bed and if I decide to flip your friend Robin, there isn't a damn thing you or her husband can do. When I'm finished with her I'll have her eating out of the garbage can because I told her to." Paul took his fork and stuck it in an oxtail the brown gravy oozing from his fork. "You ever asked yourself why Robin is even talking to me? After all, you remember the least she could do was tolerate me. You remember, I always asked you why does your friend hate me so much. Now if I call her right now she'll come over." He put his fork down, took out his cell phone and dialed a number.

"Paul…" Andria started.

Paul lifted his hand and put one finger up to silence Andria.

114

"Hi, what's up?" he said and listened. "I'm downtown. You want to come down for minute?" He paused "How far are you?" He paused again "Yeah, I'll be here for the next half hour. Okay, see you."

"This is sad." Andria looked at Paul and shook her head. "Look at what you have come to, trying to blackmail me to get into my pants."

"There is no shame in my game. When you kicked me out I stumbled. I spent countless nights thinking about you. I know I was wrong and I admit that I don't really deserve a second chance but I also know that I cannot live without you. You see, all these other women don't mean a thing to me, I could walk away from them anytime. These women are a dime a dozen but you're a gem. The mold was ground then spread over the continent after your birth. There won't ever be another you and I want you back." Paul looked Andria directly in her eyes.

"I said it once and I will say it again, you are pitiful. Not in a million years will I go back with you, and those weak lines you are spouting will not work with me. Remember, I've been there, done that. Paul, you aren't shit and the sooner these women realize that, the better off they will be." Andria twirled the straw in her drink.

"Andria, remember it's your call. Your best friend will be here in a few minutes. She has always been there for you. It's up to you to be there for her now. I give you my word if it doesn't work out I will step. I have nothing to prove by sleeping with you and I hate to approach you like this but I feel it's the only way." He picked up his fork.

"And to think I was ever in love with you. Paul, where was that side of you? Where did you hide this side of you? I can't believe I'm having this conversation with a man I almost married. You are willing to destroy someone's family to satisfy your warped ego. That's all it is, Paul. It's your ego. You are not in love with me. You don't want me back. Someone else has me now and you feel that he shouldn't. Your ego was hurt even more when Rashaun sent you home from the hospital. Now you want to get back at him. You don't want me back. You want to show Rashaun that you can have me anytime you want. And all these women are the only way you can show success for your pitiful existence. I understand you much more now that I am standing outside looking in, and to tell you the truth, there isn't much to look at from over here," Andria said, looking Paul straight in the eyes. "I gave you the credit for being a man before but I take it back. You are not a man, you are a little boy. You never made any of the transitions that eventually make a man."

"Are you finished?" Paul asked as he scooped up some rice and peas. "Your man obviously is not taking care of home because you have been doing a lot of bullshit thinking. Why don't we get a hotel room and we can separate the man from the child? Here she comes."

Andria looked around to see Robin coming into the restaurant. When she saw Andria, she looked as if she had seen the last dinosaur. Somehow, she was able to conjure up a smile as she walked to the table.

Andria stood as her friend came up to the table.

"Andria, I didn't expect to see you here," Robin said.

"To be honest, Robin, I didn't expect to see you here either," Andria said, looking at Paul who had a smirk on his face.

"Andria, like we discussed, it's all up to you. I see you haven't eaten your lunch. Do you want to take it home for you and Rashaun?" Paul asked as he signaled to the waitress.

"Good-bye, Robin. I'll call you later."

Rashaun parked his car in front of a blue 740 IL BMW, on Flatbush Avenue. The car was the flagship of BMW and cost range at least $65,000. The car was outfitted with twenty-inch rims and a very dark tint, which Rashaun doubted was legal in New York City. He saw his friend Lenny, the barber and owner of the BMW, looking through the glass door. Rashaun dropped two quarters in a meter that registered sixty minutes and walked into the barbershop.

"Hair De Mention must be doing great. I see you still have the BM," Rashaun said touched fists with Lenny.

"Life is short. A man has to live. Contrary to popular opinions there are no repeats," Lenny said as he walked over to a twelve-foot fish tank in the middle of the shop. He dropped a bag with about fifty goldfish in the tank and watched as six fish, many of them more than a foot long, made a meal of the helpless goldfish. He dropped the empty bag in the trashcan and went into the bathroom.

Rashaun took a newspaper that was lying on a black leather couch and took his seat in the barber chair. "Lenny, the man who wants to become a millionaire before he turns twenty-five," Rashaun said as Lenny walked to him, wiping his hands on a paper towel.

"It's either you do it now or wait till you're sixty and spend the money on doctors. You got to do it when the dick can rise without medication and you can indulge in the finer delicacies of life without worrying about your diet. It's said that life is foolishly wasted on the young. I don't believe in that." He wrapped white tissue around Rashaun's neck and placed a blue smock over it.

"And the BM," Rashaun said, making himself comfortable in the chair.

"The BMW is for just in case. Just in case I don't see tomorrow, I want to know that I had fun today. Occasionally, I take it upstate and I fly with the state troopers. Most people say a car is a car. These people haven't driven BMW's flagship or the Mercedes Benz 500. Anyway how's that sex case you working on?" Lenny opened a new pack of razor blades and replaced the one in the razor. He used a creamy lather on Rashaun's head.

"The case is going good but I'd rather not talk about it. I'm sure the BM makes the young girls' panties drop a lot faster too."

"Well there are some perks to owning a fine piece of machinery," Lenny said as he wiped his hands on a paper towel and picked up the razor.

"I'm sure," Rashaun said as Lenny reclined the barber chair so that Rashaun was almost lying flat. He took the razor and started from the front.

"I don't understand women. They're very confusing. You'll meet a woman and you'll tell her exactly how things will be. I don't believe in lying to women. It only creates unnecessary tension and makes you a fiction writer. I remember last year when I was with my baby's mother and I had this other thing on the side. I'm upstairs with this girl that I had been banging off and on, and who should show up at my door?"

"Your baby's mother?"

"Exactly. I look outside. It's 11:30 at night and I promised the girl that I would drop her at the train station because she had to go to work. Praise God that I live in a three-apartment building. At first, I tried to delay going out so that my girl would see that I wasn't home and go home. You would think after fifteen minutes she would leave but no she kept ringing the bell. And the other girl is telling me she needs to leave because she doesn't want to be late for work. So you know what I had to do?"

"What, Lenny?"

"While coming down the stairs I tripped on purpose, I tumbled down two flights of stairs and I got up limping. The girl got really concerned and she wanted to stay with me or take me to the hospital. I told her no, I would go upstairs and put some ice on it. Finally, she left and I ran back up the stairs and went to my landlord's apartment. I told her that I had to pretend I was shoveling her snow because I was in a jam. She knew exactly what I meant. So I went to her backyard shoveled some snow and then I walked around to the front like I was about to

118

shovel there. I saw my girlfriend and I told her that I was in the back shoveling. And you know what happened from then on, right?"

"You had to do your landlord."

"No man, I had to shovel the snow around the apartment for the rest of the winter. Shit, I'm so happy I don't have a woman right now."

"But how's your back?"

"Rashaun, get up and go free that poor boy," Lenny said, bringing the seat up.

"That wasn't a true story, was it?" Rashaun asked, looking at himself in the mirror.

"You see that mark on my back, that's where a splinter dug into me on my way down the stairs."

Rashaun took some money from his money clip and gave it to Lenny. "For the BM."

"Shit it takes a lot more than this to pay for the BM but everything counts," Lenny said as he escorted Rashaun to the front door.

"Your honor, I was not aware of this witness," Rashaun said as he sat in the judge's chamber. Kim sat in a similar red leather chair a few feet to his right.

"Your honor, this witness came forward yesterday and I would like her to testify," Kim said, looking over at Rashaun.

"Ms. Rivers, you are quite aware of the fact that the defense has to receive sufficient time to prepare. I will adjourn the case until tomorrow for the defense to prepare. That's all. You both are dismissed," the judge said and rose from his black leather chair. "And Ms. Rivers, please don't pull any stunt like that in my courtroom again."

Kim stepped in front of Rashaun brushing him on his side as they were leaving the room. "If you want to touch me, just ask. I just might let you." Kim looked up at him and gave him a wicked smile. "I'm free for dinner tonight. We can get together for old times' sake, if you can handle it."

"Unlike you, I have a client whose life depends on me. I am not on this power trip," Rashaun said, stepping in front of her.

"That has always been your problem, Rashaun. You take life too seriously. You have an adjustable bolt up your ass and you keep tightening it. Take that shit out and for once in your life exhale," she said, increasing her pace to keep up with Rashaun.

"The problem with exhaling with a woman like you around is that I might never be able to inhale again," Rashaun said as they split and went to their respective tables.

Rashaun sat next to Tyrone and leaned over to whisper in his ear "Do you know Natalie Phillips?"

"Yes," Tyrone said. "We used to go together."

"Why didn't you tell me about her?"

"Natalie moved to Atlanta about four years ago. I didn't think it was relevant."

"Tyrone, just tell me everything you know. Let me worry about what's relevant. You don't know Kim. If you pissed on the sidewalk last year she'll find out," Rashaun said as he sat up as the judge walked back into the courtroom.

The judge adjourned the case as promised. Rashaun walked out with Tyrone to the elevator that would take them to the street level. As they stood waiting for the elevator a woman who looked to be in her early sixties came up to them. Rashaun and Tyrone both looked at her.

"I want you to get the electric chair," she said, pointing at Tyrone. "And you, I have a special gift for you after the trial. You, the defender of the wicked, the Lord has sent me to punish you."

Tyrone pulled back when the woman began talking. Rashaun just looked at her as if he could see right through her. He had been threatened so many times as a lawyer that it didn't faze him anymore.

The woman went over to another elevator still looking at Tyrone and Rashaun.

Rashaun tapped his friend on the shoulder "Don't worry about her. She's just venting. Let's go get something to eat. We have to talk about Natalie."

Rashaun ordered a turkey burger deluxe, which came with french fries and a soda. Tyrone went for a cheeseburger with a small soup and apple juice. The waiter put two glasses of water in front of them.

"You want my water?" Tyrone asked.

"Yeah, I need to clean my system," Rashaun said, taking a straw and putting it in the glass of water. He liked to drink three glasses of water with each meal. He took a long pull on the straw, drinking almost half the glass. "New York water, if it don't kill you, it will make you pissed off."

"You wanted to know about Natalie."

"Yeah, tell me everything."

"Natalie should've been a man. She's a pure player. My mistake was falling in love with her."

"When was that?"

"A few years before we became friends," Tyrone said, leaning back for the waiter to put their food on the table.

"Tyrone, you have a magnet for attracting female players, don't you?"

"Shit happens."

"Go ahead."

"I lived with Natalie for a little less than two years. During that time I think she fucked about twenty guys."

"And you didn't know?."

"The girl was a nurse, you know how their schedules fluctuate. This month they are working three days on, four days off. Next month it's a five-day shift. I took her word for it. It wasn't until this brother called my house and asked to speak to Natalie. I usually don't ask questions if a man asks to speak to my woman but that day I did. Then the brother asked me who I was so I told him. He said that I was stupid. He told me he beat up that meat the night before. He said he pounded it like a battering ram. He said she was a freak and especially liked to lick brothers' assholes."

"So what happened?" Rashaun asked as he bit into his turkey burger.

"That night when she came home we had it out," Tyrone said adjusting his hamburger bun so that it fit over the melted cheese.

"You didn't flip on her and beat her up or anything like that did you?" Rashaun asked taking a fry and dipping it into a pool of ketchup he had put on the side of his plate.

"I have never hit a woman in my life and I have no intention of doing so," Tyrone said before biting into his cheeseburger. "I can hardly sleep at night thinking of Judy. I wake up in cold sweat, my head spinning. Sometimes I just want to end it all. I want to take a knife and slit my wrists."

Rashaun watched his friend and he felt a deep sadness. He didn't know what to say. Tyrone was hurting in the worse way. "Tyrone, I think you need some help. I don't know if you can make it through the trial."

"I need more help than that. I need a fucking new life!" Tyrone shouted, his eyes welling with tears.

"You guys okay here," the waiter asked.

"Yes, we're fine," Rashaun said, looking around at the audience their conversation had drawn.

"Rashaun, you don't know what it's like to be me. Look at me, I've lost so much weight. You know what I find myself doing."

"What?"

"I talk to myself. I hold long conversations with myself."

"Tyrone, we all do that sometimes."

"How long will this trial last, Rashaun? I don't know how long I can hold up. I find myself slipping and it's not happening slowly."

"To be honest with you, I don't know. With Kim, time holds no importance. She will bring in as many witnesses as

122

possible. I think you need some help. I have a psychiatrist friend. I'll ask her if she can work with you."

"Thanks, man, I don't know what I would do without you. I know you're giving a lot more than you have to and for that I will be eternally grateful." Tyrone pushed the plate with the half-eaten burger aside and placed his drink in front of him, stirring the ice in the glass.

"Tyrone, I wouldn't have taken this case if I didn't believe in your innocence. We go way back and I know you wouldn't willfully hurt someone. What happened between you and Judy was an accident; it could've happened to anyone. You guys got carried away and the result was a tragedy. I think you have blamed yourself for the whole incident but that's not right. It takes two to tango and with sex that's one hundred percent true unless you're talking about masturbation."

Tyrone smiled for the first time since they sat down for lunch. "You mean jerking off," he said, loosening up a little bit. "I used to enjoy that, just me and a porno tape."

"Who needs porno? Memories will suffice," Rashaun said, taking the last bite of his turkey burger. "We have to head back now, back to Ms. Rivers."

"Rashaun, I think Kim still likes you."

"Yeah, maybe this time she'd like to finish the job." Rashaun pointed to the middle of his forehead "She wants to put a bullet right there."

Rashaun paid the waiter who had reappeared when he and Tyrone stood. He waited an extra minute for the receipt. Andria was keeping a record of his expenditures and she would be very upset if he came home without the receipt. Rashaun and Tyrone walked down Court Street enjoying the light chill of a fall day. Rashaun missed his old friend. He needed to give Tyrone a reason to want to live again. He hoped his psychiatrist friend Jackie would be able to do just that. He hadn't spoken to her in a long time but he knew she would be there for him.

Andria didn't want to wake up. She was feeling too good snuggled below Rashaun's right arm, her right leg crossed over his feet. She heard the voice again but she chose to ignore it. Yes, she had promised him that she was going jogging but morning was far away. She felt him touching her legs ever so softly and she wondered if they were going to do something besides jogging. When he kissed her on the lips she opened her eyes because she was positive that they weren't going jogging. When she lifted her foot to continue the foreplay, he quickly got off the bed. "You tricked me," she said, lying back on the bed with a pillow over her head.

Rashaun hit her softly on her exposed butt with his shirt. "Time to do five miles in Prospect Park."

She sat up on the bed wide awake "Five miles. I promised to do half a mile, maybe three quarters if the weather is nice, and I do mean nice, maybe eighty degrees."

"Andria, there won't be any eighty-degree falls in New York."

"Exactly."

She got off the bed and headed to the bathroom.

"Morning breath," Rashaun teased, grinning so that Andria could see his teeth.

"You didn't call it morning breath a few minutes ago when your mouth was all over it."

"I was checking for gingivitis."

"With your tongue?"

"Yeah. It's the most sensitive part of the mouth."

"Uh-huh," Andria murmured as she began to brush her teeth.

124

Rashaun felt the cool, crisp fall air hit his face as he effortlessly jogged up the hill. Just him and nature, enjoying each other. He looked back to see two figures ambling along. He increased his pace knowing that he would complete a full lap around Prospect Park before Andria and Paula got up the hill. Andria had made one phone call before she left the house and he was sure that it was to Paula. When they got to the park and they began to jog, Andria and Paula had done about ten minutes when they told him to go ahead, they would catch up with him later.

"I thought they were so happy," Paula said as she sipped on a bottle of water.

"I think they're still happy, that's why I don't want Paul messing up their relationship," Andria said, looking at Rashaun disappearing in the distance.

"So what you going to do?"

"I tried talking to him but he wants to sleep with me."

"Are you serious? He said that?"

Andria started to throw punches as she remembered a lady in the exercise video doing. "I wish I wasn't. Imagine me sleeping with Paul again."

"Paul is off the last chain. To come out and ask you to sleep with him like that. Who does he think he is?" Paula asked, joining Andria in throwing punches.

"Paul has changed a lot since we broke up. He was never like that."

"Girl, they don't ever change. Their true colors just come out later," Paula said, adding uppercuts to the straight punches.

"Paula, what are you doing?" Andria asked.

"Hitting them in their balls. That's the only way they will learn." Paula continued to throw two punches and a hard uppercut.

"I think I'll join you." Andria started to include uppercuts with her punches.

Two guys jogging by slowed down a little when they saw Andria and Paula. One of them was tall and extremely thin and the other one looked like he had eaten whole chicken too many times.

"Ladies, what are you doing?" the whole-chicken eater asked.

"Hitting them in the balls and ripping them out," Paula replied.

"Lesbians, let's go," the skinny one said and they started to increase their speed. "You can't find a good black woman these days."

"That's why I started dating Chinese women. Oriental women know how to treat their men."

Andria and Paula continued their antics for a few more minutes before their hands fell limply at their sides.

"Paula, what got you out of your bed this morning?" Andria asked. "And don't tell me it's the exercise."

Paula ignored Andria and continued walking.

"Paula!" Andria shouted.

"I heard you the first time."

"So?"

"I'm pregnant."

"So, you did it," Andria said, trying to get eye contact with her friend.

"Now that I'm pregnant I'm not to sure if I did the right thing."

"Paula, you did tell Isaiah that you were trying to get pregnant."

"Of course, Andria, and he knows about the pregnancy. He's all excited about it. I think he really wants the child."

Andria started walking fast. She didn't want Rashaun to meet them at almost the same spot he had left them. "What can I say? I'm happy for you and I think you'll make a great mother. I hope that Isaiah stands by you and you guys can make it work."

Paula stopped abruptly. "Where is all this coming from? A few weeks ago you almost threw me out of your car when I mentioned that I wanted to have a child with Isaiah now you're almost applauding it."

"I won't go as far as to say I'm applauding it but a lot has changed. I realize in this world that nothing is etched in stone. A man can be your savior one day and your executioner the next. Happiness is fleeting and it comes in all different packages. Sometimes you just have to seize the moment. Look at Paul and I, we could have been married with kids now, and *wallop* he starts doing his thing. I would be screwed."

"Yeah, I know what you mean. By the way where's Rashaun?" Paula asked.

Andria looked ahead and even the two men who had interrupted them earlier had disappeared over the hill.

"Oh shit. Let's go."

"What?" Andria asked.

"Look behind us," Paula said.

"Damn I will never hear the last of this from Rashaun," she said as she recognized Rashaun's unmistakable gait.

"Ms. Phillips, how do you know the defendant, Tyrone Wheatley?" Kim asked as she walked toward Natalie on the witness stand.

"He's my ex-boyfriend," Natalie said, looking directly at Tyrone.

"How long were you in a relationship with the defendant?"

"Two lousy years," she answered still staring at Tyrone.

Tyrone put his head down.

Rashaun leaned over and whispered in Tyrone's ear, "Don't let her see the effect she's having on you."

Tyrone lifted his head but averted his eyes to the judge.

"Why do you say that? Was the defendant a bad person."

"You can say that," Natalie said.

"You can say what?"

"Tyrone was a lousy lover."

"When you say lousy, what exactly do you mean?"

Natalie inhaled deeply and sighed loudly. "Tyrone is what you would call a one-minute man. He jumps on top of you, humps like a rabbit and then rolls over. The only thing he did with any decency is oral sex and that does nothing for me."

"So you were dissatisfied with Tyrone's—let me put it mildly— lovemaking skills?"

"That's putting it very mildly."

"Was there anytime when Tyrone surprised you with his lovemaking skills?" Kim asked.

"Yes, there was this one time."

"Can you tell the court what happened?"

"Well I was seeing this butcher. He was called Big Meat, if you know what I mean."

"Was that while you were living with Mr. Wheatley?"

"Yes. Life is short. I don't believe in putting up with bullshit. Women, you don't have to put up with lousy lovers. I sure didn't."

"Go ahead, Ms. Phillips."

"Well, I don't know what came over Big Meat but he called my house and told Tyrone about us. That evening when I came home Tyrone was totally pissed. He started arguing with me and cursing me. So I told him that if he wasn't such a creampuff in bed maybe I wouldn't have to go around and look for dick."

"What happened then?"

"At first Tyrone raised his hand to hit me but I think he thought better of it. Let me tell you all one thing, if Tyrone had hit me he wouldn't be on trial. I would've been upstate with a girlfriend. But he didn't hit me, instead he ripped my clothes off. I swear I never saw his dick so big. That evening I was fucked, and I mean fucked. I don't remember exactly when we stopped but I felt the most intense searing orgasm of my life. At first when he started without me being lubricated and all it was hurting like hell but the funny thing is at the end of the pain there was this spike of pleasure. The harder he drove in me the sharper the pain and the more intense the pleasure. It was as if he was hitting a special nerve within my vaginal wall. I don't know what happened but I felt a blinding pain and that was followed by the greatest pleasure I have felt my whole life. It was after that I lost consciousness. It was as if my brain got an overdose of pleasure and pain at the same time."

"Ms. Phillips, did you at any point think that the defendant was trying to hurt you?"

"Of course he was. Tyrone was trying to kill me."

"You believed that the defendant was trying to kill you throughout that particular sexual episode?"

"Hell yeah, but he don't know pussy can't done. The dick will break and fall off first before the pussy done. Babies come out of our stuff. What comes out of a dick? Pee and some sperm."

"It's your belief that the defendant uses his penis to inflict pain on his partner?"

"Yes."

"No more questions, your honor."

"Does the defense wish to cross-examine the witness?"

Rashaun briefly spoke to Tyrone before standing up. "Yes, your honor."

"Go ahead, Mr. Jones," the judge said.

"Ms. Phillips, during that sexual episode you described did you at anytime ask Mr. Wheatley to stop?"

"No."

"Did you complain that you were in pain?"

"No."

"Did you end the relationship after that?"

"No."

"So, a man tries to kill you in bed and you don't end the relationship."

"We made up after that."

Rashaun shook his head. "You're telling the court that after a man tries to kill you, you made up with him?"

"Yes, I thought maybe we could work it out."

"Obviously, you did not work things out."

"Obviously," Natalie said sarcastically.

"One more question, Ms. Phillips, did you think that Mr. Wheatley was a lousy lover that night he supposedly tried to kill you."

"I don't know."

"No more questions, your honor."

The judge turned to Natalie. "You can step down now, Ms. Phillips."

"Anything you say, your honor," she said and gave him an I-want-to-try-you look and followed the judge's order.

Rashaun sliced a chicken leg and filled it with seasoning. It was Saturday afternoon and he had promised Andria a special Bajan dinner. He took some pre-seasoned flying fish a friend of his mother's had brought back from Barbados and fried it in olive oil then he had created a stew with tomatoes, onions, garlic and green and red peppers. He tossed the fish in there and left it to simmer in a covered deep skillet. He finished seasoning the chicken and covered it with ketchup before putting it in the preheated oven.

"Thanks for the help, baby," he said when he found Andria standing in the living room looking out the window.

Rashaun came up behind her and slipped his hands around her waist. "Penny for your thoughts?"

"I'm concerned about Robin. She doesn't know what kind of person Paul is. He is not a nice person."

"Wasn't Robin with you when you went through all that drama with Paul?"

"Yes, but I don't know what's going on with her at home, and Paul, of course, is taking full advantage of her situation. I feel so helpless. It's like a car accident you see about to happen and you know that people will get hurt but you're powerless to stop it," Andria said, resting her head lightly on Rashaun's shoulder.

Rashaun tightened his hold on Andria's waist. "Andria, the important thing is that you tried. If I were you I would concentrate more on Robin than Paul. By the way, where is he living these days?"

"I heard he moved back with his mother in that big apartment building on Brooklyn and Lefferts Avenue. The apartments in that building are twice the size of most one-family houses."

"Hey, stop sulking. Come on let's go and eat," Rashaun said, leading Andria into the kitchen.

"Wait a minute I have to go to the bathroom." She loosened her hand from Rashaun's grip and headed to the bathroom.

She came back with a bottle of Pepto-Bismol and shook it in Rashaun's face.

"I don't believe you. You doubt the skills of a world-renowned chef,." Rashaun said, putting the plates on the table. "Just for that I'll give you bird-size pieces."

"You do that and I will call your mother and tell her that you're starving me. Now you know you don't want to get your mom upset."

"You wouldn't dare."

"Try me," Andria said. She sat down and picked up her knife and fork and clinked them.

"I don't do that anymore," Rashaun said as he put the dishes down on the table.

"Yeah right, go put on some music." Andria asked as Rashaun continued to set the table.

"You are not even Mrs. Jones yet but you're already giving orders," Rashaun said as he went to sift through the CD rack. He found Randy Crawford's *Naked and True* CD and put it in their Phillips mini stereo player. As he sat down, "Cajun Moon" started to play.

131

"Now that's what I am talking about,"" Andria said. She said a quick prayer.

Rashaun looked at her and smiled. He realized he had missed her playfulness, the way she smiled and the cute things she said. He wondered how he could ever have gotten mad at her. Andria had an innocent face, and it made him feel guilty to even speak harshly to her. And boy did she have an appetite. She ate as if it was her last meal before fasting. He sat there with his fork in his hand watching Andria, as his mother would say chow down. She had filled her plate until a fly could not find a clean part of the plate to rest its legs. "I definitely think you should go on a diet."

"Why?" she asked, her mouth filled with food.

"And you need table manners, too, talking with your mouth full."

"You know that means you shouldn't be talking to me while I'm eating," she said and continued to eat.

Rashaun dug into the rice and peas and joined Andria in chowing down.

The black BMW 740IL eased into the graveled parking lot. The windows were tinted midnight black and the twenty-inch gold rims signified the car's extravagance. The owner pulled between a green Grand Jeep and an old Chevy Impala.

"Mr. Roundtree, this is a beautiful car," Rashaun said, getting out of the passenger side of the 740IL.

"Yeah, I like it," Mr. Roundtree said as he went to the trunk and pulled out a small black London Fog bag. "I especially like the protection package that affords me a little protection in this hostile world. They say it protects against most high projectile weapons, including the nine-millimeter. I'm very happy that no one has tried to test the armor protection on this vehicle."

"I love these cars. Can't afford them but love them nonetheless. The base model with armor runs about 125 G. That's a pretty sum."

Mr. Roundtree pressed the button on the silent alarm. "I don't believe in buying the base model of a vehicle."

Mr. Roundtree and Rashaun walked past a man with a portable radio blasting the reggae song "We are Just Friends." He was working on a boat named *Alaska*.

"What's up, Wayne? Still trying to get it out there?" Mr. Roundtree shouted.

"Soon I'll be racing you down the channel," Wayne responded as he continued to work on the boat.

"I'm sure you will, Wayne. Just make sure you get insurance this time so I don't have to drag you and your boat through the ocean," Mr. Roundtree said as he opened the wooden discolored door of the clubhouse. Rashaun followed him as he went into the refrigerator at the back of the clubhouse. He opened his bag and stacked the refrigerator with Budweiser and soda. He took a Coke from the ones that were already cold and offered one to Rashaun who instead opted for a can of ginger ale. They walked out of the back door of the clubhouse onto an unleveled lawn. To the right there was a sink with two men cleaning fish.

"Hector, you did good today, ah?" Mr. Roundtree said, heading toward the water.

"Yeah, I think I caught the last of the blues. Carlos here caught a few black fish. You want some?" Hector asked.

"No. I caught a few yesterday. I'm just going for a ride. Enjoy. Maybe I'll go out with you guys this weekend," Mr. Roundtree said as he stepped onto the small wooden bridge that led to the wharf which held about sixty boats with many different names including *Big Daddy, Your Mama, Fries, Midnight Dragon, Shaker, Stripper* and *Baldy*. Rashaun saw six boats all parked next to one another that looked the same.

"They all look alike to you, don't they?" Mr. Roundtree asked as he went to a black-and-white boat.

133

"Yeah," Rashaun said, following Mr. Roundtree onto a boat named *Misunderstood*.

"Well the boats that all look alike range from two to twenty years old and cost anywhere from $10,000 to $200,000. If you step inside you'll see the difference between these boats. A major part is the engine and the brand.

"You know from the time I got to this country I wanted a boat. Unlike most people, my American dream wasn't a house or a fancy car, no, it was a boat. A sixty-foot luxury yacht to be precise. I can't afford it yet but this forty-footer comes close," Mr. Roundtree said as he started the engine. "Go ahead take a look around."

The forty-footer had four captain seats on the first level. Rashaun sat down in one briefly and he could see himself relaxing in it for a lifetime. At the back of the seats were two big, open chests. Rashaun looked up at Mr. Roundtree who had assumed his seat in a big captain's chair above the four seats on the main deck. Rashaun opened the door to the bottom deck and was greeted by a queen-size bed outfitted with purple silk sheets; next to the bed were a black couch and a small end table. Rashaun walked down to the bedroom and on the right was a marbled standing shower with gold-plated faucets. Next to the shower was a door, which Rashaun opened slightly and peered inside to see a full-size toilet and standing shower with a mirror and large vanity dresser to the left. On the floor was a gold magazine rack with a variety of magazines.

He closed the door and turned around to be greeted by a medium-sized black refrigerator and a black four-burner stove. There was also a small sink with white faucets next to the stove. Rashaun walked to the bed and pressed down on it to test the firmness. From the look and feel of it he knew that Mr. Roundtree had paid a pretty penny. The room was decorated with three African paintings. Rashaun sat down on the couch and the painting of a boy and his father at the beach with a small rowing boat was directly in front of him. The painting was flushed with the wall. The second painting to the right of him, it was a fisherman with a large fish presumably a shark with bloodied teeth. Rashaun stood and turned around to see the painting of a man and a woman making love on the bow of a ship. Rashaun stepped lightly on the almond-colored carpet looking back briefly to see if his shoes had left any stains. He walked back up and went to join Mr. Roundtree who had started to back the boat out of the dock.

There wasn't a ripple in the water as *Misunderstood* moved ahead. A flock of seabirds circled looking for food. As they moved out of the channel Rashaun noticed a well-lit dock with cables running on big poles.

"Your neighbors seem to have their own source of electricity," Rashaun said, looking in the direction of a boat named *Stock Exchange.*

"That they do. Most of the boats cost $150,000 and up. Their clubhouse has twenty-four-hour security. There are security cameras all over the dock. The clubhouse has small rooms that are available for their guests, a nurse is on duty from seven in the morning to nine at night seven days a week. They all receive cable on their boats and they have a chef available from 7:00 A.M. to 8:00 P.M. in the clubhouse. There is valet parking and only club members are allowed in the clubhouse unless reservations are made for a guest. They have a lot more amenities that I cannot think of right now, " Mr. Roundtree said as he steered his boat between the large poles that supported a bridge.

"How much does that cost them?" Rashaun asked.

"Eight thousand a year."

"It seems like you looked into it."

"Yeah, I did when I moved my boat from Freeport, Long Island, to here. But once I met the guys here and I found out the owner of this clubhouse was black my decision was made. We'll take a spin out to Manhattan Beach and back, maybe then you can tell me what I can do for you," Mr. Roundtree said as he pulled back the throttle on the boat and the bow lifted and then settled back down as it cut the water.

Rashaun took a seat next to Mr. Roundtree and began to wonder if he was doing the right thing.

Rashaun had decided to help Andria with her little problem with Paul. He knew many people he could call on to do what he wanted but Mr. Roundtree seemed to be the only one who would not require a favor in return.

Rashaun believed that the life we live is filled with unsavory decisions. He understood not everything was about right or wrong, and some times the end justified the means. He applauded Andria for trying to help her friend by going the non-combative route but that only worked on some people. But some people don't really listen when you say don't do that it's bad. Sometimes a more punishing route had to be taken. In his days as an assistant district attorney, he had seen so many people's life get messed up by repeat criminal offenders. Their punishment for the crime was some time spent on the island. And they would come back out and do the same thing. Their criminal activity wasn't stopped until they ended up in a wheelchair or they lost someone close to them. Life is about lessons and some we learn too late, others we never learn.

Mr. Roundtree had parked the boat right outside the Hudson and he had brought a bottle of Lambrusco red wine. He and Rashaun sipped on the wine as the boat rocked steadily on the unstable surface.

"I need a favor," Rashaun said, looking toward a long crane looming over an unfinished building.

"I kind of guessed that. You know I have a favor for you, so go ahead," Mr. Roundtree said, sipping on the wine.

"How clean is this boat?" Rashaun asked.

"As clean as my mother's house on a Sunday morning. I have this guy sweep it for bugs twice a day. You didn't see him when we came but he was in the clubhouse."

"I have this guy who's creating a problem."

"Do you want him to become a ghost? I always recommend that because unlike popular belief we only have one life. We are not coming back as a vegetable or a cat."

136

"No, nothing that drastic. I just want him to stay away from someone," Rashaun said swirling the wine in his glass.

"The thing about pests is that they don't go away unless you squash them or break their legs. I personally prefer squashing. But it's your favor and I'll abide by what you say but remember I don't recommend it."

"I understand," Rashaun said, drinking the last of the wine and waiting for Mr. Roundtree to refill his glass.

"Do you have a name and address?"

"Yeah I'll give it to you when we're getting off."

"Don't say it out loud. Write it on a piece of paper and throw it over there," Mr. Roundtree said, pointing to the corner of the back of the boat.

Rashaun took a piece of paper from his pocket and wrote down Paul's name and his mother's address and a small note. He threw the paper where Mr. Roundtree had pointed.

"How is that case you're working on?" Mr. Roundtree asked, starting the engine. He let it idle and bent down to pick up the paper Rashaun had thrown on the floor. He read it, ripped it into small pieces, and threw it overboard.

"It's going fine," Rashaun said, not wishing to discuss the case with Mr. Roundtree. "No payback on this, huh?"

"I gave you my word. This is a repay of an old death. You worked your magic to get me off, now I'm doing what I do best," he said, turning the boat around.

The men drove back in silence, Mr. Roundtree in the captain's chair smoking a Cuban cigar, Rashaun seated in one of the four chairs at the back watching Manhattan disappear. The calmness of the water was suddenly gone, now the boat climbed waves that caused an uneven ride. Rashaun wasn't really concerned because he had already done what he came to do. The end would justify the means.

"Hilda, stop the car. Let's go out and talk to her," Andria said as they drove by Sheffield Street in the back of Pennsylvania Avenue. The street was littered with prostitutes and the coldness of the fall day did not stop them from wearing shorts and skirts that left most of their butts exposed.

"She just lost it after the World Trade Center bombing. You know her man worked on the one hundred and fifth floor," Hilda said bringing the car closer to the curb.

"Sharon!" Robin shouted leaning halfway outside the small Honda Civic.

Sharon dressed in a red negligee top and a short skirt with slits on the sides turned around to look at the women in the car. When she recognized them she headed over in her four-inch high shoes.

"What you girls up to tonight? I know this is not your scene," she said, bending down to the passenger side right next to Andria.

"Sharon, why don't you come with us? You don't have to do this to yourself," Andria said, reaching out to hold Sharon's hand.

"I like it here. This is life," she said, opening her arms wide.

"Sharon, why are you trying to kill yourself? You're college educated, you had a good job and I'm sure you can find another one." Robin reached out to touch Sharon.

"And then what, Robin, live in fear for my life? Every time I hear a siren, my heart skips a beat. I didn't quit my job because I didn't want to do it anymore, I quit because I couldn't sit at a desk and wait any longer. If I'm going to die, I don't want to burn to death or leap out of a hundred-story building. No, I like it out here in the open where the breeze is fresh and White Castle is right around the corner. Bishop was a good man, and a good man doesn't deserve to die like that. Do you know I met Bishop at the World Trade Center? No, I don't think you knew that. I know he was married but he treated me good and that's all I ask of any man. Now I don't care. Nothing anyone can do to me can hurt me,." Sharon said as she pulled away from Robin and Andria.

"Move the fucking car, bitch," a voice shouted followed by the repeated blowing of car horn. Andria looked back to see about twenty cars lined up behind theirs.

"I think you guys should go now. Don't worry about me, I'll be all right," she said and started to walk away from the car.

"Sharon, you promised to call me on Sunday. Don't forget," Hilda said as she put the car into drive.

'We have to do something," Andria said as she slumped in the front seat. "We can't just leave her out on the street like that."

"Believe me I've tried. I took her to counseling and they sent a counselor to her house. Her parents spoke to her, everyone in the family tried. Sharon just made up her mind up that there was nothing worth living for. She is trying to kill herself. In addition to losing her boyfriend, she lost many friends in that 9/11 attack. I think that man meant a lot more to her than we could ever imagine. They have been together for more than ten years, which is more than most marriages," Hilda said as she headed down Pennsylvania Avenue.

"This 9/11 thing has had a crazy effect on people's life. Lance, one of Rashaun's friends, is engaged to be married," Andria said.

"Isn't he the guy you don't like, Andria?" Paula asked.

"Yeah, the one who thinks he's God's gift to every woman on earth. September 911 or not I don't think that marriage will last a year," Andria said.

"You never know. Sometimes it takes something drastic to change a person's life. The marriage could last a lifetime," Robin said as she looked out of the window. "God knows I

139

thought I had a good marriage and all of a sudden I don't know."

"Lance is too much of a pretty boy to get married. Believe me, sooner or later that 911 thing is going to wear off and everybody will be back to normal," Paula said.

"I hope you're right, Paula. I hope it's not too late for some of us. Sometimes you can't go back to heal scars because some just don't heal. Every night I go to bed I stay up and I pray for Sharon. She's out here with the animals. Whenever the phone rings I hope it's her saying that she doesn't want to do this anymore, but I also hope it's not the police saying that they found her with her throat cut in an alley." Hilda trembled as she tried controlling her emotions and the wheel of the car at the same time.

"You okay, Hilda? Do you want me to drive?" Andria asked.

"I'm fine let's get to BBQ's before all of New York gets there," she said, turning up the Bob Marley's *No Woman No Cry* CD.

Andria watched as an Acura Legend, a Toyota Avalon and a Nissan Maxima all passed them in the middle lane. She thought about asking Hilda if she wanted her to drive but thought better of that when she looked over at Hilda gripping the wheel as if it was a railing on the *Titanic*. Hilda was obviously troubled; of the four of them in the car Hilda was the one closest to Sharon. Combine that with the fact that Hilda and her husband had not been living in paradise, and Andria could understand Hilda's tension.

Andria had her own problems. Robin was about to throw away her marriage. Rashaun was defending the man who killed her friend, intentional or not; and her doctor told her that if she ever got pregnant she might have to make a terrible decision. If she kept the baby she might have to decide between her life and the baby's. Rashaun had always talked about having a family and as their wedding approached he had been talking about kids a lot more. Andria was overjoyed when they reached third Ave and Seventy-second Street, she saw a pink Sentra pulled out of a parking spot by a meter.

"Hilda, over there," Andria said, pointing to the pink mobile pulling out. Hilda banged a Volkswagen Beetle and a Dodge Focus as she parallel between the two.

"Andria, here are the keys. You don't drink so that makes you the designated driver," Hilda said as she opened the door and stepped out.

The ladies waited thirty minutes before they got a table close to the front of the restaurant.

"This place is always so noisy," Andria said as she sat down next to Robin.

"I like it. It's very lively," Paula said as he scanned the menu.

"Paula, nothing on the BBQ's menu has change. Why are you looking so intensely at the menu?" Robin asked she placed her menu in the middle of the table.

"Well I see they have cold poached salmon, that's new," Paula said as she continues to gaze at the menu.

"That's been there forever, and if you order it you will realize why it's all the way at the bottom of the menu," Robin countered.

"All I want is one of those Texas-sized pina coladas with two 150 shots," Hilda said as she looked around for a waiter.

"I wish I could have a drink," Paula said.

"Why can't you?" Robin asked.

"Well this is the reason I asked you guys out. I have something important to tell you," Paula said, looking up from the menu.

"You're pregnant." Hilda said, not taking her eyes off the couple at the next table with two brightly colored drinks,. "And you want to know if you should keep it."

"You got the first part right but the second part is already a given. I'm going to keep my baby," Paula said, looking annoyed.

"And that's your final answer," Hilda said as the waiter came to the table.

"Will you ladies be having a drink before dinner?" he asked, pulling out a small writing pad from his back pocket.

"Most definitely!" Hilda said, drawing the waiter's attention.

"The drink special is a mango daiquiri with a shot of Alize," he said.

"A shot of Alize? Are you serious?" Hilda stared at the waiter in disbelief. "Alize barely has enough alcohol in a full glass much less a shot."

"Yes, ma'am, or you can order from the drink menu." He took the menu and pointed to the drinks section at the top.

"I want a pina colada with two shots of 150-proof Jamaican rum," Hilda said, placing the menu back down on the table.

"Ma'am we do not recommend drinking when you're pregnant," the waiter said, waiting for Hilda to change her order.

"Do I look pregnant to you?" Hilda asked, raising her voice even higher than most of the chatterboxes in the room.

"I'm sorry, ma'am. I'll put your order through." He made a note on his pad.

"And next time ask first before you try to save the human race," Hilda said and turned her attention back to the couple drinking the multicolored drinks.

"I'll have a Texas-sized Blue Hawaiian and bring us onion rings for an appetizer," Robin said.

"Do you want a shot with that for two dollars more?" the waiter asked.

"Did she ask for a shot with that?" Hilda looked at the waiter as if she was about to swat him away.

The waiter quickly took the remaining orders. Andria ordered cranberry juice and Paula settled for a Pepsi.

"Where do they get these people from? They think it's their right to save the world. Telling me I'm pregnant. I should've slapped the little boy," Hilda said.

"I was surprised that he didn't ask me for ID. I went with Paul to TGI Friday's and this waitress asked me for ID. I think they are getting ridiculous with that ID checking these days." Robin took a small mirror from her purse and flipped it open. "I know I don't look a day over twenty-one."

"Time is not that generous," Andria said as she dug into the mountain of onion rings the Spanish busboy had delivered to the table.

"Wait till you have your second and third child. All of a sudden you aged in five-year increments," Hilda said, smiling as she saw the waiter coming back with four drinks. He passed by them and went to another table.

"I thought those were our drinks," Andria said disappointed.

"That little runt did that on purpose. I'm sure of it," Hilda said throwing him a dirty look.

"So what do you guys think about me being pregnant?" Paula asked.

"What is there to think about? You're a big woman. I'm sure you can take care of a baby. Is it for that little boy that you're with?" Hilda asked, watching the waiter approach with six drinks.

"Yes, it's for Isaiah. Who else would it be for?" Paula sounded irritated by Hilda's question.

"Didn't mean to offend you. I just didn't think you and Isaiah were in for the long haul. Does he want a child at this age?" Hilda asked giving the waiter a killer look as he deposited their drinks.

"Yeah, Isaiah is more excited than I am. He said he's going to quit his job at McDonald's and look for something with higher pay," Paula said, sounding a bit excited.

"What he's going to get a job at Wendy's with benefits?" Robin asked as Andria and Hilda tried to muffle their laughter with their drinks.

"What's up with you hanging out with Andria's ex? Trouble at home, Robin?" Paula said as she sipped on her drink.

Suddenly, there was nothing left to be said as each woman concentrated on her drink and the dwindling mountain of onion rings. The waiter returned a short while later to take their orders for dinner. Hilda ordered another pina colada with another shot of 150-proof rum. This time Robin got a shot of her own. Andria and Paula asked the waiter to refill their water glasses.

When the food arrived fifteen minutes later the conversation turned to more current events. They spoke about their fear of another terrorist attack and the way Mayor Rudolph Giuliani was receiving hero worship for a job the most illiterate of people would have accomplished. Hilda wanted to teach the waiter a lesson by reporting his behavior to his supervisor but the other ladies talked her out of it. She instead settled on giving him a dollar tip although Andria and Paula objected.

"Why are we even going to this nonsense?" Andria pulled a white skirt up to her stomach.

Rashaun tightened a black belt around his waist. "Because my friend is getting married."

"Getting married to whom? You said it yourself, Lance picks up women like change in the supermarket."

"I guess he found the right one."

"Right one? Lance wouldn't know the right one if she brought him a gold-filled cake. He would take the filling then go on to the next one. People like Lance should never get married."

"Andria, I'm not a judge nor the creator. Lance asked me to attend his wedding and I'm going."

"Would you go rob a store if your friends ask you to?"

"Andria, let me not answer that question because this will lead to an unnecessary argument. I keep telling you I can't tell anyone how to live his or her life. I'm having enough trouble getting through mine. I'm not like you, I'm not going around judging people telling them something is right or wrong. I've seen marriages where the bride and groom could not stand to be separated from each other for a New York minute break up after six months. On the other hand, I have seen marriages where the couples are total opposites and people give their marriage no chance in hell to last. Guess what, their marriages last more than ten years and these days that is a milestone. I'm as shocked as you to find out that Lance is getting married but what I won't do is speak badly of the union." Rashaun finished putting on his shirt. He looked over at Andria to ask for a suggestion of a jacket to compliment his attire but when he saw her snatching a red blouse from the closet, he thought better about asking her for advice.

"I don't know what's happening these days. People around me are changing so drastically. A never today is a maybe tomorrow. I'm totally frustrated and scared. People are changing and they're changing too fast for me." Andria left the room and went into the bathroom.

Rashaun sat on the bed looking out the window at the sun peeking through the clouds. The last time he spoke to Lance was about two weeks earlier and he hadn't even mentioned any serious girl. A few days ago Lance had called and told him about the wedding. Lance told Rashaun not to worry about gifts because he knew his financial situation and the lack of time. He pleaded with Rashaun to convince Tyrone to come to the wedding. Rashaun finally talked Tyrone into attending the wedding after trial on Friday.

Andria walked in looking her beautiful self. "How do I look?" she asked, walking around the bed to stand in front of Rashaun.

His eyes traveled from her head to her feet then he reached out and made a circle in the air.

Andria turned around and struck a pose with her head in the air.

"Ugly, ugly, real ugly," he said, picking his phone up from the charger. "But I guess I got to work with what I got."

"Okay then, let's see how fast I can pick up a man at this wedding. I think you'll be driving home alone tonight,." Andria said, turning off the light in the bedroom and following Rashaun out of the door.

They reached Tyrone's house in record time and Rashaun ran inside to get his friend.

"Hi, Andria," Tyrone said, opening the back door of the car.

"How you doing, Tyrone?" Andria asked turning to look at him. Tyrone was dressed in a white suit with a red tie. Andria quickly glanced at Rashaun who just looked at her and shrugged.

The wedding was in Mills Basin, one of the most expensive neighborhoods in Brooklyn, with the price of houses ranging from five hundred thousand to ten million dollars. Rashaun drove down Ralph Avenue past Avenue U and made a turn on Mill Basin Street.

"The address is 221 Mill Basin Street," Andria said, glancing at a pad.

"Lance hit the jackpot," Rashaun said as he tried to get around the limousines packed on the street. He pulled up to the front of the house and waited for the valet to finish parking a black Jaguar.

Andria peered out at the address number making sure it was correct. "Now I understand," Andria looked at the 221 gold- plated numbers next to the big French doors.

"I don't think I'm ready for this, Rashaun." Tyrone sat slumped in the backseat, his white suit contrasting sharply against the car's black leather seats.

Rashaun tapped lightly on the steering wheel. "Relax, Tyrone, this is a small wedding. I doubt these people know anything about you or me."

Andria flipped down the visor and clicked the light next to the vanity mirror. "I knew I should have bought a dress for this. I'll stand out like an ugly duck." She turned her head to the left then the right and brought her face all the way up to the mirror. Satisfied with at least the way her face looked she closed the visor.

Rashaun gave the valet his keys and stepped out of the car. Andria followed suit smoothing her skirt. The driver got in the car and looked back at Tyrone who was still contemplating his next move.

Andria and Rashaun looked back at Tyrone. He pushed himself off the seat and opened the back door.

Rashaun and Andria collectively breathed a deep sigh of relief as they moved to the side of the road to wait for Tyrone. The valet looked at him as if he had just seen the Pope at a strip club.

Rashaun, Andria and Tyrone walked toward the French doors. The left side of the door opened slightly and a man in a black tux asked for their names. Rashaun told him and the man quickly scanned the list and scratched off their names. He opened the door fully and they stepped onto the marbled driveway.

"Champagne?" a waiter in a tux asked as they walked in. He balanced a tray with about ten glasses next to his shoulder. Andria nodded as Rashaun and Tyrone took two glasses from of the waiter.

The marbled driveway was spacious enough for at least four cars. A white lady with a long pink dress with ruffles at the bottom walked past them down the driveway.

"Did you see that necklace," Andria muttered, her eyes still on the white lady. "There were enough diamonds in it to support the economy of Barbados."

"Very funny," Rashaun said, walking up the steps to the front door. Tyrone kept looking around as if expecting a major surprise.

The door opened suddenly and Lance came out with a black tuxedo.

"You guys finally made it," he said.

Andria looked around at what she thought only existed on *MTV Cribs*. About fifty feet to her left was a winding mahogany staircase that led to God knew what. Just below that staircase was two beige leather couches with a small glass table between them. On the table was a brightly colored vase with an assortment of flowers.

"I see, so did you." Rashaun looked up at the huge crystal chandelier that hung over a small table which was surrounded by black metallic-looking chairs. A Persian rug with African drawings lay underneath the table. The marbled floors had Egyptian characters and symbols imprinted on its rustic surface.

Lance put his arm around Tyrone's neck. "Glad you could make it. How you doing?"

"I'm alive," Tyrone said.

"Well before you leave, I hope you're more than okay." Lance walked to the back of the room with his arm still slung around Tyrone.

Andria and Rashaun followed Lance and Tyrone past another chandelier hanging over an even bigger table surrounded by twelve mahogany chairs. To their left was a hallway that was presently occupied by two waiters filled with champagne glasses. The door leading toward the backyard had an ADT alarm keypad with blinking green lights indicating that somewhere was open.

"I think she's white," Andria whispered, pulling on Rashaun's arm.

"She is not." Rashaun knew that not even September 11 would make Lance marry a white woman. Lance had never forgiven his white grandfather for raping his black grandmother. It was that fact that made him hate the whiteness in him. Yet, it was that mixture of whiteness that made black women fall at his feet. Lance once told Rashaun that he would die before he ever

148

married a white woman. Two of Lance's brothers had married white women and to this day he didn't speak to them.

"Want to bet on it?" Andria looked back and saw a white-headed white man following them.

"What are we betting, and please make it appealing," Rashaun smiled as they walked down the steps toward the backyard.

"Candles, hot wax." Andria ran her right hand over Rashaun's baldhead.

"If your mom only knew," he said, stopping briefly to admire a waterfall.

"Okay, and for me, seven days of you in an apron."

"An apron? What kind of apron?"

"Hey, did I ask you what you were going to do with a candle?"

"No, because I already told you about the movie I saw with a woman pouring hot wax on a man. It looked interesting. I want to try it."

"You know me, I'm game for a lot of things behind closed doors. But you're talking about pain and pleasure here." Rashaun had heard the R&B music when he first entered the backyard but now it was getting much louder as Michael Jackson tried to rock someone's world. "But a bet is a bet and I accept."

"There you are!" Exclaimed a very thin woman in her late thirties with long, flowing black hair. "We were looking all over for you, I was wondering if you had gotten cold feet and run out on me."

Lance and Tyrone had stopped as soon as the woman came around the turn in the yard. Rashaun and Andria immerse in their own conversation almost bumped into Tyrone and Lance.

"Honey, you know I would never do that." Lance kissed the woman on her cheek "I went to get my friends, I didn't want them getting lost in your father's yard."

"Oh, these are your other friends. Lance, you are so popular. Peter and George have not left the bar since they got here." She slid her arm around Lance's.

Lance turned to face Andria and Rashaun. "Claudia, this is Tyrone."

"Nice to meet you, Tyrone." She reached out her bony fingers to shake Tyrone's hand.

"And this is Rashaun and Andria." Lance hugged Claudia closer.

"You're the lawyer that Lance spoke so highly of. Well I'm glad to finally meet you. You're currently working on a sex case, right?" Claudia said, holding on to Rashaun's hand.

"Something like that." Rashaun responded

"I love your dress. Is it a Versace?" Andria took Claudia by the hand and turned her around.

"No, but my parents will kill me if we don't get back to the wedding. My mother must be going crazy looking for me right now." Claudia slipped her hand into Lance's and started to walk back with the others following.

Lance looked back and gave a wicked smile to Andria and Rashaun.

"Of course, you know that you won't be wearing anything under that apron. I'm going to the Pink Pussycat store in Manhattan on Sunday. I heard they have a wide assortment of costumes. My sex chef for the week. I will definitely be having a lot of fun." Rashaun lightly smacked Andria on her butt as they tried to catch up with the group.

"I think you cheated."

"No, I didn't. You said you wanted to bet. I didn't even know what you wanted to bet. I was just being a good man and following your wishes."

"Lance is your friend. You knew something that I didn't."

"Maybe, but does that nullify the bet?"

"It doesn't but it does call for a compromise."

"What kind of compromise?" Rashaun asked as they approached a large gathering under a big clear tent.

"We'll talk about it when we get home." Andria glanced at the altar covered in white cloth. Behind it were four older people she assumed were the parents of Lance and Claudia's parents.

"We thought you guys weren't coming," Peter said, walking over with his wife and George to meet Rashaun, Tyrone and Andria.

Rashaun looked over at George.

"My wife wouldn't come. She said it would be hypocritical. I wanted to bring my son but she said she was taking him to a birthday party." George clutched a drink.

George looked over at Lance and his future wife standing next to the altar.

"Where is the groom?" Peter asked. "I'm still mad at him, we didn't even get a chance to throw him a bachelor's party."

"I doubt Lance needed us to throw a bachelor party, I'm sure he had a few of them before today," George said.

"Did he take you guys down to the boat yet, that's where the reception will be held. I heard there is nothing but seafood, including caviar, lobster, shrimp, clams, oysters—if it comes from the sea they have it on that boat," Peter said, looking past the podium to a yacht rocking in the water.

"They have another bar on the boat." George gulped down the rest of his drink and headed back to the bar. "What you drinking, Rashaun?"

"Well seeing that Andria is driving I think I'll have an amaretto sour." Rashaun said.

"And you, Tyrone?" George looked over at Tyrone. "Tyrone!"

Tyrone was staring at the altar as if transfixed by it. "Get me a cranberry juice. I'm taking medication."

Rashaun looked at Tyrone strangely. He wasn't aware that Tyrone was under any kind of medication.

"Andria, are you going to have your usual, rum straight up?" George asked knowing that Andria does not drink hard liquor.

"I see you and your friends have the same sense of humor. What did you guys do, go to stupid school," Andria said, looking at Rashaun who seemed preoccupied

"Andria, this is between you and George. Why are you bringing me into it?" Rashaun asked.

"I think they're about to have a fight," Peter's wife said, backing away from Rashaun and Andria.

"Ladies and gentlemen, please take your seats. The wedding will begin in ten minutes." The speakers that hung outside the corners of the tent amplified the loud booming voice.

"Can I borrow him for a minute?" Lance asked as he got between Andria and Rashaun who was headed toward the chairs. Andria continued walking toward the tent and Rashaun and Lance went in the opposite direction.

"I need a favor," Lance said.

"What? I don't have any rice," Rashaun said. "And I definitely cannot drive a boat in a getaway."

"Nothing like that," Lance said, looking around.

"Lance, don't tell me you realize that you don't love Claudia all of a sudden and you need my law skills to get out of it."

"What does love have to do with marriage? You're not stupid. You know me better than that. This little event here has nothing to do with love. This is a business deal like most marriages these days. Rashaun, I lost the will to love a long time ago, I'm marrying Claudia because she has money. She's not stupid. She knows that too. Her father already had me sign a prenup. He's stupid, too, because I'm not concern with what I'm leaving with. I intend to get as much as possible when I'm in the marriage, not when I leave it."

Rashaun shook his head. "Lance, you are a piece of work."

152

"No, Rashaun, you're a piece of work. You're all caught up in that love and shit. Andria is cute and everything but what does she bring to the table? I know her parents don't have any major money. You are a black lawyer, you hook up with the right person you could be set for life. Love is a passing cloud. Before you know it, it's gone and the only thing you have to show for it is your wet clothes. With me I don't have worry about darkening the sky and when it's over I can look back and say I had a great ride.

"Claudia wants a showpiece. As long as I'm there to be her showpiece, everything is great. I have no plans to give up my other women. Look at that skinny thing. What can I do with that? Anyway, my brother was supposed to show up but I haven't seen him. Do you mind standing in as my best man?" Lance glance back at the people seated under the tent. "I know this is not your thing, especially under these circumstances but I would really appreciate it."

Rashaun slammed his fist into his hand. "Lance, you are fucked up. You go and put me in a fucked-up situation. I didn't know you were getting married until a few days ago and obviously you don't care for the woman. I'm not passing judgment on you or your future wife but sometimes a man likes to feel like he is doing the right thing. In this case I know I'm not doing the right thing, yet you're my friend and I can't leave you in a ditch."

"Thanks, man. Here's the ring." Lance took the ring out of his pocket and put it in Rashaun's hand. "I knew you wouldn't let me down."

Rashaun looked at the diamond-encrusted ring. He grabbed Lance by the arm "You didn't buy this, did you?"

"Of course not. You think I would take a hundred grand and put it down on a ring for some woman? Claudia bought her own ring. I'll see you up front," Lance said and turned and walked back to the tent.

Rashaun stood looking out at the bay. Lance and Claudia knew exactly what they were getting into yet it didn't

153

seem right. He was brought up to believe that a marriage was a union of two souls yearning to remain inseparable, yet time had forfeited that belief. As young men, he and his friends roamed, satisfying their huge appetite for the opposite sex but they were men now and time has change. This was the time they were suppose to think about the twilight of their lives and try to meet someone with whom they would share a sunset on a rocking chair. Yet all around him it wasn't so. His friends were living the same lives they always did.

He was defending Tyrone for murder. George had been kicked out of his house because his wife found out that he was cheating. Peter was considering divorce, and dick enlargement or pussy reduction or all three. And Lance was about to marry a woman for money. Rashaun headed toward the tent, there wasn't enough seafood and alcohol on that boat to take away the bad taste in his mouth. He stopped by Andria's chair and whispered the situation in her ear and continued to the front to stand next to Lance.

"You're a married man now, Lance." Pedro had arrived after the wedding.

Lance looked at Pedro as if he was the first Jamaican UFO. "Pedro, you Jamaicans don't know anything about time. Look at the time you pulled in here. Where's that big mama of yours?"

"My baby is home taking care of business. I might be the next one down the aisle." Pedro pulled a stool closer to the outside bar.

"Your baby is home cooking a chicken, that's what she is doing," George said as he looked at his watch.

"Have a hot date?" Rashaun asked George.

"Why didn't you bring her here?" Lance asked George.

George looked at Rashaun then Lance "Why you guys all in a brother's business?"

"Yep, she's ugly." Pedro had started on his second ball-buster mix. It was a combination of Jamaican over proof rum,

Grenadian Rivers and Barbadian Clarks with a touch of lemon juice.

"Well at least he is not home whacking off on memories." Lance put his right hand next to his penis and made a jerking motion.

"There is no such thing as an ugly pussy. Maybe the woman might be ugly but never the pussy." Rashaun pushed down on his stomach. "Compliments to the chef, the food is excellent."

"And we didn't go on the boat yet," Tyrone added, dumping an empty plate.

"Fuck the food. I want another ball-buster mix," Pedro said, motioning to the bartender.

"I want her, that one right over there." George said motioning with his shoulders to a young waitress serving salmon wrapped in pitas.

"She works for Claudia's parents," Lance said, looking around.

"You fucked her already, didn't you, Lance?" George turned his attention from the waitress to Lance.

"Of course he did. Do you think Lance will let something like that pass by?" Rashaun looked over to where Andria was talking to Claudia.

"She gave me a blow job, that was it. I didn't fuck her. I won't disrespect my wife like that. Not in her parents' house. What kind of person you guys think I am?"

"He fucked her," Pedro said, rejoining the conversation after along sip of his drink.

"All right, maybe once in the kitchen. I got up to have a late-night-snack. I didn't know she would be in there with a little nightgown on. I wasn't even gonna hit it but she kept talking shit about why I'm I messing with that bony thing. She asked me if I was afraid of a real woman, so I showed her I wasn't.

"You don't approve, do you?" Claudia asked Andria.

"What are you talking about, approve of what?" Andria asked, trying her best to separate the salmon from the pita. "This is a beautiful home."

"Don't eat too much of that stuff. We still have to go on the boat. This house belonged to my grandparents; they bought it a long time ago. They were like the early Rockefellers in the black community. They owned countless buildings and businesses. When they died, it was willed to my father. Who took some of the income from the houses and invested it on Wall Street, getting out just before the market crumbled. I think he's investing again because he believes whatever goes up must come down and what comes down will rise again. You still didn't answer my question." Claudia chewed heavily on a piece of gum.

"You and Lance, you mean?" Andria really didn't want to have this conversation.

"Yeah."

"What is there for me to approve or disapprove? He's your husband."

"Look at me, Andria. I'm not the most attractive person on this earth. I rarely go on dates and when I do most men only see the Benjamins."

"And Lance is different?" Finally Andria had separated the pita from the salmon.

"He's the only one who made me feel good about myself. I know Lance won't be faithful to me. I might be ugly but I'm not stupid. All I want from him is for him to continue to make me feel a little bit special every now and then."

"You don't want much, do you?"

"It's a lot more than most people get in their lifetime."

"Maybe so, but don't you think there's someone for everyone out there and maybe a little patience might be well rewarded." Andria popped the salmon in her mouth and started on another piece.

Claudia took the gum out of her mouth and put it in an empty plastic cup held.

"Congratulations!" A woman in a red frilly dress stooped down and kissed Claudia on the cheek, "I wish you many years of happiness."

"Thank you, Saundra and Buck," Claudia said, acknowledging the man who had a stupid grin plastered on his face. The couple made small talk and walked away.

"She hates my gut. She went around telling everyone that I'm a lesbian. Back to you, Andria. Do you believe in fairytales?" Claudia asked.

"No, but I do believe in love. When all is said and done that's all we've got."

"I used to feel the same way you do but life has taught me another lesson. Fairytales are for fairies and you can see a lot of them if you go in the village late at night. They bat their eyes and they twist and turn their hands in unnatural ways for their gender. And you know what with all that twisting and turning and unnatural gestures they get nothing accomplished because fairytales don't come true. Sometimes in life you have to accept what life has to give and make the most of it, otherwise you'll end up on the porch one day thinking *I shoulda*. I'm going to take what Lance has to give and make the best life I can with him because there is no chariot in the distance. I'll walk proudly with my man and for those who have him for one or two nights they'll know that he belongs to me. I already paid off his Mercedes Benz, and whatever else he has that needs paying off I will gladly oblige and I will walk with my head held high with my husband on my arm."

"Yes!" Andria exclaimed as she finally got the pita off the salmon. "Here comes your husband and for what it's worth I wish you health and happiness. I've only known you for a short time but I think you're a wonderful person."

"Hey, let me get your number. We could go shopping sometime," Claudia said.

Andria looked at her as if she was crazy. She couldn't imagine going shopping with Claudia. She was definitely not a Bloomingdale's or Nordstrom person. "Lance has it. He calls at least three times a week."

"Okay I'll get it from him."

Andria stood as Lance came up to them. "Lance."

"Andria, I hope you weren't telling my wife any bad things about me." He kissed Claudia on the cheek.

Andria looked at him and wondered how long that affection was going to last. "Nothing more than she already knows. Where's Rashaun?"

"I think he and the boys are at the bar," Lance replied. "When you see them tell them we'll meet them at the boat.

Andria tapped her pen lightly on the notepad as she waited for her supervisor. The oval silver clock showed 11:10. Her meeting was supposed to start at eleven. Across from Andria was China and her boyfriend, Keenan. With his curly Indian hair and dark complexion Keenan was obviously mixed with something. When he had walked in earlier, Andria was a little taken aback by his politeness. He had introduced himself and waited until she told him and his girl to sit. Keenan pulled out the chair for China then made sure she was comfortably seated before he sat down. Andria was starting to wonder if the agency had done the right thing in taking Kelly out of her home.

The door opened and Mrs. Brown walked in. "I'm sorry for the delay. I got stuck on the phone," she said and sat next to Andria.

"Mrs. Brown, this is China and Keenan," Andria said.

Keenan reached over and shook Mrs. Brown's hand. "Nice to meet you," he said and sat back. China nodded.

"Go ahead, Andria." Mrs. Brown opened a manila folder and started to read.

"Mrs. Brown, Keenan has agreed to talk to the psychiatrist but he doesn't want to go to counseling. I told him that the counseling was part of the process he would have to go through to get Kelly back." Andria kept her eyes on the couple in front of her.

"Mr. Keenan, can you tell me why you are refusing to see the counselor?" Mrs. Brown asked.

"I said it before, I did not hit Kelly. I admit that I wasn't too happy with taking care of another man's child but I have gotten over that. I love Kelly. An accident happened at home and the school authority made an abuse case out of it." Keenan shook his head. "I just got this new job and if they find out that I'm seeing someone for abusing a child, I will be fired

159

immediately. I love China but I cannot afford to lose my job over something I didn't do. I just can't."

"But Mr. Keenan, the child had multiple bruises on her body. How do you explain that?" Mrs. Brown asked, underlining something in the folder.

"I can't and I won't try to. All I'm saying is that I am aware of one incident where Kelly was hurt while playing. Kelly is a young child. She will have accidents and other mishaps as she continues to grow. I don't understand you people. If we leave the kids locked up in a room, you'll call that neglect and if we let them play and they get hurt you'll call it abuse. How do you expect us to raise our kids?" Keenan put his hands up in frustration. "I came to this country when I was fifteen, I worked hard and I help my parents until they moved back to Guyana a few years ago. I never got into any trouble, never even been arrested. I met China a few years ago and we decided to make a go of a relationship. Like I said before, I wasn't too happy about her having a child but I understood that it was a package deal. As long as the father and me have no beef, everything is cool. I have gotten very fond of Kelly, I missed that little girl. I told you guys I didn't hurt her and she didn't accuse me but you'll take her away from us nonetheless, now you'll want me to attend counseling. Like I said, I'm willing to meet with the psychiatrist and if that doesn't work out, I don't know."

"Mr. Keenan, our job is not to separate families, it is to keep them together," Ms. Brown said closing the folder.

"You could have fooled me," Keenan retorted.

"However, if we see some improprieties we will try and fix them. You seem like a hardworking young man and I will give you the benefit of the doubt. We will have you meet with the psychiatrist and upon his recommendation we will decide whether the child will be able to have weekend visits to your home. If the psychiatrist agrees, we will try that for three months before we return the child to you. During that time we will make unannounced visits and Kelly will remain under New

York State care until she turns eighteen. Andria will prepare the paperwork for you to meet with the psychiatrist." Mrs. Brown picked up her folder and stood. "Thank you for coming," she said and walked out.

"China and Keenan, you do understand that the psychiatrist could refuse to let you see Kelly after the meeting?" Andria asked as she took out a few forms she had between the sheets of a pad.

"I understand," Keenan said reaching for China's hand.

"Me too," China added, looking into her boyfriend's eyes.

"I wish you guys the best and I hope everything works out," Andria said, sliding the forms over to China and Keenan.

Keenan took the pages and signed them before giving them to China. When they were both finished he slid them back to Andria. "I would like a copy," he said.

"Fine. Give me a minute and I'll be right back." Andria gathered the forms and stood.

"Ms. Jackson, how long will this take?" China asked.

"I'd say about three weeks." Andria stopped in front of the door. "We have three psychiatrists working for us so it depends on their schedules."

"I miss my daughter, and I want her home. I don't trust these homes," China said.

"Kelly is in a good foster home. Don't worry about it. I'm sure she will be back home with you soon. I'm going to copy these papers, I'll be right back." Andria walked out.

"Dr. Boston, how long have you been the Kings County Medical Examiner?" Kim asked.

"Ten years," Dr Boston, a pencil-thin woman in her early forties, responded.

"In fact, you were not only the first black woman hired to head the medical examiner unit in New York City, you were the first woman period. Quite an accomplishment." Kim stood about six feet from the witness box.

"Thank you," Dr. Boston took a sip of water.

"Do you normally do autopsies? You are the head of the department."

"Well if you have any idea about New York City and the death rate you would know that there are never enough medical examiners. I try to help out as much as possible." Dr. Boston looked directly at the judge as she made her response.

"Do you remember working on the autopsy for Judy Francis?"

"Yes. In my years as a medical examiner I have seen very few sexual deaths that rival Mrs. Francis."

"How?"

"Well it was the injury that Mrs. Francis had sustained."

"Dr. Boston, I am showing you what was previously marked as People Exhibit 1." Kim took a photograph from a large envelope and handed it to Dr. Boston. "Do you recognize it?"

"It is a photograph that I took of the insides of Mrs. Francis' vagina."

"Does the picture fairly and accurately represent Mrs. Francis' vagina on that day?"

"Yes." Dr. Boston said.

"I would like to move People's Exhibit 1 into evidence. Dr. Boston, can you please describe the picture?"

"Well it is the inside of a woman's vagina. As you can see there are welts and a   big red slash on the inside lower right hand corner of the vagina."

"Is this a normal representation of a woman's vagina after intercourse?"

"Yeah, if she was run over by a bulldozer."

"So it is not normal?"

"No. The bruises that were present in Mrs. Francis' vagina were consistent with sodomy there were also tearing and perforations of the vaginal tissues."

162

"Was there any evidence of foreign objects besides a penis being inserted in Mrs. Francis' vagina?"

"No."

"Dr. Boston, what exactly killed Mrs. Francis?"

"Well, Mrs. Francis died from rupture of the vessels in the vagina walls."

"Dr. Boston, what state of mind would a person have to be in to do such a thing?"

Rashaun stood immediately "Objection, your honor. The witness is a medical examiner not a psychiatrist."

"Sustained, Ms. Rivers." The judge gave Kim a disapproving look.

"Dr. Boston, is it fair to say that in order for such damage to be inflicted, the person causing the damage has to be very angry?"

"Yes."

"Or deranged?" Kim added.

"Your honor," Rashaun exclaimed.

"Ms. Rivers, please maintain a proper line of questioning." The judge again looked at Kim disapprovingly.

"Dr. Boston, have you seen other cases or been informed of similar cases involving rape?"

"Objection!"

"I'm sorry, I mean sex." Kim shot a glance at Rashaun and Tyrone.

"Recently we have been seeing a lot more cases of this kind of death caused by brutal sex. I think too many people are taking this as a joke. People have to be aware of their partner's intention before consenting to intercourse." Dr. Boston paused to take a sip of water. "Today we see the extreme of Blackfunk, where death is the result. I have read many articles where irreversible damage has been done to the woman's vagina and she didn't die."

"So it is your expert opinion that Mrs. Judy Francis died from injuries sustained during sex with the defendant, Tyrone Wheatley?"

"Yes."

"Dr. Boston, in your line of work, have you seen many terrible deaths?" Rashaun walking up to the witness stand.

"Yes. Sometimes you don't know how it was possible for a human being to do that to another human. And car accidents are the worse."

"Correct me if I am wrong but as head of the New York City medical examiner's office most deaths are given to you in a report form. Am I correct?"

"Yes."

"Over the last three months, how many deaths have been a result of Blackfunk?"

Dr. Boston took a notebook out and sifted through the pages. "None."

"So it is fair to conclude, that Blackfunk deaths are not as popular like let's say suicide, gunshot or accidents?"

"I suppose you can say that but one death a year from anything except natural or health-related causes is too much."

"Dr. Boston, were there any bruises on the deceased's body that would be consistent with resistance?"

"No."

"Stretch marks on her stomach?"

"Yes. Mrs. Francis had recently given birth."

"How recent?"

"Irrelevant, your honor."

"Your honor, it is important to show the condition of the deceased's body before having sex with Mr. Wheatley."

"I will allow it. Answer the question, Dr. Boston."

"I would say about three to five months."

"Closer to three, Dr. Boston," Rashaun said and walked back to the defense table.

Andria stepped out of the doctor's office and closed the door. Tears began to flow and cascade down her cheeks onto

164

the floor. She had waited so long for the news but now that it was given to her, a well of emotion came over her. She had to concentrate on putting one foot in front of the other as she walked outside. She took a tissue from her handbag and wiped the remnants of the tears from her cheeks and eyes. She hadn't been feeling well for the last few weeks but lately she had been afraid to go to the doctor. Finally, Rashaun had said either she went voluntarily or he was going to carry her. Her blurry eyes could hardly make out the list of foods and drinks the doctor said she couldn't have. The doctor's list must be a generic list that they give to all patient's because her doctor knew that she didn't smoke and alcohol was only consume in rare occasions.

"Hey, miss, are you okay?" a short, curly-haired guy asked.

"I'm fine," Andria answered.

"You sure are. You want a ride somewhere? My car is over there." He pointed to a gray Altima with tinted windows parked across the street.

Andria looked him over. He couldn't be more than nineteen. He was dressed in a maroon velour suit with matching Timberland boots.

"How old are you?"

"Ma, how old do I look?" He lifted his pants off the ground.

"Fifteen." Andria felt like having some fun.

"I ain't no fifteen. Ma, you got to be seventeen to drive in this city. And I been driving for years. What you concerned about my age for? Don't you know that's just a number? The only number you should be concerned about is the hundred-dollar bills I'm going to use to take your fine self shopping. So if you don't want to take a ride, the least you could do is give me the digits."

"Shouldn't you be in school getting an education?" Andria started to walk with the young man by her side.

"Education is for herbs. I ain't no herb," he said, looking up at her as he walked.

"So what do you do?"

"I do the God-given hustle, Ma. Anything you want little Soon gon' get it to you."

"Are you Chinese?"

"No, Ma, I ain't Chinese but I service the black community as if I was. It's as if I'm Chinese because anything a black person wants they could come get it from me."

Andria spotted a cab and hailed it. "Well I don't want anything today, Soon."

The young man stopped and waited with Andria as the cabdriver made an illegal U-turn. "So give Soon the digits, Ma."

"Do you have a pen?"

"I don't need one. I got a cell, Ma." He slipped a maroon phone from his waist and flipped it open.

"Don't call me tonight. My man will be at home. Call me six tomorrow morning," Andria said, giving him the number to Kings County Psychiatric building.

He smiled. "I got you, Ma. Let me pay the bills. We gon' do the playing."

Rashaun lifted Andria off the floor and held her in his arms, his face beaming. "I can't believe it."

She had never seen him so happy; the stupid smile on his face was intoxicating. She found herself smiling too. She had shed tears of joy earlier and now she and her man had stupid grins on their faces.

"I have names," he said as he held her hand and they walked into the living room.

"I'm sure you do," she said, squeezing his hand.

He stopped before they got to the couch. "When are you due?"

"Seven months from now."

"Are you sure?"

Andria looked into his piercing eyes. "That's what the doctor told me."

He smiled. "Okay, I guess I deserved that one." He put a throw pillow in the back of her head.

"Don't tell me you are going to start to treat me like an invalid. I'm only about two months pregnant."

"Okay I'm going to make you do the laundry and cook seven days a week, watch me use the bathroom."

"Okay, I get your point I'm not going to treat you like you're pregnant." He sat down next to her and started to play with her hair.

She looked at him and she knew he would. "I think I will enjoy being pregnant." She leaned back into his lap.

"I had a dream a few nights ago and when I woke up I could have sworn it was real."

"Tell me about it," Andria said, making herself comfortable.

"I was dressing this little boy to take him out to the park. It had snowed and it was cold outside so I was making sure that his ears and hands were well covered. After I finished dressing him and was ready to take him out to the park, the phone rang. I lifted him and carried him with me to the phone. When I picked up the phone it was my friend asking me what time I was bringing her son over. I looked at the child in my arms and I could've sworn that he was my child. It was at that point that I woke up and looked around for him." Rashaun gently massaged Andria's shoulders.

"I want you to make a promise to me." Andria sat up off the couch. "I have seen too many children suffering because of conflict between the parents. I don't want that to happen to our child."

"It won't."

"I doubt it ever will but life is funny and you never know what will happen a few years down the line. I know you are a man of your word and if you say something you will try your best to make it happen. I cannot predict the future and neither can you, so I want this promise."

"What is it?"

"I want you to promise that no matter what happens between me and you that it won't affect our child or children, if we have twins. I want you to promise that you won't use the kid to get at me in any way or form." She brushed his cheeks with her fingertips.

"I will go one step farther. Not only am I going to make that promise not to let anything get between the love we have for our child or children but I will also promise you that if my life has to be sacrificed for either one of you, I will gladly do it. I have only made that promised once before in my life and it was a promise to my mother. I promise I will give my life for hers. This promise is not fortified on a piece of paper but it is written in my heart. It is a promise between the Creator and us. You, my mother and my child are the three people in my life I would kill or die for."

Andria stared Rashaun in the eyes and she realized that he meant every word. For the first time she realized that their love had transcended time and life. "What's wrong?" she asked as he turned away from her.

"In my joy of being a father I forgot about your operation and the doctor's advice to you. I don't want to lose you for my child. Didn't the doctor tell you that there might have to be a choice between you and the child? I don't want you to have to make that decision."

"Rashaun, I spoke to the doctor. She said that I don't have anything to worry about. She said I could go ahead and have as many children as I want providing I could take care of them," she said.

"Okay then after this one, I want two girls and two more boys so we are shooting for a total of five. You could handle that, can't you?"

"Well, while you're at it maybe we can adopt five more boys and two girls and have a basketball and volleyball team."

"Hey, you want to give it a shot? I'm game."

"You are hilarious, aren't you?" Andria laid her head back in his lap and lifted her legs onto the end of the couch so that they hung loosely off the side.

"I'm just happy that's all and a happy man sometimes make a fool of himself. You made a wish of mine come true and I cannot say enough or do enough to thank you. I can't wait for the day when I can teach him."

"Wait, who said it was a him." She pushed his chin up with her right fist.

"You don't have to say it's a boy, I know it is."

"And if it's a girl?"

"Then I will take all my love for Mommy and give it to her."

"Yeah right, you can't resist this good thing here," she said, arching her back.

"Okay you're right. Now who's your daddy?" he asked, lifting her up of the couch and walking toward the room, her feet dangling over his hands.

"Rashaun, I forgot to tell you, the doctor said no sex until after the baby is born. You don't mind, do you?"

"Oops." He acted as if he was about to drop her on the floor.

"And you said you love me." Andria punched him in the stomach with her left hand.

"You are spoiled because you know I do." He laid her down on the bed and started to remove her blouse.

"Ice cream."

"What?"

"Ice cream. I have a craving for ice cream and celery sticks."

"Wait, ice cream doesn't go with celery sticks."

"I don't know if they go together but I want butter pecan ice cream and celery sticks."

"But I have to go to the supermarket to get it."

"Well I have to carry twenty-five extra pounds with me for a few months so run along."

"I see this is going to be a long pregnancy."

"You betcha and before you go, bring me some water," Andria said, lifting the covers.

"You are pushing it," Rashaun said as he tied his shoelaces and kissed Andria on the lips and started to walk out the door.

"One, two, three…" Andria shouted.

"What are you doing?"

"Counting how many seconds it's going to take you to call your mother and tell her."

He had already taken out his cell phone and started to dial his mother's number, "You lose," he shouted back at Andria as he closed the apartment door.

"And you haven't heard from him since?" Andria moved the phone from her right ear to her left holding it in the crook of her neck. It gave her the freedom of both hands, she used the right to remove Mrs. London folder from the drawer.

"Paul used to call me at least once a week but I haven't heard from him in weeks. I tried calling him at his mother's house but she said he left and she doesn't know where he is." Robin sounded very concern.

"What can I tell you? I haven't heard from Paul and I doubt I will. The last conversation we had wasn't a pleasant one and to be honest with you I don't want to hear from Paul again." Andria looked at the clock on the wall. Mrs. London should be there any minute.

"I hope nothing happened to him."

"Paul? I doubt very much that anything happened to Paul. He must have left town to visit some woman. Paul must be on a beach right now sipping on Bahama Mamas. I think you have a lot more important things to be concerned with than that loser." Andria started to jot down some notes for herself.

"I guess you're right. I've been spending a lot more time with my family these days. My husband makes it his duty to come home at a reasonable hour and he plans a lot more family outings. We went to the movies the other day. I can't remember the last time we went."

"You see, I knew you guys had something special. Your husband loves you and your son to death and I doubt he wants to give you guys up. I think many things happen for the best. I don't think Paul was good for you. He would have made you leave your husband then he would have left you. I am telling you, Paul has scales and whether he is a fish or a snake, it doesn't matter. He's still slippery." Andria looked at the door, expecting a knock at anytime.

"My son is a completely different child when his father is around. Sometimes he hardly acknowledges me. You should see him walking with his dad's briefcase as if he had a job to go to. He worships that man. I..."

"Robin, sorry I have to go. My appointment is at the door. I'll call you later." Andria hung up and went to open the door.

"Good afternoon, Ms. Jackson," Mrs. London said and sat in the chair next to Andria's desk.

"How are you today, Mrs. London?" Andria sat behind her desk.

"Well I'm better than I was yesterday. That baby didn't want to go to sleep for nothing. All he did was kick and kick all night. I think he will be a basketball player. You never know, he might be another Allan Iverson. I want to be there when the millions start flowing. I want him to look proudly at his mom and feel special because she didn't give him away." Mrs. London's eyes lit up as if she was dreaming about the big time. "This baby, I'm telling you is a very special child."

Andria looked at her and under normal circumstances, she would have believed the woman who sat next to her but this was not normal. "Did you keep your appointment with the doctor?"

"Yes, I did. I told you I'm not playing around with this baby, I don't even want to be around people when they're smoking. Just yesterday, I had to kick my friend out of my house. She came in smoking and when I told her to put it out, she made a stink. So I told her she had to leave. My baby is not gonna get asthma or none of those lung sicknesses. No, my baby has to have good lungs so that he can jump high and beat them off the dribble." Mrs. London patted her stomach lightly "I think he was listening because he kicked again."

"The doctor said that you are due in a few weeks, Kings County is where you been going to see your obstetrician, right?" Andria underlined *Kings County* on her pad.

"Yeah, but the insurance company just change me to Kings County for this child. I have always had my children at St. Mary's hospital on Atlantic Avenue. I like the doctors there. They treat you like you're somebody there. They don't care how rich or poor you are, they just treat you with respect. My husband likes that hospital too."

"Your husband is back?" Andria asked.

"Yeah, he's back. My husband doesn't leave home for too long." Mrs. London pulled out a subway fare card from her purse.

"When did your husband come back?"

"I need more Metro Cards. I used the last fare on my way here," she said, ignoring Andria's question.

"Mrs. London, if the person in charge of Metro Cards is here I will see if she can give you an extra one. You know you are not supposed to get another one until next month. The city is becoming very strict with it's fare cards. Soon they might cut it out completely."

"It's that new mayor, isn't it? He comes into office and he wants to run the city as if it's a business. He wants to cut here and cut there, talking about the city is in debt. New York City could never be in debt, all the tourists that come here every year. Since 9/11 they just want to cut everything for the poor people, like we don't have to live too. Poor people need to travel too. We have to go buy food and clothes and whatever else people do. Look at me, what am I suppose to do walk with my big belly." She pushed herself up higher into the chair.

Andria looked at her and wondered how someone could reach that point in her life.

"You've been pregnant, have you, Ms. Jackson?" Mrs. London asked.

"We are not here to talk about me, Mrs. London." Andria had no desire to discuss her personal life with a client. "This meeting is to ensure that everything is going well with you and the baby. If there is anything else you want to discuss about you or your baby's health, feel free to do so."

Mrs. London sighed heavily.

Andria watched and waited.

Mrs. London looked at Andria and looked away.

"I don't want him to leave but whenever he comes he always brings drugs with him." Mrs. London slumped down in her chair.

"You mean your husband brings drugs in the house?" Andria asked.

"He doesn't buy any food but he eats everything and I have nothing for me and the baby to eat. And you know this baby is special, I can't allow my husband to do that to this baby. I got to protect this baby."

"Mrs. London, why didn't you mention that before?"

"Because I know you guys too well. You guys are gonna have him locked up." She looked at Andria expectantly.

"Mrs. London, we are not the police. We cannot stop your husband from using drugs. The only thing we could do is recommend a drug rehab center for him but he doesn't have to go." Andria jotted down the information on the drugs in the house. "By bringing drugs in the house your husband is endangering your life and the life of your baby. Does his friends take drugs with him in the house too?"

"Yes. He has one friend name Spin who can smell when there are drugs in the house. Whenever my husband comes home Spin is in my house the next day. Spin is a tall skinny motherfucker, whose eyes are always red. Spin will take a hit and then do a complete spin like he's in the Temptations band or something. His mouth is stinking too and all he drinks is milk. After he leaves the house, I have to use Clorox on all the cups to clean the germs. I don't want you guys to put my husband in jail because I love him."

"We will have to try to get him in a clinic."

"He was in a clinic before. He got kicked out for selling drugs in rehab. You know if you are a smart drug dealer, you can make a lot of money in a rehab clinic. I think when my husband left the rehab clinic he had about 20 G's on him. He made off like a bandit in the clinic," Mrs. London said proudly.

"You not taking drugs now are you, Mrs. London?" Andria asked.

"Of course not. I'm pregnant." Mrs. London seemed upset at the question.

"Yeah, but every other time you were pregnant you were taking drugs."

"Those were with my other children, not with this one, I told you I'm not letting anything happen to this child. This child is God's gift."

"Every child is God's gift, Mrs. London. It is what you do with the child after you receive the gift that makes a difference." Andria checked her watch. She would have to meet with her supervisor to this discuss the drugs in the home. She knew exactly what her supervisor would say. She had to call the police.

"What are you going to do about my husband?"

"I have to discuss it with my supervisor." Andria closed the folder. "Does he deal too?"

"A little."

Andria knew that would make a big difference with the cops. The cops liked to go after dealers who supplied the market as opposed to users. User's, occasionally, to keep the mayor of their back they would sweep up some known drug users but that was usually a waste of paperwork. The users usually went to prison or rehab and continued their drug use.

Mrs. London stood. "Ms. Jackson, can I have the Metro Card?

Andria hated to do it but she went into her purse and took out her own card, "Here, Mrs. London. There are a few more rides left on this card but you cannot overuse your card. I will not do that again."

Mrs. London snatched the card and stuck it in her purse.

"See you in two weeks at the same time." Andria stood to lead her out the door.

"Yes, Ms. Jackson." Mrs. London opened the door and exited without waiting for Andria to open the door.

Andria sat back at her desk and rubbed her stomach. "I have so many dreams and hopes for you, little one. I want to give you the world and guide you on a path that will make your life a joy. I don't want the life for you that I had, no I want your father to be there. I want your mother and your father together, raising you. My wish for you is a joyous childhood away from the traumas that destroy young minds and create little monsters."

A tear ran down Andria's right cheek. There was a knock on the door and she quickly composed herself and welcomed the person in. It was Patrick, Paul's best friend from college. Andria hasn't seen him since she and Paul broke up.

"How are you?" she asked.

"I'm good, very good," he said and came over and hugged her.

"How did you get past the receptionist?"

"I told her I was your brother and I was surprising you at work."

"Patrick, you were always a good liar."

He sat down in the seat that was recently vacated by Mrs. London. "This is New York, the truth doesn't even get you a job at Burger King."

"So what do I owe this visit?" she asked.

"It's Paul. He wants to see you."

"I don't think so, Patrick. I don't want anything to do with Paul."

"He said he might be moving out of the city in a few months and he wants to get everything cleared up before he leaves." Patrick took out a piece of paper from his pocket and put it on Andria's desk.

She looked at the paper but didn't pick it up. "Where is Paul?"

"He's staying with me. I think he ran into some trouble with some people so he is laying low before he leaves town."

"What kind of trouble?"

"I don't know. He won't say but I think it's pretty rough because someone gave him a beating."

"Is he all right?"

"As far as I can see, a little bitter and frightened but okay."

"He must have messed with someone's wife."

"I don't know, he didn't tell me."

"I'm sorry, Patrick, but I have no interest in seeing Paul."

Patrick stood to leave. "Andria, I can't tell you what to do but let me tell you what I know. Paul loves you and he regret what happened between you two but I don't think that can be change now. He knew he fucked up when he hurt you and lost you. I know you have moved on with your life but he hasn't been able to. Whatever you do, just remember there is no harm in talking to someone to clear the air. I got to go. My wife is downstairs waiting for me." Patrick left.

"I'm still not going to talk to him," she said to no one but herself.

Rashaun kissed Mrs. Wheatley on the cheek. "Good morning. I think I smell some saltfish, and I know wherever there is saltfish there is bakes." Rashaun gave Mrs. Wheatley his briefcase to put in the closet.

Rashaun had gotten the invitation from Mrs. Wheatley to stop by for breakfast before court. He had left a few minutes after Andria because proceedings weren't going to start until eleven. Rashaun looked at the table, there were five plates and utensils on the table.

"I see you noticed the extra setting. It's for Tyrone's sister. I know you don't know her. She's his half sister." Mrs. Wheatley had begun to put the food on the table.

"Tyrone never mentioned a sister to me." Rashaun leaned on the back of one of the chairs.

"He doesn't know her too well. She always lived with her mother. She just started practicing medicine in Washington. Her father is very proud of her, he is in the room talking to her now."

"Rashaun, do you want to go and wash your hands and sit at the table? I don't know when they'll be coming out," Mrs. Wheatley said putting a large hot cup of Grenadian cocoa chocolate on the table.

"I think I'll go and get Tyrone. I'm sure he's in his room watching cartoons." Rashaun headed down the hall toward Tyrone's room.

"Oh, and Rashaun thanks for referring Tyrone to the psychiatrist. She has done a wonderful job with him. Go into his room, you will see the change." Mrs. Wheatley took a gallon of orange juice and set it in the middle of the table.

Rashaun knocked on Tyrone's door.

Tyrone opened the door dressed in a brown pinstriped suit with a brown silk tie.

"Have you met my sister?" Tyrone asked as Rashaun walked into the room.

"Interesting paint job, Tyrone. Are you competing for the circus?" Rashaun asked, surveying the green-and-yellow room.

"It's a change." Tyrone picked up a pair of Nike sneakers and pushed them under his bed. "I guess you didn't meet my sister, if you did you would be talking about her right now."

"Why, she has horns in her head?"

"Nothing like that. She is the star child in my father's eyes. He paid for her to go to medical school. To him, her being a doctor is the biggest accomplishment in his life. I can't blame him. Look what happened to me." Tyrone sat down on the side of his bed and looked at his well-shined black shoes.

"Tyrone, you are not a failure. You are an engineer for Christ's sake. You know how many people wish they had your kind of skills? Granted, you are going through some hard times, but everything will work itself out. Before you know it you will be back making the big bucks. Let's go eat some of your mother's bakes and saltfish." Rashaun walked out the room and Tyrone closely followed.

I see you boys finally made it out the room," Mrs. Wheatley said from the head of table.

"Rashaun, you haven't met my daughter, have you?" Mr. Wheatley, a big man about two hundred and sixty pounds asked, standing from the seat opposite his wife.

"No, I haven't," Rashaun was staring at the young woman that was standing over the kitchen sink. Judging from the back, Tyrone's sister was definitely in competition with Tyra Banks in the ass department. The tight black stretch jeans that she wore made the most of her small waist and her large hips.

"Rashaun Jones." She turned around and walked toward Rashaun. "I'm Yvonne, Tyrone's younger sister."

Rashaun felt like a schoolboy. He was taken completely by surprise. His mouth was open and his right hand barely made it out to shake the beautiful woman's hand

"Rashaun, my daughter is a doctor in D.C. She's in her first year of practice as a gynecologist." Mr. Wheatley spoke in a deep baritone voice, the pride evident in each word.

178

"Tyrone didn't tell me that he had such a beautiful sister," Rashaun understated.

"I've seen your picture in the newspaper but, Mr. Jones, you are a feast to the human eye." Her smile had the perfection of a dental commercial.

"Rashaun please." Rashaun found himself blushing.

"Well now that the introductions have been made I think we can start eating," Mr. Wheatley said as he motioned for everyone to sit down.

"Not before we bow our heads in prayer," Mrs. Wheatley added.

While Mr. and Mrs. Wheatley occupied the chairs at both ends of the table Rashaun and Tyrone sat opposite from Yvonne. Rashaun didn't know if he was looking at Yvonne because she sat directly in front of him or if he was drawn to her magnetic beauty. The breakfast itself was uneventful but very tasty. The topic of Tyrone's fate never came up, instead most of the conversation was centered on Yvonne's medical career.

Rashaun found out that Yvonne attended at Howard University and graduated in the top ten percent of her class. She went on to Georgetown medical school. She had recently taken a leave of absence from her job in D.C. to visit her family.

After breakfast Rashaun and Tyrone decided to travel together and the Wheatleys were to follow with their daughter Yvonne.

"My sister likes you," Tyrone said as he got into the car with Rashaun.

"Uh-huh," Rashaun mumbled as he started the car.

Tyrone smiled. "She keeps calling you dark chocolate."

"It's that what you guys left the kitchen and went in the room to talk about?" Rashaun eased the car out of the driveway.

"She wanted the info on you. I think she was surprised that you didn't come on to her. She is not used to that. Besides the initial drooling you basically dismissed her," Tyrone said as he turned to put on his seat belt.

"Wait a minute, Tyrone. This is your sister we're talking about. You wouldn't mind me messing with her?" Rashaun asked.

"Please, man, don't you think I have more important things to worry about, besides I don't really know my sister and I really don't give a fuck who she sleeps with. You are my lawyer and my friend. If a little bit of pussy makes you a better lawyer, I'll pay for the hotel bill." Tyrone laughed at his own indulgence in humor. "Man, that psychiatrist is finally showing me a lot of things I didn't see before. Again, I'm thankful to you regardless of the out come of the case."

"Tyrone, don't start getting sentimental on me. Let's talk about your sister."

"Uh- huh."

"Your sister is a very beautiful woman but you know my situation. I'm engaged to Andria and we're going to have a baby. I love Andria, and I don't think I'm going to start playing games. I have waited a lifetime for Andria and the shit is going to fuck up, it's not going to be because I can't control my dick. Did you tell her that I was involved?" Rashaun asked.

"I told her but she wasn't listening. I don't think she will take no for an answer. The little I know about my sister is that she is very determined. She wasn't the smartest or the prettiest girl growing up but her perseverance and determination are what got her to where she is."

"You don't get to look like that from perseverance and determination."

"You should see pictures of Yvonne when she was a child. She was fat and dumpy looking."

Rashaun made a half circle around the Brooklyn public library at Grand Army Plaza. He glanced over at the waterfall in the middle of the circle. How many times had he seen wedding parties taking pictures there? He had mentioned taking pictures there to Andria but she wasn't interested. She said it was too ghetto. She had seen a place on Long Island in a wedding video she wanted to take pictures there.

180

"So what are you going to do with my sister?" Tyrone asked.

"Nothing. You can tell her I'm not interested."

"Well you are going to have to tell her that yourself. She's planning to see you after the trial today." Tyrone looked up at the big clock overlooking the Atlantic Avenue train station.

"Wait. I didn't make plans to see your sister after work. I'm meeting Andria downtown to go and look at some bridesmaid dresses." Rashaun slammed on the brakes, stopping barely six inches from the car in front of him.

"I know you don't want to go and look at no damn dresses," Tyrone stated.

"No, but I have started to compromise. It's what's going to make our relationship work. Besides I love to see Andria's face when she is doing stuff like that. I doubt my opinion is going to matter but she wants it anyway," Rashaun said as he thought about Andria going through each and every dress.

"Well just tell my sister you have another appointment. Don't tell her it's with your girl because she might want to come with you all."

"Yeah, right." Rashaun looked in the rearview mirror, searching for Mr. Wheatley in his black Toyota Avalon. All he saw was one of the new silver PT cruisers.

"Can't your sister find a doctor or someone in her field to get with?"

Tyrone brushed his hands over his face. "My sister could get anyone she wants. It so happens that for now she wants you."

"Like I said that's a problem." Rashaun looked at his watch and the red light on Livingston Street. He had twenty minutes to park and get inside the courthouse. The parking garage was a few yards away and the courthouse was about five minutes walking from the parking lot. In any other place that would be more than enough time to get there but in New York luck had to be on his side.

"I didn't know she was still going to use the videotape." Rashaun sat back while Kim brought the videotape into evidence. "She wants to hit hard for her sendoff."

"Is she going to show the complete videotape?" Tyrone asked. "My parents and my sister are all in court today. Rashaun, can you do anything?" Tyrone pleaded.

Rashaun reached over and grabbed Tyrone by the shoulder, "I know this is going to be tough but it's best we deal with this now. I didn't think she was still going to use the tape but obviously she is not happy with her case at this point. This videotape might also be good for you, Tyrone," Rashaun said not totally convinced. "Maybe you will be able to see that this whole thing was not your fault. I don't think you meant to hurt Judy and you will see that in the tape. I did."

"Rashaun, you're a good friend but I'm sorry I don't think seeing myself fuck a woman to death will be therapeutic," Tyrone said, glancing back.

"Tyrone, we can call for a fifteen-minute break and you can go and speak with your parents."

A small cloud seemed to have lifted off Tyrone's face. "I would appreciate that," he said.

"Your honor, may we approach the bench?" Rashaun asked, rising from his chair.

Modern technology had made it so that the video could be set up to show on four television sets. Kim held a pointer and a remote control for the VCR. If it weren't for the nature of the case someone walking into the room would think that Kim was a schoolteacher. There was a big difference between the abc's of a teacher's work and the sexually provocative nature of the video. The small Bose cube speakers positioned throughout the front of the courtroom was linked a Carver theatre receiver one of the best on the market.

In the witness stand an audio specialist was sworn in to decipher some of the less audible sounds on the video. Rashaun looked back to see Tyrone's sister had stayed to witness the rest of the proceedings. Tyrone's parents were absent.

After the re-identifying of the videotape as the one recorded by Tyrone on the evening of the incident, Kim started the tape.

Tyrone's voice was heard welcoming Judy into his apartment. There was nothing but the inside of Tyrone's bedroom shown at that time.

"So why did you come here?" Tyrone asked Judy.

"I came to get my umbrella," Judy answered.

"You came all the way over here to get that three-dollar umbrella?" Tyrone asked skeptically.

"Why you think I come here, because I want you? Why the fuck would I go back to something I gave up in the first case?" Judy stormed into the room.

"Whatever, bitch. Just take the umbrella and leave." Tyrone was the first person to be on the screen. He had on a muscle shirt that showed of his muscles. It was a far cry from the skinny little boy who was seated at the defense table.

"That's right, nigger, go into the room and hide because you can't handle the truth." Judy was seen on the screen for the first time. She was dressed in a miniskirt, tight-fitting T-shirt that had Gucci written on the front and judging by the way she walked, heels were the shoes of the day.

"Damn, she looks good," a male voice shouted from the courtroom.

"Just leave, Judy," Tyrone said as he sat on the bed.

"I'm going to leave because there is nothing here for me, you tiny dick motherfucker." Judy walked up to Tyrone and lifted his face so that he would look at her.

"Leave. I'm telling you for the last time." he said.

"What the fuck you going to do, huh, Pokemon dick? I left you because you couldn't handle this." Judy turned around and slapped her ass.

183

Kim paused the tape. "The rest of the tape is very sexually graphic so if this kind of material would offend you, I will suggest you leave right now."

No one left the courtroom.

The judge adjusted his seat.

"You know what, Tyrone, I regretted cheating on my husband because you just couldn't measure up. You got two things going against you, your dick is small and you cum in under three minutes. Shit, sometimes you empty in a New York minute."

Rashaun looked at Tyrone who had his head down on the table. He had done that from the time Kim started the tape. But Rashaun knew that what he wasn't seeing he was hearing loud and clear. In the video Judy continued to question Tyrone's manhood while she flaunted herself in front of him. Tyrone sat on the bed, his teeth clenched tightly.

"I would have killed the bitch," someone in the courtroom shouted.

The judge stood briefly "Sir, another outburst like that and you will be escorted out of the courtroom. Continue, Ms. Rivers."

Kim had paused the tape briefly.

"I'm going to kill you, bitch." Tyrone said as he grabbed Judy by the hair and pulled her onto the bed.

"Oh shit," a woman in the audience exclaimed.

Kim paused the tape, then rewound it. She played over the scene where Tyrone grabbed Judy by the hair and flung her unto the bed.

"Mr. Perkins, would you repeat what the defendant said to the victim." Kim asked.

"He said 'I'm going to kill you, bitch,' " Mr. Perkins gladly repeated.

"Thank you, Mr. Perkins." Kim hit play on the remote again and replayed the scene where Tyrone grabbed Judy and threw her to the bed.

"That's all you got punk? Are you going to be a man for the first time in your life?" Judy screamed as Tyrone stood over her holding her by the hair. Tyrone ripped off his shirt and every muscle in his body stood out. He pulled Judy's short skirt up and with one motion he reached down and ripped off her panties. He squeezed them in his hand like a trophy.

"Are you finally going to fuck me or are you going to play with the pussy like you use to?" Judy smiled at him, taking great pleasure in Tyrone's pain.

With his left hand holding onto her hair, he flipped her over to her stomach. Her skirt had fallen back over her ass, but he flipped it back over her waist. He stood for a minute to release his penis.

"The brother is packing," a woman in the audience, exclaimed.

Kim paused the tape and looked at the judge.

The rest of the people in the courtroom awaited the judge's response.

The judge looked at Kim as if wondering why she had stopped the tape. He signaled for her to continue without reprimanding the person who made the intrusion.

"I told you don't fuck with me. I'm going to hurt you. I warned you to not to fuck with me." Tyrone entered Judy with the savagery of a mountain lion biting into its prey. Judy's scream echoed throughout the courtroom.

"Please," Judy whispered.

Kim stopped the tape.

She rewound it to just before Judy's scream and played it until Judy whispered please. "Mr. Perkins, can you decipher what the victim just said?"

"She said 'please,' " Mr. Perkins spoke loud so that his voice echoed in the small courtroom.

"Thank you, Mr. Perkins." Kim again restarted the tape.

"Bitch, I warned you now I'm going to kill your ass." Tyrone shouted this time he rammed into Judy with long hard strokes. There was a pause in the tape and suddenly a close up of Tyrone's face. His eyes seemed to have turned green.

Kim stopped the tape.

"Your honor, men and women of the jury, I had the guys in the audio video department zoom into the defendant's eyes to show his tremendous rage. If you look at his eyes you can see that they correspond to his words and his actions." Kim looked at the judge to see if he wanted her to continue.

"Well, people, that will be all for today, we will adjourn until 9:00 A.M. tomorrow." With that said the judge bang his gavel, stood and court was dismissed.

Hilda had called Andria and told her that Sharon had wanted to meet with them to discuss her future. Sharon's family had disowned her when she took up street walking and her friends were all she had.

Andria sat next to Debbie who was undecided on whether to go back to Trinidad or stay and work in New York. Unlike most West Indians who would have to hide from the INS until they could get someone to marry them or a job to sponsor them Debbie would receive automatic citizenship. Her parents had promised to give her a million dollars to come to deposit in a bank account, which would make her an instant US citizen. It was on condition that she pursues an MBA and return home after five years to take over the family restaurant business.

"No, thank you." Andria declined the box of fried chicken Hilda was pushing in front of her.

"What, you scared it's going to harm your baby?" Sharon asked.

"Nope. I never ate that greasy fried chicken when I wasn't pregnant. I definitely won't eat it now that I am," Andria answered. The smell of the chicken alone seemed to be wreaking havoc on her stomach. She inhaled deeply, hoping that the instant nausea would go away.

186

"Are you pregnant?" Debbie asked.

"Yes."

"How many months?" Debbie seemed fascinated.

"Four and a half," Andria answered.

"I was pregnant once. I had a miscarriage after the fourth month." Debbie was pensive in her recollection.

"What happened?" Andria inquired.

"My boyfriend and I were having problems and one morning I woke up and my water had broken. That was it, I lost he baby." Debbie reached over, took the ketchup and squeezed it on the chicken. "After that my boyfriend left too. It was one of the loneliest times of my life."

"Okay, guys, I did call you guys over here for a reason," Sharon said, demanding the attention of the group.

"Yo, baby, you working?" a tall man with a wedding band on his left hand asked Debbie.

Debbie just looked at him.

"Get the fuck out of here. Does she look like a whore?" Sharon asked, dismissing the man with her hand. "They will jump on anything that's fresh. In this business, you lose your freshness in a minute and the motherfuckers move on to the next one. Some of them only want to fuck the fifteen and under."

"They are sick," Hilda said.

"Yeah. They are and most of them you find out here are married men. The white ones are the worst. They leave their untouchable white wife in the suburbs and come down here and ask you to do some sick shit. One John asked me to pee on his face."

"You did it?" Andria asked.

"Hell yeah, it was the easiest hundred-dollar bill I ever made." Sharon watched two young girls walk into the restaurant. They looked at her and rolled their eyes.

"You know them?" Hilda asked.

"Yeah, we had some beef when their pimp wanted to stab me," she answered

The two girls went to the young boys that were playing dominos. Andria watched as they took out their money from their bras and gave it to them. "Those two guys over there are pimps?" Andria asked incredulously.

"Yeah, and they are the most ruthless. They beat the shit out of those girls for interfering when they were talking to me. I think they took them to the hospital when they were finished. I heard they belong to one of the gangs, either the Brooklyn Killers or Brownsville Madmen. They run their shit tight though. It's like they have a corporation with stocks. The head guy is much older, I saw him once. He looks like he is in his late forties." Sharon averted her eyes when the guys looked over at her table.

"Sharon, you got to get out of this life," Andria said feeling very uncomfortable in the restaurant.

"Yeah, Sharon. Anything you want I will give you. Just get out of here," Hilda added. She reached over and held Sharon's hand.

"Sharon, you know my parents got money, so whatever you want I'll get it for you." Debbie shot a glance at the two young pimps counting the money the girls had given them.

"I'm getting out," Sharon said.

"Rashaun knows this psychiatrist. She works with a lot of people affected by 9/11…" Andria said.

"Andria, she said she's getting out." Hilda's face lit up.

"She is?" Andria repeated.

"Yes, Andria, I'm getting out but I'm not staying in New York," Sharon said.

"Where are you going?" Debbie asked, a look of concern on her face.

Sharon looked around at her friends and with regret said, "I'm moving to Atlanta."

"Atlanta? Who do you know in Atlanta?" Hilda asked.

"Chris."

"Chris who?" Andria chimed in.

"Chris Tucker, the comedian from *Friday* and *Rush Hour*," Sharon said sarcastically.

"You serious?" Debbie's eyes were about to pop out of their sockets.

"No. She's not," Hilda, said.

"No. His name is Chris Valentine and he's a computer consultant for the army or navy, one of the arm services, I can't remember which," Sharon said.

"That's great," Andria said as she finally found a reason to smile in this restaurant of wasted lives.

"How do you know he is not a serial killer or something?" Hilda asked.

Sharon looked across at the table with the pimps and the prostitutes. Another two had walked in and slumped down on the plastic chairs. "Who do you think I've been dealing with the last few weeks, the Harlem Boys Choir?."

"I guess you're right but you have to give me all the information on him. Just in case something happens I can find him and cut off his balls." Hilda wasn't smiling; she meant every word.

"I will. I know you're serious too." Sharon looked appreciatively at her friend.

"When are you thinking of moving?" Andria asked.

"I'm out of here by the weekend. I have to try to restart my life. I want to clean my slate and start over. I don't even know if I can do it, but I am going to try." Sharon looked uncertain.

"Are you going to tell him what you did here?" Debbie asked.

"Of course not, Debbie. That would be stupid." Hilda gave Debbie a look reserve for people with no comprehension.

"Debbie, I'm honest but I'm not stupid. I already did a complete physical in which they checked for every sexually transmitted disease known to man. I was given a clean bill of health so I will go and see what life is like in Atlanta," Sharon said.

"So why did you have us meet you here?" Hilda asked. "Don't tell me you're going to work here tonight."

"No. I told you I'm out of this life. I had to come here and meet some friends I had made on the street. I couldn't leave without saying good-bye to them. Excuse me. There's Nicole." Sharon stood. "Her husband left her and her part-time receptionist job can't cover the mortgage and feed the kids."

"So she turns to prostitution?" Andria was again dumbfounded.

"Don't knock it until you try it, Andria," Sharon said as she left the table.

Andria kept staring at Nicole who Sharon had greeted with a big hug.

"Andria," Hilda shouted.

Andria looked startled, "Why you shouting at me?"

"Because you don't know how to mind your own business and I have something to tell you."

Reluctantly Andria focused her attention on Hilda. "This better be good."

"I don't know if this is good or bad but I'm going to run a test on my husband. I need to know if he really wants to stay with me," Hilda said.

"What are you going to do?" Debbie asked.

"I'm going to write a letter absolving him of the right to pay child support for our three children. If he wants to leave and he was scared of paying child support then he won't have anything to worry about."

"Hilda, you sure you want to do that? What happens if he does leave? Can you support the children on your own? I forgot how much managers make but you would need to make over a hundred grand to support the children." Andria didn't know exactly how she arrived at that figure but a guess to keep a friend grounded is always good.

"Andria, since when have you become an expert on taking care of children? The one you have in your stomach isn't even kicking yet, you better hold up before you go running your mouth."

"Okay, don't listen to me. Here comes Sharon. Tell her about your remarkable plan." Andria reverted her eyes back to Nicole.

"What did I miss?" Sharon asked as she took her seat.

"Hilda's remarkable plan to start collecting food stamps if her husband isn't willing to stay with her." Andria alternated her attention between Nicole and the young prostitutes and their pimp.

"Are you sure that's what you want to do?" Sharon asked Hilda.

"Sharon, I don't want a man who doesn't want to be with me and my kids," Hilda said.

"Aren't they your husband's kids too?" Debbie askcd.

"Yeah, but lately he's been acting like they're only mine," Hilda answered.

"He just gave her a knife," Andria said as she saw one of the young men with a red jacket on slip a knife to one of the girls.

"Who you talking about?" Sharon asked, scanning the room.

Andria pointed to the young man in the red jacket. "Him."

"Andria, put your hand down. You don't point at people," Sharon said focus on the young people at the table.

The young girl with the knife got up from the table and walked over to Nicole.

One of the people at the table started a fire in the fried-chicken box. They threw the box up in the air and screamed fire. The old security guard made a move to the table to put out the fire. Andria glanced back and forth between the three at the table and the one standing by Nicole.

"Sharon, look," Andria, said as she saw the girl with the knife in her hand reach over and grabbed Nicole by the hair.

"Nicole," Sharon shouted.

Sharon's warning went unheard because the young girl brought the knife around Nicole's neck in a half circle. Sharon jumped up from her seat and headed toward Nicole.

Andria watched with her mouth open.

The young woman put her knife back in her bag and quickly exited the restaurant.

Sharon slipped her hand around Nicole's throat in a futile attempt to stop the blood that came gushing out.

"What should we do?" Andria asked as she watched the three young people get up from the table and leave.

"Call an ambulance," Sharon shouted at the security guard who was removing the burned box from the table.

"It's way too late," the man with the girl by the door, said as he too got up to leave.

Hilda, Andria and Debbie went over to help Sharon with Hilda.

"Y'all get out of here," Sharon said, tears flowing.

Andria stood still in shock.

Hilda grabbed both Andria and Debbie and pushed her to the door. As they made their way out, the security guard shouted at the workers behind the glass partition to call the police.

"Shouldn't we have waited to talk to the police?" Andria asked as Hilda drove the car out of the parking lot.

Hilda held on tightly to the wheel to stop her hands from shaking. "Andria, you didn't see anything. We weren't in the restaurant this evening, you hear me."

A quarter mile down Linden Boulevard the ladies saw the police car with lights flashing going in the direction of the restaurant.

"They expect to catch anyone now?" Andria asked, not really expecting an answer.

Hilda furtively looked in the rearview mirror.

"I hope nothing happened to Sharon," Andria said glancing back periodically.

Hilda finally eased her hands on the wheel. "I'm not worried about something happening to Sharon. I am worried that she might do something stupid."

"Like what?" Debbie asked.

"I don't know, but I hope she leaves this city as she said she would." Hilda concentrated on the Linden Boulevard traffic.

"She slit her throat so easily," Andria said, replaying the image in her head.

"Yeah. On the streets, life is far from precious," Hilda said as she waited at the biggest, most confusing intersection in Brooklyn where Remsen, Kings Highway and Linden met. It was always a driver's nightmare and today it was no different.

Andria couldn't forget the ease in which the young girl killed Nicole. She was sure the woman could not have been more than seventeen. Did the young woman have a family? Did her parents know that their daughter was a prostitute and a murderer? Andria looked at Hilda who seemed preoccupied with the traffic congestion. Debbie sat silently in the back seat. When she got home she was going to tell Rashaun what happened. Maybe he could help her decide her next move. She touched her stomach and whispered a silent prayer that her child would never turn out like that young killer.

"Let Tyrone cop to second degree and we can end this right now." Kim took the Tetley tea bag and dropped it in the cup of hot water.

"Are you getting nervous?" Rashaun asked as he drank from a small carton of Tropicana orange juice. He knew that Kim wanted to cut a deal when she asked him to meet her for breakfast before court. He had promised Tyrone that he wouldn't do any jail time and Kim was recommending jail time.

"He'll do about five years then get paroled." Kim sank her teeth into a bagel with cream cheese.

Rashaun looked at Kim as if she had just insulted him "That's what you called me here for."

"Rashaun, don't be pig headed. Your client killed someone. He has to be punished," Kim said as she put the bagel down.

"Kim, you should know, sex hurts." Rashaun said.

"That's a low blow. Is that what this is all about?" She looked directly at Rashaun.

"This is about getting my friend his freedom. Tyrone can't do anytime in prison, sending him to prison is like signing his death warrant. I am certain he will not make a month in there." Rashaun spread some jelly over his buttered whole-wheat toast.

"There is no way I'm going to do a plea without a jail time stipulation. I think you should worry about your client spending twenty-five to life in prison over doing a mere five years." Kim picked up the half-eaten bagel. "I don't think you should let what happened between us come between the best deal for your client."

"Kim, Tyrone is not doing any time and that's it. There will be no discussion unless we are talking about probation without any jail time attached." Rashaun looked around the table for a small straw. Kim took hers and handed it to him.

"We were good together, weren't we?" she asked quietly.

Rashaun paused from taking a sip of tea and concentrated on her.

She was looking at him with glassy eyes.

"What is that all about?" he asked.

"You never gave me a chance to explain myself," she said. "You know I never slept with him again after we broke up." She reached over to touch Rashaun's hand.

"Why are you telling me this now?" he said, pulling his hand away from her.

"Maybe if we had spoken after the incident we could have gotten past that." She said it as if it was a minor infraction on a football field. The player had jumped offside and he was given a penalty of five yards. When in fact, he believed it to be a personal foul on the sixteen-yard line, thirty seconds to go, the game tied and the best defensive player for the run was injured. It became almost impossible to stop the touchdown.

"I've lost my appetite," he said, pushing his plate to the middle of the table.

"Rashaun, you are too sensitive. We would have still been together if you had given me a chance to explain."

"Explain what?" Rashaun's body had become tense as he closed his fists tightly. "Were you drugged? Did he put a knife to your throat? What, tell me, what made you let my best friend fuck you. You had meant everything to me." He had started to raise his voice.

"Rashaun?"

"What!"

"I didn't mean to hurt you."

"Yeah, Oswald didn't mean to kill Kennedy either but he still blew him away." He sipped the orange juice slowly. He had failed. He had let her get him angry. He wasn't over what happened between them.

"Is there a – "

He didn't let her finish, "No."

"You didn't let me finish," she said.

"I don't have to, whatever you are asking the answer is no."

"Excuse me, Rashaun?" Rashaun looked up. It was Yvonne, Tyrone's sister.

Kim looked Yvonne up and down.

"I guess it's my time to leave." Kim stood.

Rashaun didn't say anything.

"Did I interrupt?" Yvonne asked.

Rashaun looked at Kim. "No, there wasn't anything going on to interrupt," he said. "Ms. Rivers was just leaving."

Kim picked up her tray and stood. "See you in court."

"I didn't know prosecutors and defense lawyers have so much love going on," Yvonne said as she sat on the seat vacated by Kim.

"We don't," Rashaun said, welcoming the distraction.

"Well there goes another woman in love with you," Yvonne said, offering her winning smile. "I guess my competition is stiff. What happen every woman wants DC."

"I doubt that." Rashaun looked at his watch.

Yvonne followed his gaze. "I know you have to be in court."

"Where is Tyrone?"

"He's with my parents. They stopped to have some breakfast and I went shopping."

"Before nine?"

"Some things can't wait with a woman," she said, rising from her seat.

"Patience is a virtue," he said, following her lead and standing up with his tray in his hand.

"Patience is a virtue for old people waiting on their Social Security check to cover their medical expenses. Patience in a young woman, in time, equals an unmarried woman at fifty looking to adopt a child for company." Yvonne led the way out of the cafeteria and as she walked by there were jealous looks from everywhere.

196

Rashaun had a very short list of defense witnesses. Frank Sebastian was his first witness.

"Mr. Sebastian, what is your medical condition right now?" Rashaun asked, as he approached the witness stand.

Mr. Sebastian leaned forward in the witness chair, putting his mouth up to the microphone. "I'm half-impotent."

"Half impotent, what exactly does that mean?" Rashaun asked, looking back at the jury.

"It means that my penis only gets partially erect."

"In other words, the blood flow in your penis keeps you semi erect?"

"No, that's not what it means. It's like I just said, my penis only gets half erect. I had an accident during sex and my penis got broken in half so the tissue that is responsible for erection in a man only goes halfway." Mr. Sebastian kept his head down as he spoke.

"Is there a medical name for your problem?"

"Yes. My doctor told me but I can't think of it now."

"Are you in a relationship right now?"

"Yes, I'm married."

"Did the incident that caused you erection problems happen before or after you got married?" Rashaun asked.

"After I got married."

"Can you tell the court exactly what happened?"

"My wife played a trick on me."

"Tell the court exactly what happened?"

"I came home from a hard day of work at the day-care center. My wife didn't hear when I walked into the house because she was on the phone in the bedroom. So I sneaked in trying to surprise her but when I got to the bedroom door I overheard part of the conversation. She was telling her sister that she had gone to bed with my brother, Reggie, my own flesh-and-blood brother. I wanted to kill her then and there, your honor, but I calmed down and I thought about it. We have two beautiful children, your honor, and I couldn't live without

197

them. I also couldn't afford child support—child support on three children is subway-begging time. If I hit her, I could end up in jail and you know what goes on in jail. So I kicked the door open and I told her what I overheard and she just looked at me. Your honor, I was boiling mad and all the blood seemed to have rushed right into my penis. So I told her, let me see Reggie compete with this. I pulled my off clothes and I swear to you I have never seen my penis so big. My wife looked at me and she had this evil grin on her face. So I say okay you smiling about it so I decided to lay it on her."

"What happened next?" Rashaun asked.

"Well you know I was laying pipe right and my wife is screaming and carrying on. The more she screams the more I get excited because I have never had sex with my wife like that before. I kept slamming into her walls or something because I kept hitting something in her womb with my penis. And the harder I hit it the more she seemed to be enjoying it so it was then that I made one last hit and it happened.

"What happened?" Rashaun asked eagerly.

"I broke my penis in half. After I heard the crack I started to ease out of my wife but her orgasm had started. I have never seen a woman have an orgasm like that before. Her eyes became totally white as if her eyeballs were turning over. She started to breathe like she was having a heart attack and her vagina just pushed me out. And she passed out too. And there I was only half of my penis was erect, the rest just hung at a ninety degree angle totally lifeless."

"What did you do then?"

"I screamed like a bitch. What the hell did you think I did?" Tears had started to fall from Mr. Sebastian's eyes. "And you know the worst part?"

"What is it?"

"My wife never slept with my brother. It was something her friends had told her about."

"What is that?"

"Her friend had told her about Blackfunk."

"So you were fooled."

"You can say that."

"Are you still with your wife, Mr. Sebastian?"

"Yes. Where can I go? What woman would want me? Remember there might be grounds for a divorce but there is nothing that will stop the child-support payment. And I I'm not leaving my home so that she can bring some other man in there for me to support."

"One last question. Do you still have sex with your wife?"

"If you can call what we do sex. But my wife still talks about that day. She said she had an orgasm that was indescribable."

Rashaun walked back to the defense table, "No further questions your honor."

"Mr. Sebastian, were you trying to hurt your wife when the aforementioned incident happen?" Kim asked, replacing Rashaun in front of the witness stand.

"Yes, but…"

"Just answer the question with a yes or a no," the judge told Mr. Sebastian.

"Did you think you accomplished that?"

"No. Look who's scarred for life." Mr. Sebastian wiped the remnants of the tears off his cheeks.

"What do you think of your penis?"

"Nothing much right now." he said, looking down at crotch. There was a lot of snickering in the courtroom.

"Did you ever think of your penis as a weapon?" Kim asked.

"No, never."

"But yet you were trying to hurt your wife with it?"

"I wasn't trying to hurt my wife, I was trying to show her that I could fuck."

"By hurting her?"

"No by fucking her good."

"No more questions."

"I would never hurt my wife."

"Mr. Sebastian, you can step down now," the judge said.

Rashaun tried to walk with the bags without hitting pedestrians in the walkway. He kept saying excuse me as he walked up the block. As he looked up and saw the two concrete lions that guarded his building he made a mental note not to go overboard shopping again. He had to talk to Andria about buying a house on Long Island because he couldn't see his child growing up in an apartment. He grew up in a house and his child was going to do the same. Elevators killed hundreds of children a year and as he pressed the button on the one in his building he was sure that he wasn't going to let his child get hurt in one.

There were so many things he wanted to buy for the baby but he wasn't sure about the sex yet so he had to buy unisex. Andria refused to do the test that would determine the child's sex. She wanted it to be a surprise. It didn't make a difference to him but he had always wanted his first child to be a son. His mother told him that the child would be a boy. He didn't know how his mother knew that but he was pretty sure that she was correct.

He put down the bags and fumbled for his keys.

"Rashaun." Andria looked at him and the two big bags by his side.

Rashaun jumped back. He hadn't expected her to open the door.

She gave him a look that said I don't know what to do with you but I still love you.

He lifted the bags and stepped in as a proud father.

"Rashaun, the baby is not born yet and I'll have to start giving away clothes. There is no more room in the apartment to keep all the stuff you've been buying," she said as she took one of the bags.

200

"Baby, these things were on sale," he said for the lack of something else to say.

"Rashaun, can you pass by a store and not pick up something for the baby?" she asked.

"I try but I see some of these things and they are so cute I can't help myself. Okay I promise you, I won't buy anything for the rest of the week," he said as he put the bag in the closet.

"Rashaun, today is Thursday," she said, trying her best not to laugh.

"I know that. What, you want me to promise for the month? I can't do that," he said as he kissed Andria and walked into the room.

"Okay, then, can I go with you next time because some of the stuff you buy is not as cute as you think," she said, giving up on her attempt to hold in the laughter.

Rashaun looked at her and realized how lucky he was. "Now you're making fun of me?" he said, trying to hold in his own laughter.

"Rashaun, even your niece, Sheila, knows that you are lousy when it comes to picking out children's clothes." Andria put her hands around his neck.

"She said that." He started to smile. "Wait till I get a hold of little miss thing."

"Well you won't have to wait long because she is on her way," Andria said. "She is spending the rest of the week and the weekend with us."

"I guess she didn't want to inform her uncle, did she?"

"Nope she wants to spend it with her aunt Andria. I think she likes hanging around older women. But she does want you to take her to the park on Saturday; I think she has a soccer game. You can drop me off at Robin's and pick me up after the game."

"Okay, ma'am." Rashaun put his hands around her waist.

"Rashaun, don't buy her everything she sees and says she wants. It's not good," Andria said, knowing his propensity for spending.

"Who me?" he asked.

"Yes, you," Andria said.

"Did you hear from Sharon?" Rashaun asked.

"Yep, she called me from Atlanta. She loves it there," Andria said as she started to walk away from him.

Rashaun followed her into the kitchen. "And you have forgotten about what you saw in the restaurant, right?' He said hoping she would agree.

"I didn't have to," she said, picking up a newspaper.

"Why?" he asked grave concern coming over him as he took the newspaper from her.

"Look on page seven. There's a picture of the girl who committed the murder." Andria said and went over to the sink.

"She was found dead?" Rashaun asked as he saw the picture of a smiling teenager with the caption casualty of gang warfare printed above her head.

"She never had a chance," Andria said as she began to take out some pans.

"Life on the street every day is a hustle to survive. What are you baking?" He asked as he looked over the flour, peeled sweet potatoes, two cans of condensed milk and an assortment of baking supplies.

"I'm waiting for Sheila to get here. We're baking potato pudding tonight," Andria said.

"Can I help?" Rashaun asked.

"The only thing you could help do is grate the potatoes." she said.

"That would work. Give me a second to change," he said and went into the bedroom. "What made you make potato pudding?" he asked.

"I never did it before so I thought I'd give it a shot," Andria said.

"Do you have the recipe?" Rashaun asked.

"No, but your mother told me all I need to know," Andria said as she covered the potatoes with a paper towel.

"Oh, I guess you don't need me to tell you anything," Rashaun said, coming out the room with a white apron over his clothes.

"Rashaun, what do you have on?" Andria asked, looking at him in mock disbelief.

"Didn't I tell you I was one of the top chefs at the palace restaurant."

"And where is the palace restaurant?"

"Well as you can tell they lost their master chef so they had to close the establishment. After that I retired from the baking business, I went into the law business," Rashaun said picking up the bowl with the potatoes.

"Now, you do the menial task of grating potatoes, wow, haven't we fallen from grace?" Andria said as she continued to rummage through the cabinet.

"Remember, young woman, no task in the process of creating a masterpiece is too small for the king of chefs." Rashaun was preparing to grate the potatoes when the bell rang.

"That must be Sheila. I'm sure she'll get a kick out of you in your apron," Andria said as she went to the door. At the same time the phone rang, so Rashaun put down the potatoes and went to the phone.

"Hello," he said.

"Hello, it's me, Yvonne. You don't mind me calling you at your house, do you?" she asked in a sexy voice.

Rashaun looked at the phone in disbelief. He wanted to hang up and go strangle Tyrone for giving Yvonne his telephone number.

"Who is it, Rashaun?" Andria asked as she helped Sheila take her bag off.

"Hold on," Rashaun said into the phone. "It's Yvonne, Tyrone's sister."

"I didn't know that Tyrone had a sister," Andria said.

"He does," Rashaun said, lifting Sheila up with his left hand for a hug.

"Uncle Rashaun, I'm getting too big for you to lift me," she said as she started to squirm in his arms. "I'm going to the kitchen to bake with Aunty Andria," she said as he put her down.

Rashaun lifted the phone back up.

"Is everything okay with Tyrone and the family?" Rashaun asked.

"Yeah, everyone is fine. I was just wondering when I'm going to meet that girlfriend of yours." Yvonne asked.

"Whenever," Rashaun answered. "Hold on. Let me ask her."

Rashaun placed the phone down and went over to Andria and Sheila. "Yvonne wants to meet you."

Andria stopped sifting the sugar.

"Why does Tyrone's sister want to meet me?" she asked.

"Your guess is as good as mine," Rashaun said.

"Who is Yvonne?" Sheila asked, looking up at Rashaun.

"She is the sister of a friend of mine," Rashaun answered.

"Why does she want to meet Aunty Andria?" Sheila asked.

Rashaun looked at her. "I don't know."

"Rashaun, you are a lawyer, why don't you tell us why she wants to meet me," Andria said as she went to the table and continued grating the potatoes.

Rashaun went back to the phone. "Hello," he said.

"I thought you had forgotten about me," Yvonne said, not sounding a bit perturbed.

Rashaun looked over at Andria had begun to grate the potato. "Let me talk to you later," he said.

"Well I'm not doing anything in New York City so I'm available anytime," she said.

"Bye." Rashaun hung up the phone.

204

Sheila came over to him. "I think you got Aunty Andria mad."

"I didn't mean to but I guess you're right," he said.

"Why don't you go and kiss her? That's what Mommy and Daddy always do." Sheila started to pull him in Andria's direction.

Rashaun looked at the emphasis Andria was putting on the potatoes and the contortion of her face.

"Sheila, I don't think this is a good time for me to kiss Andria. You go help her with the potatoes. I'm going to go and get my briefcase from the room," he said.

"You're not going to help us bake anymore," Sheila said, looking a bit disappointed.

"I think you and aunty Andria can handle that just fine," Rashaun said, "but I will help eat the pudding."

"That's what Mommy always tells Daddy, get out of the kitchen and he doesn't come back until the food is done. But Mommy lets me help her all the time," she said.

Rashaun kissed Sheila on the forehead and went into the room.

"She is beautiful, isn't she?" Yelram, the old man from court, asked Rashaun.

"Yeah, but that doesn't mean anything," Rashaun countered." I told her that I wasn't interested."

Yelram dipped his spoon into the vegetable soup, and then repeated his actions again; he wiped his mouth with a napkin.

"Rashaun, you are a very intelligent young man but sometimes you make the assumption that everyone around you repeated the first grade." Yelram interlocked his fingers on the edge of the table.

Rashaun looked at him, confused.

It was the first time Yelram had spoken to him in that manner.

"The funny thing about life is that we ask for things and when it is given to us we don't know what to do with it. You told me the story of your personal experience with Blackfunk and the way it sent you in a disastrous direction. Finally, the 'right woman' comes along. You are happy, she is happy, marriage and a baby are on their way. Now you are telling me that your woman is upset at you for being truthful to her. First, you know and I know that if this girl Yvonne were ugly there was no way she would be calling you at home. Second, you're flirting with Yvonne and you know it, yet you act as if you're innocent. Finally, I don't think you have any interest in Yvonne but you find her interest in you flattering. So, instead of cutting her off, you play with her emotions to boost your ego and in the meantime it is creating a problem at home." Yelram, took a long sip of water.

Rashaun looked at the calamari on his plate and realized he wasn't going to finish it.

"Rashaun, you are no different from most men out there and you are not suppose to be. However, what is going to separate you is your course of action when situations like these present themselves. What you do will determine your life's direction." Yelram followed Rashaun's eyes to a young white woman in her mid-twenties.

"That's black women's biggest problem and they don't know it. It is the evolution of the white woman," Yelram said as Rashaun quickly redirected his gaze.

"What do you mean?" Rashaun asked, feeling a little guilty.

"You saw the same thing that I just saw, the only thing is your reaction was different from mine. A white woman with a nice ass. Another brother's reaction would be that he has to talk to her hence black women's problem. You see with the onset of equal rights and the interplay of the races, the direction of the world is changing. The black man is one of the most splendid creatures on the face of the earth. He's the ultimate prize. For years through racism, separation and total control of the media the white man has presented himself as the epitome of man."

Rashaun sighed.

"But over the years things have been changing through the absorption of black culture into the main stream. Rap music and reggae are perfect examples. The white women were generally known for their tits, which were generally big, and her butt wasn't a factor. If she was to remain with the white man that would be perfectly okay but...." Yelram paused and looked over to the table at the white woman whose focus was Rashaun. "She has seen the light and hence the presence of color as oppose to the absence. Granted, that has happened, she now has to make herself appealing to the black man and, hence, his sexual powers. The evolution of the white woman that has been going on for many years did not really take into account the increase in plastic surgery. The latter being for women of enormous wealth with preconceived notions of superiority. You see the black woman's ass is not only necessary to call her mate but it also acts as a shield in the process of mating."

"Yelram, sometimes I just don't believe you," Rashaun said, shaking his head.

"Whether you believe me is irrelevant. What I want you to do is open up your eyes and think. So as I was saying, the shield I'm talking about is the thrust from behind. When engaging in sex and the man is at the back, which is most black men's favorite position, as he thrusts his penis into the woman it prevents complete penetration, therefore, limiting the damaging effect on the woman's vagina. You see, black women being the partner of the black man were born with the...let's say for lack of a better word...big ass. Now that white women have decided to encroach themselves on the black man hence experiencing the epitome of man she has to adopt. On the other side of that issue is the cosmetic increase in the white man's penis. The white man, realizing he was losing his woman, has come out with numerous ways to stop the inevitable. He has developed medicine that will increase his muscle mass on a tremendous level and he has develop surgery techniques to increase the girth and length of his penis."

"Hey, my friend was thinking of that surgery."

"Of course, there are always exceptions to the rule. Yet, I commend your friend who chose to follow that route instead of engaging in the act of homosexuality, which leads to unspeakable deceases and the destruction of our people in Africa and the Caribbean. It is, indeed, a sad state of affairs for our people in that region whose death has come as a result of the introduction of the white man's problem on another people."

Rashaun looked at Yelram and drummed his fingers on the table.

"I'm sorry I went out on a tangent but sometimes I get caught up. While I am not apologizing for the transferring of knowledge I do want to return to our original conversation. Like I said before, while I don't think that you have interest in other women besides Andria I think you should be more understanding of her feelings. Remember, this is the woman who is carrying your child and hence your name in your life's absence. What you have to do is reach for that next level only then would you be the man that I know you can be. In life, sometimes it takes a major incident for that change to happen. At other times it's a gradual process and when you do get there, you will know. I remembered when I—." Yelram stopped himself before going on. "I digress again. Rashaun go home and tell the woman of your life that your life is complete with her."

"Are you staying here?" Rashaun asked.

"Yeah, I think I will."

Rashaun motioned the waitress over, he spoke to her briefly then left a fifty-dollar bill on the table. He pulled his coat tighter to his neck as he braced himself for the coldness of New York.

"You should of never given him that option." Paula said as the women walked down the stairs from the restaurant.

"I don't blame you, Hilda. I don't want no man living with me that doesn't want to be there, regardless of the situation." Robin pulled her bag up so that it wouldn't get caught in the railing as she headed down the stairs.

"I agree with Paula. I don't think that you should have given him that option," Andria said as she put the credit-card slip from paying for the lunch into her purse.

Hilda concentrated on the steep stairs as she made her way down behind Robin. "It took him one week to leave. I spoke to him on Thursday and the next Thursday he was gone. All he left was his cell phone number. But I found out where he is," Hilda said as she stopped with the rest of the women in front of a bridal shop.

"He moved in with his mother? As all men do," Paula said.

"Andria, why are you beating yourself over the head? your wedding dress is perfect." Robin said

"He moved in with this woman and her four kids," Hilda said.

"You lie," Paula said.

"That's why I told you that you shouldn't give up that option. You see, even if he left the house I'm telling you no woman would take him if he had to pay all that child support," Andria said.

"We did not even get a divorce yet and the motherfucker is in another woman's house." The anger in Hilda's voice contrasted deeply with her multicolored festive blouse. "And to know that I was with that man for all these years and look what he went and did to me. What would have happened if I didn't save money for my children? Lord, I would have been collecting food stamps or whoring like that lady who was killed in the restaurant."

Robin, noticing that Hilda was about to break down, slipped her hand over her shoulders. "It's okay, Hilda. Everything will work out."

"Do you see any men out there going after a thirty plus woman with three kids? Most men don't even want you if you have one, much less three. I gave this man the best years of my life and look what he left me with," Hilda said.

"He needs to be shot like a useless bull," Paula said as she made the first move to leave the bridal window.

"Hilda, sometimes things happen for the better." Andria said, hoping her comments would cheer her friend up.

"He left his kids. What kind of man walks out on his three kids?" Hilda accepted the support of Robin's arm and together the women headed to Macy's. "But you know what, I have something in store for him. I will make him regret the day he was born."

"That's the spirit, girl. We are survivors and we are all going to make it," Paula said.

Andria looked at Paula, puzzled. "Paula, isn't there a song like that."

"I never heard it, if there is one and if it's a hit then I should be collecting royalties," Paula said, marching ahead of the group.

"Sometimes I think Paula has left this planet." Andria said. "Ladies, I need to find a wedding dress for a pregnant woman, myself."

The three women laughed together as they went through the swinging doors of Macy's department store.

"I miss my family," George said as he leaned on his Lincoln Navigator.

Rashaun stood below the lone tree on the block.

"I finally got what I thought I wanted and I want what I gave up," George said, inhaling deeply.

"George, why are you talking in tongues? Have you received a special blessing or something?" Rashaun watched a cop patrol car inch down the block.

"I'm serious. I realize running women is not for me anymore—been there done that over and over. I miss my son coming and waking me up in the morning to watch cartoons. He is so funny. He taps me and asks me if I'm sleeping. He doesn't go and bother his mother, no, every Saturday morning he wakes me up to watch cartoons. Sometimes I come in at five on Saturday morning and by seven he's there tapping me. And once he gets me in front the TV you think he would let me sleep. No, every minute I nod off he touches me. I miss that."

"I feel for you, my brother," Rashaun said.

"And my wife, I didn't realize what I had until I started to deal with what I didn't have. I believe that most women are evil. Over the last few months, I have met some evil creatures," George said, shaking his head.

"And you fucked them all," Rashaun said.

"I told you I'm not all about that anymore. I don't even fuck most of these girls anymore," George said.

Rashaun took his cell phone out and started to dial.

George looked at him.

"Rashaun, what are you doing?" George asked.

"I'm calling Joanne. I think you're ready to go back home," Rashaun said.

"Just because I turned down some pussy," George said, giving Rashaun a confused look.

"George, think about it, when have you ever turned down pussy?"

"In college. I turned down Celia."

"George, you met her outside a VD clinic after you got treat for gonorrhea. And the only reason you didn't fuck her was because you didn't have any condoms."

"Well that was a long time ago."

"My point exactly."

George opened the door of his SUV and took a cloth and started to wipe the side of the truck. "Seriously though, I want to go home to my family. I'm going to call her and set up a meeting to go and talk to her about coming back. Joanne had mentioned getting counseling before. Maybe it's time."

"Hey, get me a piece of cloth because the way you're going, you'll spend the rest of the evening here cleaning the car."

George went back into the truck and took out a gray piece of cloth. "Catch." He threw it at Rashaun who caught it in the air.

"Why don't you take your family on a trip?"

"Where?"

"Grenada. It is a beautiful Island, the only thing you have to watch out for is the sand flies and mosquitoes," Rashaun said.

"You really think Madam Unida could help me?" George asked.

"She helped me and if she can't, you would have had a nice vacation with your family," Rashaun said, rubbing vigorously.

"You think Joanne would go for that?" George asked.

"Knowing your wife, I think she will do whatever it takes to make the marriage work. I told you before and I'm telling you again, you have a good wife there. If I were you, I would do whatever it takes to grow old with her," Rashaun said, wiping the taillights on the truck.

"I will."

"George, why did you have to buy this big-ass truck?" Rashaun asked as he started on the back bumper.

"I guess I won't need it anymore." George pulled out the floor mat. "Naw, I like it. I'm keeping my truck."

"Okay, I just don't want to hear your name mentioned in the same breath as that R&B singer."

"No. Besides being out of the game I don't pick the flowers when they are budding, I pick them when they have blossomed and ready to be picked," George said, shaking the mat. "Forget about R. Kelly. What's up with Tyrone's sister."

"Nothing," Rashaun said.

212

"This is the second time in life I have to separate myself from you, the first I'm sure you remembered when you left that girl in your bed. I met Yvonne the other day and if her shoe didn't have some dirt on it I would have started licking from that point up. This girl is absolutely gorgeous. For the life of me, I can't understand what she sees in your black ass but she does like you. I was trying to kick it to her and she kept asking me questions about you. She calls you D.C. for Christ's sake. I am not putting down Andria and I know my wife is beautiful but Yvonne would drop the sales of Viagra," George said, panting as he continued to buff the car.

"Timing, in life it means everything. A few years ago, I would be on that like white on paper. I love Andria and I'm not going to jeopardize that even though I enjoy the ego push." Rashaun flap the cloth to get some of the dirt off.

"You are my hero. I hope one day I will have that willpower. Next time I'm paying someone to clean this fucking car. I can't spend the rest of my life cleaning a fucking truck," George said as he went to the hood of the car.

"You are the only person I know who starts cleaning a car from the sides and leaves the hood for the last," Rashaun said.

"If I did it any other way I wouldn't finish."

Rashaun felt the first drop hit his head.

He looked up.

The sky had become very cloudy.

"Motherfucker, I can't believe this." George cursed

Rashaun threw the cloth at George who caught it and threw it inside the truck.

"I guess that's it," Rashaun said.

"Do you believe this shit?" George said as he watch the rain hit his car.

"Did you check out the weather this morning?" Rashaun asked.

"This morning I was in Jersey and I definitely wasn't thinking of the weather," he said.

"Well guess what?" Rashaun asked.

"What?"

"It's raining."

The men jumped into the Navigator.

"Let's go by Sally's restaurant," George said as he brought the truck's powerful engine to life.

"Sounds good to me," Rashaun said and grabbed his seat belt.

As soon as the men pulled out, the rain came down in torrents. George continued to curse the weather as they drove through the streets of Brooklyn. When they parked illegally in the Auto Zone parking lot next to Sally's the rain stopped. This only angered George more. Only his mother was speared his venomous tongue.

"It feels really good to get someone out of the system," Mrs. Brown said as she signed off on the folder Andria had given her.

"Yes. China will be very happy to have her family back together again," Andria said as she sat down on one of two chairs facing Mrs. Brown's desk.

"Pregnancy looks good on you Andria. This is your first, right?" Mrs. Brown asked.

"Yes, it is," Andria said,feeling a little bit embarrassed.

"Well you know a child is God's blessing, but we hardly see that in our line of work. But I truly believed that it is a blessing. Most of our clients see children as unwanted burdens. I guess when you look at where they are coming from you can understand their attitude. I always wanted a child but I guess it wasn't in the cards. Now, I'm way too old and my husband is looking at the sunshine state."

"Why didn't you adopt?" Andria asked.

"I don't know, I just never thought of it. We kept trying and trying to have one by natural means. The doctor couldn't find anything wrong with either one of us but I just wouldn't get pregnant. Finally, my husband and I gave up. But sometimes I think it is for the best," Mrs. Brown said with a look of contentment.

"I'm sometimes scared of the future for my child but I guess our parents and their parents before that went through the same thing." Andria rubbed her stomach unconsciously.

"With a child, there is never the right time. There will always be changes going on in the world. I always believe that a parent can only teach a child what he knows. There is no way that anyone can protect his or her children from the world at large. What a parent can do is be a good guide. I don't believe in sheltering the child because that will lead to exposure by the wrong individual. You don't want your child learning about sex from an unscrupulous teacher. What you want to do is give your child maximum exposure but with an explanation."

Andria did not expect a lecture on child rearing when she brought the papers for her supervisor to sign but Mrs. Brown obviously had a lot on her mind.

Mrs. Brown continued, "You see there are a lot of parents out there who knows absolutely nothing about child rearing. I call some of them TV moms-- they basically do everything they see on a sitcom. In the eighties a lot of parents loss control of their children by following *The Cosby Show* model. The application of the Cosby family model in the wrong environment—let's say the projects—fails miserably. The peer pressure that is exerted on a child in that environment couldn't be replicated on the show. A person's mere existence is a constant fight in some of these environments. Your fiancé is a lawyer, ah?" Mrs. Brown asked.

"Yes, he is."

"Obviously from the way you act at work he does treat you right. Except for those one or two times when you have been totally stressed. I'm not saying that it had anything to do with him." Mrs. Brown did not waver in her concentration on Andria.

"I did not know I was being watched at work," Andria said, her voice showing her growing anger.

"Andria, we are all being watched. A person who thinks that he is not the subject of someone's discussion at work is a fool. I'm sure you or your office mates have said something about me sometime or the other."

Andria started to blush.

"Don't blush because it is expected. Your attitude at home and at work will determine how your child sees life. Your fiancé is looking forward to having the child?" Mrs. Brown asked.

"He hasn't stopped buying baby clothes," Andria said, smiling.

216

"Once you get that from your man the rest is easy sailing. You don't have to tell me that he will require the best for his child. You don't have to tell me that he will teach and spend time with the child. A man who makes preparation for his child has already accepted the child in his life. We know especially in our area of work once a man finds out that there was conception he is already out the door. He wants absolutely no part of raising a child. The next few years he most likely will spend trying to forget that somewhere there is a child with his DNA. The law has been aggressive in bringing these men back into their children's lives by having them pay child support. But child support doesn't make a parent. Child support might add a few extras on the kitchen table but the support is lacking. Ask any good parent whether they want more child support from a man or a father for their child."

Mrs. Brown's phone rang and she picked it up. "Hold on," she whispered into the phone.

Andria took the folder off Mrs. Brown's desk. "I'l talk to you later," she said and walked out the office. Andria dropped the folder down on her desk and headed to the door. She had received a call from Hilda earlier to meet for a lunch date. Hilda sounded very distraught so they had made arrangements to meet at The Inn on Atlantic Avenue. As soon as Andria got out of the front door a cab was just letting out a young white woman who looked to be in her early twenties and a black child maybe six or seven years old. Andria stood next to the car door as they exited.

"Mommy, where are we going?" The child was dressed in a blue jumper suit with a puffy black jacket.

The young woman looked very pale. "We're going to meet your mommy."

"I thought you were my mommy," the child quickly responded.

Andria closed the cab door. "The Inn," she said to the cabdriver.

"The West Indian restaurant on Atlantic Avenue?" he asked.

"Yes."

"Nice restaurant. The price is a little high but I guess that's what you pay when you live in this neighborhood." He looked back at Andria and continued, "The waitresses are something, aren't they?"

"Um-huh," Andria muttered and looked out the window.

"Not to say that you aren't a beauty yourself. First child?" he asked.

Andria wasn't paying any attention to the cab driver. She was thinking about Hilda who had called her just before she went into the meeting with Mrs. Brown. Hilda had said that she had to talk to her about Sharon who was on her way back to New York. The cabdriver turned from Adam Street onto Atlantic Avenue and Andria looked at the tall building with bars in every window. It was one of the largest jails in Brooklyn. In the afternoon around 2:15 there would be a long line of women waiting to visit the inmates. Andria always wondered what went through the heart of a woman whose husband was sentenced to twenty-five to life.

"I have two kids myself," the cabdriver continued.

The cabdriver slowed down, "Do you want me to make a U-turn or are you going to get off here?"

Andria looked at him.

"I will make the U-turn," he said and waited for the traffic to slow down.

"Thank you." Andria said.

When she walked into the restaurant Hilda was on her second drink and it wasn't soda. Andria pulled the chair out and sat down opposite Hilda.

"What happened to you?" Hilda asked as Andria sat down.

"My boss was giving me a lecture on motherhood," Andria said, scanning the menu.

"Motherhood? I thought she didn't have any kids."

218

"She doesn't," Andria remarked.

With a wave of her right hand Hilda dismissed whatever Mrs. Brown had to say. "Girl only time and your child will determine motherhood for you."

"Anyway what's happened to Sharon. Why is she coming back to the city? The guy messed her up?" Andria asked.

"For the short time she has been there she said Chris treated her like royalty. She has not been able to say enough about him. She had finally started to get use to Atlanta when she got a letter from New York."

"What letter? Did it have anything to do with the murder in the restaurant?" Andria asked.

"No, it was nothing like that." Hilda finished her drink and motioned to the waitress.

The waitress, a slim but well-shaped young woman, sauntered over. "You guys ready to order?"

"Not yet, I want another one of these." Hilda said pointing to her glass.

"I'll order. Can I have the salmon with white rice?" Andria said.

"What do you want to drink with that?"

"Water is fine," Andria answered.

"And you, miss?" The waitress turned to Hilda.

"I'll call you when I'm ready. Just bring me my drink." Hilda used her right hand to dismiss the waitress.

The waitress rolled her eyes and walked away with her lip turned up.

"What are you doing? You trying to become a drunk?" Andria said.

"That's the least I can do after what's been happening with me. I have lost my husband to another woman with four kids. I have witnessed a brutal murder. My best friend moved away only to return HIV-positive."

"What? Sharon got AIDS?" Andria shouted, creating unwanted attention.

"Andria, would you like to broadcast it to the world?" Hilda said, taking inventory of all the eyes that were focused on their table.

Andria looked around feeling as if she had somehow betrayed her friend's trust to the world. "I'm sorry, Hilda," Andria said.

"Andria, don't worry about it. Who cares what these people in here think?" Hilda said as she leaned back for the waitress to put the drink in front of her.

"Hilda, is she sure? Did she take another test I know a lot of people have gotten false positives." Andria looked down at the food in front of her. She had totally lost her appetite. She picked up the glass of water and her hand shook so violently that she had to put it back down.

"Andria, are you okay?" Hilda asked.

"I need to go to the bathroom," Andria said as she eased herself off the chair and stood.

"Do you want me to come with you?" Hilda asked.

"No. I'll be okay." Tears had started to form under Andria's eyelids. She steadied herself with the assistance of the table and leaned briefly on the post in the middle of the restaurant as she made her way to the bathroom. Once she got into the tiny but clean unisex bathroom she closed the door. She sat down on the closed toilet bowl seat. The tears did not wait for her to snag a sheet of paper towel. The tears came down hard and heavy, sending tremors through her body and the baby she was carrying.

Andria thought about all the clients she had dealt with who had had AIDS or been HIV-positive. They were exactly that, clients. She had felt sorry for them but it didn't feel like if a rock had slammed down on her head. This was her friend Sharon, Sharon with the wisecracking mouth. Sharon had been given the death sentence. Andria had seen what HIV and AIDS had done to the people who were infected by it. There was the misconception that all those combination therapies worked but they didn't and sometimes the side effects of those therapies

220

were more than the patients could handle. Sharon had finally got out of the life on the streets. Andria was so happy when she decided to quit. She didn't care that her friend was leaving town because anything was better than what she was doing. Life was so unfair. Andria looked up at the pale white ceiling of the bathroom and wondered why the Lord was so harsh.

Lord, give her a break. She has endured so much, just give her a break, Andria prayed. When Andria left the small bathroom where man spoils were deposited her feet felt heavy but she was able to walk back to the table. When she got to the table Hilda was slumped over.

The waitress upon seeing Andria making her way back to the table hurried over to her.

"I told her she shouldn't have anymore but she wouldn't stop," the waitress said writing up the bill. Andria didn't look at the bill she just gave the woman her American Express card. She took out her cell phone and spoke to the receptionist at her job informing her that she wouldn't be returning for the rest of the day.

The waitress brought back the slip for Andria to sign.

"Do you have the number of a cab company?" Andria asked.

As if knowing that the question was about to come the waitress gave Andria a slip of paper with a number on it. "They are the best and they won't rip you off like most of the cab companies in New York."

"Thank you," Andria said and dialed the number on her cell phone. She went over and nudged Hilda.

"Where we going?" Hilda mumbled.

"Home," Andria said. "I'm taking you home."

"That's good," Hilda said. "I want to go home to my mommy."

Andria pulled out the chair and sat next to her friend running her hands over Hilda's hair. "Everything is going to be all right," she said to Hilda and herself.

"Sharon was finally happy," Hilda mumbled.

"Don't worry, Hilda. Everything is going to be all right," she said, again trying to stop the thoughts racing through her head.

The courtroom today, was as crowded as at the beginning of the trial.

"Pastor Thomas, you said that you had returned home unexpectedly," Rashaun said to the burly black man.

"Yes, I was a policeman working in Brooklyn South," Pastor Thomas replied. His voice went through the eight octaves as he spoke.

"You are not a policeman anymore?"

"No, I'm a pastor," he responded quickly.

Rashaun stopped as he was walking back to his seat. "Pastor Thomas, what you will learn today is nothing is obvious, that's why we're here."

The pastor gave an awkward smile.

"When you returned home on that faithful day, what happened?" Rashaun picked up a sheet of paper from the defense table.

"I found my wife and another man both naked, passed out on the bed. There was blood all over the bed," Pastor Thomas said.

"Did you call the police? Oh I'm sorry you were the police. Did you call for help?"

"No, before I did that I tried to revive my wife."

"Were you successful?"

"Yes, I was."

"At that point when you had revive your wife did you do anything to the man on the bed?" Rashaun asked, glancing at a piece of paper in front of him. There wasn't a damn thing on the paper.

"I was very happy to see that my wife was at least conscious." Pastor Thomas rubbed his hands nervously like most witnesses, his voice continuously changing.

222

"Conscious but in bed with a naked unconscious man? What did you do then?" Rashaun asked.

Pastor Thomas bowed his head. "She asked me not to do anything."

"What do you mean when you say do anything?"

"She said not to call for help. Everything was all right." Pastor Thomas started to shake. "I looked at her and the man on the bed in disbelief. How could everything be all right when you are lying in bed with blood all over next to a naked man? I wanted to shoot both of them then and there."

"But you didn't, why?"

"My wife pleaded with me not to. She said she invited the man home with her. She had met him in the supermarket in the produce aisle. He came on to her and she couldn't resist. He looked as if he was a killer and that turned her on. She had been hearing her girlfriends talk about Blackfunk and she wanted to try it. She told me it was the biggest topic of conversation among housewives in New York City. There was even a discussion about it on one of the talk shows. It was supposed to be an unbelievable experience."

"You are a very good man to sit down and listen to your wife in such a situation," Rashaun said, knowing that he would have done the opposite. "Why do you think you were so calm."

"Because I heard the calling and when you hear the calling you are not thinking about yourself."

"The calling?" Rashaun asked.

Pastor Thomas signed. "God shed light on my life."

"He made you see that you wife wasn't in bed with another man?"

Pastor Thomas lifted his head. "He made me see that I wasn't the man he wanted me to be. Over the years being a New York cop has driven me to do some awful things. I have stole, beaten men unnecessarily and alcohol had become my constant companion. I have neglected my wife to the point that I don't even know what undergarments she wears. God had this happen to me for a reason, to guide me to the path I have now chosen. I

223

have given up that other life and me and my wife have set out on a journey to everlasting happiness."

"You are still with your wife?" Rashaun looked at him as if he had just landed from another planet.

"Yes, I am with my wife. She is the most beautiful and forgiving woman on earth. She stood by me in my evil days, and for that I will be eternally grateful. People in the courtroom, you are never too lost for God, remember that you are never too lost for God." Pastor Thomas had stopped shaking.

"Pastor Thomas, another question. Did you know the man who had slept with your wife on that occasion?" Rashaun asked.

Once more Pastor Thomas shook his head. "Sadly to say I do, after the Divine intervened and I awoke that man on my bed, I recognized him."

"Who was he?"

"He was a perp I had arrested."

"Perp meaning criminal?" Rashaun asked.

"Yes, it is cop lingo for a criminal. He had done two years at Rikers for assault. I heard he went back a few months ago. He is also a lost soul, I do have to reach out to him because everyone needs help in finding our savior." Pastor Thomas said.

"You obviously have forgiven him." Rashaun said.

"Yes, my friend, I have forgiven him. The Lord said forgive everyone that trespasses against us," Pastor Thomas said.

Rashaun looked over at Kim who was definitely enjoying this. She had this silly smile on her face.

"Pastor Thomas, I see you have a bigger heart than most of us," Rashaun said. "Amen to that," a male voice in the courtroom shouted.

Rashaun walked back to his seat.

"Hold it, Pastor Thomas," the judge said as he saw Pastor Thomas getting ready to leave. "Ms. Rivers, do you have any questions for the witness?" the judge asked Kim.

Kim remained seated.

"Pastor Thomas, do you think your wife was looking to be hurt by that man?" Kim asked.

"No, I don't think she was. I think she was looking like so many people out there looking for the next thrill. I think we all have those urges, the urge to go beyond whatever boundaries we have limited ourselves to. It's like most people who take drugs, they all want something more. I just thought she was looking in the wrong direction. Praise God she found her way home to Him."

"Him, meaning that man?" Kim remained seated.

"No, him meaning the Lord."

"Have you had sex with your wife since the incident?"

Once more Pastor Thomas started to shake and put his head down as if looking for answers in front of him. He looked at the judge then at Rashaun.

"No, we're in counseling."

"No more questions, your honor," Kim said.

"Would the defense like to redirect?" the judge asked.

"No, your honor."

Andria sat down at the kitchen table and waited while her mother made tea for them.

"Have you been getting a lot of rest?" her mother asked as she covered the cups with two small saucers.

"I have," Andria lied. She hadn't been able to sleep since hearing about Sharon. Rashaun had been asking her what was wrong and she told him that the baby acted up sometime. He was so funny, reading to the baby at night. He claimed that a study was done that showed that you could advance a child's mental development by reading to him in the womb. So every night whether she was asleep or not Rashaun read to her stomach. He wanted their child to have all the advantages. She just wanted him to be there.

"You don't look like it, all that puffiness around your eyes." Andria's mother put the tea in front of her and sipped on hers before sitting down next to Andria.

"Andria, when you deprive yourself of sleep it affects the baby's growth. You have to take better care of yourself."

"Mommy, just last night I didn't sleep well. The baby and I will be fine," Andria said, hoping not to get into a discussion with her mother about the baby.

"You young people think you all know everything but you have never had a child. I have seen the way some kids come out when their parents don't take care of themselves. Remember, this is my only grandchild. I doubt I will see you have another one. I want you to have a healthy baby."

"I will, Mom, I will." Andria didn't know what her mother put in the tea but it tasted so much better than hers.

"I remember when I was having you."

Andria shook her head. She was hoping that her mother wouldn't get started but that hope was gone.

"I was living with your grandmother at that time, it was a year before me and your father got married. We didn't have much but your grandmother made sure that I didn't get any stress in my life. She would make sure that I went to sleep before nine-thirty and that I took a walk in the morning. I didn't go to Lamaze classes as they do today but I got my exercise. Those things were around but my mother had seven kids and none of us came out lacking so she wasn't going to let anyone tell her about having a baby. I didn't stop working until I was eight and a half months pregnant with you. My mother had me on her job. She was proud of that too. She told me that she just pushed three times and I came out. I had you at home. My mother didn't trust hospitals. She said they kill black babies or they put them on things that make them weak when they get older, so she made sure that I had you at home."

"Mom, I'm not having my baby at home," Andria said.

"I know that you won't but I believe my mother. Be careful who delivers your baby." Andria's mother held the cup in the palms of her hands. Andria always wondered how her mother held the hot cup when sometimes she couldn't even hold hers with the handle.

"Mom, I have a black GYN, who's great. She will be there when I'm ready to deliver. She told me to page her whenever I feel contractions and she will get to the hospital. So stop worrying," Andria said and finished drinking her tea.

"Have you been drinking the tea I gave you?" Andria's mother asked.

"Yeah, I drink it when I remember."

Andria's mother took Andria's unfinished tea from in front of her, went to the sink and quickly washed the cup. Her mother had finished drinking hers. Her mother had done that numerous times when she was younger.

"Mom, I hadn't finish with the tea."

"Andria, how many times must I tell you that it makes no sense drinking cold tea. You keep playing with it until it gets cold then you want to drink it. That doesn't make any sense at all." Andria's mother dried her hand on a multicolored kitchen towel.

"Mom, they did studies that show that you don't have to burn your mouth with tea for it to be good for you. Warm tea is just as good as hot tea."

"Then why boil it and pour it hot?" her mother asked.

"Just because they poured the tea when it is hot, that doesn't mean you have to drink it that way." Andria realized she was fighting a losing battle. When a person reaches a certain age, things stopped changing. She knew her mother would continue to make the best tea and drink it as hot as she could.

"Andria, I have been around much longer than you have. Listen to your mother," she said and headed out of the kitchen.

"I have to call Rashaun to pick me up," Andria said and pulled out her cell phone.

"Use the phone in the kitchen," her mother shouted.

"That's okay, I'll use my cell phone it's free."

"Suit yourself." Andria's mother sounded irritated. "Where is Rashaun anyway?"

"Mom, I'm on the phone," Andria shouted. Andria quickly spoke to Rashaun put the phone back into her bag and went to join her mother.

"Don't you watch TV? They say that those phones give cancer," Andria's mother said. "I'm sorry for the young people, there is an invention everyday and everything is just destroying the earth. Just the other day I heard they cloned a cat. A cat. The only people that will clone a cat are rich people. Lord have mercy on us all," she said.

Andria loved her mother but she always got upset when she visited her. She believed that her mother actually enjoyed upsetting her. She looked at her mother's hair and realized that it was turning white. She couldn't imagine her mother with white hair. And her mother always talks about dying these days. Andria wasn't sure if she wanted attention from her or it was just the way she was feeling. Andria went to the dresser and took out a comb and brush.

"Mom, sit down. Let me comb your hair," Andria said, going over to the big TV chair next to the bed.

"My hair is fine," Andria's mother said, sitting down on the chair. "Can you hand me the towel over there to put in my lap?" she asked, pointing to a red towel with white stripes next to the armoire.

Andria picked up the towel and gave it to her mother who spread it in her lap. Andria went back to the dresser and got the grease that she had given her mother who loved the smell of shea butter grease. There was a little twinkle in her mother's eyes as she put the grease on the towel in her mother's lap. Andria took the comb and started to take out the two plaits she had put in her hair a few weeks ago.

"When is Rashaun coming?"

"He said in about an hour," Andria replied.

Her mother looked up. "It's going to take more than and hour to grease and plait my hair," she said.

228

"I know, Mom. Rashaun will not be here in an hour. Rashaun never says that he will be longer than an hour. I bet you he doesn't get here in under two hours," Andria said as she continued to undo her hair.

Her mother pressed on the remote and a game show came up.

"Cable was the best thing they invented, now I can see all my game shows," she said as she settled in her chair.

Andria looked up at the old man on the TV screen, she had never seen him before. She wondered if the people who acted like fools when they are selected to participate were embarrassed when they returned to their hometown. She had a vivid imagination about the townspeople cursing at them because they made an ass of themselves and their town on television. New Yorkers didn't have that problem though. It seemed anything a New Yorker did was cutting edge. Andria sighed deeply and reserved herself to watching a game show. Two hours seemed like such a long time. Maybe this time Rashaun would surprise her and come early. No, she doubted that, especially if he was hanging out with Lance or George. Lance hadn't changed one bit since he got married. Now, sometimes when he came to pick up Rashaun he might have the Jaguar or the Land Rover. And he always had a different woman in the car. Well his wife knew what she was getting herself into.

"I feel so special surrounded by these beautiful black men," Yvonne said as she sat next to George.

"Where is Tyrone?" Rashaun asked, "I thought he was going to meet us here."

"My brother said he wasn't able to make it because he had to go somewhere with Mom," Yvonne answered.

"Anyone told you, you would make a great model?" George said, sounding pathetic as usual.

Lance and Rashaun looked at him. He was drooling constantly over Yvonne.

Yvonne looked at him as if to say that was the best he had to offer.

"Yeah, I have been told that one too many times," she said. "Lance, Tyrone told me that you were married but I don't see any wedding ring. What happened? You don't wear your wedding ring?" Yvonne asked.

Lance twirled the straw in his drink. "Me and my wife separated," he said, maintaining his cool composure.

Rashaun and George looked at him as if it was the first time they had seen him since childhood.

"I'm sorry to hear that," Yvonne said, "What happened?"

Rashaun and George simultaneously put their hand under their chin waiting for Lance's reply.

"I think we both realized that we weren't ready for that big commitment so we decided to separate for now. What about you? Do you have someone?" Lance asked. He gave Rashaun and George a conquering smile.

"I have a fiancé but I'm not too sure if he is the one. I feel that I'm settling and I don't want to do that." Yvonne smoothed her already perfect eyebrow. "What do you think, Rashaun?"

Rashaun was totally enjoying the interplay between Lance and Yvonne.

George was not pleased.

"It depends on what you are looking for and what he is giving," Rashaun answered.

"Rashaun is so diplomatic, I don't think you should ever have to settle." Lance said.

"Especially a woman as beautiful as yourself," George added. He blushed when Yvonne smiled at him.

"Someone bring this puppy some milk," Lance said, motioning to George.

"I don't know. Sometimes you think a person is right for you then you meet someone else and they turn your insides out."

Rashaun was hoping that she didn't look at him.

She did.

And it was quite obvious to the two other men at the table that she was talking about Rashaun.

"I think that if one person could do that to you, there is another one who can do the same thing," Lance said. "Sometimes it's not worth chasing at things that are not available. It is just a waste of time."

Rashaun shook his head. "I do believe that Lance has a very good point there. I totally agree with him."

"But you never know until you try," George added.

Both men looked at him.

"George, you are right. I believe wherever there is a will, there is away." Yvonne drank the last of her drink.

Lance motioned for the waitress. "Can we have another round?" he asked.

"Yvonne, so are you in town for the trial or will you be staying in the Big Apple." Lance asked.

"Well I did leave to come and make sure my brother was being taken care of by his lawyer. And thanks to Rashaun, I don't have that to worry about that I know Tyrone is in good hands." She reached over and squeezed Rashaun hands. "I also came to clear my head and I don't think that is working. It seems that there is a reason for my insecurities. I don't think I'm ready to get married."

"Marriage is a big step. You definitely cannot run into it," Lance said. "I think that's what happened to me and my wife. We rushed into the marriage and that's why we are separated now.

"So you don't live with her at the moment?" Yvonne asked.

"Oh, I still live in the same house with her for 'appearance' but for all practical reasons, it's over." Lance started on the new drink the waiter had just brought to the table.

"I hate that appearance issue. I had a boyfriend once and he went around with me as if I were a showpiece. Don't get me wrong, I appreciate the fact that men find me attractive I just hate it when that is the only thing they dwell on. It's like give me a break, everyone can see it you don't have to throw it down their throat. And to be honest he was a lousy fuck."

Everyone at the table looked at her in shock.

Lance smiled. "What happened he was too small or too quick at the gun? The bullets flew out before the gun was raised huh?" Lance asked, leaning back as he feasted his eyes on Yvonne.

"He was a black man."

"I guess size wasn't the problem," Rashaun said.

"How do you know that?" George asked.

"Because she said that he was a black man, emphasis on black." Rashaun stirred his drink. "Are you listening George?"

"He was too gentle. He treated me like an egg. He never wanted to try anything too perverted. I just wanted to have a good time. I don't want to be made love to all the time. Sometimes I want it nasty."

"You should definitely get it nasty," Lance said. "That's the problem with some men. They don't know how to treat a woman, they go from one extreme to the other. I believe in staying in the middle, sometimes hard sometimes soft."

"That's what a woman wants, a brother who understands," Yvonne said. She reached out and shook Lance's hand.

Lance held on to her hand, rubbing in the middle of her palm.

Yvonne pulled her hand back.

There was an awkward silence at the table.

"Andria is going to kill me. I told her I was going to be there an hour ago," Rashaun said, standing up.

"Rashaun, can I bum a ride with you unless it is out of the way?" Yvonne asked.

"Why don't you stay with George and Lance and have dinner?" Rashaun countered.

"No, I'm expecting an important call at home and the person doesn't have my cell number," she answered.

"You got the tab, Lance?" Rashaun asked.

"Yeah, I got it," Lance replied.

"Hold on a second. Let me go to the ladies' room." Yvonne took her purse and disappeared.

"You the man, Rashaun. Her eyes are closed to everybody else."

"Why now? All these years nothing like this ever happen." Rashaun said looking in the direction of the bathroom. "George, you better go back to your wife because your lines are not working."

"What did I do?"

"I think I could flip her but I need her alone. Four is definitely a crowd. Rashaun, why don't you hook shit up. Unless you change your mind and decide to dip in the pudding one last time," Lance said.

"No, man I'll do my best to set shit up. Sorry George, you weren't even in the park on game day," Rashaun said.

"Here she comes. Do your thing." Lance said.

Yvonne as always had the attention of the men and some of the women as she walked through the bar. "You ready?" she asked Rashaun.

"After you," Rashaun said and pointed the way.

"See you guys," she said to Lance and George.

Rashaun got into the car and pulled the door shut and slipped his seat belt on.

"Lance isn't really separated, is he?" Yvonne asked as he started the car.

Rashaun played like he didn't hear the question. "Are you going straight home?" he asked.

"Why, you taking me somewhere?" she asked.

He wasn't going to look over at her.

The place wasn't right.

A woman like that you have to talk to in public places with a lot of people.

"I told you my fiancé is waiting for me," Rashaun said and pulled out of the parking spot.

"Where is she?"

"Why?"

"Because that'll determine how fast you have to get home."

"She is at the doctor. It's a routine checkup for the baby." He didn't know why he lied but he did.

"Are you excited?" Yvonne asked.

"About what?"

"The baby, what else?"

"Yeah, it's one of the blessings in my life," Rashaun answered, pulling away from a slow-moving beige Camry.

"The other being Andria." Yvonne adjusted the seat back.

Rashaun kept his eyes on the road. "Andria and my mother," Rashaun added.

"A mama's boy?" Yvonne quirked.

"Whatever you want to call it," Rashaun said as he brushed an imaginary speck of dirt from his eyes. In the process he peeked over at her long, smooth legs.

"So what are you going to do about us?"

He could tell that she was looking at him.

The stoplight was taking so long, only in Brooklyn. In Florida or Atlanta the stoplight would never take so long.

"There is no us?"

Yvonne started to clap.

It startled him.

"Rashaun, why are you fighting the inevitable? Don't get me wrong, I admire you for that but I fell for you when I saw your picture in the newspaper. And I remember the first time I heard your voice at my father's house. I was doing something over the sink. My body shook uncontrollably. I was hoping and praying that you felt the same way I felt about you. I think it took me forever to turn around and look at you. I was hoping that my face did not betray my feelings. Then I turned around and I could tell that the feelings were mutual." She spoke slowly choosing her words carefully and enunciating.

He didn't look at her because it might betray the lust in his eyes.

Betrayal was a plague right now and it was running all over the car.

"Let me tell you what you already know," he said, keeping his eyes focused on the road. The trees that were planted on Eastern Parkway made the borough look regal in the evening. "You are a beautiful woman and most men, including myself, would go crazy about you. But, I've finally found something that I have been searching for all my life. She's the answer to my prayers and my dreams. I couldn't ask for more in a woman. Until now, no one has even threatened my commitment to her."

"Rashaun—"

"Let me finish," he said a bit irritated.

"Pull over and continue," she said.

He pulled up opposite the tennis court next to the park.

She brought her seat up.

He took off his seat belt.

"Can I?" she asked, pointing to the radio.

"Yeah," he said only looking at her hand.

She changed from 107.5 to 101.9 FM.

"As I was saying…"

"Rashaun, can you look at me when you talk," she said, turning around to him. "We're not driving anymore so that shouldn't be a problem." Driving and talking had never been a problem for him.

He wanted to say no and start the car up and drive off.

He could feel her eyes on him.

But he didn't turn.

235

In the cafeteria he had looked all over the place instead of those eyes.

He took a quick glance over at her like a little boy sneaking a peek. He was a man. There was no reason to act liked a child. He had walk away from pussy before with nothing at stake. He had to reach deep within himself.

"Rashaun, I don't want to break up your relationship. I admire the fact that you have found the right one. But I also think that I have found the right one and it is not my fiancé. I knew that when I met you."

"But I'm in a relationship. I have made a promise to Andria."

"You know what, Rashaun, just forget about it." She sounded flustered.

He looked over at her and saw her hands were covering her face.

He reached over and gently pulled them away. He should have stopped there.

She looked over at him.

He was losing it or maybe he had lost it.

She pushed his seat back.

He didn't stop her.

He should've stopped her. He should have told her that he was in love.

His hands were left outstretched. He never pulled them back after he had taken her hands from her face.

She moved those long beautiful legs.

He looked out the window.

The park was dangerous at night.

This is Brooklyn. A man should go home to his woman in Brooklyn not hang out by the park with a gorgeous woman. Trouble, was headed his way for sure.

He felt her moving around.

He kept watching two old men play tennis. It was late they should go home to their families. Soon they won't be able to see. They should leave the game and go home to the haven of

236

their families. There had to be someone waiting for them. They needed to call home and tell them not to worry they are on their way home.

She stretched one foot over his left leg.

He had already accepted the reaction of his manhood. Johnny was ready.

Marriage is the union of two people with hopes of forsaking all others.

Life threw a lot of temptations to break up that union.

His face was hot.

She came over and straddled him in the car.

He couldn't control his body, which had a reaction of it's own. He felt her heat through his pants as she sat down on him.

Her hand reached over and gently nudged his face.

This was it.

In his head he started singing, an old club song, *The roof, the roof is on fire. We don't need now water let the motherfucker burn.*

His hand circled her tiny waist. He should not have done that, sitting outside this dangerous park. He pulled her blouse out of her skirt.

She cradled his face in her warm hands.

He looked up at her.

The rest of the world had disappeared. There were only two people in this world.

The cars had stopped driving by. The two old men were not playing tennis on the court across the street.

As she brought her face down to his, he reached up to touch those lips of many dreams. Strawberries, diamonds, setting sun, they had nothing in common but those lips were a penny thrown from heaven.

Her lips were warm, gentle and sweet.

His blood was racing.

High blood pressure is the one of the top killers of black men. A stroke was eminent if not for pleasure for betrayal. A stroke outside this dangerous park in the early evening was to be his fate.

Their upper bodies clasped and there was no way for oxygen to slip through.

The drums started to beat in his head or maybe it was just his heart.

The strength came from nowhere.

He released his lips from hers and gently pushed her away from him.

The car had developed its own tint. It was a human reaction tint. It was impossible to see out and no one could see in.

He opened the door and fell out like a drunk. One foot touched the black tar as he waited for her to ease up. That gave him time to reacquaint himself to this world.

"Rashaun..."

He closed the door. He walked around the car to the sidewalk. The cars zoomed down Buffalo Street. He went to the fence and leaned against it. He didn't know when his shirt became open but it was. Summer had brought its own heat as he took of his shirt.

In life there are choices. He could go in the car and continue what they had started. He could stop a cab and send her home in it. There was a motel off Pennsylvania Avenue and another one on the conduit. And finally he could go back to the car and drive her home, which was what he intended to do in the first place.

"Fuck it," he said to no one in particular and went back into the car.

"Rashaun, you came home and changed your clothes earlier today," Andria asked as she got into the car.

"Yeah, I got out of court early so I thought I would do a few things before I met the guys at the bar," he said.

"I see you stopped at the car wash," she said, sniffing at the heavy deodorant in the car. "Why did you have them put so much deodorant in the car? I hate that heavy perfumed smell."

"Well you know these people, you tell them to do the car and they go crazy," Rashaun said. "Your mother looks good."

"Yeah. I think she's really excited about the baby." She looked in the backseat. "I'm surprised there is no shopping bags in the back of the car."

"Well I listened to you. You keep telling me that you'll start giving away the clothes if I keep buying any more," he said.

"Hey what happened to my kiss? I'm pregnant now so you don't want to kiss me anymore?" Andria asked, pouting.

Rashaun reached over and kissed Andria lightly on the lips.

"That's better," Andria said and pushed the seat back. "Now I can go to sleep while you drive us home."

He smiled as he saw her close her eyes and adjust the seatbelt over her stomach. He had watched her sleep the first time they slept together and it was one of the most beautiful things he had ever seen. And years later it was still beautiful to watch her sleep. She had a habit of curling her mouth to the left. As he drove through the streets of Brooklyn he realized that he was a very lucky man.

Funk II
Fourteen

"They are waiting for you in Mrs. Brown's office," Carol said pointing down the hall as if Andria did not know where the office was. Carol was about nineteen and had recently been hired to take over from Susan, Andria's friend, who moved on to become a receptionist in a law firm.

Andria was on her way into the doctor's office when she got call from one of the few workers that had her cell phone number. Andria didn't believe in giving out her private number. She had seen too many people become prisoners to their cell phones. She hardly ever kept her cell phone on but because of the pregnancy Rashaun told her to keep it on. And even then she usually cut it off. But as fate would have it she had it on today.

Andria knocked on Mrs. Brown's office door.

"Come in," Mrs. Brown said, her voice raspy in urgency.

Andria walked in to see two policemen standing next to Mrs. Brown's desk. Now she understood why she got all those funny looks as she walked through the office.

"Good morning." Andria motioned to Mrs. Brown and the two cops.

"Andria, this is Officer Lopez and Officer Handin from the 895 Precinct. I don't know if you heard the news about the hostage situation on Bergen Street but these officers were sent to get you. I, of course, will be going with you," Mrs. Brown said as she reached for her bag.

"What hostage situation?" Andria asked, pulling a chair out and sitting down.

"Oh, I'm sorry, Andria. I didn't tell you the full story. There was a drug bust this morning at 227 Bergen Street in apartment 912."

"I know that apartment."

"Yes, you do. It's Mrs. London's apartment."

240

"Are she and the baby okay?" Andria asked, feeling a little flustered.

"Well that is the problem, apparently Mrs. London had the baby out of the hospital."

"She did." Andria was shocked.

"Now when the cops went to do the bust she thought they were coming after her baby so she took the baby and ran up to the roof."

"That's a fifteen-story building."

"Yes, ma'am, it is. She is threatening to jump if we try to take the baby away. Our negotiators have tried to talk her into releasing the baby but she refused. She said she wanted to talk to you. We understand your condition and we'll take the necessary precautions to make sure you or the baby don't get hurt," Officer Handin said, putting on his hat.

"Ma'am, we'll understand if you do not want to get yourself involved in this situation." Officer Lopez maintained excellent posture as he spoke even though his gut protruded through the tight uniform. "This is a life-and-death situation. We need to know if you can come with us right away or we will have to leave."

Andria got up off the chair. "I'll go."

"Would you like some help, ma'am?" Officer Handin asked as Andria steadied herself.

"No I'll be okay," Andria said as she buttoned up her jacket.

Mrs. Brown opened the door and held it as Andria and the cops walked out.

Andria couldn't remember the last time she had ridden in a police car. She and Mrs. Brown sat with their knees next to each other to maximize the legroom in the car. As the police car with its siren blaring raced through Brooklyn, onlookers peered inside to see who was in the backseat.

"Step aside, coming through," Officer Lopez said as they made their way through the onlookers that had gathered in front the building.

"That's her sister," a man with a Yankee baseball cap said, pointing to Andria.

"Yeah, I saw her go to the apartment yesterday," a woman next to him concurred.

Andria knew she wasn't in the vicinity of the building the day before.

After they passed through the crowd being held at bay by the cops, the reporters stood looking up at the apartment.

Andria glanced up and saw the figure of a woman. Due to her approaching angle she couldn't tell what the woman held, but common sense told her that it had to be Mrs. London with the baby.

"I can't walk up to the fifteenth floor," Andria said.

"That's okay, ma'am, the elevator was repaired about two hours ago," Officer Handin responded.

"That elevator never works."

"Sometimes it takes news like this to get the landlord in these buildings to carry out repairs." Officer Lopez sounded as if he had seen it one too many times.

"Ma'am, I would like you to stay here while we go up with Ms. Jackson," Officer Handin said to Mrs. Brown. "We don't want the scene to get too crowded."

"I'm Ms. Jackson's supervisor and I am not leaving her alone, so either we both go up or none of us will." Mrs. Brown stood back while the elevator doors opened.

Officer Handin looked at Andria then at Mrs. Brown and held the door while the ladies entered. He followed Officer Lopez into the elevator then pressed the button for the fifteenth floor. The occupants remained in total silence as the elevator moaned and grunted as it ascended.

The elevator door opened and Officer Lopez was the first to get off. He went out into the mass confusion of cops-- some dressed in uniforms, business suits, plain clothes and Swat attire. The roof was flat with steam rising from vents located on opposite ends of the roof. Andria and Mrs. Brown followed the officers to a group of cops dressed in business suits with the

242

exception; of a big, surly officer with a row of stripes on his police uniform.

The officers were busy in discussion and they didn't see the group approaching.

"Lieutenant Scott." Officer Handin's voice rose above the chattering of the people on the roof.

"Lieutenant Scott," This time Officer Handin got the attention of all the cops on the roof.

"Yes." The short officer decked out in a police uniform turned around. The others glanced around for a second or two then continued their discussions.

"Lieutenant Scott, this is Andria Jackson, the social worker the jumper is asking to speak to." Officer Handin stepped back as Andria came up to the lieutenant.

"She's pregnant," Lieutenant Scott said looking at Andria's stomach. "Just what we need, another baby drama."

The lieutenant turned around to the group and whispered something. A tall, skinny white man dressed in a dark gray suit came forward smiling, his hand outstretched to Andria.

"My name is Dr. Kendrix. I'm in charge of the negotiation. Can we step to the side to talk for a minute?" he asked.

Andria shook the doctor's hand and looked around. It was obvious that Mrs. London wasn't on this side of the roof. She followed the doctor a few yards away from the group.

"Andria, this is a very delicate situation here, one that might not end favorably. What I'm saying is that someone might die and in most of these cases someone usually dies. The file on Mrs. London shows that social services has tried to help her but she remains dependent. Her son has the best chance of being productive."

"You are trying to tell me that Mrs. London is expendable? Who gives you the right to make that decision?"

Dr. Kendrix shook his head. "I'm not trying to fight with you. We do not have that time. There will be no debate on society here because there are two lives hanging in the balance.

What I am saying is that you have a woman holding a baby on the edge of a roof that is fifteen stories high. I would love it if you can tell her to move away and we can take both mother and son to the hospital but from talking to her I don't think that will be possible."

Andria turned away from him, " Dr. Kendrix, I'm ready to talk to Mrs. London."

"Okay, fine. Please try to save the baby first. If you can get her to put the baby down, we'll try to rescue her." Mr. Kendrix shook his legs in an attempt to get rid of invincible ruffles.

Andria walked to the other side of the building where about ten other policemen were huddle in a group about fifteen feet from Mrs. London and her baby. As Andria approached, Mrs. London took one foot off the roof railing. The group with the exception of Andria joined the rest of the policemen watching Mrs. London and her baby.

"Stop right there, Andria," Mrs. London shouted.

"Okay, Mrs. London, how are you?" Andria didn't know what else to say, she had had tense situations with clients before but never like this.

"All I want to do is keep my baby. I tell you, he's going to be a star," Mrs. London said rocking the baby ever so gently.

"I believe you, Mrs. London, but you have to get away from the edge of the roof."

"No, I won't. If I do that they'll lock me up," Mrs. London shouted at Andria. "And it is all your fault."

"No, Mrs. London, I want what's best for you and the baby too," Andria said.

"And you think what's best for the baby is to put him in a foster where he can be raped and abused. How do you think all my children ended up in prison? Do you think they were born bad?"

"No, Mrs. London, I think there is good and bad in everything. I promise I will find the best home for your child."

"You won't have to because my baby will come with me wherever I go." Mrs. London put her right foot back on the edge of the roof.

"Mrs. London, get away from the edge of the roof. You might slip and fall."

"All I want for my child is the best. I want him to go to the best schools, live in the nice neighborhoods and go to one of those Ivy League schools to play basketball." Mrs. London looked down at the baby who had begun to cry.

Andria wondered if the baby was dressed properly.

"Mrs. London, the baby is crying, maybe he's sick."

"He is fine. He is just fine," she said, continuing to rock the baby.

"He needs feeding. Do you want to sit down and feed him?" Andria said.

"You're trying to trick me like the policeman," Mrs. London said.

"No, Mrs. London, I just don't want the baby to get sick. You have been outside for hours. Maybe you could come in and get warm and feed the baby." Andria started to edge closer.

"Stay right there. I can feed the baby myself," Mrs. London said as she opened her shirt and slipped a nipple in the baby's mouth. "You see. I am feeding him right here."

"I see, Mrs. London, but you can't stay out here for the rest of your life," Andria said, starting to feel a slight shiver from the cool spring air.

"I told them I'm not responsible for my husband's drug dealing. I didn't tell him to bring drugs in the house. I have no control over my husband; he is gone half of the time. But they come breaking into my house to take my husband and my baby away. I won't let them do it. I won't let Satan get my child."

"Satan won't get your child, Mrs. London, I'll make sure of that. I will make sure nothing happens to him. I promise." Andria pleaded.

"Andria, I know you mean well but you don't understand. You think taking the baby away from me is the

245

right thing to do, but it's not. I can offer a lot more to the baby than any of those foster homes. This baby is special and I won't let anything happen to him. But no one will listen to me. I know if I get off this ledge right now they will take the baby from me and put me in a hospital. I won't ever see him again."

Andria knew Mrs. London was right. This had gone way beyond her. The media must have splattered the story all over the news. There was no way that Mrs. London was going to see the baby again. But Andria had to think about saving lives. She couldn't be concerned about what happened in the future. Right now she had to try to get Mrs. London away from the edge.

"Mrs. London, I spoke to the police," Andria said, glancing back at the officers huddled around. " They said that they wouldn't take the baby away from you."

The officers nodded in unison.

"They're lying, Andria. You know that as well as I do. New York City police officers are all liars." Mrs. London sat down on a maroon stone about twelve inches wide that went all around the edge of the roof.

"I know they're liars but the media is here. If they promise you in front of the media then they will have to stick to it."

"No they won't. I'm the story for today. Tomorrow I will be forgotten and so will their promise. Andria, I lived in this city too long to not know about New York cops. I'm sure they don't mind if I fall off the roof right now. Look at all their white faces, just one less nigger to arrest." Mrs. London looked over at the group of policemen as she spoke.

"No, Mrs. London, this time it is going to be different. I promise you. I won't give up on you and your son. Give me a chance to show how I can help. I cannot promise you that they won't take away your child initially but once you show them what a good mother you can be, your son will be right back with you. I promise," Andria said not sure why she was promising things she had no control over. "Look at me, I'm pregnant too."

246

"I know. That's why I wanted o talk to you. I knew you would understand. But your situation is different. There is no one trying to take your baby away. I'm sure you are planning to send your child to the best schools and live in the best neighborhoods. I want that for my child but it is just a dream. I have been in the system all my life and I will die in the system the same way my mother died in it. I can hope and dream for a better life than that but it won't happen in this lifetime. Do you know my son's name?"

"No."

"It's Elijah."

"Beautiful name. I'm sure he'll be very famous one day."

"Not if I don't take care of him. No one will take care of him like I will. I won't allow anyone to take carc of him."

Andria moved to the right. She was starting to feel the weight of the pregnancy.

"Here." Andria didn't hear him approaching but Dr. Kendrix brought a chair for her. "Try to get her to give you the baby. You are doing good," he whispered and went back to the group.

"Mrs. London, can I hold Elijah?" Andria asked. "I promise I won't give him to the cops.

"No, Andria. Under normal circumstances I would bring him over to play with your child but these aren't normal circumstances. I alone will get to hold little Elijah." Mrs. London looked down at her son.

"Let's change that, Mrs. London. Give your son a chance to play with my child when he or she is born. Step away from the edge and give your child a chance to live. Come with me," she said, stretching her hand out.

"No, Andria. You know my son will never get a chance to play with your child because he would be brought up in the system and from one system he will transfer to another. You know the fate of my children. Their files are in your office. Most of them are in prison. I will not let them put Elijah in

247

prison." Mrs. London rubbed her nose against Elijah's face. "Mommy will not let them put you in prison."

"Mrs. London, there has got to be a better way. Don't do this to yourself and your son. Life has thrown some curves your way like it has done to all of us but you can't give up now. You are a fighter—our people are fighters—but you have to be alive to fight."

"Andria, I've fought all my life. I'm tired of fighting. I'm glad that you were able to come over and talk. Even though I wasn't too fond of you I think you are a good person. All my life, bad people have surrounded me. It is good to see a good person. I told you from the beginning that this child was special and I won't let anyone take him away from me. I think you should go now and leave with a clean conscience. You have worked hard and you have done your best for me." Mrs. London stood.

"Please, Mrs. London don't do it. I'm begging you don't do it." Andria edged a step closer, tears beginning to fall from her eyes. "Let me hold the baby. Give Elijah to me, I promise I will take good care of him," Andria pleaded.

Mrs. London lifted her son in the air.

Andria heard the patter of steps behind her.

"Lord, forgive us." Mrs. London started to pray, keeping the child up in the air.

Andria saw the two officers that she had met earlier next to her. This time they were stripped of their guns, belt and all other material that the cops carried with them on patrol.

She knew immediately what they were going to do.

They looked back at their commanding officer for the signal.

Mrs. London continued to pray.

The baby began to cry.

The officers stepped forward.

Andria prayed silently.

Mrs. London turned around and looked over the edge of the roof.

The officers looked back as they awaited the signal.

Andria sat on the chair.

Mrs. London turned and ran to her left.

The officers took off.

Andria put her head down and prayed; this time she did it aloud.

Rashaun picked up the phone just before he headed out the door. "Hello," he said impatiently.

"Rashaun, this is Yvonne. We have a problem."

Rashaun reached Tyrone's house thirty minutes after he hung up the phone. When he drove up the driveway he saw Yvonne coming out the front door.

"Yeah, Tyrone is gone." He spoke into the cell phone. "But I know you are at work so I don't expect you to help me look for him."

"Fuck the Board of Ed. There isn't much you can do for these kids anyway," George said over the phone.

"Good so I will cover the hot spots. You can cover the regular places."

"I'm going to give Peter a call and see if he is available. I know he will be because he doesn't do anything on that job anyway. And since he left his wife, all the boy's been doing is moping around. At least this will keep him busy for a sec or two."

"I forgot Pete left his wife. I've been so caught up with this case. Did she do the operation?"

"No, she refused. She told him that it was on him. I guess he felt differently."

"Next time we have to make sure that Pete gets a taste before he buys the whole meal."

"You know how some restaurants are, they don't want you to taste the meal."

"For Pete's sake he has to leave those restaurants alone. Anyway call me. My cell will be on."

Rashaun clicked the red end button as Yvonne came up to him.

"I didn't know where to look because I haven't really hung out with my brother." Yvonne was dressed in DKNY jeans with an Armani Exchange sweater.

"He could be anywhere right now," Rashaun said as he walked into the house.

"Did he talk to you this morning?" Rashaun asked.

"No, I passed by this morning and I saw him getting ready so I thought he had called you or something. My father looked out this morning and he saw him running down the street. My father put his clothes on and ran after him but he was already gone. He and my step mom went out to look for him. I told them I would wait for you so we can go and look for him together. I...."

Rashaun's cell phone started to ring.

He put a finger up to silence Yvonne.

"Andria?"

"Rashaun, are you busy?" Andria asked.

"Yeah, Tyrone seems to have run away and we have court in a few hours," he said.

"Well go ahead and look for him."

"Are you okay?" he asked.

"Yeah. I'll be all right. We'll talk later."

"Are you sure you're okay?" Rashaun asked.

"I've seen better days but I'm going to Hilda's house. I'll see you later. Call me on the cell when you find Tyrone."

Rashaun heard call waiting and checked the caller ID. It was George.

"I got George on the other line so I'll buzz you later." He pressed the green send button as he stepped into the car.

Yvonne jumped into the passenger seat.

"Yeah, George. What's up?"

"I got Pete, we're going to check Port Authority."

"Okay, I'll drive through LaGuardia and JFK then I'll stop by the all-day spot. Maybe he's reminiscing."

250

"Tell that sweet thing at the spot that I didn't forget about her," George said.

Rashaun clicked the red button on the cell phone and hooked it up to the car charger.

Yvonne pulled her seat belt over her shoulder and Rashaun backed out of the driveway.

"That was such a dumb thing for Tyrone to do," she said.

"Pressure can be quite overwhelming, Tyrone is not the first person to try to skip out coming to the end of a trial. When I was with the firm, I had this one client from Jamaica who was on trial for a kidnapping and aggravated assault. He skipped town the night before the verdict was read. I saw him up here the other day and he had a new identity. It's not easy when you are looking to spend the rest of your life in jail. That case was a rough one. I think he would have gone to jail for sometime." Rashaun looked at his watch. Court was starting in two hours. "We'll hit the airports first."

"Okay," Yvonne said, becoming very pensive.

"What's on your mind?" Rashaun asked as he eased onto the Belt Parkway from Rockaway Avenue.

"You're the first man who ever walked away from me," she said.

"You're talking about me dropping you home after we left the park?" Rashaun asked scanning the road ahead.

"Yeah, most men would have fucked me right there or have taken me to a hotel. But you didn't," Yvonne said, looking miffed.

"Believe me it wasn't easy. It took everything I had to get back in the car and take you home. Even when I was driving you home I still felt like going until I got to that motel in Queens."

"So what stopped you?" she asked.

"Me. I told myself I don't want to get back into that life again. I want to give this relationship with Andria an honest try. I read this book by this tennis player."

251

"Who, Ashe, Days of Glory?"

"Yeah."

"I read it too."

"I want to be able to say the same thing that he said before he died."

"What's that?"

"He said he had never been unfaithful to his wife. I think that is a big accomplishment in this day and age. It doesn't seem like much but to me it shows a lot of character."

"I think you are well on your way to accomplishing that. It's all about ego and you have a big one."

Rashaun couldn't help but smile.

She continued, "You know I'm right. You're the first person I met who has a ego bigger than mine."

"Life hasn't been easy," Rashaun said as he looked at the signs for the different air carriers."

"With all these carriers how will you choose which terminal to go to?" Yvonne asked.

Rashaun looked over at her.

"You really don't know your brother, do you?"

"We've been apart for a long time."

"Tyrone only travels on one airline."

"Which one?"

"Delta. He refuses to travel on anything else regardless of the fare. I remember once we were going to Miami carnival and American Airlines had this great special around one hundred dollars roundtrip. Everyone went and got tickets but Tyrone. He took Delta and the ticket was $250."

Rashaun pulled up to the domestic departure gates.

"Take over," he said, putting the car in park, "If they ask you to move, drive around and meet me here in fifteen."

Andria got of on the Flatbush/Nostrand exit on the 1 train. She preferred to take the number five train, which usually runs express, but it wasn't running this time of the day.

After walking out of the station Andria stopped by the Golden Krust restaurant to pick up some beef patties and coco bread that she was positive Hilda and Sharon would devour in less than five minutes. As soon as she got out of the bakery she heard the horn of a gypsy cab driver with two older ladies who were watching with inquiring eyes as Andria made her way into the back seat. Andria felt she should have told them that the child she was carrying did not belong to their husbands or any relative associated with their great family.

"Glenwood and Eighty-sixth Street," she said to the driver.

"I don't go that far." The driver replied in a heavy West Indian accent.

"Okay," Andria began to make preparations to leave the cab.

"But seeing you in that condition, I'll do it today," he said and began to slowly edge the car down Nostrand Avenue. He blew the horn to attract the attention of a few people he saw standing on the side of the street but they ignored him. With a big sigh he headed down Glenwood Avenue with an incomplete load.

Andria got off at the end of Eighty-Sixth Street and made her way up the block. Hilda's two-family house was located in the middle of the street. She had rented the first floor to an Arab couple who had taken great pains to show their patriotism with American flags on each window of the house. Andria walked up the two-step landing before heading to the second floor. She rang the doorbell, which was loud enough so that someone walking on the street could hear it clearly.

The door opened and Sharon dressed in faded FUBU jeans and Spelman College sweatshirt came out to greet Andria.

"What's up, girl? I know you thought you guys got rid of me," Sharon said pulling Andria into the house.

Andria looked puzzled. She expected to see a depressed person not this happy person that greeted her.

"You guys were drinking in the middle of the day?" She asked as she sat beside Hilda on the couch.

"Nope. This is how we behave when the kids are not here," Hilda said. "*All My Children* is on."

"Wait I'm out there busting my butt with my pregnant self and you guys are home having a good ole time?"

"Andria it's one o'clock and you left work already."

"Well girl, that's a whole different story. Today there was nothing but drama from the time I got to work to when I left. I could have gotten a police escort to your house but I know about your nosy neighbors. I don't want them to start talking more than they already do," Andria said giving Sharon the bag with the patties and coco bread.

"I can't believe you bought beef patties and coco bread look at me I'm already three hundred pounds," Hilda said.

"So I'll have yours," Sharon said as she put her beef patty between the coco bread.

"You better give me that bag," Hilda said, making an attempt to grab the brown bag from Sharon.

"What about your weight, Hilda?" Andria asked.

"I just have to look for a skinny man who appreciates a little meat on a woman's bones."

"Well, I don't care I'm going to get skinny anyway once that AIDS take me. But it's all right." Sharon slumped down on the sofa next to Andria.

"Please, girl, I don't ever think you are gonna be skinny, not as long as there is food out there. That big ass of yours isn't going nowhere," Hilda said as she stood long enough to grab the bag from Sharon.

"What does a pregnant woman have to do to get something to drink in here?" Andria said, looking at Sharon and Hilda.

"Get it yourself," Hilda said as she took a huge bite of her patty. Unlike Sharon she ate hers without the coco bread.

"Andria, you are a few months pregnant, yet you act like you are about to have the baby tomorrow," Sharon said walking to the kitchen.

"You guys just don't know what it's like to carry a child," Andria said, making herself comfortable on the couch.

"Andria, this bullshit you trying might work on Rashaun but it is not going to work on me. I stayed at work for eight and a half months when I was pregnant with my first child. I know what it's like to have a child," Hilda said, wiping the crumbs from her mouth.

"Here we go, baby," Sharon said, giving Andria a glass of apple juice.

"Apple juice!" Andria looked up at her.

Sharon continued on to her place on the loveseat. "Yeah, because you are acting like a big baby."

"Can you add some water to it? It's a little bit too strong," Andria said, taking a sip and pointing at the glass.

"Andria!" Sharon shouted.

A phone began to ring and everyone turned to look at their cell phones.

Sharon flipped hers open and stuck out her tongue to the rest of them.

"Chris." Her face changed. "Hold on." She walked out of the house onto the porch.

Andria and Hilda looked at each other, not saying anything.

"How's she doing?" Andria asked Hilda when Sharon went out the door.

Hilda put the coco bread back into the bag and placed the bag on the center table.

"She goes and comes. Today she seemed to be in a great mood. Yesterday she wanted to end it all. She has been seeing this specialist and he is trying the combination-therapy drugs."

"I can't imagine what she is going through. She hasn't even started to live yet and she has to prepare for death. I thought she told Chris about it," Andria said.

"She left him a letter but she didn't talk to him face-to-face. I think she told him to go and get tested."

"You think he did? That's why he's calling her?"

Hilda got up of the sofa. "I hope he is negative because Sharon will die if she finds out that he is positive. You want some more juice?"

"No, this is fine. How you doing otherwise?" Andria asked.

"Well it's difficult explaining to the kids why their father isn't here but they seem to be coping. They don't know about Sharon, and I have no intention of telling them because they are so happy she is here. She spoils them rotten and she helps them with their homework and everything."

"That's good. It will keep her mind off things," Andria said. "Does she need money or anything?"

"I think she is okay for now."

Sharon came back into the room and closed the door slowly.

"I guess you guys know that was Chris. He got the results back."

Hilda had stopped on her way to the sofa.

Andria barely held on to her glass.

"He's negative. The doctor told him he has to do a follow up test but for now he is negative." Sharon walked back to her seat.

"Well why are you looking so sad?" Hilda asked.

"He wants me to come back and live with him," she said.

"That's good," Andria said.

"That's what's wrong about this whole thing. Chris is very good. He deserves better than what I have to give to him," Sharon said.

"Sharon, it's not your choice. Who's to say that you aren't the best thing for him?" Hilda said.

"Love is a strange thing, Sharon. There is no accounting for where it's coming from. It takes a lot for a man to love a

256

woman and when he loves us in spite of our faults it's a blessing. I think you should go and curl yourself in that man's arms because there aren't too many of good men around."

"I could attest to that," Hilda said.

"I don't know what to do. I didn't think I would ever hear from him again and he calls me crying on the phone. He said how much he missed me."

"Crying? I never got any man to cry over me before," Hilda said. "What do you do that I don't?"

"Hang from the ceiling," Sharon said, her face starting to relax.

"Talking about hanging from the ceiling. You will never know what Rashaun did to me last night."

"What?" Hilda asked.

"I told the fool I wanted to make love and he went to the closet."

Sharon snickered. "Don't tell me he came back with whips and chains. I didn't think you guys got that kinky."

"Sharon!" Andria shouted.

"Okay, go ahead," Sharon said, still smiling.

"The boy came back naked except for his weightlifting belt around his waist talking about if he had to do work, he had to be prepared. He didn't want to hurt his back."

"No, you aren't serious?" Hilda said, laughing.

"Rashaun is a riot," Sharon said.

"I made him suffer for that. Every opportunity I got I put my full weight on him. When he was finished the whole room smelled like Flex-all. It was the funniest thing. You should see him, rubbing every muscle in his body."

"You and Rashaun are a match, I would say heaven but that would be giving the Lord bad credit," Hilda said.

"What's up with Debbie?"

"Well..." Hilda said.

"That covers the airports," Rashaun said as he got into the car. "I hate LaGuardia. Flights are always delayed there."

"This is the hub for most of the small airlines," Yvonne said as she strapped on her seatbelt for the third time, nestling the shoulder harness between her firm breasts.

"Let me prepare you for where we are going next. This place is call Night and Day. It is not legitimate so we enter at our own risk. Cops can raid it at any time and whoever gets caught, they have to deal with it. It is not a strip club or a lap-dance club, in this place anything goes 24/7. Now it's fine if you don't want to go in there, you can wait in the car."

"And miss the excitement? I don't think so," Yvonne said.

"I warned you."

"What do you think goes on in Washington? You forgot that's where President Clinton had his office and the mayor was Marion Barry."

"You got me there. What can be more corrupted than a group of politicians?" Rashaun said, looking at his watch and accelerating.

They got off on Farmers Boulevard and Rashaun drove through some residential areas until he got to a corner store.

"This is a corner store," Yvonne said. "We got plenty of those in Washington."

"We're definitely not here to buy cigarettes," Rashaun said as he got out of the car.

"Something is definitely wrong." Yvonne said looking at the big Blackman behind the counter. "Not too many black people own corner stores. Even I know that as a little girl growing up in New York."

"Give me a minute," Rashaun said and went up to the man behind the counter with a bag of Doritos.

"Get me a pack of Trident," Yvonne said as Rashaun walked away.

"Let's go," Rashaun said to Yvonne a few moments and began walking to the balk of the store. When he got there he looked through a small glass window and waited.

Yvonne stood next to him looking around constantly.

There was some loud clinking noise as locks were opened.

Rashaun and Yvonne stepped in and were greeted by two big fat guys obviously on a diet of fried chicken.

Rashaun went into a shoulder length stance and spread his hands for the searcher. The fatter of the two patted him down reaching way between his balls. Behind him and unseen until now was a young girl about twenty-one years old.

"Twenty dollars?" she said.

"Hey, watch it," Yvonne said as the man that had search Rashaun earlier attempted to do the same to her.

"Sorry, babes, I didn't know you were sensitive there," he said as he passed his hands between her legs.

"You going to lick your finger after you finish," Yvonne said as she walked away from the bouncer.

The big man shivered and said, "Uh, I like them spicy," his squeaky voice betraying his intimidating presence. Rashaun waited for Yvonne to catch up with him and they headed downstairs.

As they walked downstairs, the wooden stairs creaked and the wall in its pastel gray invited only the lonely. At the bottom of the steps they met another bouncer who looked them completely over before they proceeded.

The basement was crowded; there were men of all ages in suits among those who seemed to have spent their lives on a street corner. There was even a few white men sprinkled around the room like pepper spray. Yvonne, upon her entrance became the only woman with more than a G-string and a see-through bra on.

"Fresh meat," a young man shouted at Yvonne as she and Rashaun made their way through the intoxicated crowd. At a makeshift bar on the right side of the basement a young girl made a combination of drinks that essentially mixed orange juice, soda or ice with a variety of hard liquor. Behind her were stacks of Heineken. On the counter was a cup with a few five-and-one-dollar bills thrown in. She flashed a smile that beckoned the hands of a dentist to straighten teeth that had never been touched by a hygienist. On a stage made up of plywood and pieces of four by four two women explored the crevices of each other's bodies. The men, gyrating and shouting, threw money at them, while others tried to put their money in places reserved for the birth of a child. A few chairs that lined the walls of the basement were occupied with men sitting and women gyrating on top the men.

"I'll be right back." Rashaun turned to leave Yvonne for a second but then he saw the hungry eyes feasting on her. "On second thought, come with me." He grabbed her by the hand and went to the deejay booth.

"Rashaun." A young man in his late twenties stood up from a seat he had next to the deejay who was busily going through The Notorious Big collection.

"Lennox, my brother," Rashaun greeted the young man with a hug and a slap on the back.

"What you doing in here? I thought you gave this life up," he said, keeping his eyes on Yvonne. "Don't tell me you brought someone who's looking for work."

Rashaun looked at Lennox and then at Yvonne. "No man. You can't pay for this here."

"Don't sleep on Sex gorgeous I could pay for a lot more than you think."

"I need to get to the rooms."

"She freaky like that. She needs an audience," Lennox said, gazing up and down Yvonne's body.

"Nothing like that. I'm looking for Ty. Did you see him come in?"

"Naw but let me take you back. I think the only one you know back there is the plumber."

Rashaun and Yvonne followed Lennox to a back door with a big guy standing to the right. When he saw them he opened up the door. In the room there were mattresses thrown all over the floor. Rashaun immediately recognized the plumber from his building who was fucking one girl doggie style while she ate another girl's pussy.

"The plumber," Rashaun shouted. "You taking care of business.

"I'm on the job, Black. I'm on the job," he said as he continued to fuck the girl from behind. Next to him was a white couple with a black girl. The white man was fucking the black girl while the black girl ate the white girl's pussy. There were about nine other couples in the room, each engaged in some form of sex.

"He's not here," Rashaun said, scanning the room.

"You think he's in a private room?" Lennox asked.

"Naw, Tyrone would never go into those rooms. It's too freaky in there and he's too cheap to pay the extra hundred," Rashaun said and turned around.

"You know your way out, right, Black."

"Yeah, I got it," Rashaun said and turned around.

"Sexy, you can come back anytime. I'll make sure you get VIP treatment." Lennox said to Yvonne.

"No, thank you," Yvonne said and followed Rashaun out the door.

"It feels nice and fresh out here," Yvonne said as they emerged out of the basement onto the street.

"I'm going to call your house. Maybe he went back home," Rashaun said as he pulled out his cell as they walked to the car.

Rashaun spoke briefly into the phone.

"Let's go. He's home," he turned and said to Yvonne.

"Rashaun, you ever been with any of these women down there?" Yvonne asked as she went around to the passenger side.

Rashaun looked over the car at her. "That was another life," he said and got into the car.

"Drink that, girl. It's good for the baby." Rashaun's mother hovered over the table.

Andria looked at the liquid in the glass, which didn't look like anything she had seen.

"Mom, do you want me to drink that now?" she asked, said hoping that she wouldn't have to drink it.

"It is unsweetened mauby bark. I boiled it myself."

"I like mauby. Rashaun and I had it in Grenada."

"Those Grenadians like too much sugar. They make everything sweet, sweet," she said, pouring herself a glass. "Go ahead. Drink it"

Andria watched as Albertina drank the dark brown liquid.

Andria did the same but instead of drinking and swallowing she spit the drink all over the table. "This thing is extremely bitter," she said, getting up and running to the sink to drink some water. She finished the water and opened the refrigerator and poured a glass of orange juice and quickly drank it.

Albertina took a rag from the side of the sink and cleaned the table.

"You and Rashaun are made for each other. He did the same thing when I gave it to him." Albertina drank the rest of Andria's drink. "What are you doing here? Aren't you suppose to be at work?"

"I was at work earlier but we had an emergency and my supervisor told me to take the rest of the day off. I was at my friend's house earlier but they went shopping so I decide to come and visit you," Andria said.

"Well you know my house is always open for you, and I don't care if you and Rashaun are mad at each other. I'm always here for you," Albertina said and sat down next to Andria.

"I know that Mama Albertina, and Rashaun knows that," Andria said.

"So how is my grandchild doing?" Albertina asked.

"Good. The doctor told me I should be able to have a normal pregnancy."

"That's great. I can't wait to see my grandchild. You know Rashaun is my favorite."

"That I do know and believe me I know I come second where you're concerned but this is one time that I don't mind," Andria said.

"I told him to stop telling people that I'm first, but that boy's head is hard." He is a good kid though and if you treat him good he will be good to you."

"I'll definitely do that."

"And don't do like those modern woman do because a woman that has a list of *I don't do that* will always be by herself. Rashaun likes home cooked food and I know you can cook, so do that for him. Make sure he doesn't eat leftovers more than twice a week. Women these days don't know that the small things that they do will make a relationship last. They run around spending hours in the beauty salon trying to look pretty. They put on more false hair than Diana Ross and they think that will make them keep a man." Albertina spoke with a serious tone as if giving a lecture to a new pupil.

Andria knew that saying anything at the moment was futile so she kept her mouth shut. Mama Albertina face had just begun to get the wrinkles associated with age and a life of hard work. With a lot of urging from Rashaun she only worked two days a week but cooked and clean seven days a week. Rashaun wanted her to quit completely but she would not survive at home doing nothing. Andria had never visited and seen any dishes in the sink. Mama Albertina always say that if you can't keep your sink clean then your clothes must be dirty. Andria never understood that logic but she learned from her mother that you never question your elders.

263

"But I'm sure you know how to treat a man because my son can't stop talking about you. He told me that you have to work on preparing fish though."

"He did," Andria said screwing up her face.

"Rashaun only likes the way I prepare fish. It wasn't until late that he started eating it in restaurants. Fish is a very difficult thing to prepare. It requires complete seasoning and perfect timing in the oven or on the stove. Most people either overcook or undercook it. Growing up we always had fresh fish but in the United States we have to take whatever the China man says is fresh. If you are cooking fish, you should season it the night before and it has to be cooked on a slow fire so the seasoning gets into it. It took me a long time before my mother let me cook fish. Fish is the way to a West Indian man's heart."

That's because you parents raised your boys like that, Andria said to herself.

Mama Albertina went into the refrigerator and brought out a bowl covered in foil paper. She set it on the table and slowly peeled the foil from around the bowl.

Andria picked up the distinct smell of salmon but not the way she seasoned it. This one had a special clean scent.

"It smells good," Andria said.

"It's because of the secret seasoning. I don't give anyone this seasoning but because you're marrying my favorite son and I like you a lot, I'll give it to you." Mama Albertina went into the cupboard and brought out a bottle with something yellow in it.

"For each pound of fish you put a pinch of this seasoning," she said, handing the bottle to Andria. "And remember, do not overcook the fish. Twenty minutes is the limit to baking fish in the oven. Make sure the oven is preheated. Today everyone is measuring things before they put it in the pot, a good cook never has to measure anything. He can tell by lifting something what he needs to put in. it doesn't matter if he is making a dish for the first time or for the thousandth time. It is all done by feel. Did Rashaun tell you that I had a restaurant in Barbados?" Albertina asked.

Andria picked up the bottle with the seasoning with no name on it and turned it around in her hand. "No."

"Rashaun was too young to work in the shop but we have spoken about it on many occasions. My specialty was fish with that special seasoning you are holding. People use to come from all over Barbados for my fish," she said proudly."

"Why didn't you open one in New York?" Andria asked.

"I use to get the fresh fish the night before and season it. In New York you don't know if the fish is from yesterday or last week. People use to be able to tell by looking for the blood inside the fish but the fish markets found out and they put blood in the stale fish now. You can't trust anyone."

"I could vouch for that," Andria said.

At the same time the phone rang and Andria spoke to the person on the other line for a few minutes.

"It's Rashaun," Andria said. "He's just getting out of court."

"I'm going to make something for you guys. Ask him what time he'll be getting here," Mama Albertina said and went into the bathroom to wash her hands.

"He'll be here around six," Andria shouted.

"That's good, we can cook something together," she said, walking back to the kitchen.

Andria gave the phone to Mama Albertina.

Mama Albertina spoke to Rashaun briefly then hung up the phone smiling.

"That husband of yours. He is spoiled rotten."

"I can see that it's not only him that spoiled," Andria said, getting up to help Mama Albertina prepare dinner.

Rashaun and Yvonne walked ahead of Tyrone and his parents down the steps of the courthouse.

"It was really good how you use the videotape to show that Judy was encouraging Tyrone to fuck her hard," Yvonne said. "Even her facial expressions you twisted it around."

"You heard it on the tape. She kept saying more and more. I did not make it up."

"Yes, but you did do a little bit of embellishing and your audio expert is a little bit suspect. I think both of you rehearsed the whole thing. I'm not saying that this is wrong, because the most important thing is to get my brother off. And I believe that it was an accident. Tyrone did not purposely mean to hurt that woman." Yvonne took great caution walking down the steps in her high-heeled boots. She wore black leggings with an open-cut white blouse with no bra.

Rashaun hoped that no cameramen took any pictures while they were walking out of court. It would be difficult explaining Yvonne to Andria. He had made a promise to himself that he wouldn't lie to Andria. To him, that didn't mean that he told her everything because sometimes there were certain things that were better left unsaid. Rashaun moved his briefcase from his right hand to his left as they passed a group of cops who believed that not only the streets of New York belonged to them but also every other place they went. Rashaun knew better than to challenge the cops', their license to kill a black man was an unwritten rule.

"A person's facial expression and language while having sex can sometimes be misconstrued. I don't know your expressions during sex but sometimes you can swear that someone is being hurt when in fact they are in ecstasy. Please don't stop if said fast enough becomes please stop and if a man stops then he would never hear the end of it. I was with this one girl and every time we did it she would be in tears and by her screams during the whole thing you could swear I was trying to kill her. But she absolutely enjoyed having sex." Rashaun stepped around a bum who had deposited himself in the middle of the sidewalk. "Judy said a lot of things in the video but not once did she cry out for help. The last look on Judy's face

266

before she collapsed on the bed was not a look of pain but rather total pleasure. Did you see the way her body shook before she passed out? Come on. You're trying to tell me that was a woman being abused."

"Rashaun, you're a good lawyer, and I'm not doubting that there is some relevance to what you are saying. But sometimes in that video I saw a woman in a lot of pain bordering on cruelty. Granted, if Tyrone would have stopped she would have insulted him but do you think Judy wanted this to go that far?"

"I'm not saying that she did but I don't think Tyrone wanted that either. I am very sorry about what happened to Judy but I believed that it was an accident and it should be ruled as such. Anyway I have to go in the opposite direction," Rashaun said, stopping for Tyrone and his parents to catch up with them."

"I understand the wife is waiting."

"You got it," he said, smiling.

"Can I come along?" Yvonne asked.

"You're trying to replace Chris Rock, aren't you?"

"Can't stop a girl from trying."

Rashaun said good-bye to Tyrone and his parents and headed for the parking lot located under the Brooklyn Marriott. He had had a good day in court and he was feeling good about himself. He was also happy to go and see the two women he loved the most in the world. At first he wasn't sure that his mother was going to like Andria but that had worked out wonderfully. In fact, sometimes his mother wanted to see her future daughter- in-law more than him. Mentally Rashaun was already married to Andria and he treated her as such. To him a piece of paper signified nothing more than the city receiving more money from him. He would never mention that to Andria because he knew how much she looked forward to their wedding.

"We broke up last night." Paula held a cup of Jamaican peppermint tea in her hand as the long red nightgown dragged on the mahogany floor. The floor was the only thing in the apartment building, which was recently converted to a coop that was worth the $150,000 that the company was asking. Paula had rejected every offer made to get her out of the building, now they had resorted to sending her threatening letters.

Andria didn't know what to say. "Maybe it's temporary." She hoped she had said the right thing.

"I don't think so. He already has another girlfriend and she's older."

"How old is she?" Andria didn't know if it was right to ask but she wanted to know.

"Forty."

"Forty! Isn't he only twenty?" Andria asked, easing out of the chair.

"Well he was old enough to go with me and father a child." Paula gave an uncomfortable laugh. "And I thought that me being in my early thirties was too old for him. Men, young or old, are all the same."

Andria remained silent, drumming her fingers on the back of the couch. She didn't believe in Paula's relationship at first but then she saw that it was working out and that made her happy. Now the breakup happened and Paula was back to square one but with an extra package to tote around.

"So what are your plans for the weekend?" Andria asked.

"What can be my plans? Grocery shopping, maybe read a good book."

"*A Fool's Paradise* is good."

"Who's the author?"

"Nancy Flowers Wilson."

"Maybe I'll try it."

"I have to go and drop Robin and her family at the airport."

"You drove here?"

"Yeah. I told Rashaun I needed the car today so he took the train in to work."

"Robin seemed to be back tight with her husband again. I am happy for them."

"I think they both had to realize what they were about to lose and once they did, they decided to put the work into it."

Paula looked out of the window.

Again Andria was at a lost for words.

"Do you think something will ever work out for me?" Paula asked.

"I think it already did." Andria got up and walked to the window to stand by her friend. "Remember a few years ago all we were thinking about was going out to party. Now, look we both are being blessed with kids. Regardless of what happen between Rashaun, and me I'm very happy to be a mother. And believe me, I will love this child with my life."

Paula nodded.

"You are right. Sometimes we get all caught up with what we don't have and we forget to be thankful for what we do have." She smiled for the first time since Andria had came into the apartment. "I am going to be a mother, and who knows maybe Isaiah might come back or we," she said, patting her stomach. "Just got to move on."

"That's the spirit," Andria said. "You going to walk me to the door?"

"Yeah, I need all the exercise I can get," Paula said and walked with Andria to the door.

The old lady who sat in the witness chair could have been two hundred years old if not for the fact that the oldest person in the *Guinness Book of World Records* was 129. Age

269

had lined her face in a way that no plastic surgeon could remove. But, you could tell by the way she sat up on the witness stand that she was a proud black woman happy to have made it to the twenty-first century. Her thin-framed glasses rested lightly on her nose as she waited for Rashaun.

"Ms. Fatima, do you know why you are here?" Rashaun asked.

"Yes. To testify about an incident in my childhood." She was proud to show that her memory was still intact.

"Do you know what that incident was?"

"No, but if you ask me a question, I'll be happy to answer it."

There was some snickering in the courtroom at Ms. Fatima feistiness.

"Let's talk about the thirty black men that were hung around the house of the master one Sunday morning."

"Oh, that was a terrible tragedy. None of those young men needed to die."

"Can you tell us what happened?"

"Well I was very young at the time but our parents brought the kids together and told us the story."

"Go ahead. Tell us the story that your parents told you."

"Well our parents did not tell us everything at that time but later on when I was older I heard the rest of it. But this story was not unique to our time. Men were being killed just for looking at white women. It all started when the misses saw Timbut in the yard one day. Timbut was a young man a little past his twenty-first birthday. He hated the white man and he refused to go into his house. Can I have some water?" Ms. Fatima asked.

"There's a glass with water in front of you. You can have it," the judge said.

"No, I want some fresh water. Those that they sell in the bottle without the seal broken. You see, living this long has taught me a lot."

"Bailiff, can you get Ms. Fatima a bottle of water from the vending machine? Thank you," the judge said. "Ma'am, your water will be here soon."

"As I was saying—" Ms. Fatima took a white handkerchief and wiped her forehead— "most of the young women adored Timbut because he was strong and muscular with thick black lips. Like you, lawyer man," she said pointing to Rashaun, "but he wore much less clothes during those times because it was always so hot. So the missus who was the boss wife asked Timbut to work in the house but he refused. She did not mention that to the boss, otherwise he would have killed Timbut."

The bailiff brought the water and opened it in front of Ms. Fatima who thanked him before he went back to his position.

"One night while the boss had gone away the missus came out to Timbut while he was lying by the pond. And story has it that she threatened to get him hung if he didn't make love to her. As I told you, Timbut did not like white people. In fact he hated white people. That night outside on the grass Timbut did it so hard to the boss wife that she passed out. After he finished he left her bleeding and ran away up until today no one has heard from him. A boy found the missus and he went to his mother for help. They cleaned the Missus up and they brought her inside and laid her down on her bed. When the boss came back and he found his wife in bed he screamed bloody murder. One of the house niggers said that a young field niggers sex her. The house slave identified Timbut but he was already gone. The boss said he would make a lesson out of it. That same night the boss killed his wife and thirty other young black men who worked on the plantation. He ordered the slaves to bury his wife and all the slaves in one big hole."

The courtroom was completely silent after Ms. Fatima had finished her story.

Rashaun had heard it before from his grandfather but this was the first time he had actually heard someone who was actually there tell it. It made a world of difference. As he looked at the far away look in Fatima's eyes he knew she had just traveled back to that time.

"Later when we were old enough to do it we found out that what happened between the missus and Timbut was called Blackfunk. It's an uncontrollable rage between a man and a woman consenting to give all they have and take all that's given to them. There is a monument in Virginia at the site where the missus and thirty black men lay buried."

There was no applause when Ms. Fatima finished her story. Everyone in the courtroom appeared occupied with their own thoughts. A dark cloud had descended on that courtroom as if the one white woman and the thirty black men had come back to ask, why me? The eeriness of the silence only fed the imagination of those who had lost without reason. The question that cried out to be answered was who is to blame when two adults get together to share an ice cream or nitric acid.

Rashaun and Andria had set the wedding date for after the trial so no questions were hanging over their day. They wanted it to be a joyous occasion for everyone.

As time passed even though Andria never forgot about her friend Judy she was coming to terms with Judy's death and Rashaun's role in the defense of his friend. Now, she actually understood that Rashaun didn't condone what happened o Judy and in fact he was very sorry. He, however, did not see Tyrone as a murderer and, therefore, had made a decision to defend him. She knew that if the shoe were on the other foot, she would have mounted the best defense for her friend. When she looked at Tyrone she also saw the hurt in his eyes as if he carried the whole incident in his heart. At times he seemed as if he is about to give up on life. Andria didn't want him to die either. Somehow she wanted peace for everyone involved. Judy's husband, Steve, had taken the baby and moved to Orlando promising Andria that he would visit sometime in the future. Andria knew he would never return to New York City because the memories were too much for him to endure.

Andria had taken two weeks vacation from work to clear her mind because the last few weeks had been so stressful. Mrs. London had died when she fell of the roof but the baby had survived because he had fallen in the safety net the officers had put up below. Now, she understood why Mrs. London ran in the opposite direction. She didn't want her son to be raised in the system and in the end she made sure that that was the only way he was going to survive. Andria knew the same net that was spread out to catch the falling boy would eventually strangle him with its long tentacles.

Andria sat home not really paying attention to the game show that her mother loved to watch but listening for the phone to ring. When it finally rang, the loudness startled her.

She got up disorientated and looked around for the cordless.

"Andria, open the door." She started to talk back into the phone but then she realized that the voice was coming from both phone and the front door. "Andria, I want to talk to you before I leave. Please open the door," Paul shouted.

She clicked off the phone and she went to the door. "Paul, what do you want?"

"I'm leaving town. I want to talk to you before I leave."

"I don't think that this is a good idea," she said.

"Andria, I know I messed up and I acted like a fool but would you let me in so that I can say that I'm sorry?"

Andria didn't know what to do or say. "When are you leaving?"

"After I leave here." There was urgency in his voice that made her very uncomfortable. If Paul knew that she was pregnant what would he do?

"Please Andria, don't let us part like this."

She thought about calling Robin but she remembered that Robin had gone on vacation. She wanted to call Paula but Paula was spending the weekend at her mother's. She didn't want to bother Hilda because she had enough on her mind preparing to take her husband to court for child support. Hilda had visited a lawyer and found out that the letter she had given her husband wasn't worth the paper it was written on. Her eyes had nearly jumped out of the socket when she saw the amount her husband would be paying her monthly for child support based on the seventeen percent per kid. Andria and Sharon wanted him to pay her spousal support too but Hilda didn't want him jumping off Brooklyn Bridge. Sharon had gone back to Atlanta with Chris. And Rashaun, Rashaun was closing out the case Tyrone's case today.

"Yes, yes," Rashaun shouted as the not-guilty verdict was read aloud in court. He turned and hugged the solemn Tyrone. He looked back and Ms. Wheatley's eyes were filled

274

with tears of joy; Mr. Wheatley and Yvonne hugged each other. Yvonne winked at Rashaun when he caught her eye.

"Can I talk to you after the celebration?" Kim had walked up to the table from the opposite side. Rashaun was a little startled when he heard her voice.

"I was planning to go home right after but I guess I can stop by your office," he said, trying to read her eyes but there was no emotion.

"I'll see you then," she said and walked away.

Paul sat at the table, his right hand around a glass of orange juice. The last time he was given a glass of orange juice by a married woman he never finished it. But that was a long time ago.

"I'm moving to Texas."

"Sometimes a change of scenery does wonders for some people." Andria was thinking about Sharon and Chris.

"I don't want to go to no fucking Texas but the last few months haven't been too good for me. I think since we broke up things have taken a nosedive."

"Sorry to hear that," Andria said with no emotion.

Paul looked deep into her eyes.

"Any feelings left for me to hold on to?"

Andria understood what he meant completely. "Nothing."

"A man does a lot of things in his life that he is not very proud of. Over the last few years I have done everything to hurt you and everything to love you. I admit I have used every person at my disposal to get to you but you seemed to have moved on."

"I have."

"Lawyers. You know they're liars."

"Coming from you, that's a compliment."

"I guess I deserve that."

"You deserve a lot more but that's not my call," Andria said, looking at the clock over Paul's head.

"I don't think that I will be able to live without you," he said as he reached over and put his hand in hers.

She whisked her hand away and put it in her lap.

"Paul, I think it's time for you to leave."

"No," he said and slammed his hand down on the table.

Andria almost fell off the chair as she pulled back. She looked at Paul and saw anger in his face she had never seen before. She looked at the phone on the couch and then at the door. Where was Rashaun?

Rashaun emptied his pockets and went through the metal detector as the court officer handed him a pass to see DA Kim Rivers.

"She is one fine piece of work," the young court officer said, smiling at Rashaun. "I would love to spend a weekend in the Bahamas with her."

"Yeah, I know what you mean," Rashaun said and kept walking toward the elevator.

He got off the elevator and walked pass the cubicles of the assistant DAs most of them recent law school graduates. He walked all the way to the back where Kim's office stood overlooking Jay Street knocked lightly on the door.

"Come in," she said.

He walked in to see Kim sitting on a very large office chair, one similar but more expensive than his.

"I see you've come a long way," he said, putting his briefcase down and helping himself to one of the two small black leather chairs she had in her office.

"Not far enough but then that's another story. Do you want something to drink?" she asked.

"No, I'm going to dinner with the Wheatleys' later and I intend to celebrate."

"I could make you a cup of tea."

"Kim, I could spend the rest of the day chatting with you but that would take time away from my woman at home. I have already put her through so much with this trial and it's time for me to go home and be with her."

"That's what I always liked about you, Rashaun. You know how to make a woman feel special."

"Obviously I didn't do it well enough with you."

"I guess I deserved that."

Kim got up off the chair and walked around the table.

Rashaun's mouth dropped. Now he understood why she asked him to lock the door when he came in.

"Kim!" he said, starting to rise from the table.

"Did you think I was going to let a social worker take you away from me? I know you want me. Your dick is already hard." She came over and sat on her desk with her feet on the arms of Rashaun's chair She had on only a slip.

Rashaun knew he shouldn't look but he did anyway. No panties and a shaved pussy were staring him in the face. He started to count backwards from one hundred, he didn't know who told him that that would help but he was doing it.

He reached up and grabbed Kim by the arms and lifted her completely of the table and kicked the chair back so hard that it slammed into the wall.

He put her on the floor, her knees on the brown-and-white carpet.

He walked back to where the chair had fallen, taking his jacket off and throwing it on the fallen chair.

"Crawl," he said as he unbuttoned his pants.

"Rashaun," she said looking up at him.

As she did he unzipped his pants and pulled out his erect penis.

"You want it," he said.

"Yes. You know I do," she said, inching forward.

As she did so he jerked on his penis.

"You hurt me bad," he said.

"I know and I'm sorry," she said, licking her lips.

"Why?" he asked.

"I don't know," she said.

"Lift your slip up over your ass," he said

Kim did as she was told.

"Anything for you. I promise I'll do anything to make you love me again."

"Take your hand and stick it between your pussy and lick it."

Once more she did as she was told. "Please, Rashaun."

"You nearly destroyed my life."

"I will make it up to you."

"Take off your blouse and throw it over here.

She quickly took the blouse that was already opened and threw it at him.

He caught it and threw it over the big black chair she was sitting on earlier.

"How much do you want me?"

"With all my heart."

"Turn around," he said.

"Yes," she said and she did.

"Now spread your ass apart with both your hands."

"Rashaun, what are you going to do?"

"I'm going to do what you did to me but only this time I'll give you a choice."

"Rashaun, just love me one more time."

He looked over and saw a soda bottle on her desk.

"Wet your finger and rub it between your asshole then put your head down and close your eyes."

She did.

He put his penis back into his pants. He walked around her and grabbed the empty bottle. He walked back to her.

Paul had begun to ramble and it was making Andria more and more uncomfortable. He started to pace around the table.

"Paul, Rashaun is going to be home any minute now and it won't be good if he finds you here."

278

"Please. What is that punk ass lawyer boyfriend of yours going to do? Throw a law book at me? I'm not afraid of your charcoal lover."

"Paul, leave now or else I'm going to have to call the police." Andria said rising and walking to the phone.

"Andria, put the fucking phone down."

Andria started to dial.

Paul grabbed the phone from her and threw it against the wall.

"Andria, I've lost my manhood."

"What?" She turned around and looked at him.

"Come over here!" he said angrily.

Rashaun put the bottle down in front of Kim's closed eyes.

He reached over to the chair and picked up his jacket and then his briefcase. He walked to the door and unlocked it.

"Rashaun!" Kim opened her eyes when she heard the door being unlocked.

"Kim, take this bottle and fuck yourself. I'm going home to my future wife," he said and walked out the door.

Kim quickly picked up the bottle and ran of out of the door into the hallway.

She threw the bottle down the hall and it smashed on the ground a few feet from Rashaun.

"Rashaun, you'll pay for this if this is the last thing I do," she shouted.

As Rashaun continued to walk down the hall a few of the assistant district attorneys were staring at Kim who was topless with only a slip on. Rashaun didn't turn back. He ignored the venom that was coming from her mouth until it subsided with the slamming of a door. He looked at the time. Andria would have a fit.

"Andria, not only did they beat me and tell me to stay away from Robin. This is what they did," Paul said, reaching down to his belt.

Andria got up quickly and moved away from the table.

Paul quickly followed her.

"Paul, I don't want to see that."

"This is what they did to my manhood, those sick fucks," he said, grabbing Andria by the neck.

Rashaun turned the key in the lock slowly trying to think about what he would say when he saw Andria. The first thing she was going to asked him was why he hadn't call. As soon as he pushed the door opened he heard the angry man's voice then Andria's scream. Rashaun quickly threw his briefcase to the floor and reached above the door to the small ledge he had made for quick access to his gun. The nine millimeter was in his hand with the safety off.

"Rashaun, no!" Andria shouted.

Paul still held her by the neck as he tried to unzip his pants.

When Paul heard Andria shout Rashaun's name he raised his head to look at Rashaun.

"What the fuck you going to do with that? Kill me? I'm already dead, motherfucker, and if I'm going my motherfucking woman is going with me," Paul said choking Andria as he advanced to Rashaun. "Those motherfuckers cut right around my dick. What kind of man you think I can be after that. Ah."

"Let go of her," Rashaun said, his voice hoarse.

"Fuck you, motherfucker. She was my woman before you came in the picture and she will be mine again." Paul jerked Andria's head viciously.

The first bullet tore into Paul's left shoulder making a clean exit to the back of the wall.

Andria screamed and Paul pulled at her even more viciously.

The second bullet tore into Paul's throat and left him grasping. Paul's hands fell to his side.

Rashaun's eyes had become glazed as the bullets rifled through the air again and again. Paul slumped down to the ground as Rashaun let the gun slip away from his hand.

Andria fell soon after Paul, landing at an awkward angle over him.

Rashaun's head was drooped to one side but he saw Andria fall.

"No!" he shouted and leaped over to her.

He picked her up and looked into her lifeless eyes. He took his right hand and slapped her to see if that would jar her awake. He examined her to see if he saw a bullet hole. He lifted her up into his arms and it was then that he saw the blood dripping.

"God help her!" he shouted and began to walk toward the door.

It was then the cops burst into the apartment.

"Everyone freeze," a small female officer, shouted, her hand barely able to hold the gun.

"Get an ambulance," Rashaun shouted as tears ran down his face. "Get her a fucking ambulance," he repeated.

Rashaun knelt down on the floor, his pants picking up the dirt of a cold New York jail cell.

"Please, Lord, if there is a life to be taken, let it be mine. Lord spare Andria's life and the life of our unborn. I know I'm not a praying man but grant me this wish and I will never ask for anything else in my life. Take my life but let her live."

"Rashaun, you have a visitor." a correction officer shouted, followed by the rustling of keys.

Rashaun walked toward the cell door.

"Son!" his mother said, tears starting to flow from her eyes.

Seeing the tears in his mother's eyes Rashaun started to cry. As soon as the door was opened he grabbed her and hugged her tightly as he used to do when he was a little boy. "Mommy, I'm sorry," he said, the tears falling onto her dress.

"It's okay. Everything will be all right."

"I think I killed her."

"No, son, you didn't." Rashaun pulled away from his mother.

"Andria is okay?" he asked, looking into his mother's face for answers.

"Yes, Andria is a strong woman, she's doing fine. The doctor said it was only a flesh wound on the side."

"And the baby?"

"The baby, too, is doing okay. They should be coming out of the hospital anytime now."

Rashaun kissed his mother all over. He was like a happy schoolboy again. His face and entire demeanor changed from a few moments ago.

"I would have never forgiven myself if anything happened to them," he said as he sat down on the bed with his mother.

"I'm on my way to the hospital. Do you want me to tell Andria anything?"

"Yes, Mom, just tell her that my love for her will never die. One more thing, Mom, can you call this number for me?" Rashaun asked and turned to the guard outside his cell. "Officer, can I get a pen and a piece of paper?"

Rashaun wrote a name and number on the piece of paper the guard gave to him.

"Yelram? Who is Yelram?"

"Mom, just tell him what happened to me."

After his mother had left, Rashaun sat in his cell smiling. He had just gotten off the floor thanking God for saving his family.

"Rashaun, you have another visitor."

Again, the jingling of keys.

Rashaun walked to the Iron Gate but the guard didn't come and open the door.

"I told you that I would get you back," Kim said as she stood in front the cell door dressed in a tight-fitting black jeans and a green blouse.

Rashaun looked at her without saying a word.

"Now you'll regret that you ever fucked with me and don't think apologizing will make a difference. I let you win that case with your boy Tyrone but this time I'll tie a rope around your balls and hang you up to dry. I thought we could have had something but instead you humiliated me in front of all my peers. I'm telling you, you will wish you were never born when I'm finished with you."

"Kim, I have no regrets and I offer no apologies for my actions with you and if I had to do it over again maybe I would have shoved the bottle up your ass because I know you like shit like that. And remember before you start pulling on the rope make sure that same rope is not connected to your neck. There are a lot of news agencies that would pay a lot to see a district

283

attorney starring in her own x-rated movie." Rashaun turned and walked away from Kim, standing with his back facing the door.

"You wouldn't dare!" she said.

"My family comes first." He said not turning around.

"We will see." She said and walked away.

Rashaun slept peacefully on the small bed in his cell that night. Him, Andria and their child occupied most of his dreams. The loud clanging of cell doors awaked him early in the morning, he quickly brushed his teeth and washed his face.

"Rashaun, you have a visitor." Kendrick, one of the correction officers said.

Rashaun hurried to the door and waited patiently for Kendrick to open the door. He felt nervous and excited at the same time. Kendrick opened the door and step back. Rashaun saw Andria walking to the door ever so slowly. She stopped a few feet away from the open door. Rashaun started to walk toward her.

"Rashaun, don't touch me," Andria said, her voice carrying a serious tone.

Rashaun stood back as if he was hit by a thunderbolt. He didn't know what to do with himself. He just looked at her. The light sweet smell of her body lotion permeated the air like an intoxicating drug. He needed to hold her so badly.

"What?" he said it as a question and at the same time a statement.

"Rashaun." She walked into the cell.

The guard pushed the door in and went back to his post.

Rashaun stood there uncertain of what to do with himself.

"Rashaun, I just came from the hospital. My side hurts. I don't want you hugging me and rupturing the wound," she said, reaching out to hold his hand.

"I was so worried about you," he said, taking in all her sweetness. "I didn't know what I would have done if I had lost you." He kissed her softly on the lips.

"You don't think that you'll get rid of me that easily, do you?" she said, running her hands all over his body.

"I never want to get rid of you. I think you have mixed your blood with mine."

"Yep and the end result is right here," she said, rubbing her stomach.

Rashaun dropped down on his knees and kissed her stomach. "How you doing little man?" he asked his face a picture of pride and joy.

"Rashaun none of that in here." Andria said, looking around.

"Andria," he said, standing up and looking into her soft eyes.

"I hope you don't think being in here will stop our wedding," she said.

"Never that. I'll marry you anytime, anywhere," he said, giving her a soft hug, "How do you feel?"

"I feel fine. Albertina came and picked me up from the hospital. She had me move into her house."

"I knew my mother wouldn't let you go back to the apartment."

"Albertina worked out all the moving arrangements. Now, I have this big bed and no one to fight with at night."

"Hey, you should be happy. You have the blanket all to yourself."

"I'm not. I prefer to fight you for it at night."

"And you always win because every time I wake up in the morning you are totally wrapped up in the blanket."

"Woman power," Andria said, pushing her hands up in the air.

"Baby, I'll be home soon, I promise you." He kissed her one more time on her delicate lips.

Andria knew that he meant it. She believed him when he said he would be home soon. As she circled his waist and he laid his head on her shoulder she realized that she and this man were going to grow old together. Nothing in this world was going to take away that feeling deep in her soul for this man. He would forever be her man.

"I have some good news and some bad news." George said, sitting down on the bed.

"Bad news first." Rashaun said.

"Tyrone was taken to the G-building at Kings county."

"I saw that coming and I couldn't do a damn thing about it."

"I went there yesterday, the place is a crazy house."

"George the G-building at Kings County hospital is for crazy people."

"Yeah well Lance and the rest of the guys went and see him today, I think they will stop by here tomorrow."

"Tyrone, he thinks the meek shall inherit the earth, he doesn't know the meek fertilizes the earth."

"What?"

"No it was just something someone told me a long time ago. What's the good news?"

"My wife…"

"So you back with Joanne." Rashaun said to George.

"Yeah, it's about that time. I didn't realized what I had until I nearly lost it."

"What about nature?"

"Most of these women out here will get you nowhere fast. There are one or two good ones, when you find them you have to hold on to them tightly. I have a good woman and a beautiful child. I got to step up to the plate and do the right thing."

"It won't be easy, George. Remember you are a pussyholic."

"I know. That's why I'm taking that trip when you get out," George said.

"Where are you going?" Rashaun asked.

"Grenada, I told you I was going to try that cleansing thing."

"You are serious."

"Very."

The correction officer walked up to the gate. "Rashaun, you have another visitor.

"I guess that means I have to leave," George said, getting up from the bed. "I will come by and check you tomorrow."

"Sounds good," Rashaun said, hugging his friend before he left.

The guard came and escorted George out. He then returned with Yelram who walked in and shook hands with Rashaun. They both sat down on the bed.

"It seemed my whole life I've been trying to run away from this place," Rashaun said, looking around the cell.

"All of us black men have been trying to do the same thing. It seems like jails are always in our backyard. But I won't let it take you," Yelram said, his voice taking on a threatening tone.

"So you will take my case?" Rashaun asked.

"I have already started on your case, Rashaun."

"Thank you," Rashaun said.

"Rashaun, you have a family to go to. Your woman will be giving birth to a child whom you have to guide. You cannot do that in here. You have to be out there to take control of your family, accept the responsibility for it's direction. You see, there are already too many single mothers and irresponsible dads in our culture. The black man has gotten lazy and he has left the direction of the family in his woman's hands. The program and life has shown us that this is not a good decision."

"What is the program?" Rashaun asked.

"You'll learn more about it later. What we have to work on is getting you back to your family so that another black family is not left without a leader. Look at our young boys and girls today. They are lost. Most of the fathers have left home and some of those who remain are non-existent, meaning they are there in body only. You have to go and be the man so that your woman and your child will respect you and in turn they will understand their role in society. Too many jails are filled with black men whose families are put into a circle that creates weak men and disrespectful women. A young woman will always have difficulties respecting a man if she has never seen a man in a responsible role. It is up to you to accept the responsibility for your family and guide it's members in the right direction. Until we do that as a people our young children will always be dying on the streets."

Yelram inhaled deeply.

Rashaun sighed.

"The role of a black woman should not be head of the household. She is that way because we have given her no other choice. It takes a man to accept responsibility and too many of us are too lazy and too caught up in other things to do that. And as a result, we lose our families. We create young men who lack direction and young women with no structure and the end result is a cycle of nothingness. On my way here I saw this couple shouting at each other on the side of the street. Her main threat to him was that she would take him to court for child support. Since when did having more material things become a substitute for guidance and being a role model? I'll tell you what will become of this relationship—the woman will take the father to court, he would have to lose a percentage of his salary and the children will remain in the same situation, fatherless. Now tell me how that helps our situation as a people"

Yelram did not wait for Rashaun's response. "Rashaun, I have confidence in you. That's why I will ensure that you get off on these charges. A man must always defend his family."

288

"But I killed another black man. Aren't I continuing the system of violence we inflict on each other?"

Yelram shook his head. "Rashaun, if I thought that you killed another man for looking at you the wrong way I wouldn't be here. A man who does not kill or do whatever he has to do to protect his family is not deserving of life. A man has every right to defend his household, and I believe that's just what you did. You will realize in the program that there have to be sacrifices. Some people are useless in our struggle. These people who if they cannot become useful, they will have to be pushed aside. You know the best way to control a black man? Put another black man over him and called him boss. These bosses will make sure that you do not even breathe the same air the white man breathes. This is what the white man has done so effectively in addition to taking away our manhood, but that is another story."

After Yelram left, Rashaun sat in his jail cell and contemplated his future. The road ahead would have a lot of twists and turns and the incline might even be too much but he had no choice but to give it his best shot. As Yelram said he had a family to guide.

Kim was dressed in a short red miniskirt with two white stripes on the sides. The policemen going toward their car to start the evening shift were stepping all over each other looking at her. Kim looked at them and continued on her way to the door of the stationhouse. She had gotten use to men and women falling all over themselves when she walked. She had gotten the call from the detective on her cell phone about an hour ago. They had caught a drug dealer with five kilos and he was interested in copping a plea. Normally Kim would send one of the assistant DA's to handle this situation but when the detective told her that the perpetrator had information on the man killed by the lawyer she decided to pay a personal visit.

The Italian desk cop directed her to the black detective sitting at the corner desk wearing an extra, extra large Fubu shirt. When he saw her coming, he stood. A chorus of "damn" echoed through the room as she walked toward his desk. Kim was also used to that.

"Detective James," Kim said, putting out her hand.

"Yes, DA Rivers. Your reputation precedes you and all of it correct. They said that you were the most beautiful woman in Brooklyn."

"Thank you. I'm flattered but you know why I am here." She said, ignoring his gesture to sit down. "Did you put him in a soundproof room?"

"Yes. He's right down the hall and totally secured to our special interrogation chair."

"Can you make sure that I'm not disturbed when I'm inside with him?"

"It's not advisable and it is against department regulation but…"

Kim finished the sentence for him, "But you will do it for me."

"Yes, I will."

"Well let's go," Kim said and turned around and headed down the hall.

"I hope you don't take this the wrong way," the detective said, "Jennifer Lopez has a nice ass, Halle Berry has a beautiful ass but baby, your ass will make the world holla back."

"No offense taken," Kim said, smiling.

"I have these two tickets for a seven-day Caribbean cruise in September. I would be flattered if you could go with me."

"What would your wife say?" Kim asked, looking at the white ring print where he had taken off his wedding band.

"Oh, that was a friendship ring that I had to cut off because it was messing with the circulation in my finger," he said as he opened the door to the interrogation room.

"Let me talk to you after I'm finished here," Kim said, going in and closing the door.

The short prisoner with a round body and tubby legs and hands sat handcuff to an iron chair in the middle of the room. The room held absolutely no other furniture.

Kim smiled. She saw the lust and the saliva dripping from his mouth.

"They call me Penguin. I would shake your hand but as you can see I can't do that," the man said

She liked that he talked first, that meant he was a talker. Talkers were generally stupid. They would always say something that they didn't want to say.

"I told the officer that I wanted a plea but after looking at you, I want a taste."

"A taste of what?" Kim asked, standing in front of him her legs shoulder-length apart.

"You see, Miss, my whole life I have spent fucking prostitutes and ghetto bitches. The closest I have come to high-class pussy is when one of these women from Wall Street goes crazy over drugs and start to roam the streets. By that time they are already beat up but you could at least say you fucked something that doesn't live in the ghetto. I'm also looking at twenty-five to life because it is my third offense and you know the politics of the law system—send the black men away for as long as possible. So I know with a plea bargain I'm at least looking at ten years upstate. So you know what, I want something to hold unto while I jerk my meat because I ain't into that faggot shit. Put bluntly, I want to taste your pussy."

"I could have them throw the book at you for that comment," She said.

"But you won't because there had to be a reason for you to come down here. I haven't been arrested more than two hours now and you're here already, so it's either promotion or bad blood. Me, I don't care one way or the other."

"What are you offering?"

"Information, only no testifying, I have a lot of stuff on one of Brooklyn's biggest ex-drug dealers but I'm sure when you guys are finished he won't be an ex-dealer anymore. We also went and handled a situation for a lawyer friend of his. The black one that recently got the Blackfunk boy free. You see I read the newspapers."

Kim could feel herself getting wet just thinking about hanging Rashaun up by the balls. "What situation with the lawyer are you talking about?"

"Before I go any further I need a taste."

Kim looked deeply in his eyes. Then she slowly lowered her G-string. She lifted her skirt up in front of Penguin.

Penguin started to squirm in his chair, pulling hard against the handcuffs that bound his hands and his feet.

With her skirt lifted and her pussy lips pulled apart by her left hand she took her right hand and passed it between her wet pussy lips.

Penguin stretched his head out at an unnatural angle.

Kim slipped her finger into his mouth.

Penguin sucked on her finger as if he had found the last water hole in the desert.

When Kim pulled her finger out it was blood red.

"Now as you promised," she said pulling her G-string up to her knees and leaving it there.

Penguin started to talk. He spoke about his boss, Mr. Roundtree, and how he and two other men paid a visit to Paul's mother's house as a favor owed to Rashaun the lawyer who had gotten him off on a murder case. When he was finished Kim had jotted down the whole incident, including Mr. Roundtree taking a razor and cutting a line right around Paul's penis and promising to come back and cut it completely off if he didn't leave Robin alone. Penguin talked so much that he told her about other deals in which he carried out contract killings for Mr. Roundtree.

"But I won't testify," he said, ending his story.

Once more Kim removed her panties completely and rested them in his lap. The thought of sending Rashaun to jail for the rest of his life had made her soaking wet.

"You want a real taste?"

"Yes, please," Penguin, said, licking his lips.

She walked closer to him.

His tongue came out like a dog and he stretched his head forward.

"How much do you want it?" she asked once again taking her finger and running it through her pussy. It came out dripping.

"Please I'll do anything even if I'm signing my death warrant. I don't care. I want it bad." Penguin tried to pull the chair forward.

Kim came up to him suddenly, and buried her pussy in his mouth.

Penguin went crazy and licked uncontrollable.

"Rashaun, I'm going to get you," she shouted as her body began to jerk up and down as her orgasm sent her head spinning.

A small dark wet circle laid imprinted on Penguin pants as Kim stepped away from him.

"Will you testify?" she asked with the serious tone of a prosecuting attorney.

"Yes, I'll testify to everything. Just tell me what you want and I'll do it," Penguin said.

"What happened in there?" the detective asked as Kim walked out of the precinct bathroom. "The perp. is talking like crazy, even telling us things we didn't ask him about."

"Just keep him safe, I have a big score to settle," She said as she started walking out the door.

"What about the cruise?"

"Take your wife and children. Their picture is on your desk."

"That's my sister and her kids." He shouted at her.

"Yes and I'm a nun," She said quietly as she headed down the precinct steps.

MICHAEL PRESLEY'S
Tears on a Sunday Afternoon
COMING IN 2003

I was pushed through the revolving exit door of the office building by two ladies rushing to leave the building. As I walked through the corridor leading to the elevators I was constantly bumped by hoards of people heading to the revolving doors. I looked at my gold Movado watch and realized it was ten after five. I navigated to the line of elevators that carried the workers up and down every day. I stepped aside as more than a dozen businesspeople in suits pushed themselves off one of the elevators. They hurried passed me as if in a rush to get to the streets. I guess the streets of New York were not as dangerous as advertised. I had been in the building earlier to set up a project with a group of engineers from our office. It was an extensive project that would require long, tedious hours. It was similar to one we had done in Staten Island a few weeks ago. It was during that visit that I met one of the secretaries, Donna Smith. She had been with the company for five years. One of my coworkers, Brian, a tall dark fellow from Brooklyn introduced me. The first hour we were in the building Brian had spent at least forty-five minutes trying to talk to Donna. I paid very little attention to the both of them because unlike me, Brian was single and the world was his oyster.

Brian and I had eaten lunch together since I came onboard Reason Consulting, the largest black engineering firm in New York. Engineers at Reason were not hired based on their résumé but from recommendations by one of their board members. My father-in-law had me working there a few months after the wedding. During our lunch at Au Bon Pan, Brian told me that Donna was dripping for me. I looked at him as if he was crazy. I hadn't said a word to the woman and she was "dripping for me."

Brian was a cool guy; he didn't have a jealous bone in his body. He told me that he tried talking to her but she was only interested in me. So after speaking to Brian I went over to her. When I got to her desk she stood and shook my hand. I must tell you I was very impressed. She was about five feet nine inches tall, dark complexion with a body that almost any man would crawl after. I said almost any man, not me. I have had those women who men have killed themselves over.

During our conversation she told me to hold on because she had to file an important document. When she turned around I'll just say that she was a black man's butter. She told me that she couldn't really talk to me and asked if I could come back and see her after work. Now you know why I am going into a building that most people are trying to leave. As I took the elevator up to the sixtieth floor I was wondering where to take her for dinner. I eat out frequently so my head was spinning with choices —maybe I would let her decide. I eat almost anything so it wouldn't make a difference to me.

It was approximately five-fifteen when I knocked on the office door. She came in and led me to a couch in front of her desk and told me to wait. A few minutes passed and a man I hadn't seen before came out and spoke to her briefly as he walked out of the office. He had a large Kenneth Cole briefcase in his right hand and upon further inspection I noticed a gold handcuff kept the briefcase in place.

"I'm so wound up," she said as she slumped down in her chair.

"That's work— five days a week, then two days to think about it then five days back at work," I said, looking at her from a distance.

"You're very beautiful," she said, sitting on the edge of the chair.

I have heard that comment from the time I was old enough to remember it. It had gotten me into and out of trouble. I think sometimes I could get away with murder because of my looks, the result of a crime perpetuated on my mother when she was incarcerated at the Delvin Correctional Facility upstate New York. Three white correction officers raped her. After I was born my mother took her life.

"I know," I said, smiling. "Thanks for the compliment."

"You're mixed aren't you?" she asked. "With that curly hair and those blue eyes you've got to be."

"Yeah, my father is white and my mother is a southern girl."

"So who did you inherit that over six-feet slender frame from, your mother or father?"

"I don't know." I was being honest because I was never told who my father was. I guess nobody wanted to set up DNA tests for three white men.

She stood and walked to the front of the desk. "Come over here. Let me see how much taller you are than me."

I guess she was into games. Normally, I wouldn't play but this one was worth it. I stood in front of her, her hard nipples pushing against my shirt. She smelled like fresh-picked apricots.

She looked up at me, her luscious red lips glistening against the dark pigmentation of her face.

"I…"

It was all she got out of her mouth as my lips joined hers. She should have slapped me then. Maybe I should have slapped myself for making such assumptions but neither of us did. Instead her mouth feasted on mine as my hand went to the front of her blouse. The snaps came apart like dry- rotted steel wool the kind my grandmother gave me to do the dishes. I pulled her blouse off her shoulders and it fell onto her desk. She pulled me towards her, her breasts rubbing against my white Guess T-shirt. Her hand traveled down my chest toward my dick and she started to rub it through my pants.

"I knew you were packing, looks and a big dick what more can a girl ask for?" she said as I helped her pull my shirt over my head. She started to make her way down my chest, leaving a trail of red lip marks. She unbuckled my pants and slid my pants down. She gently brushed the outsides of my legs with her fingertips as she reached up to pull off my Calvin Klein boxers. I stepped to the side as she gathered my clothes and put them on the couch. I stood naked on the sixtieth floor in an office building in the heart of Manhattan.

"You have what I want in my husband," she said as I started to remove her clothes. I started playing with her breasts and slowly made my way down to her skirt. I lifted it up and worked my way between her legs. My right hand moved over the front of her panties. They were moist. I moved them to the side and slipped my finger inside of her, she was dripping wet. I played with her for a few seconds more before I moved my hand to her butt. She was wearing a thong, an old song played in my head but it quickly faded like the artist who performed it. We continued to kiss until I flipped her around and in so doing her hands scattered all the things she had on her desk. I took her hand away from my dick and slid on one of the condoms that I had bought from Duane Reade earlier. I grabbed her by the hair, her weave feeling like that same steel wool but it shedded much more. I pushed her head down in front the desk. Her two hands held onto the desk for support. I entered her with the force and the vengeance of a man lost to himself and the world. She screamed and rocked the desk as she spread her legs even wider for more support. As she did that a picture fell off the desk and shattered. She was in the picture with a man and two young boys. I looked at it and then at her butt. I slammed into her a few more times until I sent a million of my kids to their death against the walls of rubber. She fell to the floor as I gave my last push.

"I needed that. You have a cell phone?" she asked, putting her clothes on.

"It's 917-777-7777."

"All those sevens?"

"It's better than sixes."

I followed her cue and started to get dress. She quickly put my phone number in her Palm organizer. She didn't offer hers and I didn't ask for it. I finished dressing before her and headed to the door.

"Wait for me she said. I have to clean up this mess and make one phone call." She started straightening the desk. "I think this is yours." She wrapped the used condom in tissues and gave it to me. I put it in my pocket.

"I nearly forgot that," I said.

"If you were an NBA basketball player I might have kept it," she said smiling. She picked up the phone and dialed a number quickly. She spoke briefly in a language I didn't understand.

"Only an engineer," I said and sat down on the couch. It was 6:30.

"Damn! This is the third time this week this has happened." She threw the bits of broken glass from the picture frame into the small garbage pail and placed it back under her desk. "These ninety-nine cent stores are getting rich off me replacing frames."

I waited for her to finish and we took the elevator down to the first floor.

"Good night Mrs. August," the security guard a potbellied with a man heavy West Indian accent, said as we exited the building. When we got outside there was a tall attractive blond white lady waiting for us.

"Thank you," Donna said and waved good-bye to me as she went to join the white lady who looked me up and down before she and Donna slipped into a black limousine waiting at the curb.

I walked two blocks south then one east, which took me to the entrance of the Carton Bar. I went inside and as usual there was a combination of suits and casuals. I sat at the bar and the bartender came over.

"Hennessy on the rock's," I said, and he turned back before reaching me.

I swiveled the chair around so that I could look at the people like me who found themselves needing a drink at seven in the evening. To my left was a white man about fifty-five years old in a postal uniform sipping on a drink that was as clear as water. I didn't think it was water because that would mean he had to drink a lot of those little glasses before he satisfied his thirst. As if on cue, he tapped his glass and the bartender gave him a refill on the way to bringing my drink. A little bit farther down from him were two white boys who may had just reached the legal drinking age in New York City. They had a pitcher of beer and about six shots glasses in front of them. They seemed to be having a good time. I looked over at the tables away from the bar and noticed a couple who seemed to be lost in New York and young black women— my guess neither was a day over twenty-five. They both had identical hairstyles long weaves running down their back. They kept looking at me and giggling. One held what I thought was a mozzarella cheese stick, which she twirled around like a baton. I turned back and took a long sip of my drink.

I had recently turned thirty-four and I had been married for four years now. I had a three-year-old son and I was one of the few blacks living in the exclusive Mills Basin section of Brooklyn. I loved my daughter with every drop of blood that circulated through my system and kept me alive every day.

"Excuse me?" I felt the slight tap on my shoulder. I put my drink down and once more swiveled in my chair. It was one of the girls I had noticed earlier. She was the bigger of the two. I would guess she was five-eight and weighed about 145 pounds.

"Yes." My face showed no emotion.

"My friend wants to fuck you." I looked over at her friend who was holding the cheese stick. She had this big smile on her face.

"And you?" I asked.

"I wouldn't mind," she said, playing with my curly hair.

"How much?" I asked.

She stopped playing with my hair and stood back.

"How much?" she repeated as if her repetition would dissipate the question.

"There's got to be something in it for me," I said.

"How about both of us together," she said, signaling her friend who was starting to get up.

"Been there, done that too many times, so unless your shit got gold fillings, this conversation is over."

"I'll be right back," she said and headed over to her friend.

I took a sip of my drink and rested a hundred-dollar bill under the glass.

"We're willing to do $400 but you have to buy a bottle of Courvoisier as a birthday gift to my friend." She said a stupid smile on her face, "Like the song…"

"I hate the song but I will buy the bottle. Let's go," I said, leaving the bartender with a hundred dollar bill for a $6.50 drink.

I drove into my driveway at Mills Lane at 10:00 P.M. parking my S500 next to the red convertible X type Jaguar in the driveway. As I stepped onto the pavement, a large black pit bull came trotting toward me. I stooped and rubbed the dog on the top of his head. He rubbed against my pants leg, walked with me to the large French doors and stood back as I opened the door.

"Thanks for picking up Emerald from the school. You didn't have to leave as soon as we came home." My wife stood in the middle of the living room. Her right eye was black and swollen.

"Is Emerald asleep?" I asked.

"Like you care. He's has been asleep since eight-thirty." She said.

"I'm taking him to the zoo tomorrow," I said as I took off my shoes.

"Laura, come here," a husky female voice beckoned from the kitchen.

I followed my wife.

"I thought I told you I don't want all that mayonnaise on my sandwich" the woman sitting at the kitchen table in a red nightgown said as my wife picked up the sandwich. She was the housekeeper and my wife lover. "You know I don't like hitting you but you don't listen."

"Sorry Annette, I'll do it over," my wife said.

I went to the refrigerator and took out a Heineken. As I passed by Annette stood. She was a little bit shorter than Donna and God had created ugly.

She looked at me, challenging me with her eyes.

I opened the bottle and leaned against the counter, staring Annette down.

"What! You want to do something about this," she said, pointing to Laura. "Go ahead and see if you won't be arrested for spousal abuse."

"Just as long as you keep your hands where they won't be cut off. If I ever come home and find my child with so much as a scratch on his arm, I will take that artificial dick and shove it down your throat."

"Stop it, both of you!" Laura screamed. "Donald. Dad said he wants to see you tomorrow."

I walked out of the kitchen with the Heineken. I went up the stairs passed the master bedroom into a room littered with an assortment of toys. I knelt next to the bed where my child lay fast asleep. I held the Heineken in my right hand as I used my left hand to move her curly hair away from his eyes. I kissed him in the middle of his forehead. A small tear escaped from my eye onto his bed.

"I love you," I said and stood. I left the room and headed down to the last room at the end of the hall. I put the bottle next to the cases of empty ones in the walk-in-closet. I sat by the window looking out at the darkness of the night. I knew what I had to do. Maybe tomorrow I could stand up to my father-in-law and tell him what I was unable to for four years.

BLACKFUNK III
IS COMING!